STOLEN SILENCE

LUCINDA KEMMER

Contents

1. Chapter 1   1

2. Chapter 2   15

3. Chapter 3   28

4. Chapter 4   36

5. Chapter 5   43

6. Chapter 6   55

7. Chapter 7   63

8. Chapter 8   72

9. Chapter 9   81

10. Chapter 10   93

11. Chapter 11   112

12. Chapter 12   122

13. Chapter 13   135

14. Chapter 14   141

15. Chapter 15   147

16. Chapter 16   157

17. Chapter 17   164

18. Chapter 18   170

19.	Chapter 19	183
20.	Chapter 20	189
21.	Chapter 21	205
22.	Chapter 22	213
23.	Chapter 23	223
24.	Chapter 24	232
25.	Chapter 25	247
26.	Chapter 26	259
27.	Chapter 27	278
28.	Chapter 28	286
29.	Chapter 29	300
30.	Chapter 30	312
31.	Chapter 31	326
32.	Chapter 32	338
33.	Chapter 33	351
34.	Chapter 34	365
35.	Chapter 35	375
36.	Epilogue	392

1

CHAPTER 1

I was alone; locked in this basement for days, weeks, and maybe even months. I'm so used to loneliness now that the very thought of being around people scares the hell out of me. I guess that's why he is in one corner of the dimly lit asylum while I'm in the other.

He coughs suddenly, making me jump. With a frustrated sigh, I lean the back of my head against the wall then close my eyes to calm down.

Ever since the brown eyed man took me I haven't been able to adjust to sudden noises. No matter how minimal they are. From a small cough to the door abruptly opening, I jump at everything.

Anyway, I- we were alone but it sure felt like I was alone because he hasn't spoken yet. He hasn't said one word. Even when I tried to make conversation with him yesterday he never responded. Instead he just stared aimlessly at the wall with his back to me. Never allowing his appearance to show and never allowing his voice to bounce off the gloomy brick walls. With his shoulders hunched he starts to softly bang his head on the wall. This action makes me think he's isn't fairing well with the first week. I can't blame him though, my first day here I couldn't stop crying.

My eyes open and a wave of air infiltrates my constricted lungs, forcing a loud gasp to pierce the silence. For a second I mistake the darkness of this place for my shadowy room at home. Giving my eyes a minute to adjust I notice the wood boards where the ceiling is supposed to be.

Sitting up, all I can see are walls. Four brick walls shrouded in still darkness. The unpleasant stench of mold and mildew fills my nostrils with such vehemence that I have to cover my nose. My butt starts aching and I don't know why. Feeling around, I realize that it is because I'm sitting on an old, dirty, full sized mattress. I try to squint to see more but it's too dark so I use my other senses. Placing my hands on the cold floor I scan the room to feel my surroundings.

After a few seconds of listening to eerie quiet and gliding my hands across the cold hard floor and brick walls I can now make an accurate guess. From the musty smell, the leaky sink a few feet to my left, and the lack of light and air, I conclude that I'm in a basement. And judging by how wet the mattress is I'm going to assume that it's drenched in my sweat. Gross. I move off the mattress to sit on the cold cemented floor.

A relieved sigh parts from my lips. That feels refreshing against my hot, clammy skin. You would think that my pajama shorts and tee shirt would help keep me cool but that isn't the case.

I blink a few more times while wiping my forehead with the back of my small hand. Beads of sweat slide down my entire body like an endless stream, mostly tickling my face. It's really hot and stuffy down here. Like boiler room hot. I should be used to this because I live in Florida but I've never sweltered this much. Sweltering...come to think of it, the first day of summer break is today so wherever I am must be near home. Home.

Noticing the stairs a few feet away from me, I quickly get up to run to them but I'm stopped short by something around my right ankle. Falling to the hard cement, my entire body feels like I've been running a marathon. I'm sweaty, out of breath and my chest hurts. How can I feel like this if I just woke up? Was I sedated? And where are my parents? Last time I saw them they were...oh no. He killed them, the burglar murdered my parents in cold blood. My body trembles vigorously. I have to get out of here. I have to get free before he kills me too. I lunge toward the stairs again only to fall flat on my face. I release a low grunt before slowly getting back up.

Glancing behind me, my eyes focus on what is actually holding me back. Once again, my fears are confirmed when I see the rusted cuff link still in place, locked securely around my ankle. Shifting my eyes from the cuff around my ankle to the brick wall, I see the chain is connected to it. Squinting harder, I can see the small hole in the wall with the chain sticking out. The chain is about the size of two arms length. Each piece working against me. Trapping me here.

"Come on!" I pull on the rusty chain, trying to break free and the harder I pull the more everything sinks in. I'm still trapped, still chained to the hard brick wall, and still panicking while pulling with all of my might. With each vigorous pull I cry out from the pinch of the cuff link chafing against my ankle. I sob until my throat burns while pulling harder and faster until my ankle bleeds.

"Someone help...please help... me!" I shout while crying uncontrollably. It's so powerful that it echoes off the drab walls and blocks out the constant rattling of my binds.

The sound of the door opening causes my body to stiffen. A small light shines on me from the opened door. My eyes widen at the sight of my captor as he slowly descends each step. He's taller than me for sure. And although I'm not quite sure what his exact height is, I do know that he's taller than my 5'4. He's dressed in all black and from what I can see his entire face is covered with a mask. For each step he declines, I scoot back further. I don't trust this man so by the time he has reached the last step, I'm pressed against the wall in alarmed fear. My heart is beating loud enough for the both of us and my hands won't stop shaking.

I watch as he bends down to my eye level and fans my face with a heavy sigh. His hand goes up to stroke my cheek and I have the hardest time swallowing.

"Name?" he questions while gently moving from my cheek to my arms. I try to identify him but no matter how hard I squint I still can't see much because his mask only reveals his brown almond shaped eyes, small nostrils, and thin light pink lips.

"Tell me your name." his thin lips move slowly as I stare in horror.

My mind is blank. I can't think, I can't speak, and I can't move my lips. I'm lost for words because of how scared I am. I've been kidnapped. How could this happen? When did this happen?

I whimper when his hand grasps my trachea tightly, pinning my head against the wall and blocking my airways.

"Tell me your fucking name," he demands through gritted teeth. With each second passing he squeezes harder, forcing stinging tears to pour from my soul.

"O-Olivia," I stammer with frightened eyes while my hands try to pry his from around my neck.

His dark eyes bore into mine while he analyzes me. The look in his eyes sends chills down my spine. They're narrowed while his lips are slightly parted. I try to read his body language but it's difficult because he isn't revealing much. Most of his face is covered while his strong grip around my neck prevents me from moving my head.

"I...told you...my name." I can barely breathe because his hand is still around my neck.

"Yeah, I heard you." There's humor in his tone when he releases my neck. He's still too close for my liking but I am relieved that my airways are clear. I inhale a shaky breath while my hands instantly rub where the bruise has formed.

"Olivia...Olivia..." he murmurs.

I remain silent while he stares at me with his head slightly cocked to the side. It's a mix between sadistic and lustful. My large blue eyes remain locked on his as he inspects my sweaty, scared form. After too long of petrified silence I decide to do what anyone else would do.

"Don't...Don't kill me. Please, I won't tell anyone if you let me go." My pleading eyes are frantically searching his; trying to find some sort of remorse. Trying to convince him to let me go.

He brings his gloved hands to my cheeks, stroking them lightly with his thumbs and making bile rise in my throat. I have to close my glassy eyes to force it back down before I'm able to speak again.

"I...I promise I won't talk to the police. Just please..." I beg with salty tears spilling over. I don't want to die like my parents. And besides the fact that I'm only sixteen, I don't want to die here in this dreadful asylum.

"Hmm," he hums in thought.

"Now that you say that, I could reconsider...I have a better idea." the creepy man grins deliriously, giving me another round of startled chills."Better than letting you go."

What? What could be better than letting me go? Is he thinking of keeping me here In this dim, depressing prison?

He answers my thoughts by softly kissing my forehead then standing up. It leaves an acidic linger; his kiss is as foul as he is.

"Wait, you can't leave me down here! I want to go home." My shaky voice falters.

"You can't go home. I've made my decision and it's final," he smirks triumphantly. "I always take something from my robberies. Just think of yourself as my personal souvenir."

He said that before. Before he took me from my warm, safe home he chimed those exact same words and I refuse to accept them.

"No, please don't leave me down here!" I crawl to where he's standing to beg, "Please don't leave me down here." I grab the bottom of his jeans as tears pour out like an opened flood gate.

"Don't cry Livie," he bends down to my shaking form then grabs my hands, gently caressing them. His musty, sweaty scent makes me wrinkle my nose while the words 'Livie' echo in my throbbing head. All of the blood in my veins is rushing to my head while his nickname plants a seed in my memory.

"Because that makes you weak. And the weak never make it." His voice is solemn. He isn't going to let me leave.

My heart drops to my stomach when I realize the severity of danger I'm in. I'm about to be locked down here with no one knowing where I am or if I'm even alive. This strange man can kill me...or do much worse. He could do so many unthinkable things to me and that thought alone sends my mind into a deeper pit of darkness. I can't stay down here. I have to try to get upstairs. At least I could get a layout of the house if I'm upstairs.

"Can I go upstairs. You can lock me in a room up there...please." My voice cracks. This time I'm on my knees while my hands are clasped together. I've resorted to begging.

"Don't make me regret letting you live." his tone is one of disgust as he looks down on me with folded arms.

I'm about to plead when I remember what he said earlier: "Don't cry Livie, Because that makes you weak. And the weak never make it."

So if crying is a sign of weakness then maybe he thinks begging is too. I can't be weak because he'll kill me if I am. At that thought, my hands instantly fall to my side while my shoulders slouch.

"If you're good then maybe one day I'll let you come upstairs." Grabbing the back of my head he brings me closer to him, inhaling my scent. I'm frozen like a statue until he pulls away, allowing me to scoot back to the wall.

I hear a soft,

"Get some rest Livie."

The sound of loud footsteps ascend the creaky steps before the door slams shut. My mind remains empty when I wrap my arms around my knees. I'm left in the dark , humid basement. Alone, frightened and full of ferment grief.

He coughs again, knocking me out of my flashback. This time he coughs in a series before sniffling. I know he's been crying and trying to cover it with a cough. I also know that he's exhausted because there is only one mattress in here, and it's on my side. The side he refuses to come near.

Maybe I could help him feel better. I'll just ask him his name. I mean he's been here for about a week and hasn't spoken since. If we get acquainted then it will be easier to explain how everything works so he doesn't get chastised by...him.

"So..." I trail off with uncertainty. I'm not that confident speaking and I don't know if he heard me. Heck, I don't even know if I heard myself. I mean my voice is raspy and low from not using it in so long. If I had to guess I would say that I've gone a few months without talking.

"So uh, what should I call you?...I mean what's your name?" I ask more clearly and concisely.

Silence.

"You don't have to tell me now, maybe another time." I shrug it off. Maybe he's an introvert. I used to be one too until I started to miss conversation.

"Hey, do you know what month we're in? Because I've lost count, you know from being locked in this dump." I laugh awkwardly, trying to lighten the cryptic mood.

Still silence.

"Hmm, I think first semester is starting. It's September right? What grade are you in? I'm supposed to start my senior year." I ramble, trying to make small talk.

I hear nothing but silence until he clears his throat. Anticipating what his voice sounds like, I wait eagerly to hear what he has to say.

"Hey, I have a question for you." his voice sounds like a foreign dream. It's foreign because I haven't had anyone to talk to in months, and it feels like a dream because I never thought this moment would come. This moment when I would actually have someone to talk to. I better answer while he's still in the mood to converse.

"Yeah?"

"Can you stop talking? Just shut up...please, yeah please." he sighs with annoyance.

I frown because even though it wasn't quite the response I was hoping for, it was a response nonetheless. At least he was somewhat polite. Somewhat.

I hear the door creak so I scoot back to the wall. As our captor descends each step I notice that guy has made no efforts to move. Is he even afraid?

Before I can pull my leg back the man grips it with a strong vice. My breaths are rugged while his are steady. He usually comes down here with a plate of food but I don't see or smell any.

"Today is your lucky day Livie."

He unlocks my chain and an unfamiliar feeling of freedom over-whelms me. I can move my ankle.

"Remember I'm giving you a second chance. I don't want a re-peat." He points at me with a warning look so I nod my head. No freedom Livie. I quickly forget my previous thought because I'm not making any mistakes this time. I've already learned my lesson.

"Don't come over here asswipe." the boy sneers harshly when the man approaches him.

I gasp when his black boot goes back to kick him in his mouth. The unlucky kid coughs while I cringe. I'm all too familiar with that taste. It's probably blood.

"Language Jake, there's a lady present." he chuckles to himself while lifting the boy up.

So his name is Jake? Now I know two things about him; his name is Jake and his mouth needs to be washed out with soap.

"Livie lead the way." he orders, forcing my body to react before my mind can. Mentally drained and physically tired, I climb off the mattress and head to the stairs. I stand at the bottom, looking up at the open door with the bright sunlight shining through. Freedom is through that door. Or so I thought. The last time I was upstairs I tried to run and he caught me. I was beaten until he felt like stopping, and starved for four days. And after, he left me down here without showering for two months. It had been my first week here, and my first and last attempt at escaping. That memory alone is one I will never forget.

"I said go upstairs." his tone is one of stern warning so I immediately obey. My bare feet touch the oak wood stairs, allowing the rough planks of wood to poke my cracked heels.

They creak as we ascend. Every small sound is magnified while my eyes squint from the harsh light.

Soon I enter the kitchen. I have no idea what he wants me to do or where he wants me to go so I turn to him for guidance. I see that they're still behind me. The man holds a squirming Jake by the forearm while pointing to a light wood table with three blue chairs. All I can do is stare at everything in disgust. The floor is so dirty that I think the dirt is literally glued to it, making it a completely different color than the original off white tiles. The light blue walls have food and dirt stains while fist holes decorate them. The stove hasn't been cleaned in years. There's a sink full of dishes and I think I just saw a cockroach crawling on them. Gross.

"Sit." he demands urgently, making my body react quickly. I sit down but Jake doesn't. He stands in defiance. Now that we're in the bright kitchen I can get a good look. His smooth hair is golden brown with a swooped bang. It's kind of intriguing how his golden brown hair compliments his emerald green eyes. My plain blue eyes don't mesh well with my dirty blond hair.

"If I have to say it again things won't go well." the tall, average weight man threatens. And this time I can get a good look at him too. His dark brown hair is combed back in a slick way while his brown eyes glisten with devilish excitement. I notice his nose is medium sized while his lips are thin. His five o' clock shadow adds mystery while revealing his age: early thirties.

All I can do is watch in horror as the man punches him in the face, knocking him to the ground. But before he can kick him Jake grabs his foot, knocking him on his back. The man groans from the impact of his head hitting the floor. I hear him swear before lunging for a frightened Jake. They scuffle while my stomach growls. It's been a couple days since my last meal so I am famished. All I want to do is eat and then go back downstairs. But I'm not that lucky because just as those thoughts leave, furious cursing bounces off the walls and into my ears.

Jake is losing. He's now pinned down while the man strikes his face repeatedly. There's a loud crack until Jake kicks the older man in his gut. I watch the man lift himself up, he's clutching his side.

"Dumbass!" he roars before kicking him. Jake grunts while trying to protect his face. Both of his arms cover his face while he remains huddled in the fetal position. I don't know much about wrestling but I do know that's a smart move on Jake's part. He's waiting until the man gets tired.

I cover my mouth when I realize Jake isn't moving. The brown haired man's shoulders heave until he turns to me. My legs move and I'm out of my seat in an instant. I shake my head and hold my arms up defensively when he approaches me. His eyes are filled with wrathful anger. I try to turn and run but he roughly grabs my arm and pulls me to him.

"Everything you do to me falls back on her!" He shouts with ferocity before yanking me forward. I wail when my head hits the table in an instant, making me dizzy. Black spots appear until I blink a few times, making them disappear. My hand grips the table for support while I try to stand. My knees are wobbly and I'm still weak from being locked up in a basement for so long. My forehead is throbbing and it takes a few moments for me to catch my breath.

"Like I care what happens to her!" He shouts back before running to the door. My mind races as quickly as my heart when I realize Jake is actually alive.

The man grabs a butcher knife before lifting me up and going after him.

"D-don't kill me! I don't want to die." I plead while being dragged to the foyer.

Jake's malachite eyes stare into mine for a second before his hand hovers over the knob. He's contemplating on whether he should attempt to escape but what he doesn't realize is that the door and windows are always locked. We need keys to unlock them which we don't have. We're never leaving. We'll never get out of here and the sad part is I don't try anymore because I'm too afraid. If he had talked to me he would know that.

"If you touch that knob Livie here gets a cut. But if you obey and come back to the kitchen then no one gets hurt and everyone gets a full stomach." The man negotiates.

No, no, no. "Please, I listened to you." I plead with quivering lips while tears form. My knees are starting to hurt from being on them for so long. My head feels like someone is drilling into it.

"Stop crying. If he does what I say then you won't get hurt." The man tightly grips my shoulder with one hand while slowly gliding the blade across my throat. He hasn't cut me yet but the way the sharp edges prick my olive skin makes me aware of how serious he is about this plan. I'm hoping Jake listens so he doesn't follow through with it.

Jake stares at me indifferently for a second. And in that amount of time I can easily determine his next move because his lips stay pursed until an evil smirks curves at the corners of his mouth. My teary eyes widen when his hand grabs hold of the golden knob before twisting it roughly.

"Why won't this piece of shit open!" I hear him shout with frustration while my throat burns from being slit. The man releases his stronghold on my neck before running over to him. My shaky hands go straight to my bleeding neck while they fight.

Lifting my hands up I cry out in frenzied panic when I see the crimson liquid decorating my small fingertips. He slit my throat. He actually did it. He told me if I was good I wouldn't get hurt so why am I hurt now? What did I do wrong?

The smell of metallic blood is overwhelming. My breaths are short and quick because less oxygen is flowing to my lungs.

The more I panic, the more my weighted chest heaves. I try to stand up to get help but the loss of blood overpowers my movements. Everything I see is a doubled blur, forcing my eyes to blink so I can stable my vision. My throat burns and it's extremely difficult to swallow. Lightheaded and dizziness consume me, causing my eyes to flutter then close before my body falls limply to the ground. I can feel the coppery liquid pool from my neck as the numbness begins to settle. The vibrant pulsing in my throat forces more blood to gush out like a running faucet. My breathing is irregular while I continue panicking. The only sounds I can make are helpless gurgles before

I'm instantly immersed in a canopy of darkness; suffocating me in its' choke hold of fear.

2

CHAPTER 2

My eyelids flutter before slowly opening to a blinding light. I have to squint to shield them from the radiating light seeping into the room. Wait, light? Is that sunlight? From the angle of the sunlight dancing on my skin, I conclude that the window is to my left. So it is sun. I can't turn my head but I can feel the sun kissing my olive skin. Being in the basement so long makes me appreciate the sunlight.

After a few moments of rapid blinking my fuzzy vision clears. I'm able to see that I'm in a room. A white room with white walls. The first sound I notice is a beeping noise coming from a machine. It makes my head throb worse so I try to lift my hand to clutch my pounding head but I can't move it. What is wrong with my arm?

I hear faint talking on my right side so I assume that there's another bed in this room. Looking from my peripheral I can see that a blue curtain separates me from the other person.

Before I can ask any questions a lady with light pink scrubs walks in. Her curly blond hair flows down her back in a high ponytail while her posture indicates exhaustion. She holds a clipboard in her manicured hands and once she's finished writing she smiles at me.

I try to sit up but realize that I can't move my legs either. What is wrong with my head, arms, and legs?

"Her stitching went well and everything else seems to be fine now Mr.-"

"Thompson. Richard Thompson but you can call me Rich." the voice replies casually. It's an unpleasantly familiar voice.

"Oh okay. Well Rich, your daughter...wait, are you sure you're her father. You look-" she gives him a skeptical look before being cut off again.

"Yeah, her mom and I had her young- very young. We were 14." he lies.

I open my mouth to tell her the truth but I can't move it. I notice my arms lay limp and my efforts to move them are still futile. Even kicking my legs has become a difficult task. All of my energy is put into trying to move so I'm not surprised when I start to sweat. Swallowing heavily, I wince when my throat starts to burn again.

"Still trying to fight?" he laughs at my weak attempt to move. His lips spread wryly while my eyes travel to where the nurse stood. My face mirrors disappointment when I don't see her anymore.

And even though she's out of the room I am determined to get help so I keep trying to exert my muscles. It's like trying to move a tree. My entire body feels stiffer than a board while my forehead is drenched in sweat. The more I try to move the more my raw neck aches. The only good news is that my migraine has dulled down to a faint throb.

"Are you alright sweetie?" The same nurse, Patty walks over to me. My mouth, arms, and legs can't move but my facial muscles can.

I try to show how afraid I am but the man, Rich steps in. He's beside her, glaring daggers at me.

"She's just trying to adjust to the temporary paralysis."

Temporary? So it won't last? My eyebrows furrow while I'm in thought.

"You're paralyzed from the car accident. Pieces of broken glass slit your throat and hit a few nerves, remember?" She speaks slowly, as if I can't understand English.

He asks her how long it will last and she tells him I'll be moving around in thirty minutes.

"You know Rich, you're not that bad looking." She smirks flirtatiously with her hand on his arm.

"Yeah, I've heard that before." he mumbles whils staring at me.

"If you want, I could give you my number and we could-"

"Could you just get the discharge papers?" he snaps impatiently.

The nurse holds a look of offense before narrowing her large grey eyes. "They aren't ready yet."

"Oh, it's nothing against you...trust me." he starts to gently rub her arms. "It's just that we need to pick up her brother from practice before the storm hits." He tells her more lies and once he is sure she believes them he flirts with her until she produces papers. I watch the entire charade unfold.

Lucky for him, he's charming because she sways in with the papers. My heart races as I watch him sign my discharge papers with a victorious grin.

"Here's my number." he slips a piece of paper to her while she holds back a smile. I know it's the wrong number.

"Make sure she takes her medicine and gets some rest. Even though she's been asleep for two days I know she's exhausted," nurse Patty smiles warmly at me.

Two days? I was out for two days. So that's how he was able to paralyze me. He injected something into my body while I was sleeping. It all makes sense now; he wanted to make sure I wouldn't move or talk. But maybe this paralysis serum will wear off by the time they come to get me.

Soon two male nurses roll a wheelchair in. Without much effort, they lift me up and into the seat. My small hope diminishes to emptiness as we make a swift exit through the double sliding doors.

"I'll be right back." Rich goes to get the van, giving me another chance.

"Mmm, mmm," I try to speak again but my mouth feels like it's glued shut. I can't move my head to turn to them and they seem to be ignoring me. I can't see much from my peripheral but I can sense their boredom from the obnoxious yawning they produce.

"Just slide her in the front." He slams his car door before running over to open the passenger side.

My heart drops to my stomach and defeat etches across my features once I'm buckled in the passenger seat. He closes my door and my eyes start to water. I had a chance to be free. To be away from this psycho but he's ruined that by paralyzing me. I can't stop the anger boiling over. I want to scream but all that escapes my lips are muffled groans.

"What did I say about crying?" he grips my chin and turns my head to his. His jaw is clenched like he's holding back anger. I stare bleakly into his dark eyes until he grips my chin harder.

Closing my eyes, I choke back my sobs until nothing but small droplets brim in my eyes. The rest slide down my cheeks when I open my stinging eyes.

"Remember what I told you, crying won't help you Livie. Weak people cry so don't make me regret letting you live." he reprimands coldly.

My entire life is being torn apart all over again. I'll never have freedom again. And worst of all, I can't even turn my head to look at my surroundings. How am I supposed to get help if I don't know where he keeps me? It's embarrassing.

He turns to me with an annoyed sigh before turning my head away.

The whole drive home I tried my best to remember street names, the number of turns we made, and even landmarks, but about ten minutes into the drive he figured out what I was doing so he started taking back roads. And I know there's nothing but Florida woods, swamps and no cars on these roads. No people; no one to see me or help me. And no way of knowing exactly where I am.

By the time he pulls in the driveway the numbness of my limbs has worn off. That means the hospital is about thirty minutes or more from where he keeps me. I counted that much.

He puts the car in park then shuts off the engine. I can feel his intense gaze as he stares at me.

"What made her ask if you were okay?"

My eyes stay focused on the decayed exterior of the home in front of us. An overwhelming feeling of dread attacks me at the sight of its white panels and black shutters. The yard is full of tall trees. A beam of sunlight casts over the entire house while the rest of the yards remains clothed in shadows.

It's two stories, not including the basement. And just like the inside of the home is falling apart so is the outside. Looking at it from the outside you'd assume that it's uninhabitable. The shutters are falling apart, the windows are so old the glass is turning brown and part of the roof has a blue tarp over it. There is dirt on the side panels and the front steps have holes.

I wince when a cold hand turns my chin to the left.

"I asked you a question Livie."

If I move my mouth to speak then he'll hurt me. But if he asked me something then that means he knows my paralysis has worn off.

"Fine." He mumbles before releasing his hold and stepping out of the car.

The only sight is of his head as he walks to my side. But before he can open my door my hand goes to the lock. With a 'click' it locks into place. My heart pounds once I realize how quickly I reacted. I reacted on impulse and for that, I know there will be consequences. But for now, I have an advantage. A chance to get out of here. With that thought, I scramble to the driver side and then the back to lock the other doors.

"You get one chance to open this door." His warning tone is stern but I choose to ignore it.

Instead, I frantically search the vehicle. For what? I'm not too certain but I'm hoping to find a weapon. He starts counting down from ten but all my focus is on the old sports magazines and empty cans of beer littering the floor. As I dig through the filthy glove compartment my eyes land on an old note so I pocket it.

By the time I lift my head up my arm is grabbed abruptly. I'm flung out of the van so fast that I don't see it coming. My face plants into the dirt, forcing the pain in my aching throat to worsen. I forgot he has keys.

"I thought I knocked the fight out of you." He mumbles while dragging me across the dirt, sticks, and grass. A small rock rips off part of the bandage on my neck, forcing a few stitches to come out. I groan loudly while digging my sneakers into the rough dirt.

"Looks like it hasn't gone anywhere..." he finishes while yanking me harder. This time it's so much force used that I can literally feel my arm socket being pulled.

"Wait... wait!" It takes all of my energy to speak with a sore throat but I manage.

He ignores me by lifting me up bridal style. My legs thrash around while he carries me up the broken stairs. His fingers press harder into my side when he tells me,

"If people find out who I am then more people will die, including you."

"Please don't lock me down there!" I cling onto his grey shirt while he opens the basement door.

No matter how many months it's been I can't stand it down there. From the mice scurrying across the floor to the constant darkness looming over me. I don't want to go back and if I don't do something quick then I'll be trapped down there again.

With the white wooden door now open, he stares at me then at the dark pit below us.

"I won't try to run anymore." It takes all of my strength not to cry because once I bring out the water works he'll see me as weak. And weak people don't make it.

With a heavy exhale, he puts me down. And despite my surprise I can't help but hold a level of suspicion too. I don't trust this man.

He points a warning finger at me so I nod reassuringly. I'm not running, even if I did I wouldn't get far. I watch him dig through the dusty cabinets. Spiderwebs fill the empty space.

"Looks like we need cleaning supplies." He shoves a dirty, grimy sponge into my chest.

My fingernails dig into it while I watch him grab a tin bucket from a corner of the room. With complete focus he goes over to the old sink and places the bucket in it. The only sound in the kitchen is the rushing water filling the empty space.

"You get chores." He glances back at me. I notice his dark eyebrows lift while he smirks jubilantly.

"Since I feed you, you have to earn your keep." The soapy bucket is in his extended hand, waiting for me to take it.

With his sleeves now rolled up I notice the tattoos lining his biceps and forearms. He has falcons on one side flying down into a fiery blaze.

"What does that mean?" I point to the tattoos.

"It means mind your fuckin' business, that's what." He rolls his sleeves down. I can't see the rest but judging by his reaction, I've seen enough.

Once I finish scrubbing the trail of blood in the kitchen I move on to the foyer. My blood from two days ago is still here. It's dry now and the color is reddish brown, reminding me of the assault that took place. I shudder from the horrible memory and decide to think of something more pleasant. Like the falling leaves on the trees. The hues of yellow, orange, red, brown, and green leaves we passed by means that Summer has ended, giving way to Autumn.

The seasons are changing and that means I've been here far too long. I'm not sure if anyone is looking for me. I mean I can't really blame them if they aren't. I was a bitch to so many people last year, including my friends. It was a terrible time. My parents were going through a separation and I just couldn't deal with it. I remember telling Margaret to comb her birds nest of hair if she wanted to keep hanging out with me. It was fiery red like her personality but it always looked like she just got out of bed. That next week she avoided me like the plague.

And then my fashion guru of a friend Kelly, I remember telling her to stop acting like the class whore. She had a new boyfriend every week but I didn't know she was only replacing the father who walked out on her mom and three sisters. She slapped me for that and it shocked the hell out of me but I deserved it. Kelly and I stopped talking after that and she even went as far as to torment me everyday. She even egged my car.

And let's not forget Nathan, he would always complain about his step dad. He'd tell me how hard of a time he was having. And one day he came to school with a bruised eye. I could tell it hurt his pride because everyone saw it. Even his jock friends. He was the only jock I liked because he never acted like he was better than everyone. Margaret and Kelly swore he was in love with me but I never saw it. I didn't want to see it so instead when he confessed he had a crush on a girl and didn't know what to do I snapped and told him that I have my own problems and to quote, "shove his up his ass". Ever since eighth grade I spent most of my time being the shoulder to cry on. The last thing I wanted to discuss was his problems when I had my own. I never stopped to consider the girl he was talking about was me.

At the time I thought I was being brutally honest but now that I look back, I was being maliciously mean. I lost all three of my friends but what hurt most was losing my best friend, Margaret. I've known Kelly and Nathan since eighth grade while Margaret's been my partner in crime since elementary school. We used to do everything together but now we don't even look each other's way in the hallways. Kelly spreads rumors about me like a sick kid spreading the flu. And Nathan gets wasted or high every chance he gets. It was so bad that last year he got kicked off the lacrosse team. All of this was my fault for being selfish. I only cared about my own pain and now I feel the wrath of theirs. Friends aren't supposed to do that, they're supposed to lift each other up and be supportive but I was the opposite. I pushed them away. I never apologized and I wish I had.

After I cleaned the downstairs area of the house he put me back in the basement. I've been down here for thirty minutes now and my stomach is gurgling. I can literally feel as much as hear the acid bubbles attacking my insides.

"Where's the... bathroom?" a sudden voice croaks from the shadows.

Once I realize who is talking I grab the bucket. Holding it with both hands I try to block out the putrid smell of urine and feces by listening to my chain slide against the cement. At first it was more annoying than fingernails on a chalkboard but now I find solace in that sound. It's the only sound that keeps me sane, besides my own voice.

"Hey, here's your-" I'm pushed to the ground so suddenly that it takes a minute for my mind to process what is happening. The waste isn't on me but it covers the concrete ground a few inches away.

"He trusts you too much. You're in on this too, aren't you?"

He steps closer to me with his shoulders squared and his fists balled.

"What are you talking about?" I ask in confusion. You can go insane down here but I didn't expect him to go crazy so soon.

"Are you his friend or something?" He questions.

"What? No!" I stand up and a waft of ammonia fills my nostrils. The waste has been in that bucket way too long and now the basement will smell more like it.

"Liar!" He pushes me to the ground with swift impact.

The next thing I see is his fist connecting to my eye. I cry out while grabbing my left eye. I can literally see stars and it throbs like a pulsating heart.

His hands approach my stitched neck to inflict more pain but instead of feeling suffocated, all I feel is air.

"What the hell are you doing?" Rich growls angrily while lifting him off of me.

With my hand to my neck, I waist no time in scooting back until I'm back on the mattress, hugging myself.

"You and that bitch kidnapped me." He replies viciously before hitting the man with something heavy.

Where'd he find that? And before Rich can ask him the same thing Jake strikes him with it. Rich recoils with his hand pressed to the side of his face. They're both silent, fueled with anger. And during their small stare down I'm able to see the rectangular shaped weapon clutched between his fingers. It's a brick.

Jake holds on to it for dear life, ready to hit him again. I watch Rich take small steps toward the angry kid. And even with silence, there's still something eerie about this man. From his hushed tone when he's angry to the way his body tenses when he's ready to attack. It's the quiet before the storm and once he unleashes his storm the results are catastrophic. Fear consumes me the more I watch him.

"You're dead!" Rich lunges forward but is stopped by the brick connecting to his face. He goes down like a chopped tree and that's when Jake takes advantage. He starts wailing on him with such ferocity and strength that his efforts could even break the brick as well as someone's nose.

All I can do is watch with pity because even if he knocks Rich out, he is still chained. We are still chained.

Jake's disgruntled cry resonates and makes my eyes go wide because Rich now has the brick. He took it from Jake so quickly I didn't realize it until his distressed grunt.

He hits him with it a few times until the boy starts coughing up blood. The sound of brick sliding across the floor echoes through the basement before it stops in front of the stairs.

"If you ever touch her again I'll kill you and leave you down here to rot!" He grabs his collar before punching him in his jaw. I hear a reverberating 'crack' before his footsteps walk over to me.

"I didn't do anything!" I shout while trying to crawl backwards.

"Let me make this clear. Any pain I receive from him, you get it too!" He barks while straddling me. My heart drops to my stomach when I realize what he's about to do.

"Wait! Stop!" I try to push his hands off but he grabs my arms and pins them above my head to stop me.

His brown eyes stare into my pleading azure ones. His face is a distorted blur because of the tears flooding my eyes and streaming down my cheeks. But I can see his entire left side is bruised and bloody from being hit with a brick.

"Stop fucking crying!" he snarls while squeezing my upper thigh. "If you just-"

"I can't control what he does!" I verbalize. How can I stop him when he never talks to me? Not to mention the the way he tricked and attacked me a few minutes ago. At this rate we'll never be friends.

"Well you better start because from now on you're the leader. You're responsible for everything he does and if he messes up I'll take it out on you."

I close my eyes while my body continues to shake from fear. I've been trapped here, held prisoner for months with this man and now he wants to hit me for no apparent reason. It's not making sense.

"You got that Livie?"

I release an anguished cry when he backhands the same side my bruised eye is on. It is barely open but I can still see his shadowy face from the light shining on us.

"Yes." I pipe sadly.

3

CHAPTER 3

The next morning I awoke with my mind still reeling from yesterday's chaotic events. I didn't get much sleep because I was disrupted by Jake's heavy snoring. He's out like a light while I'm wide awake with my mind still spinning.

I was minutes from having my purity taken away and because of that "too close" encounter I don't want to be near Rich ever again. Before that I could at least be in the same room as him but now, not so much. He continued staring down at me even after I replied to his ridiculous demand that I control Jake. I only agreed because I wanted him off of me. In all honesty, I can't control him and from the looks of things, he doesn't want to be controlled anyway. I was never the leader type, out of my group of friends Nathan was the best at that.

The door slowly creaks open before bumping against the wall. The loud bang ceases Jake's snoring. He sits up; foul mouthed and grumpy.

The light from the ajar door now shines down on my average frame like a spotlight, leaving me no choice but to shield my eyes with my forearm.

"Morning Livie." I hear his creepy voice whisper.

He's so close I can feel the warmth from his body. My eyes shut tightly when he rests his forehead on mine. His rough hands glide against my arms, making goosebumps appear.

"I said good morning." One hand goes from my arm to my hair. He yanks it back with such ferocity that I can't suppress the whimper that escapes.

"Morning." I whisper. The only part of my body I can move would be my lips, everything else is stiff from fear.

"Someone needs a shower." He mumbles before pulling me up by my hair.

A frightened shriek escapes my lips while my heart pulsates. I'm pressed against his chest, too afraid too move.

"Hey, don't act like that." He massages my lips with his finger while I swallow the bile rising in my throat.

"What are you doing?" I breathe out nervously. He's never grabbed me like this before and if I don't do something quick there is no telling what his next impulsive action will be.

"Bringing you upstairs." Amusement laces his tone. It's as if he knows what he's doing; like he can sense my fear. The very fear he gets a rise out of.

Once I sit down I wait for Jakes' defiance; I wait for a repeat episode of Rich getting angry enough to throw my head into the table or my throat being cut but none of that comes. Instead he walks in limping with defeated shoulders and silent lips.

"Good boy." Rich teases once Jake sits down.

The boy sitting across from me is completely unrecognizable. His entire left side could be the American Flag. His green eyes are sullen with deep red and blue bruises underneath, while white blisters take up residence on his broken nose and cheek.

His eyes remain locked on the dirty checkered table while I continue dissecting him. With a heavy sigh, he begins drawing circles with his finger. I continue staring at him with bewildered eyes. This isn't the Jake I've been locked in the basement with; this is an entirely different boy. And I don't mean appearance wise. I'm talking about his conduct. The willful boy two days ago would have resisted but now he's...ceding. I guess it took him getting a broken nose to finally surrender. It didn't take me long; only a week. But yesterday I attempted to run; which means I didn't completely give up. Rich said he thought he knocked the fight out of me but yesterday proves what a liar he is. I still have it somewhere inside of me.

"Livie, you're on cooking duty. Jake you get breaksfast dishes." Rich orders with a newspaper in his hand.

"I don't do dishes." Jake rubs his temples in frustration. There's a hint of defiance seeping out.

"Then I guess you don't eat either." Rich retorts.

I'm still seated when someone bangs their hand on the table in front of me. With a small jump I realize it's Rich.

"Cooking duty, do I have to spell it out for your dumbass?" He gives one quick head gesture towards the stove, forcing my legs to move faster than my beating heart. I'm out of my chair in a flash.

Jake makes barking noises once I get to the stove but I ignore him. He can taunt me all he wants but I have a method to my obedience. It's not just about doing what Rich says. I'm only trying to survive. If I hadn't begged him to let me live then I'd be dead a long time ago.

The crackles and pops of the bacon sends my stomach into a hunger induced frenzy. I relish in the delicious aroma of pancakes, eggs, and bacon. There isn't much food or utensils to work with but I'm not complaining. I'm just grateful for food. Even though half of the items in the fridge were expired I just picked from the non-expired ones and hoped for the best.

Once I finish cooking, everyone grabs a plate. Jake isn't making barking noises anymore; he's digging into his food full force.

A small smile threatens to creep up but I suppress it. Instead, I draw my attention to the way he eats. It's loud and messy with no sense of table etiquette. The way he rips apart the bacon with his teeth reminds me of a lion eating the flesh of its' prey. I couldn't focus on my meal because I was too engrossed in watching him. Spoonfuls upon spoonfuls of pancakes and bacon being scarfed down all at a rapid pace.

"What?" he looks at me once he notices my gawking.

"Nothing..." I mumble while sticking my fork into some eggs.

With an agitated sigh he shakes his head before his last bite.

"Great food Livie." Rich compliments. His thin lips curve upwards while his milky eyes stare sharply at me. He's leaing against the kitchen counter adjacent to where I'm seated.

So that's why Jake was eating like it was his last meal. I was so oblivious to the fact that he hasn't eaten since he was brought here.

"You a chef?" Rich questions.

I've always wanted to be a professional chef but I'm not telling him that so I opt to lie. I shake my head with a modest smile, "I just watch Food network."

Every party I threw my friends would compliment the food. They always told me I should just forget about graduation and move to L.A. to start my career. Oh how I wish I was there right now.

Jake washes the dinner dishes while I sit patiently. I have no idea what I'm waiting for. All I know is that I was told to wait.

As soon as Jake finishes Rich comes striding in with a cardboard box. It's dusty and filled with old clothing.

"Here's your shit. Change into it after you shower."

"I don't see any jeans." I frown at the flower print dress in my hands. It's long enough to reach my ankles. The only pair of jeans I have are too small but I'd rather where them than these old skirts and dresses.

"My gram always told me some shit about girls wearing that so don't argue or you'll be wearing nothing." He points a stubby finger at me so I nod appreciatively.

"You got this crap from an old broad you call gram?" Jake asks with irritation. He's missing the point. We need clothes so we shouldn't complain.

Rich grabs his collar then pushes him against the wall. His back hits the wall with a loud thud. I try to control my fright but it overpowers me. My palms begin to sweat and my stomach churns with nervousness.

"It's not polite to talk about the dead." He says through clenched teeth while his hands remain balled into Jake's collar.

"Your gram deserves to be dead if she raised an asshole like you." Jake counters with icy narrowed eyes.

He's a jerk who is going to get himself killed one of these days. I don't even know him well and I know that much. I wish he'd go back to being agreeable. He'll be easier to control and less of a problem for me.

"Does anyone deserve to die?" He releases Jake before strolling over to me. With each step he makes toward me, my heartrate increases.

"Death is a funny thing, isn't it?--It can take anyone in its' grasp and literally suck the life out of them. It has the ultimate control over you and there's not a damn thing you can do about it." His eyes hold ire while he grabs my cheeks.

"No one deserves to die but death is inevitable. Just think of me as death." He smiles sadistically. And I have a feeling his statement is directed towards me. I begged him not to kill me because I'm afraid of death; I'm afraid of Rich.

"You fear me because I have ultimate control over your life. You and that prick's fate lie in my hands so think before you speak or act." His copper eyes shift from my startled blue ones to Jakes' tempermental form. Rich is an intimidating 5'10 with the strength of two men while Jake is around 5'7 with scrawny arms and lanky legs. Even if he did take him on in another fight, he wouldn't knock him down for long.

Once Rich finished his menacing speech, Jake and I were ordered to go upstairs to shower. This house reminds me of the type of place you'd dare your friend to spend the night in. It's just as creepy as its owner. Anyway I ended up leading the way because I know the layout. My first week here I scoped out the entire upstairs for an exit but the doors were locked and the windows were boarded. Judging by how the wooden boards are still intact I'm guessing not much has changed about the doors either.

The little light that does shine through the cracks don't help much; it's still dim in here. But the point of the boards isn't to keep light out. I've been here long enough to figure it out. It's to keep us in.

We're now in the hallway, right outside of the bathroom. I'm about to go in when he grabs my arm to stop me.

"Hey." It's not a greeting. I know that from his tone.

"What do you want?" I pull my arm away. After his little act of rebellion he is the last person I want to talk to. Even if this is the first time he's spoken to me in a cordial way.

"I've been thinking about this...locked in a basement bullshit." He shakes his head in aggravation.

"Okay..." I trail off. I think about it more than I eat. And lately, I haven't eaten much.

"Doesn't it seem suspicious to you- the way he acts like he knows you?"

He kind of does know me. I've been here with him since May, longer than Jake has. Plus, I've managed to follow the rules; more than Jake has. No surprise there.

"I mean he likes you. Why else would he give you a nickname?" he whispers quickly when he hears footsteps.

Rich liking me is like saying knives are harmless. We all know he's dangerous and the only thing he likes is causing me pain; it's obvious by the way he treats me. Before I can reply, the footsteps get louder and closer forcing me to open the bathroom door and slide in. The last thing I need is Rich thinking we're plotting something.

I hear murmurs and then Jake starts cussing.

All I can do is shake my head. When will he learn?

As I turn the shower knob I can't help but wonder why he is talking to me now. Does he see me as a team mate; a person to help him escape? Or is this another one of his tricks? Talk to me just so he can get me in trouble again? Whatever his motive is, I don't trust him either.

Once I slip out of my tee shirt and jeans I hear something hit the floor. It's light but with all that's been going on lately, I think I could hear a pen drop in a crowded room. My vision may be lacking from being locked in the dark but my sense of hearing is perfect. Looking down I recognize it as the note I shoved in pocket yesterday.

'Soon.'

Yours Truly,

-M.W.

That's it? Just one word with signed initials? As I re-read the old note I try to think of who M.W. could be but no name or face comes to mind. It's not Rich because his last name is Thompson; at least that's what he said it was. Then again, he could be lying. Shrugging my shoulders, I place it atop the dirty bathroom counter. I'll keep it anyway.

As soon as I got to the kitchen Jake was standing by the basement door, waiting for me. This is our routine now. He lets us out to shower and eat, then we go back downstairs for a day or two.

"Take a seat Livie, you're staying up here." He says with a lax demeanor. All I can do is furrow my brows in puzzled confusion.

"I thought..." I trail off with uncertainty. I'm supposed to go downstairs. That's how it's supposed to be because I broke the rules before. I tried to run.

"You said you wouldn't try to run anymore. There's no point in chaining you down there when you can sleep in the extra bedroom."

"But-"

He laughs lightly at my confused face. "You've been good so what do you say?"

4

—— ◦ ——

CHAPTER 4

With Rich behind me I remain quiet as we descend each step. I didn't need to say anything else because my decision had been made. With a small grimace, I walked over to the basement door then turned to Rich. He shrugged and simply said, "Your choice."

Now we're walking down the steps. The foul smell of mold, must, blood, sweat and urine greet me full force and it takes everything in me not to hold my nose. There is only one light at the foot of the stairs but it's so dim it's yellow. The one window is to the left, on Jake's side. I hate this drab, depressing hell but I'd rather be down here than with creepy Rich.

By the time I get to the last step I glance over at Jake's empty corner. He's huddled in a ball on the cemented floor, leaving me to assume he's asleep. There were boxes on his side but Rich moved them to my side of the room. Even if I wanted to get to them I couldn't with my short chain.

After Rich chains me he leaves, slamming the door with violent force. The mere fact that I'd rather be down here must have insulted him but I could care less. I hate him.

My lips part to yawn, reminding me of how tired I am. I didn't get much sleep last night so even though it's in the middle of the day I decide a nap would be best. I lay down on the uncomfortable spring mattress, tossing and turning for a few seconds until I find a comfortable position. With a tired sigh, I close my eyes but before I can drift off he speaks.

"Why..." his voice is small and hesitant when he questions. Maybe he's testing the waters of my emotional state. "Why did you come back down here?"

My first thought is to pretend like I'm asleep but what good would that do? He knows I didn't fall asleep that quickly. Now my second thought would be to simply tell him the reason; because although I loathe this place, I'm at peace down here. I'm comforted by my own silence; plus Rich can't get to me easily down here. At least I'm here with someone and not completely vulnerable. But because I deem those answers as selfish I don't reply at all. Instead, I sit up and adjust my body to his side of the room to listen to what he has to say.

"I just don't get it," he sighs heavily. "You had a chance to end this but you didn't." I can see his head slowly moving from side to side. So my intuition was right; he thinks I can help him escape.

"I...I don't have a chance at anything." I mumble. It's easier not to fight. Just stay here and survive.

"We can form a plan. I mean we could try. You distract him while I sneak in and kill him." He begins to ramble, on the verge of insanity.

"Kill? No, no. You can't do that." I crawl a little bit towards him before stopping. I'm keeping my distance. The last time I got too close I ended up with a black eye while he received a broken nose.

"I have my family, friends, and Gia back home. I have to see them and to do that I have to kill him," his voice edges with persistence.

"He can't be killed. If you try and fail he'll do worse to me." I start tugging the end strands of my hair while rocking. If Rich trusts me it's definitely better than him not trustng me. I want to stay on his good side and if Jake ruins that I'll suffer from Rich's cruel wrath.

"You're really afraid of him, aren't you?"

I've already admitted that much to myself. Rich scares the hell of me and it bothers me. It annoys me because there's never been a time when I had to be afraid until now. I mean I've never been in situations that leave me with bruises and emotional turmoil. I can't adjust to this and I don't know if I ever will but I do know one thing is certain; I don't want to die.

"Whatever you do to him don't drag me in it, okay? I don't want to die." I position myself to lay back down but before I can close my eyes, he talks again.

"You might as well be dead living like this! Living here in this hellhole."

The tone of his voice has increased but that doesn't stop mine from doing the same, "He feeds us. If he dies we're stuck down here with no one knowing and no way of surviving." I know it's a pathetic excuse but that's all I've got. I make up excuses to stay because I'm too much of a coward to leave.

"Do you hear yourself? Are you really that much of a fucking coward?" He snarls furiously.

Yes, I know what Rich is capable of. If he can murder my parents without one remorseful thought then he wouldn't think twice about offing me- or Jake, for that matter.

"Why can't you just forget about your family? It's obvious you're never going home. You're stuck here like me!" I'm doing him a favor; I'm saving his life. The sooner he forgets about his family the better. Mine are forgotten. No one said it's easy. It may have taken me a week to stop running but it took me even longer to stop thinking about my parents. Like I said, it's not easy.

"You take that shit back right now!" He storms over to me so I back away with my hands up defensively.

"Keep your voice down, he'll be angry if you wake him." I frantically stare at the ceiling. If you listen closely you can hear his footsteps above.

"You're down here with rats and grime while he's in a warm bed and you're really worried about waking him up?"

I nod fervently. "He could punish us or worse, kill us."

"He really screwed you up." He sighs while rubbing his temples.

"I just don't want to die." I whisper to myself while tears overlap and spill over.

"Well, you can sit here and rot if you want but I'm getting out of here. My girl needs me." He says with determination before going back to his side of the room.

"You have a girlfriend?" Someone as distant and selfish as him has a girlfriend?

"Yeah, I had a life before that bastard took me," he grumbles.

"How'd you get here? I mean why did he take you?" Despite my wanting someone to talk to, I'm genuinely curious to know how he got here.

"Trying to be the good guy...I learned the hard way to never be that way again." I can hear his discontented sigh.

He pauses briefly, taking a minute to compose himself. His body continues to face the far wall. I can tell he isn't going to turn around.

"I was hanging with Gia and some friends in the city. It was her birthday so I took her to a club."

"Is Gia your girlfriend?"

He nods so I wait for him to continue.

"While everyone else was piling in I decided to stay outside to smoke a bit. Gia didn't want to leave me but I told her I would be in soon." He chuckles but I can hear how forced it was.

"Not even a minute after she went inside I hear screaming so like a dumbass I follow it."

"I see a lady trying to fight off some jackass who is trying to steal her pocket thingy. So before I can walk up to help her he knocks her out with his fist then takes her... bag." He finds the proper term for purse.

"I figure she doesn't need my help anymore so I decide to head back but what stops me, what keeps me from going back inside is the sound of a little girl crying. I turn around to see her huddled in a corner of the alleyway. The guy hears her and approaches so I do too. Luckily I get there just in time to try to fight him off."

"Did the little girl get away?"

"Yeah, but guess who didn't." He shrugs. His back is to me but I can see his movements. His hunched shoulders indicate defeat while his voice breaks in sorrow.

Clearing his throat he continues, "He said something about bringing Livie some company before he knocked me out."

"You must be who he was talking about," he mumbles.

Is that why he thinks Rich likes me? All because he wanted to bring me some 'company'. That alone makes me hate myself more.

I'm starting to understand why Jake is so angry now. He may have sacrificed his freedom to save that poor little girl but it's my fault he's here.

"My name is Jake by the way."

"What?" I ask with furrowed brows. Staring into the isolated corner of darkness, I can't see much except for his dejected silhouette.

"You asked my name a while ago, it's Jake." He crawls over to me with his hand extended. He's talking about a week ago when I was trying to get him to talk to me.

"Oh right, I'm Livie." I smile while placing my small hand in his and shaking it. I knew his name for more than a week now but I'll let him think I never knew.

"Yeah, I never introduced myself. My mom never raised me to be rude but ever since dad was murdered I just haven't been the same." He looks up at me with regret in his eyes. I can tell he's told me too much too soon.

"I lost my twin brother when I was three." I release my secret quickly. I never told anyone other than Margaret, but now this stranger I'm trapped in a basement with knows.

The silence that follows sends my mind into a pit of regret. I probably shouldn't have told him that. He sits with his back and head against the wall. His knees are upright while his arms dangle over them. I can't see his face to determine his feelings but I can tell you that the distance between us has closed in as we sit side by side; both taking in the unrelenting darkness.

"Rich was right about one thing..."

"Which is?" I ask. My heart is somewhat relieved that he's talking again. Even if the circumstances are grim.

"Death."

He doesn't need to explain any further because that one word holds so much weight. Death is the one thing I fear the most now. Before, my greatest fear was being kidnapped but now it's the fear of dying. When my brother drowned I was right there but I was too young to understand. Now that I'm older and have witnessed my parent's unfortunate death, it seems like all of my sub- concnsious fears have been awakened. We both know Rich is right. Death is inevitable and there's not a damn thing we can do about it.

Soon after my anguished thoughts subsided, Jake broke the silence again. He went on to tell me that his family owned a bunch of oil rigs in Texas but now he lives in Florida with his mom and older brother, Jackson.

"So you're that stuck up jock I hate?" I mumble after he tells me he's team captain of the boys lacrosse team. I glance over at him, he's now laying on the mattress with his forearm over his eyes.

"I hate goodie too shoes so let's call it even." He says solemnly. I haven't told him much about me but I know exactly what he means. I'm a "goodie too shoes" in his eyes because I always follow Rich's orders. Well, if that makes me one then so be it. At least I'm not on my way to being inside of a body bag.

5

CHAPTER 5

I t was a Thursday night, the last day of school had ended and I was spending my evening consumed in watching old movies. There wasn't much on, it was as if the television was telling me to go out and have a life. But I, on the other hand was telling it to go screw itself. With all that's happened to me this year I wouldn't be caught going out anytime soon.

Anyway, the night was young; only 9:30 p.m and I was getting bored with these old movies.

"Where are they?" I peer out of my second floor window, looking for my parents but instead I'm met with glistening bright street lamps and black pavement from the earlier downpour. Ever since my neighbors were robbed two months ago the home owners association commissioned the city of Glennville to add street lamps to our neighborhood.

Anyway, I'm still looking out of my window when I see a navy blue van across the street. It isn't Mr. Dozier's car because he doesn't have one. His son drives him around. Noticing that all of the cars within a visual radius are out of their driveways except this particular one makes me a little weirded out. People have left for summer break and I've never seen this car before.

I grab my phone to dial my parents but to my dismay my dad's cell goes straight to voicemail. They must have chosen the 11 p.m. showing.

With a frustrated sigh, I head downstairs to grab a snack. Once I hit the last step I go over to the front door to make sure it's locked. We don't have a security system so all I can do is check the locks. I go to the back door and do the same. Once I'm done I feel a tiny bit safer.

When every door and window is safely secured I decide to go to bed. I'm already in my pajamas so there's no need to change. As soon as I snuggle into my warm bed my phone starts buzzing.

"Hello?" I ask suspiciously.

"Hello?" I ask again, my voice faltering.

"You shouldn't be home alone." A male voice booms into my ear.

I hang up, regretting my decision to answer in the first place. I already know it's Kelly and her gang of bullies trying to spook me.

My dream is disrupted by the scalding hot water searing my skin. I let out an ear piercing scream as the heat from the water burns my flesh. My eyes are still closed but I can feel small tremors flow through me as I writhe in discomfort. I didn't even hear him enter.

"Dumb prick!" Jake jumps up and tries to lunge for Rich but his chain stops him. My eyes travel to his exact location and my heart fills with dread when I realize he fell alseep on the mattress. The same matress I sleep on, and the only mattress in this basement.

"I said get up; you made me repeat myself so you pay the price."

The way he says it leads me to believe he's still angry. It was my choice to go back downstairs and now I'm paying for it.

"What did I say?" He painfully grips my chin. His cold eyes search mine while I shrink back.

"To- to get up." I stammer. His entire face blends in with the darkness of the basement. He smells of after shave and his hair looks disheveled.

"Then why the hell aren't you moving?" Rich glares down at me, forcing my eyes to shift to my free ankle.

Jake coughs, sending my eyes to him. He's at the foot of the stairs and from the bored look on his face he's waiting for all of this to be over with. After he told me how he got here I understand why he won't help me. I slide off the matress to stand up. My legs are a bit unsteady but I manage to get to the stairs.

On today's menu: stale bread. We're running out of food...or Rich is doing this on purpose.

"What's up with the food?" Jake glowers in Rich's direction. The only item on our plates is the stale bread. I cooked the last of the pancakes and eggs a few days ago.

"I can't afford to feed you gourmet meals so I'm down grading." He shrugs uncaringly.

My mouth begins to water as I watch him take a bite of his sausage biscuit from Hardees. I instantly feel a pang of jealousy.

"From now on you'll do chores everyday. I'm tired of doing everything around here." He takes another bite while I hold back the urge to talk back. This place hasn't been cleaned in months; maybe even years. What does he mean by everything? He doesn't do anything except take kids and hold them captive.

"Chores?" Jake asks. He's already finished his food while I'm picking at mine.

"Did I stutter?" Rich asks while wiping his mouth.

"Because I think I was clear. Did I stutter Livie?" He turns to me, expecting an answer.

My lips move but no sound comes out. I can't form words.

"What the hell is your problem man?" Jake asks infuriatedly."You keep us locked in a basement and your concern is chores?"

He laughs lightly before standing up. My chewing slows when he grabs the back of Jake's head. I see the fear in this terrified boy's eyes but it only lasts a second before flashing to anger. Jake is now leaning back in his chair with a butcher knife pressed to his throat. His breathing is heavy as he holds back the urge to fight.

"I don't want any problems now Jakey boy..." His tone is menacing and insulting just like his words.

My chewing has come to an abrupt halt now while I watch Rich trace Jake's exposed flesh with the sharp knife. He's undoubtedly afraid because his adam's apple bobs with every heavy gulp he takes. Jake winces when Rich nicks his neck. Small droplets of blood slide down his neck like an stream.

"Because if you say one more smartass thing I'll starve you and if you don't believe me, ask Livie. She was just like you. A fighter until I broke that fiery spirit of hers." He smirks knavishly in my direction. His teasing makes me feel patheic so I avert my gaze to the checkered table.

The next sound I hear is a chair screeching against the tile then someone sitting down beside me. Jake is across from me so I'm assuming it's Rich.

"Why chores? Just chain us up and call it a damn day." He argues with agitation. I look up to see his hand rubbing the small cut on his neck. Why can't he just stop asking questions?

Rich ignores him before continuing.

"Livie, since you understand you get to explain."

This is what I was told when I first got here but my attempt to leave stopped him from allowing me upstairs.

"Hey, you speak English right?" His brown eyes narrow while his fingers snap in front of my face.

"...We...we get chores because we're supposed to learn the value of hard work. He expects them to be done at the end of the day. We'll be evaluated on how well we do and if we don't do them to his liking we get points taken. The number of points we get determine how many days we eat and shower, " I mumble the last part. My shoulders hang with shame and defeat.

"That's exactly right. You have to earn your keep," he smiles proudly at me while Jake rolls his eyes.

"You should have just killed me," he speaks low enough for my ears only.

"Eat then clean this shit up. The paint's in the living room so start there when you're done with breakfast dishes." He stands up, goes to the front door and slams it. The sound of the locks clicking fills my ears.

Jake is the first into action. With no questions asked he runs straight to the door for the second time and is disappointed when he gets the same results.

"What did he do to these doors?"

During my three months locked in the basement; the three months after my escape attempt, he would bring food down to me and a few minutes later I'd hear a drill. That explains the steel door.

"They're bolted down somehow." It reminds me of a steel vault in banks except it has an actual knob instead of a wheel.

"He said you were just like me...what happened?" He asks after too long of silence. We can't get out of here and based on our convesation last night, he knows I won't help him leave anyway.

"I tried to leave once. But I didn't get far."

All I could do was run. With my legs going into overdrive and my heart booming in my chest I pushed forward. Running down the pavement to the nearest house I could find. My breathing was sporadic but that didn't stop me from focusing in on my surroundings. The sun is going down but I'm not afraid of the darkness of night. I'm afraid of the darkness lurking in his basement. It's evil, sadistic, and menacing and I never want to be in it again.

To my right are trees with thick branches and forest green leaves. To my left is a house. It's a ranch style home with brick on the front and white siding. Without another thought, I race up the driveway and to the black door.

"What's wrong sweetheart?" A woman with a thick southern drawl answers her door.

"Can I come in?" My eyes move frantically as I look around me. I'm afraid of going back there; going back to him.

"Please, you have to help me. He killed my...parents and he's going to kill me." I plead when I realize she's still staring at me as if I'm some foreign creature.

"Okay...okay sweetie, just come inside." She wraps a chubby arm around my shoulder to escort me in her home.

"Just make yourself comfortable."

And before I can get a good visual of her, she dissappears into the kitchen. I notice the grandfather clock in front of me reads 8:02 p.m. I have no idea what time I left but if I had to guess I presume I've been free for over ten minutes.

"I called the authorities. This should hold you until they arrive." She extends a plate of fresh baked sugar cookies. My favorite. I grab one and smile gratefully at her.

Her chubby cheeks puff out as she gives me a closed mouth grin. She's short with short, auburn hair and light green eyes. She's very pretty for her age.

"Are you that mising-" Her doorbell rings, interrupting her question.

"Must be the authorities." She mumbles while scurrying to the door.

I wait for the police to come in to ask me questions or put a blanket over my trembling body but as my luck would have it, none of that happens.

"Hi neighbor." She greets cheerfully.

They engage in small talk while my eyes travel to the door. I wonder who is behind it if it's not the police.

"Mrs. Adams I'm sorry for this...disturbance. My kid hasn't been the same since her mother died." An averaged sized man dressed in a black collared long sleeve shirt with denim jeans steps in. His head is bleeding but that didn't stop him from running after me.

"What happened to your head, and I never knew you had a daughter." The polite woman smiles timidly at my terrified body.

"Yeah we had her young and ever since she had to live with me she hasn't been taking it too well." He chuckles while approaching me. Once my mind confirms it's really him I try to run but he nears me with three quick strides.

I try to scream but my mouth is covered to muffle it. His arms are securely wrapped around me when he whispers, "You thought it was over, well it's not Livie. The fun is just beginning."

"He knocked the fight out me that entire week." I shudder from the painful memory of hearing my ribs shatter. "The only time he came down was to beat the crap out of me and then he'd leave. He starved and beat me for seven days. Once it was over I coudn't tell day from night and it took a month for me to get the dried blood out of my hair."

"Damn Livie." I catch a glimpse of him shaking his head with sadness. "That...that lady didn't see past him?"

"One thing you should know is that as far as neighbors go, they don't exist. There's no point in running when no one believes you." I stare off, still trying to shake myself out of my horrible flashback.

"You can try again. We can try Olivia. You can't just give up and let your life turn to-."

"I'm not trying anything but you can be my guest. See how hungry you become after two days or how excrucitatingly painful it is to feel some of your bones breaking." With heaved shoulders I finish my rant. He stares at me with shock before it changes to annoyance.

I watch him shake his head in frustration before brushing past my enraged frame and running upstairs.

Shrugging my shoulders, I decide to start painting the foyer walls. There's a can of off white paint with a roller next to the door. Lifting it up, I trail it up the wall, repeating the movements until I'm satisfied.

I hear his footsteps upstairs and then the sound of his body forcibly crashing into the door. He won't break it down because every door needs a key.

"I'm getting out of here!" He shouts to himself. It's followed by three more loud rams into the door.

All I can do is sigh. If he's going to run then I'll let him but I refuse to suffer like that again. When Rich punishes me I'll feel it for weeks, months and maybe even years.

Once I'm finished with the foyer, I move on to the living room. I'm painting when he speaks, making me jump.

"What do I have to do?" His tone is of defeat and embarrassment.

Turning my head I see his head remains down while his hands stay tucked in his pockets.

"Um...just...just paint the living room walls and-"

"No way in hell." He counters with crossed lanky arms. "Just tell me what I have to do to get out of here."

"Jake please just follow the rules." Hopefully he catches my answer to his question.

"You may be fine with working like a slave but I'm not, okay." He paces while looking at the dilapidated living room encompassing us. It's large but it needs work...a lot of work.

"Look, things go smoother when you just do what he says. You get more freedom when you follow rules." My distressed voice tries to negotiate. He freed me last week because he said he was giving me a second chance. That just proves that following rules will work in my favor-- and possibly his.

"Wanna watch t.v.?" He asks while strolling over to the torn apart brown recliner. The archaic television sits on a small black table and has an antenna sitting atop it.

"Don't touch that!" I shout but it's too late. He grabs the remote and is now sitting with his feet propped on the coffee table.

"Why?" He smirks amusingly while flipping channels.

"He's going to come back and see the remote isn't where he had it." I start to internally panic.

"You know what Livie, screw that crazy asshole." He shrugs.

The way he sits and his careless demeanor makes me want to choke him. Every time he messes up I suffer the repercussions. When will he care? He doesn't have to protect me but he could at least be considerate enough to think about the consequences of his careless actions.

"Whatever Jake." I'm on my way back to painting the wall when I hear my name.

"It was a tragic night for neighbors in this Florida community. Just a few short months ago a family of three lived in this house but only two bodies were recovered. Forty-two year old John and his thirty-nine year old wife, Mia Walters were found dead in the home on Thursday, May 28th. Now police say that a gas leak caused this fire and that smoke inhalation caused their deaths. But there was still one missing piece to this puzzle that has boggled the minds of Glennville Police and residents for four months."

The screen switches from the newswoman to the man in a navy blue suit.

"Yes it has Debbie, I've been told that the missing piece is sixteen year old Olivia Walters. Her body was never found and she was deemed missing soon after. But a recent break in the case has police now searching the Westview area."

"Is that here?" I ask but I don't recieve an answer because he is too engrossed in the television.

"One officer told us that he got a tip from a neighbor saying that a girl with similar features to Oliva ran to her door. The woman, who refused to talk to our reporter said this occured some time in June."

"Why didn't she report this sooner? I mean it's August now." The female newsanchor, Debbie inquires.

"Because her neighbor claimed to be Olivia's father."

They ask a few more questions but I tune it out after that. So Mrs. Adams finally reported him. I knew she was bound to recognize me, especially if my pictures were all over the news. They're looking for me; I have a chance at being free. I'm so ecstatic that my lips spread into an excited grin. I haven't smiled in ages and it feels good.

Jake clears his throat, forcing my eyes to land on him. He's still seated on the sofa when he speaks.

"They're looking for me too." He says with anxious eyes. That must be what he was so focused on when he turned the t.v on. "They suspect our disappearances to be related."

"Do you think we'll be found soon?" I ask with hopefullness. If police are searching then there's no need to risk escaping. We'll be better help to them if we're alive and not dead. We need to wait for them instead of impulsively trying to run. I need to tell him this because he has a habit of acting before thinking.

But before I can open my mouth again, the sound of the knob turning makes me pause. I realize Rich is going to catch us watching t.v. and this makes my stomach twist in knots.

Jake grabs my hand on his way to the kitchen, sending my legs stumbling forward. I can still hear the t.v. in the background when Rich enters.

"We're getting the hell out of here." he whispers before stretching his hand to the table to grab the butcher knife.

We're against the wall next to the garage door. He's in front of me while I'm behind him. We have a clear visual of the kitchen entrance and even though Jake has a weapon I'm still panicking. I want to back out but I have no time to tell him to rethink this or to leave me out of it so I close my eyes and swallow dryly. My heartbeat is now louder than the t.v. while my hands shake uncontrollably. He's getting closer based on his heavy footsteps. Once I open my eyes they begin to water because I see Rich glaring murderously at us. My heart sinks to my stomach while my teary eyes widen because I know this will not end well.

6

CHAPTER 6

The noise of the television combined with my thundering heart continues to overpower my frightened thoughts. I can't think, speak, or move by the time Rich enters the kitchen. All I can do is brace myself.

He strolls in with his hands behind his back and his eyes focused on the grround. There's no need to look for us because he already knew where we were to begin with.

He's a few feet away from us, making this appear to be a standoff. His eyes stay connected to the floor while his lips release a forced laugh. Lifting his head up, we're both met with his malevolent glare. His look of ill intent makes my knees buckle. The entire room is quiet except for my light breathing and Jake's heavy panting.

"Betraying me this soon Livie?" He smirks cunningly.

My teary blue eyes meet his cold brown ones, making my throat close up. His presence is strong and so is his rage. His fists are balled while his jaw remains tight, trying to hold back fury that's ready to be unleashed any second.

"I...no." I shake my head while digging my nails into the hem of my dress. The way he smirks at me sends chills down my spine. And what's worse is that I'm not sure if he's teasing or serious. His unforgiving stare continues penetrating mine until I break from it. He steps forward so I step back. I've backed so far into the wall that I feel like I should have become part of it.

"You're going to give me the key to that god damn door, you got that?" Jake authoritates with the knife in a death grip. The way he holds it in front of him with hands as pale as a ghost leads me to believe that he's never held a knife before.

"Give me the knife. You don't have the balls to stab me." He antagonizes him.

"This is a bad idea..." I speak with fear filled eyes. If Rich is not showing any signs of fear then that means he has control over everything that's happening. Jake has no idea.

"Oh yeah?" He charges at him but soon ends up on the hard floor. In one swift movement Rich has lifted the teen's flailing body and slammed him into the ground. Jake is now squirming and cursing underneath Rich's black boot.

"What was that Jake?" Rich presses his boot into his neck, causing him to howl in discomfort. I watch in horror as Rich bends down and takes the large knife from Jake's sprawled hand.

He is still trying to fight when Rich harshly digs it into his right side. I close my eyes when he cries out in pain. This is something no one should see.

"Don't play with toys you don't know how to fucking use!" He roars thunderously, making me flinch.

My eyes stay transfixed on the ominous scene between the two males. Rich pulls the knife out then jerks him up by his collar. I cover my mouth when he pushes Jake against the wall, forcing a strained growl to part from his lips. His head is drooping while he continues to bleed. I cringe from the sight of the crimson liquid seeping out of his wound and dripping onto the white tiled floor.

"Go...to hell." He breathes out tiredly. His chest moves quickly while his body shakes convulsively.

Rich presses the knife into Jake's wound and slices the rest in a downward motion. The boy's cry of agony fills my ears with a haunting sound; marching in my eardrums like a band and making me feel even more responsible for his pain. It's my fault he's here and now I'm not helping him; I'm just standing here watching him bleed.

"You first." Rich retorts before pushing him into the table.

I hear a loud crash when his back makes a violent impact into the table. His knees buckle, sending him falling down like a crumpled napkin.

Rich kicks Jake until his low grunts are replaced with strangled coughs and wheezes. His white tee shirt is stained and ripped. I notice the large amount of blood he continues coughing up and my stomach sinks deeper. I've always hated the sight of blood, especially someone elses. The sight of it is unnatural. The thick, red liquid clumps decorate the floor while small streaks appear on the wall he was against like red paint. A trail of blood is flowing from his injuries and expanding on the floor, making me want to gag.

My eyes remain focus on the gruesome fluid before me. It stops right at my feet. The very same feet that are adhered to the floor. From my trembling legs to my sweaty palms, and burning throat, I'm consumed by fear.

By this time Rich has placed Jake's small straggled body against the wall in an upright position. His eyes flutter in and out of con-sciousness while his head nods off. Staring at him, I realize he has two more stab wounds along his abdomen and he's bleeding profusely. If he doesn't get proper medical attention he'll bleed out.

I have the urge to help him so my legs move before my mind can stop me. I'm almost to his broken body when Rich grabs my hair and pulls me back. Hard.

"What did I tell you?" He pulls my hair firmer, making my eyes tear more.

"Not to-" And before I can explain myself fully my face hits the floor. I don't give myself time to focus on the pain because I'm up and running in the blink of an eye. With my breathing heavy, I head towards the stairs but I'm tackled so suddenly that the wind is literally knocked out of me.

My forehead collides with the end table on the way down, forcing my head to start aching. Groaning, I try to lift myself up but his strong grip on my ankles stops me.

"Let me go!" I scream when I feel myself being dragged across the cold, dirty floor. My nails screech against the wood floor as he continues dragging me.

"Now why in the hell would I do a stupid thing like that?" He turns me on my back. I look at his dark raised eyebrows and dark, gleaming eyes. He thinks this is funny.

"Humor me Livie. Why would I let you go?" He begins to gently glide his hand up my leg. We're in the kitchen, only a few feet away from Jake's still body.

"Because... I listened to you." I whisper hesitantly while my vision blurs from my salty tears.

He frowns while pressing his hand on my thigh so unmerciful that I'm one hundred percent positive it will leave a bruise.

"You call him trying to stab me 'listening to me'? You think you two can team up and take me down?"

"I- I didn't. We-"

"If you think for one fucking second you can beat me I'll make you remember why you can't. I broke you before and I'll do it again. Two more months Livie and I'll be having you crawling on your knees like the obedient pet you're supposed to be." He sneers venomously. My wet eyes close and a small whimper escapes when his fingertips squeeze my area.

I shiver from his foul touch, wishing I could just disappear. Jake starts coughing again so I turn my head to his location. He's still against the wall with a pool of blood surrounding him. His hand presses on one of his wounds while the other arm remains limp on his side. His eyes are closed now.

"What's one way to get you to understand, huh?" He grips my chin and turns my head to face him.

"You don't have to do anything because I understand. I told him to follow your rules!" I wince when his hand moves to my throat.

"Then why was he trying to kill me?" His expression is a mix between anger and intrigue.

"I...I don't know. He dragged me in here while you were opening the door." I start choking when he squeezes tighter. My hands grip his to get him to stop.

"Everything he does to me falls back on you." His voice is steady but his hand shakes, even shaking my stitched neck. "Remember that?"

I nod my head as best I can. He lifts me up and wraps his arms tightly around my waist. "That's why his death will be on your hands if he bleeds out."

"W-what?"

He drags me to a chair and sits me down."We're going to wait and watch."

"I'll give him a solid hour and if he's not dead then I'll make you regret following behind him. And if he dies then it's on your hands. You killed him." He smiles devilishly at me, making my eyes lower to the floor.

That's not fair at all. If he lives I'll be ravaged and if he dies, his death will be my fault because I couldn't control him. The outcomes of either scenario is grim for me.

"Come on Livie, if you ever escape me you can tell his family how their spoiled bastard of a son died because of you." He nudges me with his elbow while laughing cynically.

And just when I thought Rich was just cruel, he proves to be more than that. It's one thing to stab him several times but to watch him bleed to death and then blame me. I'm more than disgusted.

"Don't look at me like that. Reminds me too much of your mom." He remarks sharply.

My mom? How does he know what she looks like? He killed her before my parents could turn on the lights. There is no way he could see her with how dark it was that night.

"How do you know what my mom looks like?" I ask so quickly that I end up covering my mouth afterward.

My head whips to the side and a pulsing throb begins to settle once I turn to him. With my hand on my cheek I wince when he grips the back of my head and brings it forward.

"Rule one, from now on you'll only speak when I ask you a question. Starting right now you'll do everything I tell you to. No questions asked. If I tell your ass to jump your only response should be how high. Both you and him, if he lives. You got that?"

Rules? Does he think I need rules because I've become rebellious or something? From what he said previously, he already thinks Jake and I are trying to team up against him. But if only he knew that is the last thing I want to do. Jake was the one who grabbed my hand and ran into the kitchen. It was just me being in the wrong place at the wrong time. I can't control Jake, no matter how hard I try. And despite what he thinks, I am obeying him, I'm not rebelling. Why can't he see he succeeded in knocking the fight out of me?

"Hey, you got that?" His golden eyes narrow, indicating his seriousness. My head pounds the more his grip tightens, making my eyes blink several times. He asks me again, forcing me to swallow my pain and respond.

"Yes." I mumble.

There were no more problems after he slapped me. I was determined not to cause any more trouble. Even if that meant halting all questions. And believe me it was a hard task, considering how intrigued I was when he mentioned my mother. I still can't help but wonder what that was about.

Anyway, I decided that the smart thing to do would be to continue doing everything he says. Between Jake's rebellion and Rich's determination to make me a leader I already have my work cut out for me. I have too many scars to count so the last thing I need is for Rich to be angry with me.

Jake's loud, sudden coughing sends my eyes to him. It's been fifty five minutes and he is still holding on by a thread. He was about to pass out thirty minutes ago but I kept making noises with a cough or my chair. At one point I even tried to go over to him so I could shake him but once I stood up Rich grabbed my arm and threatened to take me if I went over there. I ended up sitting back down. I know I'm pathetic but when I'm faced with a choice like that, it's easier to do what Rich says.

And as selfish as it sounds, I have to protect my virginity because no one else will.

"Time's up." I speak lowly. He went over his hour limit. I know because I checked five minutes ago.

I wait to be scolded, but instead, Rich goes over to him and checks his pulse.

"Well I'll be damned. This son of a bitch is still alive." He shakes his head in awe.

I let out a sigh of relief because no one's blood is on my hands. Jake lives and I get to live with myself. I'm so thrilled I could dance. But I won't.

"He's breathing, but not for long. Go get the first aid kit." He orders.

With a small smile on my face, I make my way over to the downstairs half bathroom to retrieve the kit. By the time I enter with the small white box Rich is already performing CPR. Before I know it I hear the first aid kit fall to the floor. My heart starts to race and my palms drip with sweat the longer I watch Rich blow air into Jake's lungs. While I'm watching him lie lifeless on the kitchen floor, my first thought is I killed him. I actually took another human beings life.

7

CHAPTER 7

Watching Jake remain stagnant on the kitchen floor takes me back to the lake where my brother drowned. I remember the day he was pulled from the murky water. His eyes shut tight while his small body soaked and covered with small twigs. I was hiding behind my mom's leg when they pulled him out. I remember seeing her knees buckle as she crumpled to the ground; distraught with grief after seeing her deceased child.

And just like my brother, Jake lies immobile. Not moving, not breathing and not living. His lifeless body brings back so many horrible memories that I've tried to forget. I've tried so hard to keep them from resurfacing but now they're here; every horrofic sight, every ear piercing scream, and every bitter feeling I felt the day my brother died is back.

The longer I watch my horrific reality unfold the more I wish I could look away. The more I wish it would all go away. But unfortunately for me I can't stop staring, and the awful memories of this entire ordeal will never go away.

"Come on, come on." Rich chants.

With my hands squeezed tightly, I watch as he pumps air into Jake's lungs. His once vibrant tanned skin is now drained of all color while his sharp green eyes continue to stay shut. Not even a hint of alertness. The blood from his wounds flow out of him like a tube of ointment. Large clumps of red stain the floor around him, even staining Rich's jeans.

Before I can blink twice, Rich moves from his mouth to his chest. He starts quick chest compressions while I continue to internally panic; too afraid to let my troubled emotions show. Troubled not because of Jake's unfortunate situation, but because I'm only thinking of myself. The longer I stand here, the less I'm helping.

But even when I really ask myself if I should help, I end up feeling worse because my reply is a strict no. I stop myself from helping because I'm hoping Jake would just wake up; that these tragic events would turn in my favor, but oh how wrong I am. Instead, I'm faced with a boy who is nearly dead and an unremorseful mind telling me not to offer my assistance.

With his hands over Jake's chest he pushes harder. All of this effort and he still isn't showing any signs of vitality.

"Move." I walk over to an out of breath Rich. He gives me one quick skeptical glance before scooting over.

This is it. I kneel before Jake, positioning myself to revive him. Thank God for my mom making me attend CPR classes after my brother's death. I guess they're about to pay off.

My eyes remain closed as I descend to his parted full lips. I'm about to press my lips to his when I hear and feel coughing. Opening my eyes, I see him coughing up blood so I scoot back to give him some air.

"Nice job Livie." Rich pats me on the back while we wait for him to finish wheezing.

After I give him water, Rich carried him to the sofa. I was told to dress his wounds so that's what I'm doing now.

"Argh!" He hollers when I apply the aseptic to his deepest wound. It's the length of a pencil and the width of a finger; stretching from his upper abdomen to his lower waist.

"Sorry." I mutter while applying light pressure to another wound.

"What did he mean?" He asks after a few moments of awkward silence. This is the first he's spoken since I've been tending to his injuries. His grass colored eyes stare at the wall behind me while I patch him up. He has four more stab wounds while his right eye is swollen shut.

"Livie, what does he mean?" His voice cracks so he coughs to clear his throat.

"I don't know." I shrug while finishing up the last bandage. I know his curious gaze will pierce my soul until I talk so instead of looking at him my eyes stay focused on my task at hand.

"You know what I'm asking."

"No, I do not." I stand but I'm stopped when he grabs my arm.

"What happens... in two months?" He winces while sitting up.

"Nothing. Just leave it alone." I don't know why, of all the things to be concerned about, he'd choose that. You'd think he'd be more worried about his injuries and the fact that he nearly died fifteen minutes ago but no, he wants to know what happens in two months.

"Is it about Rich? What's he going to do?" He presses.

"Why do you care so much? Just leave it alone." I sigh loudly while putting the medical materials back into the first aid kid.

"You," Rich calls, forcing me to turn to him. "Come clean this up." He motions for me to go over to him.

As we walk back into the kitchen my mouth gapes open. I know I was just in here but I still can't overcome the gory sight before me. It looks like a crime scene. A trail of crimson liquid goes from the kitchen entrance all the way to the garage door. The table and chairs are knocked over while the crumbling wall holds small dents from when Jake was thrown against it.

"This floor ain't moppin' itself." He hands me the same tin bucket. This time it's filled with actual detergent, water, and bleach. He bought other cleaning products too which let's me know why he went out in the first place.

I can feel his eyes on me while I'm scrubbing the floor so I make a bold move to glance behind me. Our eyes meet, making me freeze.

"Staring won't clean this mess up." He speaks coldly, forcing my eyes to go back to the partially cleaned floor. The smell of blood and cleaning products intermix and makes me want to vomit. I shake it off while I scrub harder. I'm about to take a rest when something crosses my mind.

"Can...can I ask you a question?" My sudden voice echoes through the kitchen walls, leaving me shocked and still afraid but there's nothing I can do now. The words that escaped cannot be erased.

"You get one."

I'm stunned at how calmly he replied but I don't dwell on that. I need to focus on an acceptable question. Think, think, think. I rack my brain for one but I'm stumped when I can't choose the right one. Shoot, I did not think this through. I have so many questions all bottled up that if I only ask one then others will just naturally spill out.

He thrums his fingers on the the tabletop, reminding me to hurry up. I roll my eyes because knowing Rich, he would control how many questions I ask. I'll just go with the one that will help me the most right now.

"Why do you want me to control Jake so badly?"

"Have you ever had a pet before?"

I think about that before answering. I've had a pet, only one though. She was a black terrier puppy that I had to train. My parents were teaching me responsibilty but I was just to ecstatic to have a pet. I played and fed Myla but I never succeeded in training her. She ruined the dining room rug and chewed on every shoe and curtain. One day my mom took her on a walk and she attacked a man. That was the last straw because my parents sold her. They couldn't take it anymore and if I wasn't going to do what was asked then there was no point in keeping her. I was twelve when it happened.

"Yeah but what does-"

"Then it's like that. Think of Jake as your new pet. If you can train him you get to keep him."

So Jake was right when he said Rich brought some compay for me. And because he went out and basically kidnapped someone else, I have to be the one who keeps him from breaking the rules. I have to keep him in line? But I can't do that. I won't do that because I'm not a leader.

"Problem?" He's looking at my frowning face. I frown and I don't even realize it.

"What if I can't...train him?" I ask with apprehension.

"You remember what happened thirty minutes ago?" He's now standing up with intimidating crossed arms.

I nod slowly.

"Then I don't have to explain because I'll be the one cleaning up a bigger mess."

I don't need to ask anymore questions to know what he's implying. His policy is 'actions speak louder than words' and if Jake keeps being unruly then his life will end. And if I don't do what I'm told then mine will too. Based on Rich's actions today, he is serious when it comes to proving a point. Hopefully Jake will realize this and be more willing to cooperate, because if he doesn't then we might as well be digging our graves.

After scrubbing the floor until my hands and knees became raw, Rich decided it was time to lock us in the dreaded basement again. We're in here with no food, water, shower, or air. It's hot and stuffy but at least he replaced the light and removed a few boxes to make room.

With my back against the cool wall I release an exhausted sigh. The beads of sweat pour down my forehead, making it glisten under the light like diamonds in the sun. Jake is beside me, trying to rest, or so I thought.

"Look, it's August now. We need to start thinking of a plan so we can act on it."

I groan while closing my eyes because I told him to leave it alone. Now I know why he was asking about the two month thing.

"Livie, you hear me?" I can hear the tension in his voice but I ignore it. My eyes shift to catch a glimpse of him laying down with his arm behind his head. His other arm rests on his abdomen while his legs are crossed.

"We're not leaving. Why can't you get it through your thick skull?" If he still wants to leave after what Rich did then he's crazier than I thought. Doesn't he understand that it only gets worse the more he acts out.

"In two months something is going to happen. Something you won't talk about. Why not leave before then?"

"Because...because if I leave- I just can't." With my eyes closed I slouch in defeat. I'm not going to talk about what happens in two months. Heck, I don't even want to think about it.

"You saw what he did to me- to you and you still want to stay?"

I subconsciously rub my sore bandaged neck while in thought. As ironic as it seems, that's mostly why I want to stay. To prevent that from happening again. If we leave he will find us and the pain he'll cause will be so much more worse. I know that for sure.

"If you want to stay here with this crazy psycho who keeps you in a basement then fine. It's your choice but I'm getting the hell out." He seethes while sitting up. We don't have pillows so he has to use the wall for back support.

"And how do you plan on doing that?" I raise a curious eyebrow while giving a sideways glance.

"You think I'd tell you knowing damn well you could rat me out?" He mouths abruptly.

The mood in the air has changed drastically. It's gone from a small windstorm to pure turbulence. Jake and I hate each other and if anyone walked in on us, it would be very clear to see.

"I wouldn't rat...you out." I swallow the bile in my throat when I notice the grotesque dead baby mouse a few feet in front of us.

I loathe him, that is true but I'd never betray him. I'm only concerned with what he does when it affects me. If he wanted to try to escape by himself then I would let him. But because I get punished for everything he does, I'm not letting him leave. The only way he's leaving is if he does it on his own and Rich doesn't blame me.

"I know because I'm not giving you a chance to."

"What's that supposed to mean?" He says it like he doesn't believe me. One thing about me is that I'm not a liar and I hate being seen as one.

"Every time I make plans to leave you always reject them. I gave you a chance but not anymore. It's clear you're on his side. I bet you'd report me to your master before you'd help me leave." He shakes his head bitterly.

"My master?"

"I see the way he looks at you. You're his puppet and he knows it. That's why I don't trust you or him." He stares ahead with determination. His eyebrows pull together while he thinks.

"If anyone of us should be skeptical it should be me. I mean you just waltz in here with your entitlement issues thinking everything should go your way. You've done nothing but make my life worse. You're the one who isn't to be trusted." I point a small finger at him before crossing my arms.

"There's a difference between entitled and willful. Oh and as far as I'm concerned, your life was screwed up way before I got here sweetheart." His lips curve as he grins slyly at me.

But I'm not bothered by his arrogant grin, I'm more annoyed with the way he says sweetheart. It makes my blood boil. I'm five seconds away from decking him in his already bruised jaw.

"Well, if my life is screwed up then yours is too Jakey cakes." I sneer acidulously.

He glares at me with a look of vicious hate. His jaw is clenched while his dark green eyes continue to glower sharply.

"You think telling me what to do or how to do it makes you a leader but you're not. You're just some brainwashed slave." He finishes with a prevailed smirk.

"I'm not a slave to anyone." I say through gritted teeth. I'm trying to keep my emotions hidden but he's slowly making them show.

"You sure about that? Because I say otherwise." He replies matter-of-factly.

I know where this is headed so I decide to entertain his antics anyway.

"How do you know? What makes you sure I'm brainwashed?"

"The way he controls you with one look. I know your type and I feel sorry for you." He quips coolly. He isn't smirking anymore. Instead, his lips pull into a frown.

"You don't know anything about me so do me a favor and don't feel anything for me." I narrow my blue eyes at him.

"I know you're not a leader. And I also know that you'll never be able to lead me, control me, or whatever the hell you and that bastard are trying to do. So do yourself a favor and stop." He says hardheartedly.

With silence and darkness casting over us I decide to end it there. Jake's made himself clear; he isn't going to cooperate while Rich, on the other hand, wants me to make him. I don't know what to do so I do what comes naturally. I tune every movement and every creepy sound out so I can drift off to sleep.

8

CHAPTER 8

Two loud 'pops' echo through the entire house and wakes me up. With an alarmed heart and wide eyes, I quickly sit up. My phone is on my nightstand so I grab it, only to realize the battery is dead. I forgot to charge it.

Looking at my wristwatch I see it's 2:40 a.m. Oh my God, my parents. Throwing the covers back, I scramble out of bed and run straight towards the stairs.

With my hand on the rail, I start to descend but I'm stopped when I hear an unfamiliar voice.

"I loved you and you know that!" The angry male voice yells.

What is going on? I creep down a few more steps to get a better look. My body leans forward while I peek over the railing. A shocked gasp parts my lips when I see a figure covered in all black from head to toe. The longer I stare the more my eyes start to water because on the floor in front of him lies two motionless bodies.

The little light from the kitchen allows me to see the deep cherry red liquid pooling on the beige foyer rug. A jolt of pain passes through my heart, making me clutch it. Is this what heartache feels like?

I watch in horror when he bends down to a body. My mother. Her blond hair glows in the light pouring from the kitchen.

"I'm so sorry." He sobs before firing several more times.

Suppressing a scream with my mouth, I turn on my heel and sprint up the rest of the stairs. By the time I make it to the top, my heart is still beating like a drum while my breaths are short pants. I hear footsteps behind me so I run to my room.

With my hands on the door I push forward to close it but a sudden force knocks me backwards. My eyes tear more when I see the evil figure standing over me. His steps are slow and steady as he approaches my shaking body. I'm terrified and from the evil smirk plastered on his face, he's enjoying this.

My dream is interrupted by the noisy sound of glass breaking. Opening my groggy eyes, I see a figure near the window. He's hunched over, breathing tiredly. I roll my eyes because I already know who it is. I just don't know how he unlocked his chain.

"Jake!" I whisper after sitting up.

The clash of bottles and boxes being thrown around fills my ears and irritates my nerves.

"What are you doing? If you get caught-"

"Just stop talking for one second." He limps over to me. His right hand presses the bandage on his abdomen. The blood seeping through is transparent.

"I need to get to a hospital. Now I'll only ask once, are you in?"

"You're leaving?"

"No, I'm just going to stay here and bleed to death." He states dryly.

I hate his sarcasm but I know what he's saying. He needs medical attention so he's going to find it. And even though I don't think it's a good idea to leave, I also don't think I should stay here either. If Rich comes down to find me by myself I'll be accused of helping Jake leave. When Rich is angry he's impulsive and unpredictable. His anger sends chills down my quaking spine and I don't want to hang around to feel another minute of it.

I hear more bottles roll around on the floor, averting me from my thoughts. Looking up I see him looking at the window.

"Wait, I'm coming too." I start walking over to him but my body is yanked back abruptly. I land on my butt, grumbling while pulling my ankle.

"Yeah genius, you're still chained." He limps over to me with a smug smirk.

"Just get me out of this damn thing." I shake my ankle to indicate the restraint holding me captive.

He chuckles at my attempt to be brave and then slowly bends down. I hear a suppressed groan leave his lips before realizing that he's still in pain. Once I patched him up he didn't get any pain medication. He didn't get the treatment I received when my throat was slit.

He struggles to pull something from his pocket so I gently grab his arm to stop him.

"I'll get it, just tell me which pocket."

He points to his right one so I dig in it. After a few seconds of filling around I'm finally able to clutch a black bobby pin.

"Found it in the sofa." He grins mischieviously while I hold it in front of me. My eyes roam over the pin, observing every inch of potential freedom.

Closing my eyes, I inhale before sticking the pin into the keyhole. My lip throbs while I jimmy the keyhole and soon I'm tasting blood.

Ignoring the metallic taste, I twist and pry the lock, trying to dislodge the cuff. With riveted fervor, I put all of my effort into freeing myself that when it clicks and the shackle falls off I'm in a startled daze while he shakes me.

"Hey, you okay?"

Tears spill from my frightened eyes and glide down my cheeks while I blink rapidly. The small light bulb above flickers sporadically; illuminating our faces in one second while making them appear as crescents in another. He's staring at me with...concern. As if I'm some fragile human on the brink of breaking down. His dark eyebrows scrunch downward while his smoldering green eyes bore into mine. I don't think he realizes how he looks so I decide to break our staring match. Looking down at myself, I know why he was looking at me with sympathy. My knees are drawn to my chest while my arms tightly wrap around my upper body. I didn't know I was rocking.

"Because if you want to stay, you know be my guest."

The last time I was free he caught me. I'm taking a chance this time and there are two main reasons why. One being, I don't want Rich to chastise me for Jake's reckless actions, and two being that deep down inside, I want to prove Jake wrong. I'm not a brainwashed slave.

"Seriously, if you can't do this..." He trails off, unsure of how to finish his sentence.

"No." I take a few deep breaths before releasing the stronghold on my arms. My heartrate steadies while my palms rest on the cold cement floor, cooling me down in a sense.

"No," Standing up, I dust myself off while looking in his direction. "I'm coming."

His 5'7 frame is now standing near the small window. I'd have to stand on something to reach it because it's higher than me, and I'm around 5'4.

"This is the only window that's not boarded. Probably the only window down here." He analyzes it for a few seconds before throwing the beer bottle. It crashes into the window before ricocheting off and falling to the floor. It didn't even make a scratch.

"Hey if we're doing this then you might want to be a little quieter. If he wakes up-"

"Livie, if he hasn't come down here by now then he's out for the night." He winces while chucking another bottle at the old glass window. The bottle breaks once it hits the wall. Glass shards fly like glitter before falling onto the cemented floor.

"He comes down here?"

"Yeah sometimes, and you'll never guess why."

I wish he were being sardonic but something in the tone of his voice tells me he's serious.

"We need to search these boxes for something that will break that window," he swallows dryly. I notice the tiny droplets of sweat occupying his forehead. His body is leaning against the wall while he continues holding onto his side.

"I'll check again." I volunteer because from the looks of his wounded state, there isn't much he can do.

I'm about to look inside a box to my right when I hear the faint sound of footsteps above. With eery quiet lurching over us and fear on our eyes, we both look up. The footsteps stop at the door and soon after, we hear the lock jiggling. Jake starts cussing while I run to my spot.

"Pssht," he calls before I can sit.

"A little help."

I turn to see him limping slowly so I run over to him. Wrapping his arm over my shoulder, I support his weight so we can make it to the mattress. Once we get there the door flies open. With a racing heart, I quickly throw him down. He lands on his injured side which forces a pained groan to emit from his lips.

"What does he come down here for?" I whisper while rolling him on his back. He mumbles incoherencies while grimacing. I know he's in anguishing pain but if I don't move quickly we'll get caught.

"You'll figure..." He winces while I position him against the wall.

"It out soon." He finishes once I have him situated.

I'm about to demand he tell me but the creak of the stairs sends me into fast action. With shaking fingers, I lock his chain back in place before I move on to mine.

By the time Rich gets to us, we're still and silent. I'm laying down while Jake sits propped against the wall.

Peeking my eyes open, I see him looming over me. He bends down so I shut my eyes tightly. I feel his rough hand against my cheek. Stroking lightly, he glides down to my neck until he reaches my hair. His touch makes my heart pound so hard I can feel it in my head. My breathing is irregular while I'm trying not to panic.

A sudden warmth attacks my cheeks while something soft touches my foreheard. Once I open my eyes I'm met with the sight of his neck. I can feel his smooth jaw resting atop my head.

"Get off of me!" My alarmed voice rings through the room while my fists rapidly strike him.

"Hey!"

He grabs my arms and pins them above my head.

"Calm down."

My body freezes in place, too afraid of his next move.

"Please let go." I pipe when his face nears mine. If he leans an inch more then our noses will be touching.

"I thought you were someone else, that's all." He's breathing as heavily as I am while his fingers firmly press on my wrists.

The look; the dangerous desire in his eyes and the way his lips curve makes my blood run cold. Even if he thought I were someone else something tells me that he would have kept going if I hadn't said anything.

Once my wrists are free I pull them closer to me. He backs up and is about to walk out when I stop him.

"Wait!" I shout.

He stops walking which lets me know he's listening.

"He...Jake needs medical attention."

I start to shake him, only to realize he's unresponsive. His head droops down while his eyes stay shut.

"I'll be back." Rich says softly.

I don't know where he is going but my mind is working. Thoughts swarm around me like bees in a beehive. While Rich is gone, I have a chance to get the hair pin from Jake's pocket so that's what I do. I scoot to him to retrieve it from his pocket.

By the time Rich comes back Jake is barely breathing. He's going in and out of consciousness while his blood drips on the floor.

I watch Rich pull a syringe from his jacket pocket then insert it in Jake's arm. It's the paralysis drug. The same drug he gave me so I couldn't talk or run.

Once he lifts him up he heads for the stairs.

"Why do you watch me sleep?" I blurt out quickly.

He ignores me by continuing to ascend the worn steps.

"Did you mistake me for my mom?"

I hear the door slam furiously and then the loud echo of the lock clicks. The sound reminds me that I'm still trapped here and how pathetic I am to be used to this.

Now that I'm fully awake I might as well search for weapons again. The first time I did this I found a hammer in the corner. I wonder what I'll find this time. Probably nothing. Ever since the night I attacked him he's been cleaning out this horrid place.

Scanning the open space, I see three boxes to my right on Jake's old side. There were at least five before he cleared it out. I wonder why he'd leave these three.

I start to crawl to the one closest to me but I'm stopped short by my chain.

"The bobby pin." I mumble before going in my pocket.

Once I'm free, I stand to stretch my stiff muscles. They pop while I yawn, reminding me of how sore I am. With everything that has happened my mind must have mentally suppressed the pain I was in.

A shiver runs through me once I get to the box in the corner. It's been chilly down here lately and I don't know why. Maybe there's a draft somewhere.

I walk over to where the air is coming from and feel the walls for some type of opening. After a few minutes of scanning the walls with my fingers, I decide to give up. As long as I have the bobby pin I'll be able to come back.

With that thought, I move on to the box to my right. It's an average size cardboard box, nothing special. I bend down to open it and dust attacks me, forcing a coughing fit to erupt.

After fanning the dust I seacrh the box. Soon, my hand is gripping something soft and cottony. like fabric. It's a box full of old clothing.

Shaking my head, I move onto the second box. It didn't take me long to realize that it was an empty box. The last box intrigued me the most because it contained old photos. One had a woman with long brown hair teaching a class. The others had the same woman but without the class. There was a picture of her tutoring a student with neatly trimmed hair. I couldn't see any faces because they were both focused on the book on her desk.

"How is this going to help me?" I release a frustrated sigh before throwing the picture. It lands face down, allowing me to see the words on the back. Once I pick it up, my heart drops and my eyes widen when I glance over what I'm reading.

'My favorite teacher, Mrs. Walters.'

9

CHAPTER 9

With my arms crossed, I stare at the scattered pictures on the concrete floor. My eyes roam each Polaroid while my mind spins like a pinwheel.

There are five photos of the same two people. A teen boy sitting across from a woman with long, chocolate brown hair. I notice that the one in the middle is the only photo with words on the back. Those words replay in my head like a broken record.

'My favorite teacher, Mrs. Walters'

Could that be what M.W. stood for?

Pulling the slip of paper from my pocket, I trace the words with my fingertips.

'Soon.'

M.W.

it reads in a much neater handwriting than the photo.

I continue biting my lip while in thought. If M.W. means Mrs. Walters then that's just that. Nothing more. The woman in the photo is not my mother. She's just a person who looks similar to her with the same last name.

With a small, agitated sigh, I lift the box and chuck it across the room. It slams into the wall, making a small huff. With my fingers entwined in my hair, I close my eyes and slowly trace over my face. I need sleep and if I don't get any soon I'm bound to pass out. With that thought, I make my way over to my spot. Once I chain myself to the wall, I pocket the pin then lay down. But before I can close my eyes I hear the door opening.

My eyes open quickly when he exhales heavily, fanning my nape. A sudden shiver provokes my exposed arms, making goosebumps appear.

With silence encompassing us, he begins to un-lock me. I don't need to question what he's doing because I already know. It's time for breakfast. My stomach is growling because I haven't eaten in two days. But my mind, now that's a different story. My mind is full like a glass of water, just waiting for the chance to pour all of these unanswered questions out.

"Rich?"

"Hm." He stands to stretch his arms. I notice another tattoo on his left arm. I can't see it because part of his sleeve covers it.

"Are you the kid in the pictures?"

His stance is hesitant while he stares at me in awe. The expression on his his face is one of shock before he looks around him. I'm staring at the dark ring around my ankle while awaiting his response.

After a few moments of uncomfortable silence, impatience gets the best of me.

"Why can't you just talk to me! I listen to you without back talking and this is how you treat me? Like I'm some-"

"If I ignore you then that means shut the hell up." His dark eyes hold resentment while penetrating my soul. I should be terrified, but because he's only glaring at me, I feel safe enough to speak my mind.

"I'm not going to shut up when it comes to my mother. You knew her and I need to know how...or why." I say with firece conviction. "I deserve to know if I'm stuck here." I'm now standing up, mere inches from his intimidating stature.

"What stopped you from questioning me before?"

The question catches me off guard. I did not expect this, especially since I'm speaking up for myself.

"Do I have to repeat myself?" He's looking at me with scolding brown eyes. They're narrowed while his thin lips remain tight.

"You-" I close my eyes to block the tears that are about to pour out. "You threatened to cut my tongue out."

"And what else?"

"Only speak when I'm asked a question." I roll my eyes at his stupid rules. The same rules I've been following since I've been here.

"You know the rules but you haven't been following them. You're becoming...rebellious." He says the last word with disgust.

"No I'm not."

"Then how'd that box get over here?" With his muscular arms crossed, he glances at me and then towards the box to my left. I forgot I threw it over here.

When I don't reply fast enough he bends down to my eye level and grasps a fistful of hair. My scalp burns from the sudden force as my head bends back further.

"How did that fucking box get over here?" His raspy voice crescendos. The edge in his tone is more menacing than his stronghold.

I grit my teeth to prevent myself from crying out but that only lasts a second before I let an ear piercing scream vibrate the walls.

"I don't know!"

"Don't play games with me Livie. I know it was thrown from the other side of this room so how'd you get free, huh?" The way he grins makes me believe he knew what he was doing when he left these three boxes down here. It was a test and I failed because I asked about the pictures. No, no, no. This isn't happening. It's like every chance I have at freedom is destroyed by him.

But if I can convince him I never moved then Jake and I have a chance. I have to keep the bobby pin from being taken. "I never left this spot."

And just when I say that, he pins me down without warning. I'm on the floor with his hands on each side of me while his knees straddle me.

"We're going to play a game. If you tell me how you got out then I won't hurt you."

"I never lef-"

His finger presses to my lips to quiet me. With sharp, cunning brown eyes and a small grin, he whispers,

"I have a better idea. If you can get away from me then I won't hurt you."

As soon as those words part from him I feel an instant pinch on my upper thigh. My breathing quickens when his large hand smoothly slides up and down my leg. His sturdily built body lingers over mine while his palm is pressed against the concrete, shielding me from freedom.

I try to roll on my side but he uses his free hand to grab my chin. Thinking on impulse, I lift my knee to kick him but he grips it firmly.

"Not going to play by the rules, are we?"

I feel open space which tells me that he's off of me. Once I scramble up, I run toward the stairs but I'm suddenly jerked backward.

I hear a cackling laugh and then a rattling chain. He must have chained me when I wasn't looking.

"Well I can make up my own too." His creepy steps echo through the dim asylum, and with each one he takes I scoot back.

I watch him bend down to where he's now squatting in front of me. My heart sinks to the pit of my stomach when he pulls my legs forward.

"Don't!"

"Don't what?" He frowns with mock doubt. "Do this?" He pulls my legs are apart, forcing me to squirm more. His hold is too tight and even when I try to kick him he just squeezes my upper thighs.

"Ah, don't be scared Livie." He bends down to my ear to whisper, "I think you're worth the wait."

"So let's try this again."

He loosens his grip on my legs so I scoot to the wall. My chest heaves from my racing heart while beads of sweat glisten on my skin, illuminating under the light above.

"How'd you get free?" He goes over to his toolbox and begins digging through it.

My mouth becomes unbearably dry when I see the pliers in his hand. He observes it for a minute before digging for another. This time he finds the right size, a bigger size.

"If you lie to me or play dumb then I'll pull every single fucking tooth out until there's nothing but gums."

By the time he approaches me, my back is firmly pressed against the wall. I can feel every rough, uncomfortable brick poking me; taunting me and confirming how trapped I really am. I can't run and there's nowhere to hide.

"Tell me."

My lips are pressed tightly together while his thumb and index finger pinch my chin.

"Fine." He pulls my lips apart then slides his slimy finger in my mouth. With quickness, I bite down on it, refusing to let go.

"Dammit!" He growls before slapping me with the heavy pliers. I fall sideways, my head instantly connecting to the concrete. I can feel blood flow from my now aching mouth so I clutch it while groaning. I wish the pain would go away but it just lingers, only to be magnified by the sudden feel of pliers pulling my molar.

My teary eyes land on Rich's cruel ones. His angular jaw is clenched while his teeth remain gritted.

"I gave you a chance!" He pulls harder, almost uprooting my tooth. I scream out while holding onto the pliers.

"Mmm! Mmm!" I try to speak but it's muffled.

"What was that?"

He stops mid- pull with a look of disapproval. His brown eyes narrow, forcing my eyes to close. I better tell the truth if I don't want my tooth pulled out.

"I stole... a pin from the sofa when I was bandaging Jake," I mutter with failure wavering my voice.

Without another word, I wait for him to take the pin and leave me down here for a few more days, but an unexpected throb comes first. Opening my eyes, I see the front of his black shoe, only to realize it's pressed to my neck.

My throat continues to throb while I claw at his shoe. It's a burning, pulsing ache that won't diminish. The harder he presses the more my fingernails dig into his shoe, pleading for him to stop. I can barely breathe so speaking is impossible at this point. Only relentless gurgles and gags seep from my lips.

He starts to twist his foot, digging deeper into my neck, and before I know it I'm kicking and gasping for air. It's as if my soul is being sucked from my body while the pain of a thousand needles pricks my dry throat.

"Here's a tip, I know when you lie so don't. Now get up," he orders.

And just as quickly as it happened, it's over. My chest heaves while my hands clasp my sore, bruised neck. Taking deep breaths, I try to gather my bearings.

Once I'm standing, he goes in my pocket and takes the bobby pin.

"I can't risk you getting free." He utters while grabbing my upper arm.

I don't say anthing the entire walk upstairs. I'm just in a blurred daze, so when the door slams shut I'm startled out of it. Looking around, I realize I'm in the bathroom. A light pink shirt with the words, 'Superstar' in the middle sits atop a pair of denim jeans on the counter.

"He got me jeans." I whisper while tracing my fingers across the dark cotton fabric. I've never really thought about how important they are until I was forced to be without them. This may be my only pair so I'll wear them with a smile.

Moving cautiously, I turn the knob then I let the water drench my small hand, spraying me in the process. When the water is warm enough, I remove my clothing. I haven't looked in a mirror since I was punished for trying to run. Rich broke every mirror that existed in this horrid place so I have no idea how bad I look. I know I have a heart shaped face, dirty blonde hair, big, light blue eyes, a small nose and full lips like my mother. But as far as hips and chest go, I'm not very developed yet. My skin color is an olive hue just like my dad's. He's half italian.

A small pang throbs in my throat again so I rub it gingerly. I don't need a mirror to know that my bandaged neck is a completely different shade of green from my natural olive hue. The pain will go away but the scars will always remain.

Now it's breakfast and as bad as I don't want to eat, I know I have to. I have to build up my strength if I plan on leaving with Jake.

Jake is here now. From the looks of his round, bruised face and blood soaked clothing, I doubt Rich took him to a hospital. I know Jake can be a little rough around the edges and manages to make more enemies than friends, but he doesn't deserve to suffer like this.

My eyes trail his face, noticing a small wince as he bites into his cereal.

"I'll be back so don't move. I know he won't." He chuckles darkly. His sense of humor scares me. Actually, everything about him scares me and I dread being in the same room as him.

"My entire body feels like I've been rammed repeatedly." He groans while laying his forehead on the table.

"Why did he beat you again?"

I don't know why I would ask such a foolish question. Of course I know why Rich beat the crap out of him.

"If I told you I didn't know why then I'd be lying."

He runs his fingers through his tousled, honey wheat hair then continues.

"It's like he knew I had thrown those bottles before he got downstairs."

Like with me and the box. He noticed it had been moved. He probably noticed the broken glass in the corner by the window. Rich knew what he was doing.

"I thought he paralyzed you so he could take you to the hospital." At least with that, you can't feel anything.

"It was water."

My eyebrows pull into a frown while I stare at him. Water? Why would he...and that's when it hits me. Rich wanted Jake to feel every punch and kick, that's why he didn't paralyze him. It was his punishment for trying to leave.

"And what hospital? He took you to a hospital?"

My mouth forms an 'O' once I realize what I just did. This will only divide us even more. Why did I tell him that?

After a few seconds of silence, I look up to see his head leaning on the palm of his hand. He's analyzing the scratch marks on the table when he asks,

"What'd you find in the boxes?" It sounds kind of forced but I don't dwell on it. He's bothered by the fact that I went to the hospital and there's nothing I can do to fix it.

"Just old photos." I speak meekly.

"That's it? How the hell is that supposed to help us?" He says more to himself than to me.

That's exactly what I said but instead of speaking, I just shrug my shoulders.

"We need to think of way to get out of here," he asserts while thrumming his fingers on the wood table.

I'm chewing my cereal while my baby blue eyes remain glued to my bowl, hoping he lets it go.

"Now that we have that pin we can look for a secret door or something."

My un-chewed food slides down my esophagus before barricading my airways and forcing me to start coughing.

If he finds out Rich took it then I'm done for. Believe it or not, that's the only thought I have right now while I'm literally choking on my food.

"Here." He offers me his water so I take it, guzzling it down without a second thought. The cool liquid glides down my throat and clears my clogged airways.

"Thanks." I smile once I finish the bottle. I drank all of my water so I'm grateful that he shared.

"Yeah, don't mention it." He returns a half smile, making his full, pink lips spread halfway across his round face. I notice that along with his once full muscle mass, his cheeks are also starting to thin out from not eating regularly. From there, my eyes trail to his crooked, bloody nose. And then to his intriguing light green eyes. I never realized how trusting they are when he smiles.

"Hey, when you two lovebirds are done smiling at each other like lunatics come to the living room." Rich is leaning on the door frame with crossed arms and a smug smile. I see him shake his head with repulsion before turning on his heel and walking out.

"What was that about?" Jake asks with creased eyebrows. He's just as puzzled as I am.

"I said come here!" He shouts impatiently.

We exchange suspicious glances while piling into the normal sized living room. Jake continues to limp while I try to keep my knees from shaking. I have a bad feeling.

"Sit." He orders with eyes directly at me. I'm supposed to be the leader so with no questions asked, I plop down on the orange sofa.

"I don't have time for this shit." Jake is about to storm out when Rich blocks his path.

"Sit before I break your legs." He threatens casually.

He and Jake exchange malicious gazes. It's like they're fighting in some war that involves just them. They're both speaking with their eyes and from the look of Jake's defiance he isn't going to be the one to back down first.

"When I tell your dumbass to sit you do it." He grabs Jake's collar and pushes him to the floor with so much force that the wind is literally knocked out of him.

I watch in awe-struck horror as Rich stomps on Jake's bad leg repeatedly. It tears my insides to see another human being suffer like this, and with each cry of agony that fills the air, my eyes water more. This only makes me wish Rich would just lock us up downstairs. I'm comforted down there because I don't feel, see or hear pain. I can just sleep all of the bad away, only to be awakened by it the next day.

"Okay! I'm...sorry! I'm...sorry!" He's holding onto his leg while rolling around. His face is distorted from the pain he just endured.

"Next time I won't be so forgiving so do what I say the first time."

This is the first time Jake has apologized for standing up to Rich but once again, Rich isn't phased. It's as if he has no sense of remorse. No sense of feeling. Now, Jake knows as well as I do what Rich is capable of. Maybe this will change him.

After I help Jake onto the sofa, Rich explains what he's- what we're doing.

"You're both going upstairs to dye your hair, then you're going to cover those bruises and change clothes." He hands us a pile of new clothing. And judging by the appearance and fresh, new smell, they're from a department store.

"Why?" I blurt out, clearly against this idea. And besides the fact that I love my short, blond hair, it's a habit now.

"We're having visitors, that's why." He grins while loading a black gun. My eyes linger on the golden handle when he cocks it.

"That belonged to my dad." Jake whispers so suddenly that it takes me a minute to figure out what he's talking about. His eyes are intently set on the weapon in Rich's hand. If it were food, and Jake was a hungry lion then Rich would be in trouble.

"Are you sure?" I watch Rich put the gun in a holster on his backside.

"I think I'd know my dad's gun when I see it." He remarks snidely.

"Don't do anything stupid. Just wait it out." I whisper quickly while Rich approaches us. I'm starting to doubt his apology was genuine. It was probably said to throw Rich off.

I can see him from my peripheral vision. He glances at me solemnly then shakes his head in annoyance. But I don't care if he's irritated by my response. He needs to learn to think before he acts.

He doesn't make any moves by the time Rich gets to us so I assume that he's going to listen to me. It's about time.

"Go get ready kiddos, we have roles to play." He smiles wickedly at us, forcing me to swallow the lump in my throat. If he's going to do what I think he's doing then this may not end well.

10

CHAPTER 10

"**W**ho do you think the visitors are?" I ask while combing through my newly colored hair. It falls in dark waves just past my shoulders. Rich broke all of the mirrors so I'm looking at my reflection through a shattered one in his room.

"Not sure, but I do know that we need to form an escape plan anyway. We can't count on anyone saving us." Jake's hair is now dirty blond and shorter than before. I watch him run his fingers through it and note how unusual he looks with lighter hair.

"But what about the gun?" Everything changes when a gun comes into play. We're stomping on dangerous ground whether he knows it or not.

"Guns don't scare me." He admits quietly. I watch him stare off as if he's contemplating on whether he should say more.

"It's the people behind them." He looks up at me with honest eyes. It's like we're thinking the same thing.

"Which is all the more reason why we shouldn't try anything." Rich is dangerous with or without a gun, and if someone else dies then I'll break again. Jake may be hot headed, stubborn even, but believe it or not he's the only company I have here, other than creepy Rich.

"Well, if you're waiting for your knight in shining armor to come and rescue you then you're just as psychotic as he is." He shakes his head with an aggravated sigh. I watch him struggle to remove his old shirt so I walk over to help.

"I'm just saying that waiting for help that will never come is pointless." He explains, causing a glare to form on my face.

"And I'm saying that the visitors could be people who can help us. We should wait." I clutch the hem of his shirt, contemplating on tugging hard enough to emphasize my point.

"You like him, don't you?" His lips curve suddenly, sending my eyes back to my task.

"No, what makes you say that?"

"You always find a reason to stay." I can hear the uncertainty in his voice. It's as if he thinks I'm lying.

"I'm not saying we should stay, I'm only saying that it's smarter to outsmart him. I've been with him longer so one would think you'd follow my lead." My eyes look up at him and for a second, I'm immersed in my dad's emerald eyes.

"Ha! What lead?" He scoffs.

And just after he says that, my entire mood changes from hopeful to forlorn. What good is talking to him when he refuses to listen?

Without another word, I roll my eyes while removing his shirt. Earning a few stifled whimpers from him, I choose to ignore it. My eyes land on the purple bruises and bandaged cuts lining his abdomen and right side. All wounds consisting of deep red and purple shades; all polluting his naturally glowing skin with coppery blood.

"It's bad, isn't it?"

Jake hasn't looked in a mirror since he got here and I know it's affecting him. He seems like the kind of guy who is obsessed with his appearance.

"You look... like you." I say while swiftly pulling his new shirt over his head. It's a gray Nike tee.

"You won't hurt my feelings if you tell me the truth." He gives a timid half smile to reassure me.

"Well in that case..." I bite my bottom lip while frowning in thought. "You're ugly now." I hold back a grin. Satisfied that something will finally diminish his huge ego.

"So I was good looking before?" His dark eyebrows raise while he continues grinning at me. Even with a busted lip his smile is still magnetic.

I roll my eyes and decide that the conversation stops here. I know where it's headed and I refuse to stand around to be insulted by him.

"Where are you going?" he asks in a humorous tone.

I hear him call after me but I don't reply. I just slam the bathroom door shut.

After thirty minutes of attempting to fix my hair and cover up my bruises without a mirror, I just give up. As long as I don't draw attention to myself then it isn't noticeable.

Once I'm satisfied I step out. I'm now wearing a long sleeve crew neck tee. It covers my arms while the dark denim skinny's hide my damaged legs. My feet are covered by white high tops.

"Not bad, Olive."

My head snaps up when I hear that name.

"What did you just call me?" A menacing glare penetrates his eyes while I speak cautiously.

"O-live." He emphasizes the word, making me cringe. "Problem?"

"Don't call me that." The name is just as repulsive as its' taste.

He smiles at me with an amicable grin while rubbing his chin. I can tell he's gone through Rich's things. There isn't much in here, I could have told him that.

"You hate olives, don't you Olive?"

I've always hated Olives, even when my mom would make me eat them.

"That's what I'll call you then. Olive, it fits you." He limps over to me with a smug smile; obviously pleased with himself.

"Why? Is it because you like them?" I make a quick decision to pull my hair back into a ponytail before Rich gets here.

"No, because you leave an awful taste in people's mouths."

I want to punch him in his perfect face but before I can reply to his jerk-ish statement Rich walks in. And before my mind can process my actions, I'm moving backwards.

"Still afraid of me, Livie?" Rich walks closer until there's a mere two inches between us.

"You look cute." He winks at me, making my cheeks heat.

While my head is down, I take the time to look at his dark Levis. They fit him perfectly. From there, my eyes travel to his black button down, complimenting his dark hair. I notice the strong waft of aftershave and how his hair is no longer slicked back. It's all over his head; but in a good way. His sleeves are cuffed, revealing his intriguing ink. My eyebrows furrow because if he's trying to keep his identity hidden then that's the very thing that will get him caught.

"If things go well today then I won't have to use this." He holds the gun with the golden handle in his hand, tracing the outline of it with his fingertips. Now, most girls would be turned on by Rich and his badass personality but I'm not most girls.

"Please don't tell us you're going to shoot someone." I speak boldly.

He chuckles before saying, "No Livie, you're going to shoot someone."

"With my dad's gun?" Jake is shaking his head in disgust.

"If you two fuck this up, their blood will be on your hands." He points the gun at both of us to indicate how serious he is.

"Don't kill anymore people." I speak up before I can stop myself. I talk about how direct Jake is, well I'm slowly becoming that way too. I'm becoming more outspoken and I like it.

But instead of Rich scolding me, he just grins before shouting,

"Show time kiddos," as he walks out the room.

Once we get downstairs we're told to sit on the old, torn sofa. It makes my skin crawl but I don't complain, I just stare aimlessly at the four barren walls. There aren't any pictures or decorations. The only places to sit are the sofa Jake and I are currently on, and a broken recliner Rich sits in. The t.v is now gone, replaced with an empty book shelf. The walls look better. No more chipped paint or cracks. He's been working on this place.

A few minutes ago, Jake asked a few questions about the gun and the people coming, but Rich never answered him. I'm just glad Rich didn't use me to shut Jake up. Instead, he stays silent while analyzing me. Ever since the night he pecked my forehead, he hasn't taken his eyes off of me. A shudder passes through me and I fail at suppressing it. Rich notices and gives a light chuckle.

The silence in the room after that is deafening; making my ears burn from anxiety. My right leg shakes while we wait for our "visitors".

Two loud knocks at the door makes me jump slightly. I feel Jake slowly scoot to the edge of the sofa. Maybe he's planning on running when the door opens. For my sake, I hope he doesn't.

"Don't move." He aims the now loaded gun at Jake while making an "I'm watching you" motion.

"Whatever man." Jake mumbles with his head down.

"Livie, remember what we rehearsed." He looks at me so I nod. "You," he points to Jake again. "Follow her lead."

Now, I have no idea what's happening or who is at the door but I do know what Rich means. After I ran the first time he made me rehearse lines for when the police or neighbors ever came. Neighbors, police...is that-

"Hey officers, what's up?" He speaks coolly. One hand rests in his pocket while the other clutches the door knob. My head peeks over my shoulder and I'm surprised at what I see. Two police officers stand on the porch. One is a female with short, auburn hair while the other is a taller male. He's bald but makes up for it with his height and big smile.

"We got a call from this location about a possible kidnapping." The female officer says while they step in further.

They have their hands on their holsters while Rich has in his back pockets.

"Police?" I whisper to myself. I can feel Jake's eyes on me but I don't exchange his glance, My eyes roam around just like my thoughts. Police? Here in this house. I can't believe this. Freedom is so close yet so far away. What do we do?

I feel body heat beside me and before I can panic, I realize it's Jake and how extremely close he is. His hand clasps my upper thigh. It's enough to get my attention so I turn to him.

'Follow me.' he mouths to me.

The sofa becomes lighter once he and I stand up.

"You said you got a call from inside this house?" Everyone turns to me with questioning stares. I may have spoken out of turn but I don't care.

"Yeah, it was a tip about a possible kidnapping."

Why would he lead the police straight to him?

"Look officers, my kids play pranks all the time. I think that's what this is. Just some harmless prank."

That's what he's doing. He's trying to steer them away from him. I know how cunning he is. If he can convince them we're a family then it will be harder for them to suspect him.

"Well Mr.-"

"Thompson." He informs with crossed arms.

"Well Mr. Thompson, it may be harmless to you but not to the people involved. I don't think your children realize how serious a 911 call is. We spend time and tax payers money to come over here." She stares at Jake and I with stern gray eyes.

"Okay officers, if it's really this serious then take them down to the station." Rich waves his hand around nonchalantly.

"Yeah, please take me." Jake goes over to the man who is standing by the front door.

I notice the way officer Tommy has his arms crossed while watching the peculiar scene unfold. He's thinking this through like me. I know why Rich is so calm; because he's confident that his manipulative tactics will work.

"You want to go to jail, kid?" Tommy's thick brown eyebrows wrinkle into a frown.

"Not my first choice for freedom but I'll take it."

"Freedom?" The female officer, Lori asks quizzically.

"My kids haven't been the same since their mother died and they had to move in with me. They think I'm so horrible." He speaks so sympathetically that a stranger would be convinced he was telling the truth.

"So you prank call us because you hate your dad?" Tommy sighs in irritation. I can tell he isn't good with kids.

"I'm just trying to make this work. It's not easy being a single dad." He continues his lie.

"That asshole isn't our dad!" Jake is seething with rage. His cheeks are just as red as my shirt.

"How do we know that? I mean you're the ones who prank called us." Lori points at us then to herself. She thinks we're lying.

"We're not playing a prank and we didn't call you, but we're glad you're here." I say to keep Jake from making things worse. If he doesn't calm down he'll look like the spoiled teen Rich is talking about.

"If you didn't call us then who did?" She raises her perfectly waxed eyebrows while observing me.

"It's obvious who did it!" I point an accusing finger at Rich who is standing a few feet to my right. I thank God I can't see his face.

"Why would he call us to report a possible kidnapping at his house?" The male officer shakes his head.

"Forget who called! Just get us the hell out of here!" Jake tries to push the heavy set officer out of the way but he grabs him by his forearm.

"Whoa kid, calm down." Tommy orders with authority in his voice. Jake continues to try to fight, forcing Tommy to pin him against the wall.

"You don't want me to arrest you for disorderly conduct," he warns.

"Why don't you arrest him?" I point towards Rich who is now standing beside Lori. The look on his face is more than anger. It's betrayal. From the way his eyes narrow and his shoulders heave, I can sense how pissed he is. He wasn't expecting this from me.

"Why would we arrest him sweetie?" Lori walks over to me and puts her strong hand on my shoulder.

"He kidnapped us! We're his victims." I try to explain, but from the misconstrued expression on her face she isn't understanding.

"No sweetheart, your dad didn't kidnap you. He took you after your mom died." She speaks softly.

The whole room is spinning the longer I stare at the two confused officers. Can't they recognize us? Why won't they listen to us? I run my fingers through my wavy hair in frustration. A small strand of brown lays in the palm of my hand and that's when I realize the drastic changes done to me. My hair is longer and the color is darker. It's dark brown and stops just past my shoulders now. My clothing is new and covers most of my bruises.

And that's when it dawns on me what Rich meant. He made us change our appearance so it will be harder to convince the police we were kidnapped. All of the photos circulating on the news and in the papers are of me with my short, blond hair not long, dark hair.

They're still staring at me while Jake is trying to free himself from the strong grip of officer Tommy.

"You have to believe me! I'm Olivia Walters, the missing teen from the Glennville area." I know what I just said could help me or hurt me but I'm willing to take a chance. I notice Rich's eye twitching while he stares grimly at me. A small gulp slides down my throat when our eyes meet.

"Olivia Walters?" Lori rubs her chin with a curious expression. Her matte lips pressed together while in intrigued thought.

I nod fervently.

"I think you're mistaken because she's dead." Tommy is now holding Jake by his forearm. He seems to have calmed down now.

"Yeah, the FBI found her body in a small lake a few weeks ago." Officer Lori confirms.

My entire face drops at the realization that no one can help me. With my shoulders hunched and my head down, I close my eyes, trying to think of something else that will help my case.

"Is that it, officers?" He asks innocently.

"Yes sir, we just need you to fill out some paper work so we can send you a bill." Lori states factually.

"Wait! I have a birthmark on my left wrist." My eyes shift from Rich who is standing by Jake and Tommy, to Lori.

With her fingers around the knob, she turns to me.

"Let me see."

Relief floods my insides when she releases the knob. She walks over to me and with the sweetest smile, extends her open palm. I avoid Rich's intense gaze while placing my left wrist in her hand.

Her eyebrows raise while she observes it for a minute, letting the possibility of finding me alive sink in. Her angelic features hold surprise shock the longer she stares at the circular mark on my wrist.

I even pull my sleeve up further to show part of the brown bruise on my forearm.

"Mr. Thompson, we're going to take them down to the station. Just to make sure they don't prank call again." She says casually. And in that moment, I realize what she's doing. It takes all of my being to stop myself from cheering.

Without argument, they put our hands behind our backs to arrest us. It's an uncomfortable position but I don't complain, instead, my eyes travel to Jake's' to let him know not to panic. He gives a quick nod to let me know he gets it. It's what he's been waiting for too.

I wait for Rich to stop us on our way out but he just says,

"I'll meet you guys at the station."

This statement sends my thoughts into a panicked frenzy. Is he really going to meet us there or will he stop us from making it out of the driveway? I don't know the answers to those questions, but what I do know is that I'm ready to get out of here.

Before we pile into the car, Lori removes our cuffs.

"We're going to take you to a safe place now." She smiles while we scoot into the back seat.

I take the time to rub my sore wrists. Sore not only from the cuffs, but from the many times Rich gripped them too tightly.

I feel the smooth hum of the engine as we back out of the gravel driveway. Looking back, I don't see Rich so with a satisfied grin, I get comfortable. Relaxing my tense shoulders while I stare out the window, I think back to home. Will my friends and I ever be the same? And now that my parents are gone who will take me in? What good is being free if I still feel trapped on the inside?

"I saw the calendar. He's counting down days. But til' what?" Jake whispers so suddenly that I have to ask him to repeat.

Once he does, I regret even asking him. I don't want him to know about it, and honestly I have no idea how to explain it. How do I tell this guy that in less than two months my virginity will be gone forever?

"Why do you care so much?" Why does he always have to bring it up? Maybe he's bored and needs something to talk about. Or maybe he hates me enough to keep reminding me of the awful things in my life.

"I don't know, just curious."

I guess he is right. He doesn't know a thing about Rich, except for what I've told him, and that still may not be enough. I don't know why but I think they have a deeper connection. There's too much tension to say they're just random strangers.

"Olivia?"

"It's September so it's one month now. One month until my one hundred and fifty-ith night."

In one month it will be October, which means I've been here for five months. The night of October twenty eighth will mark the five month anniversary of my arrival.

"So?"

My first week here he said I should be welcomed the proper way. When I asked him what he meant he told me I'd figure it out soon enough. So the day I finally figure it out, I begged him not to do anything to me until I was ready. He agreed and said he would give me plenty of time but ultimately the decision was up to him. That was before he gave me an exact date.

"On October twenty eighth I'll be...welcomed," I sigh sadly.

"Oh...so that's the two month thing." He speaks slowly, trying to digest what I just told him. "I thought- never mind..." He trails off.

I want to ask him what he thought it meant but I choose to reply with a small,

"Yeah." I swallow dryly while tears slide down my cheeks. "One month now." The entire time I was in that house, in that basement, I had been awaiting my terrible fate. But now, I don't have to look forward to that anymore.

"Told you we'd get out of here." He tries to smile but it fades quickly. If Jake knows Rich like I do then this is far from over. Remember that bad feeling in the pit of my stomach I mentioned earlier? Well it's still here. I can't shake it and that makes me even more worried.

"What if we're not really leaving?"

I stare at the blur of green trees as we zoom down the back road. One thing I hated about the south was how far apart you can be from civilization.

A sudden roar of thunder rattles the earth, shaking the ground and my bones. I watch the sudden pour of water fall from the dark sky. Its' loud patter against the windows is bone chilling.

"What do you mean? They're taking us to the station now."

Lightning strikes near my window, making me flinch.

"They are but Rich isn't going to let us get away. Not this easily at least." My natural instincts start to kick in when I realize how dangerous this truly is. All of my bad thoughts are back full force. Who is he going to shoot with the gun? I don't want anyone else to die. Dealing with my parents' death is bad enough.

Thinking back on Rich and what he said about meeting us at the station, I quickly turn to see if he's following us.

"No Livie," Jake grabs my arm, forcing me to turn to him. "Don't start that. If he wanted to kill us he would have by-"

Jake's sentence is interrupted by several loud gun shots and then tires screeching. Everything is a blur while we hydroplane at a rapid speed. The rainwater only makes the road slicker while the intense lightning and booming thunder shake the car. Imagine driving on a dim road with low visibility and rain pouring with a vengeance. It feels like we're driving in a hurricane.

"Shit, I can't see!" The male officer swears before gripping the wheel tighter than before. He tries to steer us back on path but it ends up failing. Instead, we spin until we're rolling against the hard pavement. Our bodies jostle around as we barrel roll down a small embankment. My heart rate spikes when I feel glass prick my face. I try to hold onto the headrest but my body is abruptly jerked forward.

A sudden icy chill encompasses my entire body. My ears roar from the rush of water around me, and I have the hardest time breathing. My arms flail when I realize that I'm underwater. A huge gulp of water travels down my throat, almost suffocating me. The heaviness in my chest feels like a weight holding me down. I try to swim but every time I kick my legs I'm pulled down. Something is wrapped around my ankle, preventing me from surfacing.

I have to get to the surface before I drown so I feel around for my restraint. My fingers grip something soft like hair before realizing it's a person. A cold, pale corpse floats up until it's beside me. With a panicked scream, I wiggle my leg free until I'm able to move.

My ears ring while my lungs plead for air. Coughing and swimming is all I can do until I get to shore. With my back on the sand, I try to steady my breathing. My heart is beating as fast as my trembling hands, and it's not from the chilly water. I close my eyes but quickly open them when I see officer Tommy's dead, hazel eyes staring back at me.

When I sit up, I see his body floating aimlessly in the lake. He's face down, un-moving. The way his head bends makes me realize what killed him. The impact of those rugged rocks at the bottom of the lake. If he's dead then who else is alive?

The small, sudden crunch of sticks makes my body tense. I can't move no matter how hard I try and with each step I hear, my thoughts get worse. Rich is going to get me and take me back to that horrible place he calls a home. I don't want to go back; I just want to be free. Free from him, free from myself, free from everything.

"We have to go," He pulls my arm but I don't move. I continue to rock slowly while sobbing.

"Now Livie!" The fierce power in Jake's' voice awakens my senses. It's not Rich.

"Come on!" He yanks me up and continues pulling me through the branches and bushes in the woods. Before I know it, we're away from the lake and surrounded by trees and greenery.

"But what...what about the cops?" I ask when we come to a halt.

"They didn't make it." He replies quickly. A little too quickly for my liking.

"You didn't check, did you?"

"Look, either we get out of here or get taken again." The way his arms are wrapped around mine not only indicates his seriousness but his protectiveness as well. I don't even think he realizes it.

"And besides, someone has to live to tell the story."

It sounds harsh but he's right. If Rich gets us and the cops die then there won't be any witnesses. That's why I got taken the first time. Because I was a witness. A witness to my parents' murder.

"Dammit, we're going in circles." I run into his back when we make an abrupt stop.

"Don't look at anything." He tries to steer me away from the gruesome scene but my eyes won't let me look away.

The overturned cruiser is now rammed into a tall oak tree. It's the most surreal thing I've ever seen. The front of the car is crumpled like a piece of paper while the rest is engulfed in smoke and flames. If I look closely I can see the outline of a woman's body. Lori.

The broken window from where I was thrown out of has blood dripping on the glass edges. Is that my blood? I look down when I feel it dripping down my leg. A large glass shard, the size of my hand sticks out of my leg.

My breathing becomes staggered when I start to panic. I hate the sight of blood and what makes this worse is that it's my own blood. Is this what Jake was trying to shield me from?

"Help!... Get this thing out of my leg!" I shout while hyperventilating.

"I told you not to look at anything." He mumbles while leaning me against a tree.

"Just pull it out!" I shout while gripping my leg tightly. The crimson liquid gushes out of my painful wound. It feels like someone stabbed me with a huge needle and then slid it across my leg.

He bends down to my eye-level before sighing loudly. The hard pounding of the rain prevents me from seeing him well. We both have to squint to get a good look at one another.

"If I pull it out you could bleed out!" He shouts over the roaring thunder.

"If it stays I'll pass out!" I clutch his collar to keep my balance while I stand. The only times I've been cut would be when Rich slit my throat and now. If you counted, that's two times and I'm still not used to it.

A few feet away, a sharp flash of lightning strikes a tree, instantly uprooting it. We manage to get out of harm's way but the deafening sound it makes shakes the ground and sends quakes through me.

"We're going in circles but we have to keep moving! If we don't find a road in five minutes then I'll pull it out, okay?"

With my arm over his shoulders and his hand gripping my waist, he helps me stay up.

He's just as hurt as I am but one thing I've noticed about him, is that he's good at pushing through pain. Unlike me. I'm not sure how long we've been walking but every step we take makes my leg throb more.

"This isn't making sense."

He stops us after a while. We've been hobbling through sticks and branches for who knows how long. All I know is that I dozed off about thirty minutes ago but now I'm wide awake. A little weak but awake nonetheless. He promised we'd reach a road soon but the only thing we've run into are trees and more trees.

"What? What's... wrong?" I breathe out tiredly. My sight is blurring while my movements are sluggish. I use a tree for support.

"I...I saw him earlier. I thought he would get us but he just turned around." He scratches the back of his head while frowning. I've known him for a couple of months now so I know what that means, he's puzzled.

"Wha-what? You saw... him... and didn't... tell me?"

"You were half dead." He shrugs carelessly. "And it wasn't easy carrying you but at least you were quiet. Yeah, the peace and quiet will be missed." His full, pink lips pull into a confident smirk.

"If you saw him... and he didn't do... anything then... that means he's... following us."

"Yep," He pops the 'p'. "And watching us too." He looks around when a cardinal flies past us. The rain has died down and now it's getting dark.

I take a moment to catch my breath before making a startling conclusion.

"We're not... going to reach a road." I finally catch my breath but once again I have something else to worry about. Is Jake going to listen to me?

He groans and shakes his head out of frustration before asking,

"What makes you say that?"

"Rich is giving us two options: run into him or keep running around in the woods."

Whatever his plan is, it's definitely not intended for us to reach a road. And if we don't get help soon we might not make it to morning. For one thing, Jake's wounds are too serious to be left unattended. The deep red stains on his gray tee speak for themselves. He's still bleeding heavily.

"Let's keep moving then." He speaks with utter determination.

"I'm tired and I don't think running in the gloomy woods all night will solve anything." The numbness in my left leg has settled. I'm limping but I'm able to walk on my own. And just because I'm able to walk doesn't mean I'm going to. The blood loss is overwhelming and I have a strong desire to close my eyes.

"My dad has a lake house up here. If we get to it first we can get help before he can get us."

I nod my head while sitting down. With my arms underneath my head, I'm about to close my eyes when I'm suddenly shaken.

"You have to stay awake- we have to stay awake."

My eyes slowly open to see him hovering over me. He tries to pull me up but I lazily push him away.

"Let me sleep." I groan with a scratchy voice. If I can sleep then I'll have enough energy for tomorrow.

I feel my body slowly being lifted, forcing my eyes open. Looking around, I see that my frail structure is pressed against his chest. One of his arms is under my legs while the other rests on my back. I'm in an upright position so I can't fall asleep.

"I said we have to stay awake and I meant it."

And although I'm dog tired and in no mood for his antics, I can't find a suitable reason to be angry at him. I can't be upset because I've noticed something different about him. I don't know if he's always been this way but I do know that I'm proud of him. I'm proud because he isn't using 'I' anymore, he's using 'we'.

11

CHAPTER 11

I feel a rough texture graze my cheek, forcing my eyes open. Everything is dark around me so I use my fingers to feel around.

What am feeling for? I don't know but I'm hoping to get a better sense of where I'm at. From the soft cottony texture and the firmness of the mattress, I conclude that I'm in a bed.

Shifting my body, I experience a nagging ache where my leg was cut. Ignoring it, I reach for a lamp anyway. My fingers grasp the switch but the firm grip around my hand startles me to silence.

"Livie," the bone chilling voice whispers in my ear. A sudden feeling of uneasiness settles in my stomach. "Don't move." he orders staley.

His hand is still on mine when I feel the bed dip. I'm on my back in one quick motion while he's hovering over me.

I'm silent but my mind is yelling, screaming, and shouting at me to fight. So with that, I lift my right leg up to knee him in his groin. He doubles over, making a loud ' oomph'. I manage to crawl off the bed before he can stop me.

The pain in my leg festers, reminding me of how awful it feels to even be moving. I grit my teeth while hobbling to the door.

And just when I think I've made it, a large pair of hands suddenly wrap around my waist. His heavy body falls atop mine, forcing a pained scream to part my lips.

"Shut the hell up!" He snarls harshly while covering my mouth. I squirm underneath him but he still doesn't move. The bellowing pain in my leg has magnified because his knee digs into it.

"If you can't handle this then what's next just might kill you." He growls in my ear. The coolness of his breath sends chills down my spine. I try to crawl from under him but he grabs a wad of my hair, forcing it back.

I whimper while being lifted up. Kicking and screaming, I feel him throw me over his shoulder. This can't be happening. How'd he get in? And where is Jake?

By the time my thoughts leave, I'm already laying in the bed. All of my efforts are put into trying to break from his strong grip, so when I feel the cold barrel pressed to my cheek my body tenses.

"You know I'll use this," he threatens placidly. The gun is still pressed to my temple while his left hand trails my leg.

"It's your choice Livie, the easy way ... " he rubs his chin in amused thought before continuing,- "or the very hard way." he chuckles to himself, finding his little comment amusing.

I hear the sound of my zipper sliding down so I do what most girls would do, I squeeze my legs together.

"Wrong choice."

His sinister smirk and stalking brown eyes remind me what he is. And in that instant I realize that I did, indeed make the wrong choice.

Gripping my neck tightly, I wait for him to choke me but he just lightly grazes it with his thumb. His toxic touch and haunting stare seize my soul with just one glance. I can't look away, even if I wanted to.

There's something about him that makes me freeze up. And it's a billion times worse when I'm afraid.

"You smell nice," he compliments smoothly.

My breath catches in my throat when I feel his nose trail my neck up to my cheek. The warm heat from his exhale, makes the hair on the back of my neck stand straight. His hands are no longer on me, they're on each side of me. My eyes move quickly from him to the open space between us. He's still straddling me but I have enough room to catch him off guard.

"Get away from me!" I shout while punching him with intense force. I hear a small grunt from him before my shirt is grabbed. We hit the cold floor with a thud so powerful that it shakes the house.

I groan from the wicked pain in my sore muscles before slowly getting up.

"Fucking bitch!" He growls. I'm pulled to his chest then lifted up. His forearm is wrapped around my neck while the barrel of the gun is pressed against my cheek.

"Don't kill me...please don't kill me." I sob with despair filled eyes.

Before I can plead some more, a sudden heavy blow attacks my head. I fall to the ground limply. The room is spinning and my head pounds like someone is stomping on it. My fingers go to my temple, resulting in bloody fingertips when I place them in front of me. The crimson liquid carelessly drips down my temple before dripping on the floor.

"I'm not going to kill you but I'll make you wish I had." The hateful, infuriated glare in his dark eyes holds not only vengefulness but lust as well. And as odd as it seems, lust scares me more.

He grabs my arm, making my heart race rapidly. I stumble until I'm thrown onto the bed. Falling face first, my head ricochets off the head board, causing me to hiss.

"I own you now Livie. When will your dumbass understand?"

"When will you realize you that you can't win?"

Turning me around, he holds my neck before striking me with the gun a few more times. This time, my eyes roll in the back of my head because the pain is too unbearable. I can hardly breathe and feels like my nose is broken. The vibrant ringing in my ears won't weaken. I'm in a painful daze while he ties my hands above my head. With my eyes closed, I try to gather my bearings but the sudden feel of his rough hand on my chin forces them open.

"Look at me, Livie. I want to see your soul." His lips move slowly while his hauntingly creepy words replay in my head.

With one large inhalation, my eyes open to darkness. The clammyness of my skin provides an icky feeling that I so desperately need to get rid of. The dream. It felt so real. He was on top of me and there was nothing I could do to stop him. Fearful thoughts make their way to the front of my mind the longer I lie in bed panting. My hands are trembling while tears stain my once rosy cheeks. I hate this feeling within me; this feeling of fear and confinement.

The sound of movement from outside the door sends my body into panic mode. With a frantically beating chest, I scurry off the bed. I drop to the floor so that I can crawl under it. Or at least, that was my plan. But like most of my plans, this too is an epic fail because I somehow end up falling forward. With a loud thump, I make impact with the floor. Groaning loudly, I try to sit up but a familiar voice stops me.

"What the-"

The darkness of the room turns to light in an instant, and soon dirty sneakers are in my view, walking over to me.

"Oh, didn't mean to interrupt your makout session, Olive." He smiles widely while holding in a laugh.

In the position I'm in, it's kind of hard not to. My body is sprawled on the floor while my face is planted on the hardwood. I look so awkward.

My cheeks flush while I sit up, "Yeah, just practicing."

Looking around, I see that I'm in a room. A spacious bedroom with an owl themed bed, chest, curtains, and rug. The earthy tones mix well with the dark mahogany floors, giving it more of a rustic feel.

"Do you normally scream bloody murder before falling out of bed?" He raises his straight eyebrows while assessing me leeringly.

"Only when you ruin my dreams." I retort blatanly.

"Ah, so you're dreaming of me now?"

With his hands in his pockets, he continues eyeing me blithely. His small eyes glint while he stands confidently.

Out of all the things to say, it had to be that. I need a subject change, and fast.

Grabbing the side of the mattress, I lifty myself up. Only noticing a small ache from my movement, I sub consciously rub the medical tap covering my wounded leg.

"Um my leg, it feels...better." I take time to notice that he changed his own bandages too. A glass of water sits on the bedside table along with a bottle of Tylenol. There's a ruffled blanket sitting in the recliner. I guess he needed rest too.

"Yeah, I had to patch you up. You did the same for me so I kinda had to pay you back."

"Thanks." Noticing his stare, my eyes gravitate to his. With a hint of insecurity looming over me, I straighten my bed hair.

"I was gonna say make yourself at home, but from the looks of it, you've already done that..." He mumbles dryly.

There's something to his tone. It's like he's implying something else. With an annoyed sigh, I stare at him in disbelief. Did he just say that?

"I know I look like crap. I don't need you to make me feel worse." I cringe when I pull too hard on my hair. There are little twigs and large clumps of dirt stuck in it. It will take me hours to fix my hair.

"I never said you look like crap. Your bird's nest of hair speaks for itself." He blurts rudely.

"And your rude demeanor speaks for itself. You're an awful person and I feel sorry for your girlfriend." I chide bitterly.

Making my way over to the drawer, I decide a shower would be in my best insterest. But before I can walk to the drawer to get clothes, he grabs my arm. His fingers are lightly encircled around my wrist. It's not to inflict pain, he just wants to get my attention.

"I'm not... an awful person Livie." He speaks slowly with a somber tone, as if trying to get me to understand.

I don't look him in his alluring green eyes. It's not that I can't, it's just that I don't want to. If he's being honest then I'm afraid of how I'll feel. After staring at the floor for what seems like hours, I feel his grip loosen. His hand falls to his side just as his body steps to the side.

I silently make my way over to the drawer. Looking through it, I see a bundle of shirts. I pick the first one I see before opening the last drawer to find jeans.

"Did you call the police yet?" My voice breaks the silence while I dig through the pile of shorts and jeans.

"Um, yeah." He's shocked too based on his hesitance. "They were supposed to be here four hours ago."

The frustration in his tone forces my eyes to wander to his. He's at the door when he stares grimly at his watch, and then to me. A few more seconds of silence and he'd be gone.

"What time is it now?" I inquire curiously.

With a pair of denim shorts and a Florida Gators tee I walk over to the where he's standing.

"It's 12 a.m. You've been snoring since we got here." He mutters with his hands in his pockets.

If it's twelve in the morning and he called around eight then he's right, they were supposed to be here four hours ago. Not unless, they never got a call. My mind begins to muse as I try to decipher whatever code Rich has set up.

"I uh, left you alone because I figured you were tired." He rubs the back of his head shyly while giving a small sigh.

"Did an operator answer when you called?" Looking from the pile of used clothes in my hand to his confused face, I conclude that he's waiting for me to explain.

"A 911 operator..."

"Uh yeah, a lady answered but it sounded more automated than real." He wrinkles his nose while thinking. It's the same frown he uses when he's trying to figure something out.

"I'm going to the bathroom," is all I can say. I need time to think too. Time to figure out Rich's plan. And a nice, long shower will do just that.

On my way to the hallway, he stops me to give me a walkie talkie.

"In case the lights go out again." He says while encompassing it in my palm.

I take it and begin to notice the amount of time we hold physical and visual contact. Too long for my liking so I pull away.

"Did you run into something, other than the floor?" I hear him ask in a low voice.

What is that supposed to mean? Is he calling me ugly? The longer I simmer over his rude comment, the more anger boils inside of me. What do I say to that? Or better yet, what do I do?

I continue staring at my barefeet. This time, my fists clench while I narrow my eyes. Looking up, I see his lips slighlty part while he frowns in speculation. The playing dumb look won't work.

"Why? Does my face look just as horrible as my hair?" I ask in a sarcastically annoyed tone.

"No, seriously."

He grabs my hand before I can slap him, and leads me to the bathroom.

"Look at your chin."

Snatching my arm away from him I walk over to the bathroom mirror. I'm more so afraid than shocked at what I see. A small, barely noticeable imprint of a thumb sits on the left side of my chin. My shaky hand lightly graze over the gray bruise.

"I just thought you fell or ran into something again."

My dream. It felt so real because it was real. He grabbed my chin right before saying, "Look at me, Livie. I want to see your soul."

"What'd you just say?" He asks in a slightly worried voice. His eyebrows are raised in a questioning way while he stares fearfully at my panicked expression.

"Nothing...I mean I need to take a bath." With both hands on his angular shoulders, I spin him around before pushing him out the room. Slamming the door shut, I quickly lock it. Sliding down the wall, I close my eyes. For every breath I take, my exhalation comes out louder and shakier.

"Hey, I didn't mean to piss you off again." Sighing loudly, he twists the silver knob several times.

It can't be Rich. He isn't here. Jake locked the doors, or at least I'm hoping he did.

"Livie, come on! Just open up!"

The door shakes with every loud bang he makes, forcing my body to jump reflexively. He continues shouting and knocking while small tears brim in my azure eyes. And the more he yells, "open up" the more I get the feeling he means it in more than one way.

"Livie, I was just- I thought you knew it was..." He trails off. My ears are fully alert so I'm able to here the sincerity in his voice. He shouldn't worry about me. Wiping my tears, able to shake out of my despair filled daze.

"Thanks but I have some- female issue to tend to. I'm okay though!" I lie quickly. My monthly hasn't come yet, in fact it just left. If he knew the real reason I'm panicking he'd call me crazy. He already thinks I'm just as psychotic as Rich. So instead of explaining my nightmare, I lied to him and then kicked him out.

"Don't mention it I guess...Oh and just come downstairs when you're done." He speaks earnestly. I hear him breath a sigh of relief before his footsteps walk off.

Grabbing the edge of the counter, I steady my breathing while gingerly rubbing my bruised chin. The bathroom is the size of my room. It's huge for a bathroom. In all actuality, this entire house is enormous. Enormous enough for one to get lost in. While I run my bubble bath, my stomach twists at the thought of having an...extra visitor.

Looking behind me, I make sure the door is locked. Once I feel safer I slide my foot into the warm, soapy liquid. I soon place the rest of my sore body into the water and let my tense muscles relax. I lay my head back, letting the water engulf my body in serenity. I've always loved water. It makes me feel lighter.

Releasing a low sigh, I close my eyes with my last thought being, I hope I'm just paranoid. I hope Rich isn't here.

12

⸺ ◦ ⸺

CHAPTER 12

The heavy rain is calming me while I bathe. Scattered intervals of rumbling thunder and sharp lightning drown out my focus on this horrible situation. It's oddly funny how the one thing that scares most, soothes me.

Once I finish bathing I take the time to go back over my thoughts. If Rich is here, in this house with us then wouldn't he be quick to let us know? I mean he's cunning, which makes him great at predictinng our moves. Which could mean that he's outside, waiting for us to run straight to him. With that thought, I make a mental reminder to tell Jake my thoughts about Rich. If he is following us then we need to be ready for him.

Anyway, my next train of thoughts randomly bounce around my head like a ball in a pinball machine.

Going from my horrid nightmare to Jake's attractive smile. Shaking my head, I bite my lip while wondering why I just thought of that. He has a girlfriend. What's wrong with me?

With my head back, I decide to plunge myself deeper into the leukwarm water. My ears rush with water while my cheeks puff from holding my breath. I need to relax and this is the very thing that will help me.

While I'm under, a scene of faces quickly breeze through my mind. Like a cinema of all the people I've met in my life. Eyes, noses and lips formed into faces of all shapes and colors.

A sudden knock causes my head to quickly lift up. My breathing steadies at the sound of a soothing, motherly tone.

"If you don't get out the wrinkle monster's gonna get you." She uses her long, lean arms to lift me out of the tub.

"But I like the water mommy." I say in my innocent, four year old voice.

My wet hair clings to my face, forcing her to remove strands.

Her heart shaped face mirrors a frown before a small smile flahses across her red lips.

"Yeah, well the water will be here tomorrow night." She taps my button nose with a dainty finger.

Soon, we're out of the bathroom and I'm in my room. She dresses me in my Barbie pajamas while singing our favorite bedtime song.

"One two, straighten your room,

Three four, close your door,

Five six, pick up Liv

Seven eight, goodnight kiss

Nine ten, let rest begin"

She finishes while tucking me in.

Sighing lightly, I watch as her captivating blue eyes shine down on mine. My mommy. I smile while she gently places her forehead on my small one. Lifting my small arms, I pat her beautiful brown hair before she pulls away.

With a playful grin, she shakes her hair on my face, tickling me.

"Night, my little Liv." Her small lips spread sincerely once my eyes begin to flutter.

"Livie!"

A roar of static fills my ears before I sit up with a racing heart. The water from the tub is all over the dark tiles, making them glisten like a sea in the moonlight.

"What are you doing in there; drowning?" I hear again. What? Where is that coming from?

My eyes travel from the tiles to the counter where the walkie talkie sits. Oh shit, Jake.

Remembering the door is still locked and he can't get in, I jump up. Almost slipping on some water, I come close to falling on my face. With my hand outstretched I manage to grip the towel rack before I can do anymore damage to my bruised body.

"Olive, I have something you really need to see so stop spazzing out over your bloody problems, and get down here."

My cheeks turn bright red when I realize what he means. He thinks I'm on my period. Just what I need, more ammo for him to bully me.

Grabbing the walkie talkie with one hand, and my shorts with the other, I try to one handedly pull my shorts up.

"I'm going to kill you." I speak in my most threatening voice.

"Well, if you could get down here first then maybe I'll believe you." There's mischief to his tone which makes me want to kill him more than before.

For some reason, he knows how to grind my gears, and I hate him for that. I never knew I could hate someone as much as I hate Jake. Wait, actually I hate Rich more. Although, Jake is quickly making his way to the top of my list.

By the time I limp down the spiral stairs my paranoid thoughts about Rich being here subsides, only to be replaced with thoughts of murdering of Jake. He's in the foyer too. With the way his hair looks, wet and mangled, and they way his navy blue shirt clings to him, I conclude he had a shower too.

"Are we ready now, princess?" He mutters with a bored tone.

"You can't talk about me, you showered too."

"But I didn't take an hour."

Rolling my eyes, I walk past him to the kitchen. I'm starving so I head towards the fridge.

"Yeah, just make yourself more at home." He smirks when I take a huge bite into my turkey sandwich. I decide to ignore him while taking a few more bites.

"You said you called the police earlier?" I ask while sliding a plate his way. I'm sitting at the island counter while he stands across from me.

"Yeah," He picks it up and takes a bite. With his eyes closed, he chews slowly before suddenly stopping. With wide eyes, I watch him throw the food on the counter before leaning over to vomit.

"What is wrong with you? I didn't poison it!" I shriek with a mix of panic and frustration.

"Poison-" he coughs out, "-would be better... than that! It's expired." He breathes out tiredly.

Looking down, I see the partially sandwich in my hand. The moldy spots on the bread and cheese make my stomach churn while my entire face pales. The turkey is as slimy as a snail while the putrid smell irritates my nostrils.

Running over to the nearest place I can find, I hurl the remaining contents of my stomach into the stainless steel sink. And I was so hungry. There goes any chance of having a decent meal.

"The worst part is, yours is half eaten. It's like you didn't realize it was expired." He wipes his mouth with the back of his hand.

With my eyes to the floor, I stay silent because I'm a ptitful basket case. Either my body is used to old, expired food or I'm so hungry I just don't care anymore. Either way, I'm a sad case. I don't even want to see his face; his face of shame because I know it's directed toward me.

An abrupt warmth fills my insides when he takes my hand. Silently, we pile up the stairs, forgetting about eating altogether. I've lost my appetite for the next week.

"I called the police after I turned on the generator." He mumbles quietly. From the way his head tilts downward with his eyes appearing curious, I think he's trying to determine if I'm okay.

So if he called the police like he said he did then they should be here. If I'm right, and Rich knows we're here then we don't have much time.

"I basically barricaded every door and window." He stares at me with concern while reading the emotions on my face. "That should give us more time to get help."And just after he says this, I get the feeling he is thinking what I'm thinking.

"When did we get here?" I stare at the dismantled office.The oakwood desk is flipped over. Papers lay on the floor as if they're part of it. The walls have holes in them and the lights on the ceiling are busted out.office. It's turned upside down, as if a tornado has hit it.

"Around 8:30 p.m I think." With his hands in his pockets, he shifts on his uninjured leg.

"Then why haven't they come yet?" I mumble to myself.

Walking over to the overturned desk, I see the black phone on the hardwood floor. Picking it up, I dial 911. It doesn't even ring.

With the phone in my hand, I look at him wearily.

"Are you sure you called them? Because this phone is not working."

"What do you mean it's not working- Did you break it?" He runs over to me and briskly snatches the device from my hand.

"Really Jake? I broke a phone in 2.6 seconds?" I roll my eyes while he continues to fumble with the phone.

"I swear I called them. I mean someone answered and everything."

He's now on the messy floor, trailing the cord with his fingers. I watch him cuss before holding a busted wire in front of his exasperated face.

"The damn cord is cut." He rubs his hand through his ruffled hair while gritting his teeth.

Cut? How the hell did that happen? When did it happen? And that's when it hits me, if he barricaded this place then he's the only one who could have done something so twisted.

"What kind of sick game are you playing, huh?" I ask with narrowed eyes. My chest heaves as anger boils inside of me. I was so close to freedom and once again, it's being taken away from me.

"Hey, don't turn this around on me. I wouldn't cut our only means of communication." He holds his hands up defensively with a hurt expression.

Only means of communication. Those words bounce around in my head, echoing repeatedly.

"Do you have a computer here?"

A phone isn't the only way to communicate in this day in age. We can use a computer to reach the authorities.

He sighs heavily before saying,

"The screen is broken, but now that you're here this is what I wanted to show you."

He lifts his hands in the air as if to show me the entire room. With my brows pulled in, I continue eyeing him with bewilderment.

"This room and my parents old room are the only ones like this. Destroyed."

He shakes his head in distate while further observing the torn down office.

"It's like every memory of my dad lived in this cabin and now only broken shit remains."

He goes on to tell that his dad was murdered in this room. The murder made world news because of who his dad was, Roy Rogers, oil tycoon.

"The police say a burglar shot him but I know that isn't true. It was some business deal gone wrong." He stares out the large window behind the desk. We're on the second floor so these don't have furniture blocking them like downstairs.

"This place, this lake house used to be our everything. Mom, Dad, Jackson and I would come up here every summer."

He pauses to recollect.

"And now that he's gone, mom won't visit his grave, this place or even hang his pictures in the house."

His head is down in anguish while his hands remain dug into his pockets. I don't think I've ever seen his so...sad. Let alone, so eager to pour his emotions out. His hurt makes me want to console him. It makes me want to tell him that everything will be okay. He'll be home soon and everything will be back to normal. But the coward in me is just as afraid as he is. And I know I'd never have the courage to say anything uplifting to him.

"Who is this?" I ask while picking up the frame from the floor. He comes over to me and takes the photo from me.

"Oh, that's my uncle. My dad's younger brother."

Now that I'm looking from a better angle, I can see two young men sit on a boating deck with arms over each other's shoulders. The mane on the left looks older and has light brown hair while the other guy has dark brown hair. They favor in many ways than one. They both share the same almond shaped brown eyes, small pink lips, medium sized noses, and strong jawline. They must be brothers.

"Were you two close? You and your uncle?" I ask while noticing his uncle has the same facial hair as someone I know. I can't put my finger on it, but I have seen him before.

"Nah, I don't remember much about him. Last I heard he was serving time for stealing someone's shit."

My mouth forms an 'O' at that. Maybe I've seen him on the news. If he's a criminal then his mugshot has been on the evening news before.

"He's basically the outcast in our family. I think my dad told me how he got sent away to an all boys school in Glennville."

"Glennville?" That's where I live. Well, used to live. It was a small, quiet town in central Florida with a population of a few thousand. I wonder how much has changed since I've been gone.

"Yeah, rumor was he had an affair with his married teacher."

Married teacher? Is that the lady in the pictures? The lady tutoring the engaged student. I know who that too engaged student is. It's Rich. A younger him. It has to be him. I mean if he was sent to an all boys school and then had an affair with his teacher then that explains where those pictures came from.

"The pictures." I whisper to myself. I sub consciously dig into my pocket while staring off. I'm surprised I was able to keep this picture with all I've been through in the past few days. Lifting it up, my small fingers trail the outline of the female and male. They're both facing each other but I can still make out some of their features. Rich and the teacher both have dark brown hair. He still has that same strong jawline too.

"And look at this" Jake's loud voice breaks me from my thoughts. With an exasperated sigh, I place the pictured back into my pocket before going over to another part of the room. It's like a closet, except on each wall is huge glass case full of-

"Guns?"

"One is missing." He points to the empty space.

Looking around in awe, I'm shocked and a bit scared. There's enough guns and ammo for a third World War in here. I'm sure he wouldn't miss one gun. Hell, it might not even be missing. Maybe his older brother took it.

"Yeah but that doesn't mean-"

"Livie, I've been away from this place for eight years but I remember enough to know that my dad's guns have always been in that case. Every single one of them." He turns to me with a look of precise certainty.

"So, someone broke in and stole one. It's not that serious." We have bigger problems to worry about. Like getting out of here.

"My dad was shot and the gun he was shot with is missing. There's a connection." With his arms extended, he starts pulling on the locks.

"Between...us or the guns?" I ask slowly, trying to figure him out. He starts pulling on the locks, causing me to eye him more suspiciously. Doesn't he know that he needs a key to open the cases?

"A random robber wouldn't just come up and shoot him. It was someone he knew."

I take the time to let him sort out his thoughts. With a weary sigh, I walk out the room. Thinking back on the pictures, I run over to where I dropped the one of his dad and uncle. Staring at the picture of the handsome young men in the picture I notice somethig else. Jake looks strikingly similar to his uncle. The only difference is his lighter hair and green eyes.

"How'd you get here?" He asks so suddenly that my heart nearly jumps out of my body. With my hand on my chest, I turn to him with a look of discontent.

"Oh, I'm sorry for scaring you. Now can you tell me how you got here?"

"I...um what?" My words can't keep up with my what my mind is thinking.

"Just tell me how he got you." He rephrases, making his statment clearer.

With my eyes narrowed, I stand up with a look of defiance.

"I don't want to talk about it, okay?"

The last thing I need is to tell all of my problems to this guy who always finds a reason to blame me for everything wrong. Ever since our last argument when he told me I wasn't leader material, I've kept my guard up around him. I'm not telling him anything about me or my problems.

"Look, I just need some info. If I can figure out how we're connected to him then-"

"Why do you even care, huh?" Our focus should be on getting away from Rich, not trying to solve a murder mystery.

"Because I saw my dad, that's why." He steps closer to me with his arms folded. His stature isn't intimidating, it's relaxed.

"Your dad?" I thought he was dead.

"Yeah, I saw him in a dream so I asked him who killed him. Who was the person who murdered him and he told me the answers were all around me." He looks around, to indicate the "all around me" part of his sentence.

With a small grin, I raise my eyebrows in tentative thought.

"Don't look at me like that." His green eyes remain solemn while his dark eyebrows pull inward.

"Let me get this straight, you saw your dad in a dream and now you think we're all connected." I roll my eyes.

"Yeah. There has to be some kind of link. We're not here by fate or destiny, or whatever some people think!" He throws his hands in the air before gripping his hair in frustration.

I know what he means because I used to be one of those people. I used to think wherever life took me was where I was supposed to be because fate brought me there. But now, I'm know it's not fate that has us here-

"It's just a huge coincidence, okay? He took you because his first plan failed and me, well I'm only here because I witnessed him murdering my parents!" It flows from my lips quickly, ready to flee from my locked tongue.

The silence is an overbearing quiet, making my body warm while my eyes water. Jake is still leaning against the wall with his head back and eyes closed; letting it all sink in.

"Murdering your parents?" he mumbles while thinking. "Wait, he murdered your parents?" His sharp, malachite eyes open and shift to mine.

"I don't want to talk about it." I shift on my leg while biting the inside of my lip. It's bad enough my dreams constantly remind me of what Rich has done; I don't need anymore memories. I'm trying to forget the awfully dreadful ones I have.

"No Livie, I...I think I found a link." He strolls over to me with a calm aura.

"What are you talking about? What link? I said it's coincidence. I'm not staying here if you're going to ramble-"

"Just shutup and listen!"

My body jerks up while my eyes widen. His stance is anger mixed with agitation. I don't like it so I cross my arms with a menacing stare.

"Yelling at me won't make me listen to you!" I shout back, clear frustration on my face and in my tone.

He sighs while I close my eyes and rub my temples.

"Okay, you're right. Yelling won't help but I have something to tell you. Something I think will help us."

When I don't reply he continues anyway.

"Remember when I told you my father was murdered?"

Yeah I remember but I choose to stay silent. He senses it too so he doesn't wait for my reply. "Well, I think he's the guy who did it."

Slowly, looking up at him, I see how serious the mood has gotten. I see the anxiety and determination lining his handsome features. I see the way his jaw is pressed while he continues staring at me.

"I think Rich murdered my dad just like he murdered your parents in cold blood."

My blue eyes hold his worried ones while he continues assessing me. His arm are folded like mine and we're both standing inches apart. The only difference is his breathing is quiet and heavy while mine is just steady.

13

CHAPTER 13

"**A**re you crazy?" I blurt out after a few moments of silence. We're still in his dad's old office, standing inches apart. His eyes are no longer on mine. They're glued to the floor.

"No, but I'm starving."

Ignoring his growling stomach, and mine I ask,

"Can we just get out of here?"

Instead of trying to solve this murder, we need to focus on getting to safety. Rich is still looking for us so we need to get somewhere safe, somewhere he isn't. I know what he'll do if he catches us, that's why I'm not staying here to get caught.

"Yeah, just let me break the gun case first." He mumbles before walking to the closet.

As soon as he leaves, a sudden flash of lightning strikes outside, illuminating the room for a second before everything goes black.

"Jake!" I shout while trying to feel around the dark room. My arms and legs move aimlessly while being guided blindly. What's worse than darkness? The obvious answer is not being able to see in the darkness. It's like being blind folded with no sense of sight, only being led by what you feel with your arms outstretched. It's a terrible thing because I never know what I'll hit next.

I curse under my breath when my knee hits the overturned desk for the third time. Where the hell is he? I've been calling him but he hasn't responded. With weighted fear over me like a dreary cloud, I somehow make my way out of the room.

After stumbling a few times, I finally make it to the stairs. If I can find the generator then maybe we'll have some light. I'm about to take a step when I feel myself being roughly pulled back. Before I can scream, a hand covers my mouth. I don't think about the smell of detergent, or the way their arm is wrapped around my mid section in a painless way. All I can think about is the devil himself. Rich.

Tears unknowingly pour out while my mind spirals out of control. I can't let him win. I have to get away. I think while I twist and turn, trying to fight the perpetrator off.

"Shh! He'll hear you." A familiar, semi- deep voice whispers.

My futile attempts to fight cease when I realize it's Jake. With my hands still holding onto his forearm, I shake my head so he'll release his hold.

"He's," I swallow the hard lump in my throat at the thought if him actually being here. "He's in here?"

He nods fervently before taking my hand again. I'm not in tune with my feelings or body anymore as we run down the hallway. Our legs move swiftly, both of our feet pattering down the hall in the quiet blackness.

The longer we run, the more I can feel myself slowly slipping away. I'm in too much of a daze to know where he took us. All I know is that the powerful slam of the door made me jump.

I watch him use his flashlight to observe his surroundngs. The harsh light lands on me so I use my forearm to protect my eyes. Soon, the flashlight is in my hands. He tells me to point it to a spot in the room while he grabs the objects he needs. With a small sigh, I comply. I point the light in every direction he tells me to until he has enough items against the door.

"This should hold him until we think of something." He walks over to me with a stressed look. The light is still on him when I see how tense his shoulders are. His soft eyes land on me before quickly scanning the room again.

I look around too. Skimming the room for something that can help us. My eyes go from the family pictures on the wall, and cards that read 'Grandmother' to a queen sized bed in the corner. The simple lilac and cream colors, give me room to conclude that we're in a relative's room. His grandmother.

"Do you think he cut the power like he cut the cell phone cord?" I ask in a small, hesitant voice. Jake is sitting beside me with his head in his hands. It's been a couple of minutes since he's stopped looking for weapons. The gun he had earlier is now in front of us. It's useless because the bullets are nowhere to be found.

"I think there's something you're not telling me." The serious tone of his voice makes my eyebrows crease in confusion. He doesn't have to see me to know he needs to explain.

"The bruise on your chin. He did it, and you knew it."

He's right. Rich did bruise my chin but I thought it was a dream--until I saw it for myself. It's as real as a physical scar can get. Rich was in the room with me and now he's in this house with us.

"Something tells me you know a hell of a lot more than what you're telling me."

I know more about Rich because I actually take the time to observe. If Jake would spend his time watching Rich instead of fighting him then he'd know what I knew.

"I only know what you know, which isn't much!" I've told him what I know. Instead of trying to pick a fight with me he should be focused on getting us out of here.

"You're lying! You knew he was in here but you didn't warn me."

His eyes narrow at me, causing me to bury my head in my hands. He's right. Despite what I'd like to think, I knew Rich would be in here. From the gut feeling I've been having to the horrible nightmare that confirms his strong presence. I knew he was in here the moment I was awakened from my sleep.

"I almost ran into him, Livie! A warning would have been nice."

"I'm sorry, okay! But if I told you about my dream then you'd probably think I was crazier than what you think now." I know it's a pathetic excuse but that's all I've got left; pathetic excuses because I'm too chicken to speak up.

"When I saw your chin I knew that was real. That's not easy to pull off." He closes his eyes while resting the back of his head on the wall. His chest moves steadily while he tries to calm himself.

"Now we're stuck in here with that crazy asshole looking for us!" He growls frustratedly with his fist clenched. Now he's back to being pissed.

Silence clouds the tense air after his outburst. The only thing for me to do is stand up and pace. What do we do now? It's almost three in the morning and if we don't think of something soon, we're done for. If he catches us then we'll never see the light of day. Jake will never see his family again and I'll never get to see my friends. We'll die in that basement if he lets us live. We don't stand a chance against Rich when he finds us, and he knows it.

The sudden sound of the doorknob twisting forces my body to stiffen. With alarmed eyes and a racing heart, I start backing away.

Fear overtakes my thoughts while my legs move backwards. I don't want to go back to that awful hell house.

My body backs into another, causing my mouth to open. A hand clamps down to prevent my panicked scream while his other hand grasps my arm tightly.

"Stay quiet, I have an idea."

With my shaky hands over his, I wait for him to release his hand from my mouth.

"Remember when I tried to break the window in the basement?" He asks calmly.

Nodding my head slowly, I wait for him to continue.

"Well, we're climbing out of this one."

He goes over to the window above the rocking chair. I want to ask him how the hell we're going to do that because we're on the second floor but I stay quiet. If he has a way out, I'm taking it.

He groans while trying to lift it up. It doesn't even budge. It's like it's glued shut. He's exerting so much force that he has to grit his teeth while closing his eyes. I shudder from the pain he's feeling. I can only imagine how excruciating it feels. At this point, he's just as weak as I am.

After countless attempts to open the window, we hear loud banging from the other side of the door.

"You shouldn't have snuck out!"

Another powerful bang echoes through the room, making my bones shiver.

"Now I have to break your fucking legs!"

Two more bangs. He's now throwing his body weight against the door. And from the creaking it's making, it will be down soon.

"Help me!" Jake shouts, cuing my legs to spring into action. My hands grab the wooden part of the frame before pushing upwards.

For every sound the door makes, my body jerks sub consciously. It's like an extreme version of the hiccups. My palms sweat while my eyes remain wide with fear. If we don't get this window open we're as good as dead.

Thinking back to when we were in the basement, I remember Jake trying to break the window. Maybe that's what we have to do.

"Where... are you... going?" He pants in short breaths.

"We need something to break it." I say while going through his grandmother's closet.

"Livie,"

I turn to see him smiling with a sly grin. A small glint appears in his moss green eyes.

"You're a genius."

14

CHAPTER 14

The unnerving sound of the door being kicked repeatedly forces my hands to move as quickly as my heart. I'm now rummaging through the closet filled with old clothing and a strong stench of moth balls.

Choosing to ignore the burning in my nose- the smell is the least of my worries-I continue throwing things behind me while I sift through the cluttered closet. Why does his grandma have so many useless things? A peacock looking hat, a small box with nothing but old Vogue magazines, a few dresses, and a- golf club? It's behind a curtain of clothes. My face lights up as soon as it's within my hand.

"Livie!" I hear Jake's horrified voice scream my name. With quick feet, I spin around only to be knocked down by a heavy force.

Lifting my head off the floor, I groan while the acrid taste of blood saturates my entire mouth.

"Livie," He grins sadistically, making my entire being freeze. I know that voice. That familiarly foul voice. The same voice that awakens my biggest fears and floods my mind with undeniable dread. "No, no, no, no." I whisper while staring at him with wide eyes.

His hair covers part of his eyes while beads of sweat race down his forehead and onto his black shirt. I notice the blood on his knuckles, forcing my eyes to shift behind him. Oh no. Jake lies motionless on the floor, a huge gash above his right eye.

"I'm going to have fun with you."

I'm suddenly lifted up by his strong hands and then pinned against the wall. My lungs tighten when he squeezes my neck too hard. My mouth opens, only to emit scattered gagging noises. He's using one hand to pin me against the wall while the other is pressed on the wall. His lips gently graze my earlobe for a second before he whispers,

"So much fun but first, I have to break you."

I inhale a shaky breath when he loosens his hold around my neck. It's tight enough to keep me in place but not tight enough to choke me. That is, until a sudden intense burning attacks my lungs, forcing me to gasp for air. My throat tightens again from the unbreakable force he's using to strangle me. I can't move my lips to scream, or even fight.

From the way he cuts off my circulation, I know he plans on coming close to killing me before having his "fun."

"What did I say after I caught you the first time?" He scowls while I blink rapidly. My head is starting to feel light, causing my limbs to become limp. If he doesn't let go soon, I'll pass out.

"I'll have you bowing down to me like the obedient pet I trained you to be." With his hand now gripping the back of my hair, I feel him lay his forehead on mine.

Closing my eyes, I shiver when I feel his surprisingly soft lips trail kisses on my neck.

"Every fiber of your being belongs to me now." He whispers before inhaling deeply. The creepy act and lustful words force my horror

strickened whimpers to increase. My body shakes while he continues to inhale my scent.

I can't let him do this to me. I can't let him kill my spirit again. I
won't. It takes all of my strength to lift my hands to his face. With
my sharp fingernails ready to attack, I drag them down his face;
mimicking the nails on a chalkboard act.

A small growl parts from his lips when I finally manage to make
him bleed. He pushes me down instantly, sending my frightened
body to the hard floor. With my bloody palms on the ground, I try
to lift myself up but fail when I'm abruptly kicked in my abdomen.
I clutch my bruised stomach while wheezing painfully. The pain
is unbearble now. I want to scream out but I refuse to give him
satisfaction, plus the festering pain will worsen. He kicks again,
sending a throbbing sensation across my inner organs. With closed
eyes, I grit my teeth while feebly trying to crawl away.

"Hey, don't run from me!" He grabs my hair and pulls me back.
"I'm not going to hurt you..." I'm pressed against his chest while he
strokes my cheek. " -Much." He finishes.

The sickening nausea returns as more teardrops roll down my
cheeks. Just thinking about losing my virginity to this immoral man
makes me start hyperventilating.

With his one giant arm trapping my hands, I cringe when I feel his
other hand roam over my entire body. Slimy. Dirty. foul. I hate him.

"My Livie." He rests his chin on my head. We're sitting on the
hardwood floor. He holds me closer while I swallow the bile rising
in my throat. My hearbeat quickens when his hand trails up my leg,
stopping on my inner thigh.

"D-don't." My eyes are closed while I'm still pressed against him;
merciless tremors flow through my terrified form when he ignores

me. He releases a low chuckle at my fright before continuing to grope me. And the worst part is, I can feel his excitement. I'm beyond disgusted.

"Let the fun begin."

I squirm and squeak when his hand grips my chest too tightly. I'm unable to move, unable to fight. Fearing the worst, I brace myself for the unwanted feel of his fingers inside of me. I prepare myself to forget all of my emotions, because I don't want to feel anything with Rich.

I wait for it but it doesn't come. Opening my eyes, I'm able to see that I'm no longer trapped. Realizing my sudden freedom, I crawl to the door. Staggering up weakly, I'm about to walk out when I hear Jake shout.

"Wait for me!"

Turning my head, I see him staggering over to me with a bleeding head. His left hand grasps the back of his head while his right grips the empty gun. My eyes scan the room to unravel the scene that previously took place. From the overflow of metallic liquid dripping off the gun to the way his chest moves quickly, I realize how I was able to get free. Jake stopped him from further attacking me. He saved me from Rich's evil grasp.

"Come on, we gotta go!" He shouts before trading the gun for my hand. And once again we're holding hands. His large hand engulfs my small one as we make our way down the spiral staircase. Our hands fit like gloves, and this time, I don't have an urge to smack him or pull away. No, this time I hold his tighter.

We make it to the door and as soon as he opens it we're greeted by strong winds and heavy rain. A storm stronger than a hurricane is going on outside while one just as strong is whirling around on the inside; the inside of me.

In the midst of running out the door, I hear an earsplitting gunshot. I hear a deep voiced scream before feeling the absence of his comforting hand. The fact that his hand is no longer holding mine makes a small twinge of disappointment invade my insides.

It takes a minute for me to understand what just happened so when I turn to my right, I'm more than shocked when I see him curled up with his left arm to his chest.

The way he cluctches it, making the blood flow from his injured arm, gives me reason to believe Rich did the unthinkable. He shot him.

Bending down to his level, I try to lift him up. Our bodies are shaking and drenched in rainwater. We're both in pain, tired, hungry, and weak. But we have to keep going.

Grabbing his arm, I wince when I pull too hard, even inflicting pain on myself. Why does my arm hurt?

A booming rumble of thunder makes me flinch, but I quickly recover. I pull his arm again, cursing when he doesn't move. The small ache in arm is now a pulsing discomfort.

The heavy downpour clouds my vision so I can barely see his struggled breaths. I can only feel the ache in my right arm. I think the bullet grazed me.

"If you and him both want to live then you'll stand the fuck up and come back inside. Now."

I can feel the hard barrel press against my head before I'm suddenly falling to the wet ground. I forgot how impatient he is.

Rain falls like pellets as I lay on the dirt and stick infested earth. I took too long to answer. My eyes are wide while my chest heaves sporadically. I can feel the blood pour from the back of my head before a pounding throb seeps in. A pair of black boots come into view, causing more tears to spring in my eyes while I try to cower. I know what is going to happen. I know what he is going to do. And just as soon as my distraught thoughts leave, Rich bends down to my eye level.

The falling droplets from the sky make his sculpted face appear distorted. His eyes are a darker shade of brown; just as cruel as his intentions, while his thin lips spread wryly.

"It's time to be house broken." He mouths before his fist connects to my already bleeding face. I don't have time to scream or run. Instead, I submit to numb unconsciousness just like Jake has.

15

CHAPTER 15

"Hey Liv! Over here!" Someone calls my name, making my head snap to their location. A wide grin forces itself on my lips when I see Nathan, one of my best friends waving me over. He's leaning against the wall with a red solo cup in his hand. looking bored as hell.

"You look like you're over this." I lean against the wall next to him, making sure our arms touch.

"Where's Margaret and Kelly? Are they still coming?" He asks brashly. Looking up at him, I'm met with the weird look he gives me- half curious, half... dreading. This alone makes my eyebrows scrunch downward because they should have been here by now. I'm usually the last to arrive because I'm the youngest in our group. Plus, I had to convince my parent's Nathan was going to be here.

"They didn't make it yet?" Kelly always attends parties- well, the ones she deems as 'cool' or 'solid'.

He bites his lip while shaking his head. I watch him take a swig of whatever's in his cup before handing it to me.

"Well, they're missing the good part." I smirk while sipping the liquid from his cup. The awfully strong and bitter taste makes me grimace. It's clear what it is; Jack Daniels.

"No doubt about that." He laughs at my reaction then reaches for his cup. I hate being laughed at so I hold it closer.

With the cup to my parted lips, I guzzle down the rest of the beverage before throwing the cup down and wiping my mouth with the back of my hand.

"Whoa, slow down Liv. I don't want this to be too much for you," he speaks softly. He knows my parents trust him with my life.

"I'm not a lightweight so don't laugh at me. I just didn't realize it was JD." I cringe from the caustic taste on my tongue. I've had alcohol before, just red wine and fruity drinks.

"Sure." He grins at me with playful gray eyes. "If you're not a lightweight then prove it."

A round of cheers and applauds fill another part of the room, gaining our attention.

"Follow me." I say before pushing through crowds of dancing teenagers. The loud music blaring makes my ears throb but it's nothing compared to the small migraine threatening to creep up.

Once I'm in the kitchen I see two kegs being occupied by two girls. A blond and a brunette. They look a year or two older than me, considering I'm still fifteen. I watch in astonishement while they drink without even taking a breath. I don't know how they do it but I'm going to prove to Nathan that I'm not a lightweight.

More cheers and catcalls surround the air once they finish. With triumphant smiles, and beer dripping down their pretty faces, they high five each other. I watch them do their little hanshake before dancing into the living room. A few guys follow them but they ignore them. No doubt they're seniors.

"Who's next?"

I make my way over before my bodyguard, i.e Nathan, can stop me. I'm only here because my parents like him so I'm taking full advantage of this. I mean this is his party, afterall and if he can't handle me then he deserves whatever my parents dish him.

"I'll go too." He's now standing beside me.

Dammit. What is he doing? My eyes focus menacingly at him when he winks at me. From the way his tousled raven hair lays, scattered and still sexy, to the way his small dimples appear when his red lips part. I can see why most girls swoon over him.

Nathan wasn't built yet but he looked incredible for a sixteen year old junior in high school. No one believed he was the age he said he was.

"Don't overdo it to prove a point." He says solemnly this time.

I choose to ignore him before focusing on the keg. His small chuckle makes me realize he knows what I'm doing. I love how he can see through me sometimes.

The blonde guy who leads this little contest starts counting down, forcing me to ready myself. I'm prepared to beat Nathan if it's the last thing I do.

I awake with a powerful migraine, forcing me to clutch my head while groaning loudly. Everything hurts but the worst ail is this pounding headache. It's worse than my first hangover. Grimacing slightly, rollover only to make the pain lessen. But unfortunately for me, it worsens. You'd think I'd be accustomed to this pain but I'm not. I'll never be.

I hate the feeling of pain. Not just in a physical sense but mentally as well. I've never been this depressed in my life. Now I see how Nathan truly felt when he needed me the most. He needed me to help him through it. He needed me to tell him everything would be fine.

Looking back, I saw all of the signs but I chose to ignore it. The drinking, the mood swings, and even the suicide notes. That was the summer before his senior year though. His parents found out about his heavy depression just two months before school started back up. They saw how badly he needed help so they sent him to rehab for those two months.

He was the last person I thought would break because he was the strongest in our group. If something bothered him he knew how to handle it. Or so I thought. The one issue he couldn't fend off was his step- father. And if I was a decent person back then, then I would have been the first to help him.

But no, I was too busy being selfish. I was too involved with my own petty problems.

After a few minutes of laying in silence and sobbing, my aching head subsides to a dull thrum. Now that it's better, I'm able to focus my thoughts. Thinking more clearly, I remember Rich choking and touching me. I remember Jake practically saving me. And then I remember being hit by Rich's gun. Oh no. And Jake; where is he?

Sitting up quickly, I feel dizziness overtake my body; including my vision, so I have to close my eyes. Once I open them, my vision blurs before refocusing again. It's probably due to the previous head trauma I endured.

Anyway, the room is eerily quiet, and once again I'm immersed in complete darkness. Everything is dark around me, and it's not just the dark that scares me the most. It's the sudden sound of screaming. It's chilling to the point where my own bones shake.

From the deep voice and pained agony behind it, I'm guessing it's Jake. He's in the other room.

Running off the bed, I jolt straight for the door. Considering how dark it is and how wobbly my legs feel, I make it there in record time. Surprisingly.

As soon as I approach the door my hands grasp the cold knob before realization hits me. The door is locked. Jake's screams are close. Too close.

Looking to my left, I realize he's on the other side of the wall no the door. His screams get louder, forcing me to bang on the wall.

"Jake, calm down! Everything will- be fine." My voice wavers right in the middle of my reassurance. I hope I can convince him to stay calm. I was never good at that.

"Fuck! This...it just...it hurts so fucking much!" He groans again.

My heart aches every for every anguished outcry he makes because I can't help him. He has managed to help me but I can't even help him.

My palms are on the wall as I continue listening to his pleading. I have a feeling that if I don't get to him soon he might die.

"Jake!" I shout with desperation. He's been silent for a few minutes now, which scares me to my core.

"Don't worry about him."

A cold voice startles me, causing my body to stiffen.

"Jake," I swallow nervously. "You're getting out of here- we're getting out of here like you said!" I yell with determination. And although my mind is telling me how screwed we truly are, I can't help but hope we're right. We're getting away from Rich.

"I don't know where he's going with a broken leg." He chuckles lightly.

With anger boiling inside of me, I turn to see a nonchalant Rich sitting in the corner of the same room I was previously in. The owl themed room. He's in the recliner with the ruffled blankets, sitting ever so calmly.

A small lamp lights his side of the room, revealing his shadowed face.

"And you Livie, we both know where you're going." He cracks a heavy smile before pointing the gun at me.

A small gasp fills the air while my body becomes rigid.

"Now be a good girl and do what I tell you." With the gun pointed at me, he motions for me to move to my right. The bed.

Closing my eyes, I back further into the wall- if that's even possible. I need a plan.

"Look at me."

He's closer now because I can feel his minty breath fan my face. I've seen enough of him. Why can't he just leave me alone?

"Remember when I said I would take you."

I jump from the feel of his hand grazing downward. My eyes are still closed while his cold fingertips go from my arm to the small of my back. My breathing quickens when he pulls me closer but I don't dare open my eyes. His body is hot against mine and even though I'm pressed to his chest, I can still feel him on my thigh.

"Well, times up. Now, open those pretty eyes." He whispers in my ear huskily. I suppress a shudder when I feel his hand slip inside my blouse. Why aren't I fighting back? It's as if my body is just as stuck as my mind.

My heart hammers in my chest when he starts pushing up on me, allowing his body heat to resonate onto mine. He inhales softly, making me sink further into the wall. If his fist weren't balled in my shirt, I'd probably be able to run.

"Livie," He states in a warning tone. I'm all too familiar with that tone. He wants me to look at him but I won't. The eyes are the windows to the soul and every time I look into Rich's I see an eternal sea of wickedness. I hate him.

My eyes are still closed when I feel the cold metal on my cheek.

"If you don't open your fucking eyes now then they'll be closed permanently." He threatens through gritted teeth. Knowing how petrified I am of being shot, my eyes snap open.

Looking into his dominating eyes, I notice how powerful they are. How intriguing yet dangerous they are. How can his stare hold me prisoner too? Dread washes over me as he moves the gun to my stomach.

"Move," He grips my arm then pushes me in front of him. I stumble before he steadies me.

"Move your legs!" He roars impatiently.

My perspiring palms cling to the hem of my shirt as I walk toward the bed with my head hung low. My heart sinks the closer I get to the bed. I need a plan. I need to fight. If I could just steal the gun from him then I could shoot him and walk out of here.

Glancing back at him, I feel him grip the gun tighter before pushing it further into my back.

I don't have a chance.

Before I know it, I'm spun around with such brevity that I end up falling backwards. The mattress is soft and the sheets are cold. Just as cold as him.

"Like I was saying before; we can do this the easy way...or," He leans forward, causing my body to scoot back. This action must have angered him because grabs my knee and points the gun at it.

"Move from me one more fucking time and I'll shoot your knee cap."

My heart stops and so does the rest of my body. Only small tremors flow through me. I'm more than terrified as he glares murderously at me. My stomach churns as my mind begins to race with horrid thoughts.

"Don't hurt me. Please-" Small droplets slide down my cheeks when I feel him graze my inner thigh. His touch is acidic.

"Prove to me you're strong and it won't hurt- too much." I watch him lean closer to my quivering lips.

He grabs my chin, forcing me to pucker my lips. With the gun still in his hand, he begins trailing it along my jaw.

This act forces more tears to spill over. I can't stop myself from being afraid of him. I don't know how to be brave.

"Hey Livie, don't cry."

He releases his grip on my chin and then stands up. His tall stature is more than intimidating. It makes him appear as a shadow in the night. A thief, an attacker. Someone you'll never see coming.

"Because crying is weakness." His deep voice echoes in my head before I feel a stinging pain. The slap is so strong that I'm knocked onto my back. My vision falters between the blurry tears in my eyes and throbbing of my head.

I feel a huge weight on my body so with quick reflexes, my knee goes up to kick him in his bulge.

"Fuck!" He shouts angrily while I smirk devilishly.

It's just enough to slow him down because he clutches it while falling on his side. The clang of the gun hitting the ground awakens my senses.

While he's still cursing and rolling around on the bed, I crawl off to grab the gun.

"Stay where you are!" My shaky hands grip the gun while I try to compose myself. I've never held a gun before and I'm scared out of my mind. I guess there's a first time for everything.

"Okay," He coughs out. "Okay, I'm not going anywhere." He is now raising his hands defensively. With a small grin and narrowed eyes, he seizes mine.

I'm taken aback by his placidness. Why isn't he angry, or trying to fight me?

"Um-" Think Livie, think. I need to get out of here but the door is locked. I need a damn key. Shit.

"You want the key?"

So he does have a key. Stupid bastard. I'm about to speak when he continues.

"You're not getting the key. This lake house is just as much mine as it was my brother's." He finishes with a yawn. I watch as he stands up, alerting me to hold the gun tighter.

"Don't move Rich! I swear I'll shoot you!" I hold fierce power in my voice while I speak. It's to let him know how serious I am.

He releases a dry laugh before shrugging.

"Fine then, but just know this Livie, I used all the bullets on Jake's legs." He states precisely with his hands in his pockets.

My finger pulls the trigger reflexively but to my dismay no sound comes out. No bullet penetrates his flesh. With a gaped mouth I drop the murderous vweapon before turning on my heel.

I don't know where I'm running to, all I know is that I need to get to safety.

Before I know it, I make it to the window. It's a normal sized window beside the recliner he was previously sitting in. My eyes focus on the beauty on the other side of the window. From the trees, fog and sunrise surrounding the lake house, I conclude this window leads to the back yard. The orange and yellow hues of the sky confirms my suspicion of what time of day it is; morning.

My hands push upward, trying to open the window. I struggle for a few minutes until my hair is roughly pulled back.

"Ah, no ya don't."

I scream from the pain of feeling my hair being ripped out. Humming softly, he continues dragging me across the hardwood while I claw at his arms.

The next thing I feel is my front landing on the mattress. Lifting myself up quickly, I try to crawl forwards but he grabs my arms and pins them behind my back.

"Looks like you've made your choice. The hard way it is." He growls while tying my hands with rope.

I can't stop crying, it's so loud and so suffocating that it burns my throat and forces coughing spells to erupt. I twist and turn, even kicking. But the only thing I'm doing is making it easier for him to disrobe me.

"Please...no." I manage to whisper once he removes my shirt. "Jake...please... help me."

16

CHAPTER 16

I continue screaming and panting until my ears ring. My world is crashing down all over again. And once again, there isn't a damn thing I can do about it.

In the amount of time that has passed, I haven't felt any pain; just him all over me. Touching me, breathing on me, and even kissing me. On the surface, all of his unwanted affections are slow and gentle. But in my morphed mind, he's rough and violent; foul and immoral. A man I will forever detest.

My hands are still tied while I squirm, and even though my throat is dry, that still doesn't stop me from yelling for help.

"Help me...help!" I hiccup. "Get...get him off of me!" I scream when he begins tugging on my jeans.

In the position I'm in, he has easy access to my rear. He's sitting on my back while I'm laying on my stomach.

My head jerks back when he pulls me to his chest. "No one can help you now, Livie."

With that, he spends me around. Now I'm facing him while he holds me up by my neck. He isn't choking me, just eyeing me lustfully. The hair on my neck stands up when I realize how exposed and vulnerable I truly am. I'm only clothed in my pink bra while the waistband of my jeans hangs on my waist, revealing a small peek of my pink panties.

His eyes hold a mysterious mischief to them as he tilts his head. It's the same way he looked at me the first night he came down to the basement. The same stare that haunts my consciousness and unconsciousness. It's as if he's playing with me, and I have no idea what his next move will be. He knows this so he'll use my fear to his advantage. This is what he's always done. But this time, I won't be able to hold him off. Or can I?

"Please don't do this- please, I'm not ready." I plead while trying to swallow my fear. If he sees more tears, he'll keep going because that's how he is. He feeds off of my fear. I know that much about him.

With an amused grin, he leans closer to my ear.

"Sooner or later, I'll have you."

His words are clear and concise. Even chilling. It's not just his presence, but his promises. He means what he just said. Even if it is a double meaning. I get the feeling that he'll "have me" in more than one way. This thought sends shudders through me.

"But for now, I'll settle for this-"

My heart steadies when he releases me. I fall on my side, unable to adjust my body because of the restraints.

I don't give any thought or attention to what he's doing as I try to calm my nerves. Breathing in and out, I practice the excerises my mom taught me when in a dire situation. I need to relax. But how can I when the devil himself was seconds from taking my virginity?

I jump slightly before my body tenses at his toxic touch. He soon comes into view with a curved grin. His eyes are beautiful when he smiles, but when he grins, they're just downright creepy.

I yelp when I'm suddenly lifted up. I feel the cold surface of the headboard as my back presses against it.

"What- what are you doing?" My chest heaves in quickened intervals while I stare wide eyed at him.

"You had the police on my ass, Livie. You had them thinking that missing girl was you because of some birthmark." He spits the words out as if they are venom on his tongue.

"But they won't think that anymore. Not after I mark you."

"Ma-mark me?" I stutter, clearly baffled by what I just heard. What does he mean hell 'mark me'? I had this birthmark sense birth. No one marked me, other than God. I was born with a mark on my left wrist and he can't change that.

He ignores my panicking while making his way over to the already lit fireplace. How did that get lit? And where the hell did it come from? I don't remember a fireplace in this room.

"My father gave this to me and my older brother. He carved our initials in it so we'd always know it was ours."

He holds the charcoal colored poker up, observing it carefully.

"So guess what I'm going to do to you?" I hear the floorboards creak as he approaches me. With fear already overtaking me, I pull on my binds tighter than before.

He can't mark me, brand me or do whatever twisted thing he's trying to do. I don't want this. I don't want to feel anymore pain.

My upper body presses harder into the headboard the closer he gets.

"Come on!" I tug on the rope cutting my wrists, hoping to get some type of positive results. My eyes blur from the tears while my wrists bleed and sting. I wish I could say I'm crying because of my stinging wrists but that isn't true. I'm crying because my attempt to free myself is failing miserably.

"Sta-stay away fr-from me!" I jerk away when he reaches for my chin.

"Don't move from me." He speaks cautiously.

I ignore his command while scooting to my right. If I can prevent myself from being harmed then I'll at least be able to live with myself. I refuse to just sit here and take it.

"What did I just say?"

My right ankle is grabbed this time, forcing my left to kick rapidly in the air.

"Let me-me go!" I pant while writhing around.

And that's when it happens. The sudden feel of him tying my ankles together forces more tears to spill over. He's blocking all ways to freedom again. I can't use my hands to fight, and I can't use my feet to run. This can't be happening. Someone, please help me.

Once he's finished tying my ankles togther, he sits me in an upright position against the headboard.

I watch with trembling lips as he brings the now heated poker in front of my face. It's tip is sharp and the color of a flame. Orange with hues of red. I can tell it just came out the fire.

"If you move then I promise you it will hurt worse." He speaks casually while I continue to quake mildly.

My eyes close, allowing overlapping tears to slide down my pale cheeks. By the time I open my eyes, I wish I hadn't because of the horrid image I see. He's now hovering over my right upper thigh with the poker sits firmly in his grip.

I feel his thumb graze my inner thigh, making my heart flutter. The poker is in his right hand while his fingers continue to gently trace my inner thigh.

"Please..." I trail off, on the verge of begging. All of my emotions are intensified because I'm on high alert. I'm scared, nervous, and an all around mess. I can only imagine how my brown hair looks, disheveled and knotted, while my left side of my face is bruised.

"Once this is over, I'll show you pleasure." He chuckles darkly while narrowing his eyes.

I wish he'd knocked me out first because the agonizing pain I feel now is beyond unbearable. My screams become louder after each stroke of the poker. He's literally carving into my flesh. The inflamed poker heats my sweaty skin, and fills the room with a putrid smell that I can't describe.

Closing my teary eyes, I bite my lip while gripping the rope tighter. My toes curl when he begins the seconf letter. I can't make out what he's writing, all I know is it hurts like hell. My tensed body flinches when I bite my lip so hard I draw more blood. I don't have time to realize that he's stopped carving into me because once the heat leaves, it's back on my flesh again. Burning, searing pain rips apart my skin and my insides. It's so horrible that I can even hear the sizzling heat taunting my ears. The scorching heat that scalds and scars my delicate olive skin won't let up.

"Scream, Livie." He smirks sadistically while carving a deeper cut into me.

My throat burns as I release an ear splitting scream. The entire room is spinning so fast that my mind can't keep up with what's happening anymore. My eyes have been widened for so long that they feel stuck permanently.

I can't see, hear or think anymore as all of my senses slowly abandon me. I wish I could just pass out. Just escape what's happening but I'm in too much discomfort to do that. So, with my body jerking repeatedly, I lay in slience. Just staring off and waiting- pleading for him to stop.

This isn't enough for Rich because just as my silence fills the room he presses harder on my wound, making me whimper loudly. I'm still gripping the rope on my wrists when I start twisting around.

Someone make it stop. Make him stop. It feels like my thigh is on fire, and every movement I make irritates it.

"That's not fucking loud enough." He growls fiercely.

"Ahhh!" My heart nearly stops when I feel the sharp tip of the poker twist into a raw, tender part of my thigh. The cut is soo deep that I can even feel it graze my bone.

I continue crying loudly until he finishes. I don't even know how long it's been because I lost count after fifteen seconds into it. I think it's mid morning because the sun is now up. I'm near the window which means I can feel the sunlight seeping through. It's lighting the room with vibrant, warm hues, and kissing my skin. The feeling makes me cringe because of the throbbing, searing pain on my tender thigh.

"Now, time for part two." He smiles wickedly at me before walking out of the room.

My upper body is numb, only allowing me to feel the intensified anguish on my thigh. I can feel the crusted blood on it but I won't look. I don't want to see any of it.

He comes back in and then purposely slams the door to make me jump. My eyes are still trained on my partially unclothed body when Rich roughly pulls my head back.

"When I say look at me, I mean it." He narrows his eyes at me, forcing me to cower. The sharp, vibrating pain in my head is nothing compared to what I just endured. My eyes shift from his coffee colored ones to the moss colored ones in the chair in front of the bed. His body heaves slowly while he tries to stay awake. I notice the way his right leg sits, stagnant and limp, while blood still pools from his left arm. Jake looks awful now. And from the way his eyes roam over my body, he's saying the same about me.

"You're going to perform and he's going to be the audience."

He grins triumphantly while it takes all of my being not to throw up. I'm not cut out for the entertainment business, and I'm definitely not even supposed to be here for his enjoyment.

Jake stares at me with a mix of anger and sadness.

I can't look at him so I avert my gaze to my lap. Bad thoughts consume me as more teardrops cloud my vision.

"I got all day," Rich crosses his arms while leaning against the bed post.

Swallowing dryly, I try to shake off the nervousness settling in the pit of my stomach. I hate him so much. My eyes hold pleading while I stare at Rich.

I can't do what he's thinking of having me do. Besides the fact that I'm only sixteen, I'm also extremely tired, hurting, and too weak for his games. And even though my eyes say all of that, I get the feeling he still doesn't care.

17

—— • ——

CHAPTER 17

With my eyes closed, I lay completely still. If I can pretend like he's not here then he'll go away. Yes, that's my logic and I'm sticking to it. Ignore him until he goes away.

"Well, what are you waiting for? Do something."

My eyes are still shut but I can still see the humor in his tone. Nothing about what he's doing is in the least bit funny.

I wince when my chin is gripped roughly. Opening my teary eyes, I'm met with his disturbing glare as our foreheads touch. Imagine staring into the eyes of your other half. Your evil half. That's how I feel when I look into his eyes. Some of the qualities in Rich are what I see in myself. Selfish, secretive, and provoking. The way I treated my ex friends reflects the way Rich treats me now. Maybe Jake's right, Rich and I aren't that different.

"Get the hell up. What are you waiting for?"

"I can't move, you asshole!" I seethe with boiled rage. My loud outburst awakens Jake from his dormant state. He's now bobbing his head lightly, trying to keep himself awake.

"Well, let's solve that problem, shall we?" With a cunning grin, he walks over to me.

My whole body tenses from his close proximity; even my breathing has stopped. He seems to notice this because he winks at me before untying my restraints.

Now that I'm free I can stretch and rub my sore wrists. While I'm trying to ease the soreness of my tense muscles, I notice Jake's horribly alarming state. His black rimmed eyes droop while the rest of his body hunches over. I notice that the blood pouring from the wound in his left arm has slowed down. He is in unimaginable pain but at least he won't bleed to death. My eyes hold sympathy the longer I stare at his broken body.

From his small torso all the way down to his right leg; it's a disgusting sight. Blood is all over his body like a second skin. He's barely recognizable because Rich beat him so badly. I can only imagine how horrible it was for him because he's still healing from being stabbed a couple weeks ago.

"No need to strip, I already got that out the way." He grins smugly at my partially clothed body.

Looking down, I see that I'm only dressed in my pink bra and panties. He must have pulled my jeans off without me noticing. With my cheeks suddenly inflamed from the realization of him undressing me so quickly, I swallow nervously before looking back up. Rich is still eyeing me while Jake is doing it too- in a not so subtle way.

Once our eyes meet, his dart down to his lap, as if he's ashamed. I expect this from Rich but not from him. Just him staring at my body like I'm a piece of meat makes me want to vomit. Rich is supposed to be the perverted one, not Jake.

Tears roll down my cheeks when Rich grabs my arm and forcefully positions me on my knees. I'm still on the bed but now I'm more exposed and vulnerable. Not to mention, he awakened the throbbing burn on my thigh. I know he carved something into it but I refuse to look.

"Since you don't know what to fucking do, I'll help you."

I squeak when he takes my arms- the same arms I'm using to cover my body- and puts them around his nape. His toned chest presses against my small, sweaty one, making my heart race. When did he take his shirt off?

My eyes shut tightly when he tilts my chin up. I don't want to look at him so I shake my head vigorously while trying to pull my hands away from his neck. I manage to pull my hands away but am stopped when his grip around my wrists tightens.

"What did I say about moving from me?" He growls in my ear. His lips graze my earlobe, making me cringe.

"No, no...n-no!" I begin sobbing harder when he brings me closer. His hands go from my wrists all the way up my arms until I feel him squeeze my rear end. I'm frightened and embarassed because I can't stop this from happening. How pathetic am I, huh? I can't even cover myself and I can't fight. I need a way out of this and I need it now.

He continues to violate me while I cry. Every kiss is putrid and every touch is vile.

In no time I'm laying on my back while he straddles me. I'm caught in between him and I can't move. His hand is holding mine captive above my head while his eyes penetrate mine lustfully.

I use my body to try to lift myself up but the pressure on my wrists makes me wince. I lift myself up again, ignoring the nagging pain. I'm determined to keep my virginity.

"Don't...fight me!" He roars, making my body shrink back into the bed. My teary eyes land on his flexed biceps, and strong abdomen. I now realize how he's able to win every fight. His strength aids him in overpowering me.

"Help-help me!" I shriek right before his lips capture mine. The way his tongue roams over my mouth makes me nauseous. I twist and writhe while he continues kissing me. A burning lust, passion even, invades my mouth and pollutes my soul. Tainted, fractured, stolen. That's how I'm feeling right now.

He deepens the kiss, making my heart flutter from firght. My eyes are wide open while I groan loudly, trying to plead for him to stop. And from the way my body is reacting to this kiss, I can gladly say that my mind isn't the only thing that wants to be free.

"You're the one-- you're the prick who killed my father!" An angry, thunderous voice booms, saturating the air with deeper animosity.

Rich pauses, his fingers roam around inside of my panties, just inches from my core; just seconds from sinking into me. My body is stiff but my mind is jolting around. I can feel his lips still pressed to mine, frozen in place at what Jake just said. I grimace from the feeling of sweat and my manipulated arousal as it continues flowing under me.'Please get off of me.' I chant in my head while my heart continues hammering.

Rich sighs heavily, fanning my face with the air from his nostrils before pulling back, instantly breaking the kiss. With my lips now free, I inhale quickly, trying to make up for air I lost. I can't move away from him because his hands are now firmly clasped around my arms. He bought my hands down from above my head.

"What did you just say to me?"

I whimper because with each word he speaks, his anger forces his fingers to tighten around my arms. The feeling is of a strong pinch, and no matter how hard I try to pry his hands off, they just get tighter.

"I think you heard me, Uncle Rich."

Uncle? Wait, what? Rich is Jake's uncle? Why didn't he tell me?

Rich's icy chuckle fills the tense air and forces my body to involuntary shiver. I'm in shock from this new information. They're related? I know I saw the pictures but I never connected the dots.

"I thought you'd never figure it out, you dumb piece of shit." His hands release my arms before trailing down to my incinerated thigh. I cry out painfully before laying still on my back with wide eyes.

"So why'd you do it, huh? Why did you kill your brother?" Jake shouts, on the verge of breaking down. I can hear the turmoil in his voice.

I'm still groaning when Rich says,

"You're so fucking dramatic." The way he says it seems to mean he's talking to us both. His head cocks to the side before a demented grin spreads on his face. My eyes hold panic because I know what he's thinking.

"No, don-"

He presses his thumb on my raw wound, causing me to groan some more. It hurts when I move, and now that he's inflicting more pain, it makes it more irritated. Biting my lip, I suppress a whimper when he begins tracing it with his fingertips. The pain is crippling, forcing me to clutch my hands to try to stop them from shaking.

"Why did you kill my dad, Uncle Rich?" He practically spits the words 'uncle Rich' out. There's clear hate and hostility between this two.

His heavy body gets off of mine and I am relieved because the pain weakens, and I also get to move. It takes all of me to bite back the throbbing pain in my thigh when I move to the headboard. With my breathing still heavy, I bring my knees to my chest to hug myself.

"You wanna know what my ink means?" He's standing between us both with his arms crossed. The closed mouth smile makes me narrow my eyes at him. This isn't a game.

"This has nothing to do with my father!" Jake boils with wrath. He's angry and he wants answers. The way his body quakes while his fists ball up leads me to believe that he's a few seconds away from pounding Rich's brains out. If he could walk he would have by now, and I wouldn't be the one to stop him.

"The first three ravens symbolizes the number of people who betrayed me."

He points to his arm to show us the black ink lining it. It's the same tattoo I saw and asked him about. The same tattoo with the birds flying into fire.

"The eternal pit of fire is the price they paid for betraying me."

Jake and I remain silent while he explains.

"So, Jakey boy, the moral of the story is that your actions bring about your own suffering."

I gulp when he stares at me in particular. His brown eyes are haunting yet intriguing. I can't look away because he has me locked in. Locked in his mystifyingly disturbing eyes.

"So choose wisely, because just like death, I don't have a problem ending you."

18

CHAPTER 18

The loud music vibrated off the walls and into the crowd of dancing teenagers. With my eyes closed, I let the music sink in the more I move. It's some party playlist the dj is spinning and everyone is enjoying it.

The beat changes to a more upbeat pace, causing more people to flood into the already packed living room. We're all sweaty and close but I'm not complaining. Instead, I smile widely.

I've always loved music and dancing because freedoms of expression is improtant. In all honesty, anything dealing with the arts has always interested me. As my body moves in sync with the beat, I can feel myself letting go. The more I dance the happier I become, that is, until I ram into someone's chest.

A rumbling laugh reverberates against me, forcing my eyes to trail upwards. I go from the cream colored shirt with the sleeves rolled up to full, smiling lips and tousled, black hair.

"Nathanieeelll!" I squeal happily. He's here, he actually came. "I'm soo, soo. sooo happy you came."

"It's my party, of course I'd be here." He laughs that heart stopping laugh while I continue dancing.

"Ready to go? Your parents wanted you home by eleven."

"Nooo! You'll neva take meh alivee." I slur my words as I head towards the stairs.

"Seriously lightweight, c'mon."

I hear him sigh and then I'm suddenly grabbed around my waist.

"Let goooo." I giggle while squirming. He has a vice grip around me and it's hard to move. I forgot how strong he is, even for a sixteen year old.

"Not until you sober up." He lifts me up and over his shoulder without much effort.

"But, I'ma not...even soberrrr." I laugh loudly to the point where I'm almost snorting. I've never been this wasted before. It feels weird, like my mind isn't in control of my body anymore. Every word I think in my head comes out differently when I say it out loud.

"Yeah, I know that...Now how am I going to get you home?" He mumbles before plopping us down on his bed.

Speaking without thinking, I quickly say,

"I can't stay here."

He grins at my drunkened state while shaking his head. His eyes smolder in a playful way, making him look even more tempting.

"Wat, you can get the floor." I giggle while kicking off my sandals.

Scooting up to his pillow, I inhale deeply before sighing with content. It smells like shampoo and detergent. Just like him.

"What the hell Liv? You can't kick me out of my own bed."

"I can't...and I just did." I mumble as I snuggle into his sheets. Warm and comforting unlike my bed at home. Cold and lonely.

I hear him sigh before laying beside me. I scoot back until I'm in the heart of his chest. With his arms wrapped around me, he snuggles closer, and then places his head in the crook of my neck.

"Nathan..." I speak quietly, debating on whether or not I should ask.

"Hmm."

"Is wat Kelly and Margrit said truth?"

During our sleepovers over the summer they would tell me about how much he likes me. How the whole, at the time, sophomore class knew about it except me, the little freshman. Now, Margaret and I are entering our sophomore year while Kelly and Nathan are going to be Juniors.

Kelly told me she volunteered to help him get over his fright but the "classes" she set up didn't work. She says that he's still too afraid to ask me on a date. I never believed them before but the more I spend time with him, the more I'm kind of starting to see it. And that scares me.

I think he knows what I'm asking but he just says,

"I don't know Liv. Let's just get you sobered up."

I miss my parents. I miss my home. I miss my friends. But most importantly, I miss Nathan. All of the people I miss, cared about me the most. And now, they're all gone. No one is here for me. No one is here to tell me everything will be okay, or that I'll get away from Rich. That maybe, I'll go to prom or even graduate high school and then go to L.A. No one is here to tell me how proud my parents would have been of me. No one is here to hold me like Nathan did that night he was helping me sober up. Nope, no one who cares about me is here.

"Ah, fuck. We're back in this shithole again." He grumbles while sitting up.

I knew where we were, I just didn't want it to sink in. I knew the moment I felt the shackle around my ankle. I knew the moment I inhaled the stiff, moldy air. I knew Rich would either kill us or bring back to this hellhole. I knew this but it's still difficult to take in. Maybe if I let my tears wash away my turmoil then surely, it will go away. All of my hurt, anger and the feeling of being trapped will go away if my tears wash it away. So with that, I sit up and wipe my eyes. Just like my thoughts helped me I need to help Jake. Someone needs to be the encouraging one.

"It could be a lot worse, Jake." I spit out without thinking. What a dumb thing for me to say. Can it seriously get more worse than this?

"Have a look around, Livie. It is a lot worse!"

I want to tell him that at least we have each other, and I'm here if he needs someone, but I stay quiet. I doubt he'll want to hear that.

"How long have we been here?" I change topic because the previous conversation will just lead to arguing.

"I don't know, all I know is that you snore." He states plainly. "Like a big ass bear."

"That's not what I asked but thanks captain obvious." I mumble sarcastically. I know I snore. I just never really had to hide it because I always slept alone.

He chuckles, making my cheeks flush from the refreshing sound. At least he isn't going to bicker with me.

After a few moments of quiet, he finally says,

"Give me the bobby pin. I'm going to look for a way out."

"What?" My head snaps up to see him limping over to me. He's still chained too, which means to get out he'd need what he's asking for. The bobby pin.

"I need the bobby pin so we can get out of here. We both deserve to live, to laugh, to just enjoy life, ya know? We deserve to go home." He stares at me with sincerity which means that his determined streak is soon approaching. And when that comes, I can give up on trying to convince him to leave it alone.

"I already searched this dump. Nothing is here, except us." I rub my sore neck gingerly while cringing from the dreadful sight of the basement. It's chilly, smelly and an all around mess down here.

"I'll double check, maybe you missed something." His hand extends to receive the pin so I decide to change the subject.

"Something weird happened the night we tried to go to the hospital." I'm just going to tell him what happened the night we tried to leave.

"Like what? He finally came to his senses and realized what a dick he is?"

I stifle a laugh before pushing the loose strands of brown hair behind my ear.

"No, he...he uh, he kissed me."

"I told you he liked you." He scoots closer, forcing a tinge of excitement to flow through me.

"It wasn't like that, it felt more protective than romantic- well, at the time it did." The more I ponder on it the more I realize he pecked me on my forehead. A kiss on the forehead is a symbol of protection. I remember when my dad would read me bedtime stories and then kiss my forehead after saying goodnight.

"Maybe it was romantic and you're just too much of a stiff virgin to realize."

"What? No, I'm a virgin but I'm not...stiff, as you put it." I can let loose if I really wanted to.

"I mean you never know. Gia was a shy, hopeless virgin until I helped her get out of it." He waggles his eyebrows playfully while I shake my head. I can't stop my lips from spreading into a grin and

I'm grateful. Grateful because he has managed to make me smile, which is something I desperately needed.

"You miss her, don't you?"

He exhales slowly and then turns to me.

"I think about what she's doing and who she's with. Sometimes I wonder if..."

He trails off so I stay silent. I'm not going to press him for information. Especially something as personal as his relationship.

"Do you have someone, you know?" He looks up at me with long eyelashes. His head tilts in a curious way while he stares at me.

"To date? Oh no, I never really get into intimate relationships." I shrug nonchalantly.

"Let me guess, your dad says you can't date until your thirty?"

"I can't date until he's seventy."

We exchange laughter and for once I'm not focused on my horrible surroundings. I'm laughing and it feels good.

"How old are you?" He inquires once our laughing ceases.

"I'll be seventeen in October. What about you?"

"I turn eighteen next week." He sighs sadly while leaning against the wall. We're now side by side with our arms touching.

"You graduated?" I ask, awestruck. He looks like he's sixteen. Maybe because he hasn't been eating properly.

"Uh yeah, I graduated in May." He notices my shock, which makes a confident smirk grace his attractive pink lips.

"I had a wrestling scholarship to attend Berkeley in the fall. No chance of that happening thanks to that prick." He shakes his head while running his fingers through his longer hair. I note how weird he looks with a hint of a stubble too.

"Berkeley?"

"Yeah, something about California."

I smile because that's what I used to say. I've always wanted to live in Cali because of how beautiful it looked on t.v. I know it's kind of sad to base your future home choice on what you've seen on television, but I'm tired of the east coast. I need a change.

"I actually wanted to attend chef school in L.A."

"Really? Gia hates the west coast. We argued a few times about me moving out there."

"Well if she loves you then she wouldn't mind, right?"

He frowns in thought at my question. I don't know much about love but I do know that sometimes people make choices to better themselves. Gia shouldn't worry about him, he'll be okay.

"She's just afraid of being alone." He sighs sadly. "I'm the one who promised I'd never leave her and look where I am."

I don't know what to say to that so I stay quiet. It's easy to have a fighting spirit when you have something to live for; someone to live for. It's natural to fight when you have hope. But what hope do I have when all of my dreams have faded? When all of my family and friends are gone forever? I feel like a dark, empty pit of nothingness; just existing with no purpose whatsoever.

"What about your friends?"

"Huh?" I didn't hear him because I'm too engrossed in my turmultuous thoughts.

"You say you don't date but there's gotta be one guy who likes you." He tries to lighten the mood but it's only depressing me more. Nathan liked me but I ruined it by being selfish.

"The one guy who liked me hates my guts now."

"Why? What'd you do?" He turns to me with a teasing grin that only annoys me.

"You ask a lot of questions. And what makes you think I did anything?" Even though it's my fault, I don't need Jake knowing. He'll just label me as the 'girl who gets on everyone's bad side.'

"I've known you for almost two months now and you don't bring out the best in people. So tell me, what'd you do to make the poor guy hate you? Because I have an idea but I want to hear from you first."

"Stop trying to piss me off Jake."

"Oooh I must have hit a nerve. Is wittle Olivia gonna cry or tell her mommy on me." He teases, making my fists ball up.

I don't give him a chance to say anymore because with one quick swing, my fist connects to his nose. I'm on top of him while repetitiously driving my fist into his face. He swiftly grabs my arms before pushing me to the ground. I'm now on the bottom while he straddles me.

I try to squirm out of his hold but he just squeezes my arms tighter, inflicting more pain. My squirming makes him wince because I grazed his bad leg.

"Get off!" I growl while pointlessly fighting him. His hands still squeeze my arms while he continues sitting on my stomach.

"Apologize first." He smirks with self assurance, like he has me where he wants me.

But oh, how wrong he is. A bright idea pops into my head so before doubt can step in, I lift my head to plant my lips on his. For a minute, we're both frozen. The only sound is our heavily beating hearts. Why did I just do that?

All of my blood rushes to my face when I realize what he's doing; and what I'm continuing to do.

I should pull away. But before I can, he slowly parts his split lips. I follow after him and am surprised when our kiss deepens. He tastes good, like shockingly good, so I put my hands on his cheeks to bring him closer. Our bodies are pressed against each other while we lock lips. The longer we kiss, the more my body wants him. He starts running his fingers through my hair while my arms wrap around his nape. We move in sync; like we're both on one accord. Like we're both agreeing for once.

"Now do you want me off of you?"

He breaks the kiss for a moment to look into my eyes. I'm a bit startled but I can't look away. I steal his gaze while gently tracing the outline of his jaw. He's gorgeous.

I'm captivated by him so I can't form words in this moment. Instead, I shake my head slowly. I'm too enamored by him that it takes a minute to realize that his lips are back on mine. We succumb to the alluring feel of each other as I feel myself being lifted. My legs wrap around him so he can carry me easier.

We continue making out until I feel my back on the mattress. He feels under my shirt while his tongue grazes over mine, sending pleasured shockwaves through my body. All of my thoughts, good and bad are gone. All I'm focused on is how good he feels pressed to me. And in that moment, I feel myself slowly letting go.

The frightening sound of the door opening makes my heart drop. Jake doesn't seem to hear it because he continues kissing me. Think Livie, think.

I pat him to get him to stop but he just sucks on my bottom lip.

I hear slow, heavy steps decline the stairs so with dread, I chomp down on his tongue. He groans while we back away from each other.

"What the hell? Why'd you bite me?"

His face is distorted in confusion and annoyance. I hate that look but I needed to do it. Who knows how Rich would react if he sees us.

"Yeah Livie, why'd you bite him?"

I turn to see Rich holding a plate of what looks like four slices of cheese pizza. Its' delicious aroma agitates my stomach, forcing gurgling noises to fill the dreary air. I'm so hungry.

"You- he was attacking me!"

That's all I've got and I'm hoping Jake catches on. Rich's suspicious eyes go from mine to Jakes' confused frown.

"I was teaching you how to fight!"

Yes. He gets what I'm doing. Good, now Rich won't suspect any-thing.

"By pinning me on the mattress and making me helpless? Genius plan, instructor."

"Okay look you two, I bought food so kill each other after you eat." He slides the plate to me before walking back upstairs and locking the door.

We don't give each other a second glance as we dive into the plate of desired food. I dig into my pizza, not caring how hot it is. Jake does the same thing, making small moaning noises. He's definitely enjoying his slice.

"He bought us food." Jake speaks quietly. The way his eyes narrow while he chews makes me relate to how he feels. Rich is the kind of guy who you'd hate being grateful for.

"Told ya." I grin while savoring the wonderful taste of bread, sauce and cheese.

"But he's still a scumbag tool."

I giggle before starting on my next slice. Sauce drips down chin, creating a mess and forcing Jake to grin at me. Crap, I'm embarrassing myself. I need a napkin, which we don't have. Looking down, I use my shirt- my overly large shirt to wipe my mouth. This shirt is not mine.

"You gave me your shirt?"

His partially healed cuts and bruises are prevalent on his tan abdomen, making my eyes drop down in sadness.

"I'm sorry. You didn't have to do that."

His hand places itself over mine, forcing my eyes to land on his. With a modest smile, he says,

"It's cool. I've been wanting these abs to breathe."

After we eat we talk some more. It's mostly about our home lives. Turns out we're not too different. Even though he and Jackson, his older brother, are four years apart they're still very close. I tell him how close Waylan and I were before he died. I tell him stories about how when I fell and scraped my knee, Waylan would cry too. He told me it was twinlepathy. And when I asked what that was he pinched my cheeks then told me, "You need to get out more, sweetheart." All I could do was roll my eyes before smacking his hand away.

I soon found out that he's been to three continents; Europe, Asia and Africa. Not including the U.S. Because his dad was a businessman and oil tycoon, he was allowed to travel with him when he was younger. The only time I've traveled was to go to my grandmother's funeral in New Hampshire. Other than that, I've never been anywhere. Especially to amazing places like Europe, Asia, and Africa.

After our travel stories ended, he told me about his friends. He has three; his brother, Gia, and Dylan. Dylan is Jackson's age, twenty two, but they've always gotten along. He tells me that he and Gia met in elementary school and have been close ever since. I tried to listen with a polite smile but when he confessed how much he loved her, I couldn't help but feel a little jealous. I shouldn't feel this way because she had him first, but the sad reality is I do.

He moves on from that and I'm relieved because I don't want to hear about her anymore. What a lucky girl she is to have him. Beneath his hard exterior is a funny, sweet, ambitious guy who seems to love her. She's so lucky.

He continues telling me stories about their wild party life while I listen with astonished ears. Another thing we have in common, he has three friends while I have- well, had three. He attends wild parties while mine are milder. He likes action and horror movies like I do and his favorite subject in school is science while mine is History. Funny, I didn't take him as the nerdy science kid.

"I'm smarter than I look, Olive." He smirks at me, making my heart flutter.

"Does that explain your Berkely scholarship?" I smile tauntingly.

"Life isn't just about my good looks and smarts. Athleticism works in my favor too."

I sigh with a bored expression. Here he goes with his over saturated ego again.

"It's called humor Livie." He shakes his head with a playful grin.

"Yeah, you're such a comedian."

Yawning, I make my way over to the mattress. Food makes me tired...or maybe I'm just tired from not resting. Either way, this girl is dog tired.

My eyes get heavy but before they can fully close, I feel a giant arm wrap around my waist. I need this comfort but I can't allow it. He has a girlfriend.

"Jake..."

"I know Livie, but I think you need this just as much as I do."

With that, he pulls me closer before snuggling his head into my hair. My tense body relaxes into his as I place my hand on top of his. He's warm and soothing, and I love it. I want it. He's right, I need this just as much as he does.

19

— ◦ —

Chapter 19

I tossed and turned during the rest of the night. It was as if my body was trying to shut down while my mind kept me awake. I can't sleep. Especially now that I've been with Rich for three or four months, give or take. My insane sleep pattern is off the charts now, and I don't think I'll ever get it back.

My body jerks slightly when I feel something poke me. From the position we're in, it's easy for a boy to get...happy so with a suppressed giggle, I just lay still with a small grin. His arm is draped over my side as he sleeps semi peacefully. The light snoring feels like a soft wind on my neck and I begin to wander how on earth can he fall asleep so easily.

He pokes me again, and for the billionth time, I sigh loudly while shifting to lay on my back. I don't know what's worse, falling asleep only to see Rich invading my dreams; or, staying awake, only to be met with the dreary, depressing scene of the basement. Yet another reminder of Rich.

As my thoughts continue to spiral downward, I inch my hand closer to his. Our fingertips graze one another while I ponder on whether or not I should just grab his hand. I need him to hold my hand. I need him to reassure me that things will get better. That we won't be stuck here, in this depressing pit of weakness and pain, much longer.

My heart rate spikes when I feel his sturdy fingers wrap around my small hand, instantly interlocking our fingers.

"Can't sleep either..." He whispers tiredly. And judging from the smallness in his voice, I get a sense that it's not just a question, but an answer as well.

Tilting my head upward, I smile weakly.

"It's more than that, it's..." I trail off, regretting my words.

Not only was that bad feeling resting in the pit of my stomach again, and causing horrible jolts of pain; but the insatiable need to kiss him again kept creeping up. And even though we're holding hands, I still can't help but feel a heavy uneasiness right now. An uneasiness so strong that my fingers tremble. Something terrible is going to happen, and it's going to happen to us.

Just being back in Rich's awful grasp forces my stomach to twist, and my blood run cold. My despair filled thoughts fill my entire mind with dread, hurt, anger, turmoil. The only thing running through my tired brain is: why did he bring us here? He should have killed us by now.

"What did he carve into your thigh?"

My body tenses automatically as I try to scoot away. In one quick motion, Jake lifts himself up, with a few painful groans, before straddling me. Both of his hands are pressed against the matress while I'm stuck between them, and underneath him.

"I can't talk about it."

I can't look at it, and I can't touch it. If I talk about it then I'll feel it all over again. I'll feel the blurry tears stinging my eyes. I'll feel the searing pain of the hot poker carving into my flesh. And I'll feel the evil, unforgiving presence of Rich mocking me, taunting me with his cold, chocolate eyes. Something tells me that that was just the beginning.

I gasp loudly when I feel fingertips graze my inner thigh. It's not enough to cause harm, just enough to acknowledge their presence.

"What- what are you doing?" I ask shakily. My eyes search his for an answer. I hope he isn't going to do what Rich tried to do.

"Don't think like that, Livie. When have I ever purposefully hurt you?" He raises an eyebrow while I chew my bottom lip.

"Just because you have a witty response doesn't make it true. You purposefully hurt me with the words you say." I stare him straight in the eye, feeling a hint of courageouness.

His face drops suddenly as realization kicks in. I watch him bring his head back up to meet my eyes.

"I didn't mean to...it's just your so, so- just so naive sometimes. I'm only trying to bring out your potential." He speaks sincerely.

"Potential?" What potential do I have? I never had potential to fight, be strong, or be anything, really. And if he's referring to me running with him, then that still doesn't count. I was selfish.

In all honesty, the only reason why I ran with him was to protect myself and no one else. I knew it was only a matter of time before we got caught. So before we ran, I weighed my options; stay here and deal with Rich, or leave and get caught, only to deal with Rich. Even if I had stayed or went with Jake I would have been tormented. So either way it went, I was bound to lose. I always have been.

"Yeah," He sighs while getting up. I notice him wince while clutching his stomach. I don't wander what's wrong with him because mine hurts too.

"You have so much potential and power to be more than great. To get us out of here. I mean you're the only one who can turn this whole thing around. I see it, Rich sees it, but you don't."

Turn it around? How can I turn this around. What has happened to us both cannot be undone. We've both lost loved ones, and we were both taken. The only way out of this is exactly what Rich said, death.

"He isn't going to let us go, he'll kill us first. We're never getting out. Don't you get that?" I raise my voice without faltering.

"Have you seen the way he literally gawks at you? You remind him of someone. I mean, it's obvious Livie, he even carved something into you." He holds onto his abdomen as he paces. "Oh, and let's not forget the favortism he shows toward you. I'm his own fucking nephew and he hates my guts!"

His shout makes me jump, but my mind stays planted. He only gawks at me because he's pyschotic, or just wants to get under my skin, either way staring doesn't prove anything. And even if I did remind him of someone, wouldn't he care enough not to harm me? Deep down inside I think I know who I remind Rich of, but I'm not willing to accept it. Not now.

He clears his throat, forcing me out of my reflections.

"Favortism?" I question once I recover. "He hasn't shown me any favortism, and as far as they way he looks at me, it's only because he's some, sick, perverted freak who can't control himself." I scoff, highly offended that Jake would any indicate that I am Rich's favorite.

"Yeah, you're right,"

My eyebrows furrow from his change in tone. I watch him sit next to me and then capture my eyes with a glinting smirk.

"You're not his favorite. You're just brainwashed by him because you can't think for yourself. He knows he can control you." He crosses his arms whilst shaking his head.

"Just because your plan to leave was a fail doesn't mean you have to attack me." Look at what Rich has done to us. We'll never be the same carefree, alive teenagers again.

Jake will never be that happy-go-lucky guy with popularity and good looks, and I'll never be that happy, friendly, girl with amazing friends, and loving parents again. You know that saying, 'you never miss what is good until it's gone'? Well, I miss my mom, dad, school, my life and my friends. Even though I was a nasty person to all of them, I still miss them despite them not missing me.

"Our plan to leave failed. Remember, we're a team now, sweetheart."

My face turns red and with a look of disgust, I glare daggers at him. But before I can retort, a sudden urge to vomit forces me to run to the corner of the room. My ankle throbs before I feel my body abruptly fall forward. I don't make it far because my chain stops me. Falling on my face, I sit up. With my palms against the cool concrete and my head down, I hurl the remaining contents of my stomach out.

Once I'm done, I crawl over to the mattress, feeling a sudden round of chills. My entire body is sweating profusely but I'm not hot, I'm freezing cold. Hugging myself, I curl into a ball.

"What...what did he do...to that pizza?" He groans loudly from the far side of the room. He's still chained too.

With my mouth suddenly drier than the sahara, I try to swallow. Everything hurts, from my throbbing head to the aches in my feet. My symptoms have gone from bad to worse the longer I lay shivering on the beat up mattress. I don't know what Rich used, but it's enough to get his point across.

With a shaky breath, I call out to him.

"I'm... I'm sorry! We're sorry!"

I keep repeating it until the sound of the door slamming shut, and feet thudding down the steps alerts me of his presence.

"You think that will make me reverse it?" He bends down to my quivering body with a look of intolerance. I feel his rough hand grip my chin, forcing me to grimace. Every part of my body is overly sensitive to pain and movement.

"What...is it?" Jake pants loudly. I can't see him because I'm facing away, but I do know that he's in just as much agony as I am.

"It, is just the beginning," He smirks sinisterly while penetrating my soul with intense, garnet eyes.

With heavy foreboding and teary eyes, my panic sky rockets at the calmness in his silk like voice. It's the way he speaks before acting wickedly. It's the calm before the storm.

I have another urge to vomit, and it's not just because of my illness. The bad feeling in me tells me that if he doesn't kill us, he'll make us regret being alive.

20

CHAPTER 20

The heavy breeze sweeps the leaves away in one brisk movement, and sends my wavy hair flying. With a contented grin, my legs set into motion to retrieve the stolen leaves. Sometimes I love the wind and others times I hate it, in this case I hated it because it blew me and Waylan's pile of leaves away. Now other times, I loved it. I loved it because it was so carefree. It doesn't care what it moves or where it moves it to. The wind is free from regret because once it's finished blowing, it either stops or moves on to its' next victim.

At three years old, I never knew what that meant but I knew enough about the wind to know that it was carefree. It was just like Waylan and I. We had no regrets because whatever we moved or wherever we moved it to belonged there. Just like these pile of leaves belong in the front yard. After lunch mommy let us come outside so we could jump in the pile of leaves.

Fall is here early- at least that's what grandma tells us. We're visiting her in the southeastern part of Tennesee; a small retirement community called Ridge Mount. Her home is beautiful. It's a ranch style home with a small lake in her backyard. It's just for her and Russell, her golden retriever. Ever since my grandfather went to heaven last year, she's been living here alone. My mom visits occassionally to check on her, but for the most part, she's out with her church group.

Anyway, I love this place. The fresh air, the clear water, the beautiful animals, the friendly people, and the delicious food. But unfortunately, all good things must come to an end because we're going back home next week. I don't want to though. I want to stay here forever.

"Livia, chase lees." He orders plainly before going back to his task of piling them up.

With my arms folded, I say,

"What's the mad jack word?"

"Pwease?" He asks more sweetly. I giggle at the peanut butter stuck on his small front tooth before running after more leaves.

My twin brother and I spent the rest of the afternoon piling leaves in the backyard. We had a plan, I'd catch them while he piles them up. I had to remind him not to get too close to the water a few times. Mommy and grandma always told us to stay away from the dock and don't go near the water.

"Olivia and Waylan, I have someone here I want you to meet!" My mom calls from the deck. She usually watches us from there but I see that she has someone with her. A man.

Oh no, Waylan.

Noticing that he's near the dock, I run over to him to grab his hand. I tell him what mom said so he reluctantly follows.

"He kind of surprised me coming all this way. But I'm happy to see him regardless, this is my...friend. His name is-" She speaks hesitantly. Her golden hair shimmers in the afternoon sun. I notice how close she is to us both. She's on bended knee while holding our hands in hers.

"I'm Mr. Rhodes," He gives a friendly smile before reaching in his back pocket.

I watch him with large, blue eyes as he digs in his pocket, searching for something. He's taller than my mom, and appears to be younger than her too. Shifting my glance from the giant man standing in front of us to my mom, I notice something different about her too. Why is she so happy to see him. I can see the beam in her light cerulean eyes while she reveals pearly white teeth. I always admired how my mother looked with red lipstick. I've always wanted to wear it too but she would tell me to wait until I was older.

"Can we go to play with lees now?" Waylan whines with a bored tone. Most people say that there's a quiet twin and a loud one. Waylan is the outspoken one while I'm more timid.

My mom smiles lovingly at him before saying, "You'll play after this." She lets go of our hands before standing up. She's in between us while we wait for the guy- Mr. Rhodes to finish fumbling in his pocket.

"Ah, here it is."

He bends down, sending my hand to Waylan's. He doesn't give a second thought before holding onto my hand. With him being the older twin, he's more protective.

"Every kid loves candy, right?" He smiles with bright teeth. His face is shaved and appears to be oval shaped. I notice the way his smooth, dark brown hair sits on his head. Neatly trimmed. Waylan squeezes my hand in warning but I keep staring. I'm trying to see his eyes but can't because he's wearing shades.

Waylan continues holding my hand while we wait anxiously. Anytime he doesn't trust someone he'll always squeeze my hand.

"You want it?" He extends the sweet lollipop to my brother but he just shakes his head vigorously.

"Waylan, what's wrong with you?" My mom bends down to him with curious eyes. Her hair bounces while she explains to Waylan why we shouldn't be rude to guests.

"It's okay Mia, more for the other one, right?"

"If we don't go back to the lees soon they'll be gone." He whispers to me while I stay silent. I want to play too but I also want candy. I'm conflicted.

"Ooooh," My face lights up at the sight of a blue lollipop coming towards me.

"A beautiful ocean of blue like the color of your eyes." He smiles cunningly, forcing me to suddenly latch onto my moms leg. He's too close.

"You know, if I had a daughter she'd be just like you. Would you like living with me?" He ask quizzically while I suck on my lollipop with bewildered eyes.

"No, she would not because she has a father. I've told you this before."

My eyes widen at my mom's tone. That's her 'time out' tone.

He sighs heavily while my mom continues glaring at him. They don't give anymore attention to us so instead, I watch them attentively. Focusing in on every word they say, every hand gesture they make.

"All of that bullshit you said about leaving him Mia was a lie to begin with." He seethes through gritted teeth. His anger scares me. It's like a shaken up bottle of soda, ready to explode when opened too soon.

"We're working things out and I need you to understand. I'm getting older now, and I can't have both worlds anymore." She explains. I watch him run his fingers through his dark hair with one hand, while the other rests in his pocket.

"So your husband and spoiled brat kids are more important than me- than us?"

"Leave." She turns from him, looking at the ground. "Leave now."

"Look, I'm sorry Mia. I didn't mean that. What I meant was that they can come with us. I'll take them in as my own." His voice edges on persistence as he grabs my mom's hand.

"That's sweet Richard, but you still live with your parents. You're seventeen, remember?"

She gently rubs his shoulder before pecking his cheek. I don't understand why she would kiss him instead of daddy. I don't comprehend her affection towards this stranger.

"I know but love has no limitations. Including age. Our love has no limitations, Mia. This is the perfect timing to act on our plan. Remember, take the kids and leave. I mean look at us, we're both underappreciated and-"

"You know I can't do that anymore. When I met you things were different. You were a handsome freshman and I was your teacher. I didn't even know I was pregnant with the twins until-"

"I know, I know. You didn't know until the night he proposed." He rolls his eyes in annoyance.

"He is my husband Richard, and I love him." She buries her head in her hands. My curious eyes linger on hers. I can sense something is wrong judging from the bags underneath her tired blue eyes, and the way her disarrayed strands of golden blonde hang loosely.

"But you don't want to complicate things. You enjoyed us but now you have a family to focus on. Am I right?

He sighs heavily while my mom remains silent.

"Not just that. I'm twenty seven and you're seventeen. You should date someone younger. You deserve someone else. Someone better." She gives him a half smile, hoping that he will accept it. But as I watch his features morph from indifference to hurt, I realize that he isn't going to accept what she said.

"Remember what you discussed in class? Valentine's day three years ago, you recited some poem about forbidden love. And at the end you gave your opinion, saying that love has no limitations; including age."

"I...Rich, I'm sorry but you have to leave." She whispers softly. The few sniffles that break the silence indcate her shed tears.

"Fine, but if I can't have you then I'll take what you promised me." His cold, garnet eyes dart to me before quickly looking away.

"What? No, you can't-"

"No Mia, you can't back out of our deal. Remember, I paid off your debt and gave you everything you have now; that includes your house, car, and even your job." He narrows his eyes, mirroring a vicious look of hate.

My heartbeat speeds up while I tightly grip my mom's pantsleg.

"I won't let you take them." She stands with folded arms, fuming.

"If you want to keep your job you will. Or better yet, if you want those loansharks off that bastard you call a husband then you will."

I'm standing next to my mom, sucking on my lollipop with furrowed eyebrows. At the time, I had no idea what they were talking about but I had a feeling it was important. That it had something to do with Waylan and I.

Little did I know that while I was focusing on their conversation, my brother was focusing on something else. Something that cost him his life. I never thought in that short time away from him I'd be without him forever.

My eyes open slowly, allowing hints of sunlight to penetrate them. With a pained groan, I use my forearm to shield my eyes from the light. Sitting up, I see that I'm in a room. It's a master bedroom. Everything is black except for the duvet and sheets on the bed. They're a dark gray.

"Where am I?" I wander aloud. But before I can swing my legs to the edge of the bed, I feel a restraint on my ankle.

No. No.No.

My teeth grit when I feel the chain link chafe against my skin. This reminds me of my previous prison downstairs in the basement. Being starved and locked away for months isn't just torture; it is inhuman as well. As if Jake and I deserve it. Ha! I smirk darkly, no we don't but I know someone who does. Someone who haunts my dreams and terrorizes my reality. Someone cruel and uncaring. Someone incapable of giving and receiving love. Someone named Rich.

"From now on you'll be living upstairs with me."

My head snaps up from my task of trying to break free. Was he here this whole time?

"No, I can't live up here...with-" I start to hyperventilate when I see him stroll towards me.

"Looks like you don't have much of a choice because when I gave you one, you chose wrong."

He's now standing in front of me with a small grin.

"But I-" my mouth opens to speak but a finger places itself on my cracked lips.

"Hey, it's alright babe. He isn't dead." He reassures with a look of displeasure.

"What-" I swallow the bile threatening to rise. "What did you just call me?"

"You've been in and out for weeks. I figured you needed strength so I decided to let you rest. Especially for tomorrow." He goes over to the nightstand. I hear something that sounds similar to a spoon clanking against a cup.

"Strength for what? What...what happens tomorrow?" I interlock my fingers in a tight grip, trying to will myself to calm down. By this time he has stopped stirring whatever it is in the cup. I'm still on the bed with my back pressed into the headboard. I need to get out of here.

"Your seventeenth birthday celebration. I promised your mom that I'd make it a very special occasion."

The longer his words sink in the more my heart sinks. I can feel despair weigh down on me like a heavy boulder. Before I can speak tears begin to erupt, and then my hands start to shake. With closed eyes, I breathe inwardly but my exhales are shaky.

"Drink." He orders.

"Wha- what is-is it?" I stammer with wide, teary eyes. The last time I ate something from him, I fell awfully ill.

My head jerks forward, only to be met with his fiery eyes. Our foreheads touch, making me cringe.

"Drink or else..." He warns again.

"Mmm." I whimper when I feel his thumb and index finger seize my jaw. He presses too tightly, pinching the skin on my chin.

With my hands still quaking, I grab the hot mug. Staring at the dark brown liquid, my mind begins to fill with dread.

I look back up to meet his glare. With full apprehension, I bring the mug to my lips. Counting down from ten, I realize I can't do it.

"I don't want to go back to sleep. Please don't drug me."

And before I can react I feel the scalding heat of the beverage attack my flesh. The scorching hot liquid seeps into my pores, sending my hands to my face in a instant as I cry out.

"Things would go a lot better for you if you just learn to shut your fucking mouth!" He roars before the back of his hand meets my already throbbing cheek.

Without sound, I let the rest of my tears pour from my soul. I'm drowning in the tears I cry until I hear footsteps walk away.

"You need to be re-trained." He grumbles before a resounding slam of the door fills the air. My frightened body reacts by flinching at the harsh sound as I lay curled into a ball.

I remained in the room all day until night came. I could tell it was getting late because the shadows in the room stretched against the walls, reaching out to me. I longed to blend into the wall. To be nothing more than just invisible. Because if I were invisble I'd be safe from harm. I'd be safe from predators like Rich.

The sudden sound of the door creaking open forces my eyes to shut tight. I'm laying down, facing away from the door, and hoping he'll just turn around and walk back out.

"Come on, I know you're awake." He rubs his fingertips along my arm. The goosebumps are prevalent now.

"I know you want to shower."

My eyes open at the sound of that. If Rich is correct, and I've been asleep for weeks then that means I haven't showered either. I know

I smell putrid to outsiders, but I've grown accustomed to the smell sometimes. Half the time I don't even realize I stink. Anyway, I'm so ecstatic for a shower but I don't want him in there with me.

My heart nearly jumps out of my chest when I see a pair of brown eyes staring back at me.

"You want a shower?" He asks with a hidden smirk.

"I... uh yeah." My timidness spills out, causing him to chuckle.

"Then come on." He unlocks my chain before showing me the bathroom. I'm given a spaghetti strapped violet night gown that appears to be way too short.

"It's that or nothing." He grins while suggestively raising his eyebrows.

"But of course, I prefer the latter."

With a look of repulsion, I hold the night wear to my chest while entering the bathroom.

Everything goes by in a slow daze. As if I'm a zombie, only moving in a routine. I turn on the warm water, then I remove my dirty clothes before stepping in the shower. I wash everything away with a pleased smile. Letting the soap lather up all over me, including my hair, I scrub everything bad away. All of my pain, fear, hurt, and anger slide down the drain; relieving me of my worries for a little while.

While I shower I think about Rich and what he's doing. He's finally letting me shower again. Now if I can win back his trust then Jake and I can get out of here. My thoughts soon travel to Jake and what he's doing. I wonder if he has showered or eaten yet. I wonder if Rich was being honest when he said Jake was still alive. I wonder if Jake really likes me as much as I'm starting to like him.

Wait, am I starting to like him?

Well duh, you did kiss him. If you didn't like him then you most definitely wouldn't have kissed him, especially with the way you both smelled. Gross.

But that's the thing. Kissing him made me forget how bad we smelled. It was just that perfect- or weird, either way he took me away from this place with just one smooch.

My thoughts banter back and forth until they're interrupted by the door opening. Crap, why didn't I lock it?

My hand automatically goes to the knob to turn off the water. Looking around frantically, I realize that my towel is on the counter. An overwhelming sense of gloom showers over me when he says,

"I forgot to mention. You can take a shower, but only if I'm in there with you."

My mouth fights to stay shut while I chew my bottom lip. He's still outside of the shower while I'm on the inside, trying to figure out how to get passed him.

"From now on I'll shower with you and there's nothing you can say or do to stop me." His menacing eyes roam my body as I continue cowering. My back presses against the shower wall while my arms cover my bare chest. I had just finished scrubbing myself clean then Rich had to ruin it.

"I'm- I'm finished." I try to brush past his intimidating stature but my body jerks back violently.

"You're not finished until I say you are." He grumbles in my ear.

My breathing comes out in ragged pants when I feel his area press into my thigh. With the way I'm pressed against his chest, it's hard not to feel anything.

"Don't!"

"If you want to keep your tongue I suggest you shut up."

His lips graze my ear, forcing my quivering lips to close. I feel his hand on the small of my back while his other holds my arm with a vice grip.

I squirm but to no avail can I break away. The water from the showerhead pours down on us like rain and soon, I'm emmersed in dismay.

I'm still squirming so when his lips crash down on mine, I have no time to scream. With my frightened body paralyzed with fear, I stay completely still while he continues to violate me roughly. Pushing me against the wall, I feel his hands trail over me while his foul lips puncture my skin.This time I'm not lucky enough to feel his rough hands grope me, no. This time I have to feel him push his fingers inside of me. The pressured pain is so sudden that it forces me to scream 'no' repeatedly before I can stop myself.

Small tingles attack my scalp the more he bends my head back. My constricted chest feels cold once I place my hands over his, hoping he loosens his grip.

"Let go, you're- you're hurting me." I start sobbing louder when the pain worsens. The way his fist is balled in my hair indicates he has no intention of letting go.

"What did I say if you screamed?"

His brown eyes narrow, making my stomach twist.

"It will...get- get worse." I hiccup as tears stream down my flushed cheeks. I want to beg, scream, shout, but for some strange reason I can't. Every time I open my mouth, the only thing that escapes are alarmed gasps.

With wide eyes, I groan loudly before gripping the shower curtain tightly. I feel my muscles tighten in restraint from the force of his fingers. He pushes further, making my body spasm.

One. Two. Three.

I bite my lip, trying with all of my strength to hold back a cry of agony as he goes deeper. I'm too tight and he isn't being gentle.

"Damn...you feel amazing." He moans.

My teary eyes remain closed while he continues. Please stop. Please, please, please. I inhale giant gulps of air, hoping to calm myself. But how can I be calm when this is happening? Why is this even happening. My thoughts are interrupted when a sudden surge of pressure rises, forcing my throat to betray me. I groan again, this time louder than before.

"Livie," He speaks calmly.

I see his eyes go to me before I cower. I don't have time to know that his fingers are out, nor do I have time to react when I see a large fist come towards me.

The constant ringing in my ears keeps me from hearing anything except the rapid shower water pouring down on us. My body is yanked up and pulled forward before I can gather my bearings.

"I meant what I said, Livie. No screaming, crying, or groaning like you're miserable. You have it better than most so act like it."

My raw body convulses with each rapid penetration, making my core throb more. This time he's gripping my neck while his fingers do the rest. My toes curl and I have the hardest time breathing as he continues ramming his fingers inside of me. My eyes are closed, only willing myself to go back to innocence. To go back to the time when I was happiest. And that time was with Waylan.

I feel something rock hard near my area, forcing my panic to increase but I can't scream. I'm not going to give him the satisfaction of causing me pain. My nails dig into his torso while I brace myself for what's to come. I know it will hurt, and I know I'll scream. And once that happens, I'll be beaten to a bloody pulp.

"You like your little present?" He eyes the carving on my exposed upper thigh, making me shiver from the memory of the horrific event that occurred weeks ago.

How can that be a present? It's just a stain that can never be washed away. It won't heal over time. It will just remain stagnant on my thigh for the rest of my life. I won't escape him or the memory.

"I asked you a question." He sighs in annoyance.

Opening my eyes, I see him standing in front of me. My red, swollen eyes gawk at his wet, toned torso before blinking rapidly. My mystifed eyes hover over the artistic ink that decorates his right upper abdomen. The black ink stains his skin, marking him just as he marked me. I can still feel his fingers gliding against my mark on my upper thigh when he asks again. This time more impatiently.

"What...what does it mean?" I ask numbly. I'm in too much pain to feel anything else. I can barely stand, and I'm surprised my wobbly legs haven't forsaken me yet.

"Remember the story behind my tattoos?"

He stands comfortably while I stand cautiously. I'm still covering myself while he stands stark naked in front of me. The droplets slide down his body, making his firm body glisten.

What is wrong with me? This guy just violated me- almost raped me and I'm standing here eyeing him like he's some sex god.

Shaking my head in disgust at myself, I try to walk past him but he grabs my arm. I wince when my body is slammed against the wall. My heart skips a beat when his nose touches mine.

"If you don't answer me then we'll go again. I got all night babe and I have no problems doing more." He smirks with a hint of callousness in his voice.

I hate this insensitive bastard and Idon't have time for this. I just want to lay down. I'm tired, light headed and my private area burns intensely from his abuse.

My eyes shift from his cold ones to the blood on the shower floor. It must be from my bleeding lip.

"Ahem." He makes a noise to indicate warning.

With my eyes narrowed, and head slightly tilted, I ponder for a moment before eyeing his tats on his arm. They're a group of ravens flying into a fiery pit. He told me before that the ravens symbolize the many people who betrayed him. But-

"Who betrayed me?" I ask hesitantly while grazing it with my fin-gertips. It's about the size of my palm. The carving on my inner thigh is of two ravens flying into a pit of flames. It's the same tattoo as his, just not a tattoo exactly. It's an engraving on my flesh; taunting me and reminding me of how worthless I really am. I'll never let anyone see it or know about it. Including Jake.

"Was it you?" I ask after a long silence.

From the way he gazes at me with patient eyes, I get as sense he gave me time to think.

"Livie, I know you hate me but you can't deny the truth. I never betrayed you." He shrugs with crossed arms.

My anger boils, spilling over like an overheated pot on a stove. I don't think about the consequences before I speak.

"Taking me from everything is betraying me! Doing this- violating me is betraying me! I hate you and hope you rot in hell!" I seethe with heaving shoulders. My malicious blue eyes remain steady as I glare murderously at him.

"No! Taking what was promised to me is not betraying you!"

Promised to him? What does he mean? My confusion lingers the more my thoughts whirl around.

"That doesn't make sense. What was promised to you? And who betrayed me?" I continue glaring at him with fierce cerulean eyes. He has me intrigued and I need answers now.

"Yo still don't get it, do you?" He rubs his temples before shaking his head. This act reminds me of Jake and how he is when he is frustrated.

"It's not a matter of what was promised, but who. And I'll let you figure that last part out. They all connect." He smirks cunningly, revealing handsome features. I shake that thought because the overpowering glint in his brown eyes dig into my soul and sends a shiver through me.

21

CHAPTER 21

"**S**he did it because she loved you. Both you and your brother." He speaks suddenly, making my heart quicken.

It's been a few hours since the shower ordeal and I'm currently laying in his bed, crying my eyes out.

"You don't get it, do you?" I mumble pestulantly. He'll never understand how I'm feeling. My own mother sold me to this creep. Poor or not, that's not love. That's wrong on so many levels. And nothing he says can make this right.

Traitor, liar, thief.

That's all that's been occupying my mind since I layed down. Rich is currently sitting in the recliner, watching me ball my eyes out like a kid without candy. I know because I can feel his daunting presence and soul clenching stare. He's probably heard my earlier rambling too.

"I know I'm awful but I have an acceptable reason, okay. I was drunk earlier...still kind of am, actually." He chuckles while I remain stoic. I hate him.

"That still doesn't give you a reason to violate me like you did!" I sit up quickly with fervent anger seething through me. Facing his unearthly silhouette with a death glare, I cross my arms. He can make excuses all day but I'll never forgive him for the multiple times he nearly raped me.

"I've been trying to wait til you were eighteen, like your mother and I agreed on. But I just-"

"Shutup! Stop talking about my mother like you knew her!"

Besides the fact that I'm fed up with his lies, I'm also dreading my seventeenth birthday, which is tomorrow.

Silence captures us both while I breathe heavily. I can see him getting up and walking toward me and somehow, even in the darkness, I can see the annoying smirk plastered on his face. But I'm not afraid. I'm livid.

"Livie, I did know her. I know more about her than you do." He speaks calmly while sitting arcoss from me on the full sized bed.

Just because they were in a relationship does not mean he knew her. He is just some pervert who split up my parents.

"She wasn't the same after your brother drowned, I know that much too."

The night stand lamp now illuminates our side of the room, giving some light to me, and in a way, to this monstrosity of a situation as well.

"Just leave me alone." I pull my knees to my chest, trying to fight back tears. My throat tightens while my teary eyes burn. I don't want to hear this because old feelings and memories will resurface.

"No, you need to hear this. You have to understand that this isn't a coincidence. I need you to know that I wasn't just some random burglar in your house that night, okay?"

"Livie look at me." He grabs my hands in his before I can pull away. My head is still facing away from him while he tries to get me to look in his eyes. I'm not going to stare into the eyes of the devil.

Suddenly, my body is pinned down on the bed. Both of my arms are tightly held by his forceful hands. I'm scared but I hide my fear by chewing on my bottom lip. I know I can't fight, there's no use in trying to. So the only choice I have is to look at him. I feel cool air fan my face while his fingertips outline my skin, making me shiver.

"Look. At. Me." He asserts somberly.

With apprehension, my eyes shift to his.

"What...what are you trying to say?" I try to keep my trembling voice level but it falters. I'm on the verge of panicking. I'm afraid of the truth.

"I'm saying that everything that has happened to you, your parents, and Jake was planned. It's been planned from the start. Your dad was never part of that plan, though. So for that, I'm truly sorry."

My head spins while my heart rate spikes. I can't think about, speak about, or even believe what I'm hearing. This is so surreal. Is he apologizing for murdering my dad but not my mom?

"This isn't real." I mutter while running my fingers through my hair.

"I told you that everything was planned."

Planned? My thoughts travel back to the night Jake and I were at the lake house. He was hovered over his dad's missing gun, rambling about him.

"So let me get this straight, you saw your dad in a dream and now you think we're all connected." I roll my eyes.

"Yeah. There has to be some kind of link. We're not here by fate or destiny, or whatever some people think!" He throws his hands in the air before gripping his hair in frustration.

"Planned? You planned to kill her? To kill them?" My lips tremble while more tears pour from my soul. I'll never get to see my parents again. I'll never get to have my dad walk me down the aisle on my wedding day. And I'll never have my mom there to help me pick out wedding dresses. The rest of my teenage life will be spent alone. An orphan without parents or a home.

"I didn't kill her! By the time I got there it was too late!" He shouts, more powerful this time.

His hands are off of me so I decide to sit up. I listen silently as he continues telling me his version.

"I was only in your house to take you and your mom with me, that's it. I never planned on killing anyone." He eyes me with solemness. I don't know what to think so I avert my eyes to the sheets.

"I broke into your house -with good intention, of course- but I didn't know they were on an anniversary date so I waited."

"After about thirty minutes, I decided to go to your room to watch you. I hadn't seen you since you were twelve and I just wanted to check on you." He says it more like a father figure. The tone makes my eyebrows furrow. So he hasn't always seen me as sexually attractive? All these years I would feel a presence in my room, thinking it was Waylan when in reality it was Rich. He was looking out for me just like my brother would have. I don't know if that's creepy or sweet.

"By the time I got back downstairs, I heard giggling outside the front door."

He pauses, "At first, I thought it was you on a date or something but then I realized that I had just checked on you so it couldn't have been you. And then I heard it. I heard that prick of a father of yours." He looks distant while I stare worriedly at him.

"What were they talking about?" I ask without stopping myself.

He sighs while rubbing his temples. Could it be that bad? I narrow my eyes in curiosity.

"He was saying how sorry he was for cheating on her all of those years. He told her he was sorry for ever feeling like she deserved it."

"Oh," I hold my head down. He's right, he does know more about her than I do. I never knew my dad cheated on my mom. Is that why they separated?

Before my brother's drowning, my family was what I would call close to perfect. We bonded from the moment my brother and I came into this world. Well, that's what my mom would always tell me. And even though she spoke words, I could still feel the love through her and my dad's actions. They read to Waylan and I every night. Mom would read to me while dad would read to him.

I remember when I'd get scared Waylan would crawl in my bed and we'd laugh and share the funniest moments of that day. I remember mom and dad coming in our room to scold us and a sense of warmth filled my heart when they'd laugh with us too.

But that all changed after Waylan died. My dad worked constantly while my mom continued blaming herself for his death. I knew my dad blamed her too. We never talked about it but I feltt it. I knew my father but didn't really know him, if you know what I mean. Most mornings before I headed off to school he'd be downstairs fixing his tie. I would say hi but he would just wave me off before walking out and slamming the door shut.

Once I turned ten, I realized that my parents were just living together to keep me happy. But my happiness diminished when I realized how unhappy they really were. The fights, the arguing, the screaming. I remember it all.

They legally separated when I was eleven, and by the time I turned sixteeen they were back to casual dating.

"Yeah, I hated your dad. Especially when Mia would tell me what they'd argued about. Like I said, I hated him but I didn't plan on killing him." He shakes his head disapprovingly while I urge him to continue.

"Once he apologizes to her, I wait for her to tell him to fuck off but I don't hear that. Instead, I hear the words that hurt my soul. She apologized for trying to find him in another man. She apologized for cheating on him with me."

I watch his face contort into anger before his fist slams into the headboard.

My body automatically backs away defensively. I'm thankful he didn't see me flinch.

"So I decided to put on my black mask to confront her. I mean if she was going to mask her love for me then I was going to mask my face."

"When they entered they saw me and panicked. Your dad pulled a gun out on me before I could explain myself."

My hand goes to my mouth the more I listen.

"He was pissed, thinking I was there to take Mia but at that point I decided she could have him. I didn't want to deal with the bullshit lies anymore."

So that's what he means by the people who betrayed him. My mom being one of those people.

"He still has the gun pointed at me so I hold my hands up defensively. Mia is staring at me the entire time until she finally says: I don't want you anymore. I'm not breaking our deal because you can have Olivia. Just tell her I love her."

Just like that she gives me away? What kind of mother does that? Not the kind I thought I knew for sixteen years.

"Your dad explodes at that point, waving the gun from me to her. They continue arguing over you and finances while I try to keep them quiet. I'm surprised you didn't wake." He says modestly.

"I'm a heavy sleeper but the gun shots woke me up." I reply timidly.

With a forced half smile, he sighs before continuing, "I needed to calm him down so I walk over to them. But before I can talk him out of anything, he fires. I remember thinking it was me he had shot but I never felt pain. I stood there in shocked hurt while watching Mia, my first love limply fall to the ground."

"After that, I lunged at him. It was like all of my bottled up anger exploded on him. We fought for the gun, and in the midst a shot was fired. I'm sorry. No one deserves to lose their parents that way."

My jaw clenches while I wipe my teary eyes. So the plan was to take me. I was going to be taken even if my mom was still alive. My body goes into a steady rock the longer I ponder. I can't hate her but I can hate what she did. Even if she and my dad were struggling financially, I didn't deserve to be given to some stranger. I don't deserve this.

"Can you just let us go? Please." I hold his stare with pleading blue eyes. He's finished with his story and I'm able to understand him better. Now, will he understand me.

His features grow rigid before softening. I notice the dark stubble on his chiseled jaw, making him appear older and more handsome. From there, my eyes go to his thin lips, presssed solemnly. The look in his eyes hold something deeper. Something more meaningful.

"It's kind of too late, Livie."

My palms begin to sweat while I fear the worst.

"What do you mean too late? Just let us go. We won't report you." I remember him saying how bad he doesn't want to go back to prsion so I won't send him if he let's us go.

"I can't... I can't because I'm in love with you."

His eyes hold sterness, hiding behind a mask of raw emotions. The emotions shake my core, making me speechless. Looking back at him, I can see the hidden fear, shame, and hesitance. But the longer he stares into my eyes, seizing them, the more those hints of fear, and shame start to pass, As if he can see through to my soul. He's slowly pulling me apart while I struggle to keep my emotions in tact.

I stay frozen in disbelief while he continues admiring me. I notice the glint in his garnet eyes as he smiles a closed mouth smile at me. A loving, protective smile. There's an array of emotions in his eyes that scares me. But most importantly, I find the most powerful one, the most frightening one: love.

22

—— ◆ ——

CHAPTER 22

He's lying. He has to be lying. This is just an excuse to keep me here. He doesn't want to let me go because he's afraid I'll go to the cops on his crazy ass. And once I do that he'll get sent to prison. He's already been before and he doesn't want to return. I have no idea what sent him there and I don't plan on asking.

All I know is that his cunning and manipulative nature has me feeling more uneasy than I was before. If that's even possible.

"Look, I know what you're thinking but trust me when I say that I feel something for you. Something you might not even be prepared for." He sighs heavily, making a point to rub the back of his neck. It's as if he's ashamed of himself. As if his anger towards me has just been sexual tension.

"Can you say somethin'?"

He's not in the recliner anymore. No, he's inching towards the bed. Towards me.

"Why are you...why are you telling me this?" My voice falters while I try to keep bile from rising. This is all too much. I mean I've never been in an intimate relationship before. And now this man wants to confess his feelings for me? This soon to be seventeen year old girl who wants nothing to do with him. I can't even fathom what he wants to do with me. Or to me. It's just all too much.

Bringing my shaky knees to my chest, I stare at the clock that reads 11:47 p.m. before shifting my eyes to Rich's chin. I can't look at his pleading dark eyes. I won't.

"Livie," His voice lingers, making my name echo on his tongue. "I'm telling you this because I've decided that now is the perfect time." His eyes remain focused on me. With his strong jaw, thin lips, dark hair and eyes I can see why he'd have women swooning over him. He's attractive for an older guy, but he's meant for someone else. Someone just as old as he is.

"Perfect time? Perfect time for what?" I close my eyes to block the tears. I need to stop myself from breaking down. Maybe this is a joke. Maybe he's just playing some sick joke on me.

"What do you want for your birthday?"

My head snaps up at the sound of those unfamiliarly nice words. What is he doing? I just asked him a question and now he's avoiding it.

"Don't look at me like that. I'm answering your question. Now tell me what you want, birthday girl?" He smiles, making his eyes shimmer. The way his eyebrows raise indicate playfulness but I'm not falling into his trap.

With compressed lips, I glare at him.

"I want to get the hell out of here and away from you!" I spit with venom.

I'm still on the bed, boiling with anger while he's standing on the other side of it, eyeing me hungrily.

"You know I can't do that. Now choose again." He shrugs his shoulders with a blase smirk. I notice him flex his biceps, making my cheeks flush. Why am I blushing? My hand goes to my cheek while worriation begins to settle.

I hear a small chuckle so I send another glare to him.

"Can't or won't?"

"I told you before that I'd have you crawling on your hands and knees like the obedient pet you're supposed to be. If you keep pushing my buttons I'll make sure of it." He speaks through gritted teeth, as if he's trying to be patient with me.

The mood has gone from bad to worse. Much, much worse. His threats are just as menacing as his stare. I hate him.

"Now, what do you want for your birthday? I'll grant you one wish." A smug smile creeps up on his lips as he places his hands in his jeans pockets. I notice his laid back attire. It's a fitted black tee with light denims that also fit perfectly. His tatts are showing, making him appear more badass than he already is.

Thinking back on the pictures of he and my mom before she died I remember how clean cut he looked. He didn't have tattoos, his hair was smooth instead of rough, and his smile appeared honest, not daunting. Now, he's some heartbroken, murdering rapist who is set on making my life hell.

"If you don't choose I'll give you my present first." He trails his fingers along my leg, making me jump slightly.

Why is he so close? When did he sit beside me?

Shaking my head, I crawl out of bed. The heat from his touch is too much and the way he's gazing at me creeps me out. Looking down, I realize I'm only clothed in the purple neglige he gave me earlier. It's a v- neck, revealing a bit of cleavage- wait, cleavage? When did that get there?

Out of the corner of my eye, I see Rich smirking at me with charming eyes. He's amused.

Stupid asshole. Taking a minute to gather myself, I shift uncomfortably while pulling the black laced hem down. It's literally sitting on my behind, and if the wind blew I'd be arrested for public indecency.

"Take your time, I'm just admiring the view." He adds with a triumphant smile.

"I want," I'm very uncomfortable so I use one hand to cover my chest while the other pulls on my night gown. I want some proper clothing but I'm only allowed one wish so I choose the best one.

"I want to see Jake." I want to give him food, water, and clean clothes. And maybe, just maybe get some answers.

My legs stay stagnant on the top steps while my thoughts struggle to decipher what's happening. I'm an emotionless robot as I stay frozen on the steps. I can't believe I'm finally going to see Jake. The one boy who can push my buttons and then make me want to kiss him at the same time. The one boy who brings out the truth in me. The one boy who I now realize is slowly becoming a man. The man I'm starting to like.

I don't know if he feels the same about me, or if he even wants to see me. I mean I have been upstairs, eating and showering while he's been down here suffering. The thought of a shower makes my heart pound so I repress it. I don't need anymore memories of Rich.

I hear coughing so my covered legs set into motion. As I descend the creaky steps, a strong odor consisting of mold and must attacks my nostrils, making me cringe. I have a hard time breathing as painful nostalgia forces its way into my mind. I've always hated dark, haunting places. This place especially.

"Did he show you the paper?"

That's the first thing I hear. I expected an attack, given the last time I had food in my hand, but that doesn't come.

"What paper?" I place the plate of spaghetti and sauteed green vegetables in front of him. I cooked it before I came down here so it's safe to eat.

Once I step back, I take a minute to take in the once cluttered, suffocating asylum. It's clear some things have changed in the few weeks I've been captive upstairs. The space has completely trans-formed from horrible to half-way decent. The boxes that were in the corners of the room are now used as a fort to protect himself from the leak just above our heads. I notice the window is now boarded to keep him from trying to break it.

My heart aches when I notice the purple ring around his ankle. Poor Jake. That must have shattered his hopes just as much as his ego. He really wants to be the one to get us out, but from the way things have gone it looks like he hasn't much luck.

"They stopped looking for us, Livie. And the officers' deaths, the ones who died trying to save us were deemed a suicide."

I avert my eyes from the blood strickened wall on the side where the mattress lies. I can't make out the words.

"What? Why'd they stop?"

He stands then turns to me with a look of pity. A look that makes me feel even more worse about myself. But I can't look away from him. He has grown too. His clothes are a bit rumpled but still smell clean, nonetheless. He still has bruises lining his body but they aren't as bad as before. They're starting to blend with his tanned skin. And even though his emerald eyes are a bit sullen with heavy bags underneath, he still looks better. He's healing.

"Apparently, they already found us." He shrugs with a sense of abandonment. I get the feeling he's starting to give up. This isn't like him.

"What do you mean?" They have to keep looking for us. It shouldn't be that hard to find two missing teens. I mean sure, people go missing everyday and I'm not special. But I just need to know that someone cares. I need to know that I'll be found soon. Although most of my immediate family has passed, my dad's younger sister Casey should still be looking for me.

"Yep, they found us here- at our dad's- the article claims." He saunters to the wall with his plate in hand. I notice the small sink and toilet in the corner of the room. That wasn't there before.

"No, they can't just give up." The strong urge to cry sneaks up on, forcing me to wipe my eyes with my sleeve. Rich decided to let me change into a pair of grey sweats and a white tee.

"They can do whatever the hell they want but I'm getting the fuck out."

I shake my head at his proanity. He can be so vulgar sometimes but I guess that's what makes him, him. He's stubborn, outspoken, and courageous while I tend to be more docile, shy, and cowardly. I'm feeling inevitable hoplessness overshadow me the longer I think about how weak I truly am.

With slumped shoulders, I slide down the wall next to him. I feel our body heat while I lay my head on his shoulder. Inhaling deeply, I smile while closing my eyes. Despite all that's been happening, I feel the need for him to kiss me again.

"I've been meaning to tell you something, Livie." He speaks suddenly, making my heart flutter nervously.

Looking up in anticipation, I brace myself for the good news. This is it. He's going to tell how much he loves and needs me. How he and I should be together instead of he and Gia.

"I need you to pretend like that kiss never happened."

My face drops to sadness at those words. I know what he means but I don't know if I want to accept it.

He shrugs out of my head, leaving nothing but cold air on my cheek. I feel a sense of loss. As if I'm a deck of cards, stacked neatly until someone comes along and blows them, instantly knocking them down.

Bringing myself to speak, I clear my throat before saying.

"Okay, it's forgotten but I really need your help."

He pauses while I think of what else to say. I don't feel right lying about my feelings for him but he's right. He has a girlfriend and our kiss just complicated things even more. I need to consider his feelings. I need to consider mine too. Stay away because he'll hurt you.

"You need my help?" He laughs, making my lips spread into a grin. Did I mention how sexy his laugh is?

"With what?" He turns to me with raised brows. His full pink lips are tight while his green eyes hold bewilderment. With his scrunched nose and slightly creased brows, I conclude that he's really cute when he looks curious.

"Can you convince Rich to let me stay down here?" I say in desperation. If I have a reason to stay then maybe Rich will allow it. Jake will be my saving grace.

"He won't let you stay down here. Just go back up there and-"

"No! I don't want to go back up there!" I don't want to feel his slimy fingers all over me when we shower. I don't want to hear him call my mom's name while stroking my cheek. It's sick. He's sick.

"If you go upstairs we can find a way out for us both. That will take some time though, but, if you can make him think you're on his side again then maybe he'll give you more freedom. Remember what you said earlier? We get more freedoms when we do what he says." He quotes me, making me wish I could erase what I had said previously. That was before I found out that I'd be subjected to rape everyday.

"Don't let him take me back upstairs...I...please." I start sniffling, trying prevent the waterworks.

"I'm counting on you Livie. I mean this could be the opportuninty to set us free. Once he sees you're on his side again then you start making demands."

He doesn't get it. He doesn't know what Rich is planning once I get upstairs. The only reason I'm down here is because it's my birthday wish.

"You have to gain his trust to get us out of here." His firm hands remain on my shoulders while he tries to calm me down.

The longer I stare at him, the more my thoughts roam. So is that why he really wants me to go back up there? Because I have a chance to get us out of here? But is this for us or just him? Does he like being down here all by himself? Or, am I his saving grace? So many questions overtake my already distressed mind.

"You have to do everything he says to get us out of here."

A small frown takes residence on my face while I search his eyes. This isn't making sense. First he called me a coward for doing everything Rich demanded and now he actually wants me to? What is wrong with him? What changed his mind?

"What was your part in Rich's plan?"

I feel his hands ease off my shoulders before he turns away from me. He seems to know a lot about Rich. He is his nephew, afterall. And he also seems to be siding with him right now. This is not making sense to me. I need answers.

"Why does that matter?" He scrunches his nose in disgust while I try to compose my frustration. Why can't he just answer the question?

"It matters because Rich says we were both part of his plan from the beginning. So I need to know your part." I have a feeling he knows but just won't say it.

"So you still care about what he says?" He crosses his arms while shaking his head at me. It's kind of demeaning.

"No, it's not that. It's just not making sense. You're his nephew and he literally hates you. If you don't know why then you should at least care about finding out. "

Shrugging his shoulders, he turns to me with narrowed eyes,

"I care about getting out of here and I'll do whatever it takes to be free. So go back upstairs."

"No! I'm not going back up there!" I retort as equally annoyed as he is.

"Hey birthday girl. It's time to go." I hear Rich call out to me. I don't want to go. I refuse to go back up there.

"Thanks for the food Olive, and remember what I told you." He smirks with closed eyes.

"I hope you choke," I say through gritted teeth while being abruptly pulled up. Is this what anger feels like? My mind is saying punch him while my tears sting my already puffy eyes. Yeah, this is anger.

Wrathful anger. It's not just the stifling heat in this basement either. No, it's my body feeling inflamed with rage. I want to kill Jake.

23

CHAPTER 23

Once we get upstairs I'm instantly immersed in fear. The kind of fear that is inescapable. The fear that is inevitable because there's nothing you can do to prevent what's to come. The fear that makes your heartrate spike. The fear Rich has created to constantly stir in my heart.

I can't shake the horrible feeling that makes my stomach lurch as he closes the door, locking it too. As I back away, I can't shake the stalking feeling that makes shivers run down my spine. The dreadful feeling of Rich seizing my soul and ripping my insides out.

My arms flail around to punch him while my legs kick. In a quick, swift motion, he lifts me up and throws me on the bed. My head ricochets off the headboard, forcing a throb to emerge.

I'm frozen as I watch him remove his shirt, giving sight to toned muscle and fascinating ink. But I'm not consumed in his fit body or his art, no, I'm worried about what he'll do to mine. I'm afraid of feeling my soul bleed out as my purity is ripped away from me. I can't help but feel sick at that thought. The thought of Rich's "present" to me.

Soon I feel air on my skin, causing small hairs to prick up. How did my shirt and pants come off? Oh no. Oh no, oh no, oh no. Why didn't

I fight? I hug myself while rocking. I'm crying softly and it's affecting Rich.

I see his concerned face when he bends down to stroke my cheek. My body remains frozen when I feel his slimy fingers move from my cheek to my chin.

"Livie,"

I wince when I feel his rough hand grip my chin and tilt my head, forcing me to look up at him. His other hand rests on the cup of my bra. I shudder when I feel him pull my strap down.

"Stop." I plead with glassy eyes.

He remains silent while trying to remove the rest of my clothing. But I'm not giving up that easily.

"I said stop!" I use my hand to slap him. It's so powerful that even he is deemed speechless.

While his head is faced away from me, I take the opportunity to jump off the bed.

Looking down at my bare legs, I confirm my sorrow filled thoughts. I'm not in my tee shirt or sweats anymore, and he's not in his shirt and jeans. No, we're both halfway nude and panting. I'm panting from running while he's panting from chasing me.

"No!" I scream when my body collides to the floor with him on top. I can feel his manhood press into me, making my body stiffen.

This time he spins me around with a muderous glare etched on his face. His tousled dark hair lingers near his eyes, while his narrowed essonite eyes hint of powerful, dangerous, lust.

"I want you and I'll take you. Now get up."

I feel a cold piece of metal on my neck. A blade. The sharp blade nicks my soft flesh, forcing me to whimper and shake. He slit my throat before so he'll do it again.

Without another word, I reluctantly stand. His large hands swallow mine as he grips them forcibly.

With the knife still pressed to my throat, I focus my attention on him. His fingers trail my leg until stopping on my engraving. It's purposefully done to make me flinch. To show that he still controls me.

I hate feeling exposed. I hate this feeling of vulnerabilty.

"I still can't dismiss the fact that you broke my rules a couple of weeks ago. You ran when I warned you not to. So now, the only way to stop you is to show you why you shouldn't."

"Don't hurt me, don't hurt me, don't-" My trembling lips close when his fingers press on them.

"Shh, don't worry. You'll learn from this. Maybe even enjoy it."

He leans in for a kiss so I take the opportunity to lift my knee to kick him in his groin.

"Hey, that's not necessary,"

A shocked yelp escapes my lips when he manages to catch my kneecap in mid-air.

"I'm not hurting you so don't hurt me."

And before I know it I feel an immense amount of pressure at my entrance. Imagine a heavy bag of rocks hovering over you before suddenly being dumped all over your body.

Gasping loudly, I hold onto the first thing I can. His shoulders. He inches himself in slowly before pushing further and faster.

I cry out from the pounding ache as it penetrates my core and expands my walls. I don't like this feeling so I squeeze my legs together to try and dull it down.

He notices my grimacing and painful moaning so he pulls out.

More tears blur my vision when I feel blood slide down my legs. I'm bleeding. This hurts too much. Make it stop. When is it over? My mouth opens to scream, shout, yell but the only sound that resonates are helpless groans and coughs.

"This should help," He hands me a glass of something that reeks of strong liquor. The smell is similar to vodka. Stale and acidic.

I grab it and without hesitation, guzzle it down. The burning alcohol slides down my throat and makes me want to vomit. I cover my mouth to try to hold it in but a sudden cough forces it out. It spews all over he and I, making him narrow his eyes.

"Shit Livie,"

"I have... to puke." I stumble off the bed to make a break for the bathroom but before I can start running, he grabs my hair and pulls me to his chest.

"Not so fast. I go in with you,"

Swallowing dryly, I nod my head. My hands won't stop shaking and my stomach continues to stir. Why won't they stop shaking? And why do I feel sick? My shoulders heave while I inhale giant gulps of air. I'm hyperventilating. This is unreal.

After what felt like hours- but were probably minutes- of me vomiting my brains out while Rich held my hair, I was finally able to steady my breathing. With my back against the bathroom counter, I wipe my mouth with the back of my hand. My body is sweating profusely while my eyes are still red from crying. My naked body is secured in a postion that makes me appear less vulnerable. I'm hugging myself while Rich stares at me. There isn't any emotion in his features. I suppress a shiver.

"Don't be so nervous, it's only what you make it." He chuckles, revealing a small dimple on his right cheek.

None of this is funny. He can't just take what he wants and expect me to accept it so easily. I have a right to keep what's mine. I have the right to save it for someone special. With my quivering hands now over my face, I cry harder. I don't want this if I'm going to be up here. I'd rather be downstairs with Jake. At least I know I'm safe.

"I'll give you a minute to clean yourself."

He removes my hands from my panicked face before planting a soft, unwanted kiss on my lips.

"And lock the door if you want but just know that I can break it down." He smirks wickedly.

Before I do anything I make sure I can stand. My vaginal area feels heavy and throbs consistently. I can feel the blood on my legs but I dont't bother looking at it. I want to wash everything away. I want to scrub until I'm raw and bleeding. I feel empty. Unloved. I'm ashamed of myself.

Five minutes into roughly scrubbing myself I hear the door open. I've already brushed my teeth, now all I need to do is finish scrubbing his scent off. I need to void my mind of him. I need to drown out his evil laugh and chilling smirk. I need to erase his cold, disheartening eyes from my memory. Another tear rolls down my already stained cheek when I feel his presence behind me. He takes my hands in his to stop me.

Without anymore words he pulls me into the bedroom. My rigid body remains apprehensive but he just pulls harder.

Spinning me around, his hands rest on my hips before I feel his lips conquer mine. I release small, muffled cries while he ignores me. His hands seem to be all over me and his scent, his scent of aftershave will be a permanent mark in my memory. A memory that will forever haunt my soul and taint my being. I'll never think of aftershave the same anymore. Every time I smell it I'll think of Rich.

My body falls backwards, forcing a small squeak to escape my lips. They're bruised from his rough kisses.

Without hesitation, he enters me again. This time he doesn't go slow, or consider how much pain I'm in. No. this time he pushes harder until I release a blood curtling scream. I can't hold back anymore. This hurts way too much. I feel like I'm being stabbed repeatedly.

"Plea-please...st-stop!" I shout when I feel a grating, grinding motion that inflicts more pain. My muscles constrict while my nails dig into his skin. I'm breathing irregularly as I feel more blood flow down my legs.

"You're not wet, that's the fucking problem." He pulls out again and this time he rests his head in the crook of my neck while I keep my widen eyes focused on the ceiling. I can't do this. He can't do this.

He sighs heavily before lifting me up. I'm able to blink a few times to keep myself from passing out. I need to escape this but all I can think about is the pain. The awful, terrible, angonizing pain.

And then it happens. My mouth is forced open and then I feel something stiff enter. My eyes begin to roll in the back of my head when I feel him penetrate my throat. He tastes of salt.

"Mmm." My hands instantly go to hold his to pry them off my hair. He has a firm grip, forcing my head to move back and forth. As he pumps himself into me, I can't help but bite him.

I hear a bunch of profanities before my head whips to the side. My eye feels heavy to the point where it might not open tomorrow. My bruised lips are bleeding, filling my tongue with a metallic taste of crimson.

"I was trying to help you but I see you don't want it."

I feel myself being pushed down again, making my body panic. My legs close tightly while I try to push him off.

"No! No, no!" I use what energy I have left to fight him but my efforts are futile. My eyes widen when I see the blade in his hand. He holds it to my sore throat with controlled dominance.

"Spread your legs or I'll slit your damn throat again."

Nodding nervously, I open my trembling to give room for him. With a satisfied grin, he positions himself in a way that makes my heart sink deeper. It's going to happen again. Why me? Why this? Why now?

I start crying, only to have my mouth covered by his firm hand.

"Scream in my fucking ear again and I won't be so nice." He threatens evilly.

My mind is telling me to go numb but my body can't comprehend. All I feel is torment.

He doesn't even give me a chance to reply because the next thing I feel is an explosion of excruciating ail. He penetrates me again and again, not even stopping to see if I'm okay. With each painful thrust, my eyes and throat burns. My back arches to try to stop my convulsing body but that only magnifies the pain. Without anything to grip, I take hold of the sheets. My fist ball into them while I grit my teeth. I can feel my toes curl while my core aches.

"I love... you..." He pants out while I keep my trembling lips closed. He's still on top of me, still inside of me, but now he's leaving lingering, disgusting kisses all over my chest.

"Say it." I feel his hand suddenly capture my throat, forcing my eyes open.

The longer I look into his crazed, lustful eyes the more I get the feeling that I'll feel more pain if I stay silent. I don't want to hurt anymore. I don't like this. This is my first time losing my virginity and it's because some sicko took it. I despise him. I'll never love him. He'll always be the man I so desperately want to be away from.

A warning squeeze on my throat makes me wince. His eyes still roam my body before the sound of my small, weak voice alerts him.

"I-I lo-love...you too." I stutter out, too afraid of his next move.

This time he continues with a triumphant grin and smoldering, lewd eyes. No words are spoken. Only grunts or groans of pleasure from him while aching jolts of pain shoot through me.

He complments me, even tells me how bad he needed to feel me. But all I can do is bite my lip to try to keep myself from screaming in his ear. While he's enjoying this, I'm the one who is hating it. I'm suffering but he doesn't see that because all he sees is his pleasure. Silent tears overflow and spill out the longer he thrusts, making a point to force me to moan by gripping my rear. He continues confessing his falsified love for me while I lay numb, covered in semen, sweat and regret.

What have I done? Will this make him worse? Now he doesn't know how much I hate him because all he knows is that I said I loved him.

The sudden feel of his perspired body collapsing on mine startles me out of my thoughts.

"I promise you that it will only get better. You're mine and I'm yours forever." He whispers creepily in my ear. My eyes are still closed while my breathing remains hitched.

He plants soft kisses on me while I lay completely still.

I can't feel anything but him inside of me. I can't see anything but his soul clenching eyes, seizing my being. He feels like I love him and I can't say anything to stop him from feeling this way. I'm hopeless.

24

CHAPTER 24

Blinding lights pierce my eyes, forcing my forearm to shield them. The heat from those lights illuminate my skin, making a few beads of sweat appear. The sudden sound of the crowd cheering causes a blush to force itself on my cheeks.

"Livie!" I hear my mom call my name so I turn to see her standing backstage.

"Remember to smile and make eye contact. Be poised, be perfect." She mouths to me with a bright smile.

Nodding my head, I turn my attention to the three judges in front of us. This is the final stage of the pageant. The stage where they determine and crown the winner.

I wait patiently- with my hands interlocked behind my back and one foot forward- as our names are called. All fifteen of us give broad, pretty smiles, appearing to be perfect angels. We remain poised and perfect like how proper young ladies should be. Our hair is perfect, our skin is flawless, and our attire is impeccable.

I'm in the group aged twelve to thirteen. With me being twelve, this is my first year being placed in the pre-teen category. I know I should be nervous, going against so many prettier girls than myself, but I'm not. I've been in pageants since I was five so I'm not as nervous as I was before.

Anyway, the judges deliberate and soon they come to a decision. My teeth take hold of my bottom lip while waiting. I hear a foot tapping a few people down from me. The girl is nervous and I part of me feels sorry for her. The judges deduct points when we tap our feet.

I want to win but I'm not to the point where I'll go crazy if I lose. Like my friend Kelly. She's thirteen and feeds off of this type of thing. Her dress is a stunning shade of turquoise, complimenting her natrually strawberry blonde hair and hazel eyes. And like always, her mom is standing next to mine, coaching her as well. I never understood that. Kelly was born for this, unlike me.

Looking down, I notice how my dress looks appropriate for a twelve year old. It's cupped sleeves slightly hang off my shoulders while the scoop neck top only reveals my collarbone. I don't have much chest to show anyway so my mom made the right choice. The rest of the lilac dress falls to the floor and hides my silver heels. Yes, heels. My mom makes me wear them to gain practice for these pageants. I hate them.

"So the judges have come to a unaminous vote. Now, give another round of applause to the candidates." The announcer revs up the crowd.

I'm trying so hard to keep smiling but my gums are starting to hurt.

The judges announce the runner ups first. Third place goes to a girl with long, brown curly hair. Her name is Mira and she's really nice. I come in second and the winner, of course, is Kelly. I'm not surprised. She's so much better at this than I am.

"Good job Liv!"

"You too Kel!" We hug before running off to our families. I have my second place trophy in my manicured hands and I'm content.

Smiling proudly, I hold it up for my mom and, wait-

"Where's dad?" I ask with furrowed brows. My eyes move around the busy backstage, trying to spot my father. He should be here.

"Smile Liv!"

A bright camera flashes in front of my eyes, forcing me to blink rapidly. She took the picture when I wasn't ready. But that's the least of my worries.

"Where is he?" I speak impatiently. My dad and I rarely speak but when we do he always tells me how proud he is of me.

"He's working. You know how that goes." She shrugs it off uncaringly. The way her shiny red lips curve with a sly grin makes me question verity in her statement.

"What's going on?" I mean I know they've separated but can't he show up to my events. Doesn't he want to see me?

"Livie, no worries. We'll celebrate without him." He interjects happily. He is the man my mom is hugging. His hand is draped around her slim waist as they both smile at me.

"And who is this?" I glance at the man standing beside my mom.

They both remain quiet while I continue sizing him up. He's tall with smooth brown hair and light brown eyes. His thin lips give a modest smile, indicating his politeness.

"Liv, don't do this here." She eyes me with a hint of admonishing. The look in her sky blue eyes tells me that I'd better keep quiet.

"Now, who wants pizza and ice cream?" He tries to lighten the mood but it's not working. I want to see my dad.

"Come on Liviebug. We have some celebrating to do." She wraps her arm around my shoulder while I glower.

The entire drive to the restaurant was filled with me asking him embarassing questions and giving snide remarks. When he'd ask me what my favorite food was I'd say whatever you hate. When he'd ask if I liked him I just rolled my eyes.

My mom was clearly frustrated but she apologized to him anyway. She blamed it on me almost becoming a pre-teen. All I could do was scoff at that before saying,

"The problem isn't my age. It's his creepy ass."

From that moment on, my mom made sure I never saw him again. Or at least made sure I forgot who he was.

I spent the rest of the night tossing and turning until finally falling asleep again. And this time, my dream of my mom only lasted a minute before I was awakened by an image dark brown eyes, and a cunning smile. They say that the eyes are the mirror to your soul.

Well Rich's mirror is dirty, foul and shattered. Every time I look into his brown irises he captures my soul and drowns it in his own poison. Why do they haunt me so much? Why are they embedded in my mind permanently?

My eyes snap open to be greeted by a view of the dark ceiling. I awake in fright again. With my heart pounding and soaked skin, I look around. This is the twenty fourth week I've woken up from a nigthmare that I can't shake off. It's been six months and I still have nightmares that keep me up. Nightmares involving him.

I had nightmares before Rich sexually assaulted me but I've always been able to sleep right after. Now, not so much. It's like my traumatic experiences have awakened another part of my brain. The part that was supposed to completely forget everything.

That's how it was for me every night. Constant bad dreams and nightsweats. Most times Rich would wake up and wrap me in his arms before humming the song my mom would sing to me.

At first, he annoyed me to the point where I'd curse him or fight him, but one night he choked me until I became unconscious. That scared me enough to never fight him again. I've always been afraid to die. And now that fear is magnified because he considers himself to be death, meaning he won't hesitate to kill me.

Anyway, the days turned to weeks, and the weeks to months.

I spent my time upstairs with Rich while Jake spent the rest of his time in the basement. I wasn't allowed down there and I wasn't complaining. I was glad to be away from him. Especially after our previous argument. He only saw things how he wanted to see them. He didn't see the pain and pleading in my heartbroken eyes when I begged him to convince Rich to let me stay downstairs. No, he didn't give a shit when I told him that I didn't want to be upstairs. All he cared about was me getting us out of here. All he cared about was me sacrificing my body in hopes that Rich would let us go. And although I've already had my most sacred possession stolen by force, I still get the feeling that he won't set us free.

I know I should probably ask him but I can't bring myself to do it. Plus, as absurd as it sounds I refuse to. Not for someone as selfish as Jake. If I'm going to endure this torture then he'll have to suffer too.

The sound of Rich footseps forces me to sit up quickly. My hand goes to cover my mouth when I feel moisture come up. I close my eyes while forcing the bile back down.

"Wake up babe!" He storms in with an exuberant expression. He's so happy while I'm so miserable.

"Look who I bought for you." He pulls something...or should I say someone out of the hallway and into the gloomy room. It's Jake.

Realizing I'm not even dressed, I clutch the blanket before using it to cover myself. I hear Rich's dark chuckle while my cheeks turn a bright red.

"Still shy, Livie?" He grins at me with wild eyes, making my heart beat faster. I pull the blanket up to my neck, hoping to rid this exposed feeling.

I notice Jake's green irises focus on me. I notice his eyes roam my bare arms until they land on my petrified eyes.

"Hi," He murmurs in a barely audible tone. I've been on edge lately so every sound is intensified. I'm able to hear the softest whisper.

"Why is he here?" I narrow my eyes, forcing his eyes to shoot back to the floor. He knows I'm pissed at him. He knows I hate him just as much as Rich now.

"He is here because he wants to start over. We're all going to start over, actually."

"Olivia, meet your nephew, Jacob Rhodes." He pushes him forward, making him stumble a bit. His body is healed now and his clothes are new. His appearance tells me he looks better, but his facial expression tells me he is feeling...hopeless?

The sudden sound of a horn honking outside makes me jump.

"Shit!" Rich grabs his suit jacket before running out of the room. I forgot about his interview today. He was dressed in a white collared shirt with a navy blue jacket and matching pants.

"Well say something." He shrugs with a hint of irritation.

I glance at him, instantly feeling irked. The previous silence was comforting and now he has ruined it with his annoying ass voice.

"Something." I smirk evilly. This makes his eyes narrow while my eyes shine with happiness.

"Stop flirting with me Olive, I'm taken." He smirks back just as evilly as me before taking a seat on the bed.

My body stiffens when he nears me, forcing him to hold his head down.

"Sorry, I... I-"

"Can you just go away now?"

"Why do I have to leave? I just got here." He says stupidly.

"Fine." I mutter while wrapping the blanket tighter. I stand up and without hesitation I bolt to the bathroom.

I lean against the door before sighing heavily.

The days usually consist of me waking up, showering, cooking, eating, and then renovating the old southern house. I don't know what I'm supposed to do now since Rich left without leaving me directions. He just left me with an asshole.

Shaking my head, I turn on the shower. Before I shower I touch my scars. It's been seven months now since my first rape and I'm fully healed. Only scars remain, but none of them hurt anymore. Looking at them causes a small grimace to etch itself on my features. The slit on my neck is closed now but still holds a light pink hue. The scratches and bruises that once ached my core are now small abrasions, marked with scars.

A sudden urge to puke sneaks up on me again so I head to the toilet.

Once I'm done I step into the shower. Without acknowledeging the small baby bump, I begin a brisk, heavy scrub. I still scrub my skin raw to the point where it hurts to even touch it. I'm a patheric mess and there's no one who can help me. Hell, I can't even help myself. I'm worthless. I feel like a repeatedly used napkin. Crumpled, dirty, and stained by Rich.

The water turns cold, forcing me to get out. Ever since Rich discovered why I took lengthy showers he set the water to turn cold after ten minutes.

Once I step out I'm greeted by the sound of Jake's serious voice.

"You smell really good. Like vanilla." He's leaning against the counter with folded toned arms.

From his round jaw upward, I stare at him. His full lips have a natural pink while his nose is a bit crooked, probably from being punched in it too many times. His eyes are an intriguing green with tiny specks of gray. Squinting, I notice that they change from light to dark daily. His eyebrows are as dark as his hair and his skin has a natural tan to it. It's clear he used to spend a lot of time at the beach, unlike me. My parents were always busy working so we could never go as a family. I could have driven myself down there but who wants to go the beach by themselves?

"And you look pretty amazing too, if I do say so myself."

"What?" I follow his eyes to my naked body.

"Shit, get out!" I yell whilst covering myself with the shower curtain. Why is he even in here?

"Okay, okay. Geez Olive calm your tits." He smirks at my inflamed cheeks.

With my chest heaving, I narrow my eyes at him, piercing his gaze enough for him to know my solemnity. He leaves a towel and some clothes on the counter before closing the door.

How did I forget my towel and clothes? And why the hell is he so distracting?

After getting dressed and brushing my teeth, I make my way to the kitchen. I'm starving.

With an annoyed sigh and an eyeroll, I brush past a grinning Jake.

"That was some show this morning, huh?"

With silence engulfing the room, I start preparing my five star breakfast. It's a peanut butter and jelly sandwich. The fridge is basically empty. We're running low on food.

"This day just keeps on getting better and better." I mumble sarcastically.

This makes him laugh and hearing that pisses me off more.

"Why are you here?" I snap angrily.

"He made me come up here. I only said I wanted to start over, right my wrongs. I told him to leave me in the basement but he said he couldn't do that anymore so here I am now." He shrugs while I take a seat across from him. He's looking around in awe while I pick the crust off my bread.

Biting into my sandwich, I take a minute to let it all settle.

"It's confirmed, he really wants to torture me now." I shake my head in disapproval. Jake is the last person I want to see right now.

"Maybe it's to torture me..." He speaks softly.

My chewing slows as I stare at him in bewilderment. What does that mean? Is someone feeling guilty?

"Well if it is then it's 'cause you deserve it." Shrugging my shoulders, I rest my head on my palm.

"I like this side of you." He smirks before reaching for a piece of my sandwich. I think he's joking but what do I know? When I thought I knew the real him he proved me wrong.

"Can you not?" I speak with agitation.

"Oh, sorry." He mumbles with his head down. His hand slides back to his side of the table. I hear his stomach protest but I don't care. He can fix his own sandwich.

I continue chewing my PB and J sandwich until a sudden urge to vomit creeps up.

My chewing stops while my eyes widen.

"Liv-"

Before he can ask any questions, I bolt to the downstairs bathroom.

Once I get back, I notice him still scanning the kitchen. I've done so much cleaning and decorating that it does appear new. I basically painted, remodeled, and cleaned the entire kitchen. The rest of the house still needs work though.

"Livie, are you sick?" His words make me stop.

Clutching my shirt, I make a point to tug it down. I don't need any prying eyes seeing it. It's May now, meaning I've known about this "pregnancy" for four months. Rich has no idea, and I want to keep it that way.

"Why hasn't he taken you to a doctor yet?"

Shrugging, I stay silent. If I go to a doctor then he'll know. And if he knows then he'll be pissed. There's no telling what he'd do to me or my baby. He doesn't want kids.

"Do you want it?" He says the word "it" acidically, making my eyes flicker with hate.

"No I don't but I'm not killing him or her."

Being raised in the south it's expected to be against abortion because it's a cruel form of murder. Killing an innocent life is frowned upon. It's immoral. I mean I live in the Bible Belt which is all the more reason why I shouldn't abort the baby. I know better.

My grandparents took me to church but my parents never did. But during the times I did go, I was taught not to take a life. No matter how small. And even though I don't love it, I'm not aborting it.

"This shit is ridiculous Livie. Ever since that night you told me to piss off in the hallway I've stayed silent. I've tried to keep my distance but you can't keep this up."

If he remembers correctly, he also told me to leave him alone so it goes both ways. That was the night Rich let him upstairs to shower. He tried to talk to me and I told him to piss off. I acted like he never existed. Well, that made him angry so he told me he really didn't want to talk to me either.

"How far are you?" He sighs in defeat. He isn't going to get me to listen to him.

"I'm four months, I think. Look, you have to promise me you won't tell him. You've already betrayed me once so please don't do it again." I speak cautiously.

"I never betrayed you. I didn't know he was going to- to do that to you." His eyes linger on mine, holding a steady gaze.

"You're a liar and I hope you burn in hell." I narrow my eyes with crossed arms.

"No, I'm seriously telling the truth. He promised me he wouldn't hurt you if..." He pauses. "Just stop hating me because I'm not your enemy, okay."

"Why didn't you listen to me that night, huh? Why'd you force me to go upstairs? We both know what Rich was going to do. You knew it was the night before my birthday. You played a part in my rape and as far as I'm concerned you're just as bad as he is."

"No, I didn't. I only wanted a way out. So when he came downstairs a few days before I told him not to hurt you. I told him that would be the only way I'd let him win. Was if he promised not to hurt you." His eyes hold something. Something meaningful. Is he being honest?

"Let him win?" I ask with curious eyes. My hand rubs my firm tummy sub consciously.

"My uncle never liked being told what to do by my dad, his older brother. Now he sees this as some kind of payback." He shakes his head, allowing his long hair to shake too. I have an urge to smile but I stop myself.

"Is that your part in his plan?"

Rich wants me because I remind him of my mom while Jake is only seen as a ploy. A way to fulfill his need to control. He feels like his brother dictacted his life by telling him to break it off with my mom. Now, he wants to dictate Jakes' life. He is seeking revenge on his brother by using Jake.

"I told you we weren't here by coincidence. The night he took me he knew I'd be out and away from my mom."

"So what did he mean when he said you wanted to start over?"

He draws a heavy breath before rubbing the back of his neck gingerly.

"I apologized for all of the...trouble I caused. The rebellion, the attitude, the fights, my stubborness. I apologized and promised that I'd change."

"So is that the truth?"

"Hell no." He smiles wickedly, making my insides twist.

"What? You can't lie to him. He knows and he'll kill you." I speak frantically. I'm afraid of Rich. Jake doesn't even know.

"I'm not letting him get away with this shit, Livie. Even if it was your birthday, he shouldn't have gone through with it. Especially to make a point to me. He wants to separate us but now he's convinced that I'm not against him anymore."

"I see why you hate him so much. It's not because he murdered your dad. No, it's deeper than that. It's because you're just like him. You see yourself in him." He's a selfish, dangerous, liar. And even though he feels bad for what I went through he can't take any of it back. He can't go back in time to fix this.

"I was distant but I was never selfish. That was all you, sweetheart." He says plainly.

"Selfish? I was selfish? See, this is exactly why we fight. You need to grow up and get your head out of your ass. If I were selfish I wouldn't have tried your plan."

I tried to convince Rich that I was in love with him but it was too much. Especially since every demand I made never provided positive results. Only slaps or punches.

The look in his eyes hold surprised shock. I'm sure he knows not to piss off a pregnant woman.

"You tried my plan?"

"This is why I'm pregnant, Jake. Because he wanted me to prove how much I loved him." I don't need to say anymore because I think he gets it. That was the fifth time I was raped and I actually felt pleasure from it. I hate myself even more because of that.

"Livie, I don't know what to say. I'm so sorry. I'm sorry for being a jerk." He sighs before holding his head in his hands. His fingers grip his hair in a distressed manner.

"Whatever Jake, I don't want to hear it. It's too late." Part of me hates blaming him but another part wants him to see what his selfish actions caused. I wanted to get out of here too but I'd never make it at the expense of his safety.

"Do you want to know the real reason why I wanted to get a smoke the night Rich took me?"

My head is down while I twiddle my fingers. I refuse to look at him so I nod my head instead.

"Gia and I had a fight. We were in the club for about thirty minutes before she starts flirting with this tool."

"I was getting drinks and I come back to her giving out her number to some douchebag. So I confronted them. I punched the guy then told her that was the last time she'd bullshit me. She argued about how I didn't really see what I think I saw. I got pissed and stormed out."

So she cheated on him? What the hell? Is that why he acted so distant and cold to me that night?

"I just couldn't bring myself to cheat on her again. When I kissed you I realized that I loved her way too much to ever do that again. I'm sorry but she really needs me." He speaks solemnly.

Holding my head down, I try to hide my teary eyes. I know he's taken and I shouldn't have feelings for him, but the sad truth is that I still do. I think about him every night before I go to bed. Every time Rich holds me I pretend I'm with Jake in the basement. I pretend that he's holding me close. I imagine him protecting me.

I really like him and for some weird inexplicable reason, I want to be his. I want to be the one he loves. But he's too busy loving some-one else. Someone who doesn't even reciprocate those feelings for him.

"Are you okay?"

I feel a hand on my shoulder, forcing my eyes to focus on his dark green ones.

"It's just...it's just that I really needed you too." I can feel my throat burn from the approaching sobs. But I can't cry in front of him. I already look weak and pathetic being pregnant by my rapist.

"Well, I'm here now, Livie. I'm here to fix this. Doesn't that count?"

Nodding my head, I return his half smile. I don't know what this means but I know I like it. We're not arguing anymore and I like it.

"Okay, so what's our new plan?"

"New plan?" I stare at him with confused eyes. We're not leaving because he'll kill us first. And I don't want to die. I don't want my baby to die either.

"Yeah, we're getting out of here, remember?" He gives an encouraging smile as his hand grabs hold of mine.

"Alive?" I peer at him with expectant eyes. The need to be comforted is intensified when he starts to rub his thumb on my small hand.

"Alive is all we'll ever be." He smiles a heart stopping smile at me, revealing handsome features. Breathtaking green eyes and attractive pink lips. His smile is really magnetic. And for the first time in six months, I manage to smile a genuine smile.

25

— • —

CHAPTER 25

After breakfast we headed upstairs to start forming a logical, secure plan. I have no idea what he's thinking but I do know that if we can get outside then we have a better chance at being found.

"Thanks again for, you know." He says gratefully.

"It's better in your stomach than in the toilet." I smile weakly, still feeling a bit sick. I ended up sharing my food with him because my stomach couldn't keep it down.

"Are you sure you're four months and not two or three? I mean morning sickness would have passed by now." He says it in a manner that suggests he has been through this before.

With sad eyes, I bring my head down. I don't know how far along I am. All I know is that I haven't had my monthly in four months. I vomit throughout the entire day, and my tummy is firmer. It's a small bump that only I seem to notice. I started noticing a month ago, in April so I came to the conclusion that I must have conceived some time in January.

"Did you take a pregnancy test?"

We're at the top of the stairs, the same place it happened.

Shaking my head, I chew on my lip nervously. There aren't any pregnancy tests because I'm not supposed to get pregnant. He only buys me tampons for my period and razors to shave with. Plus, if I do manage to miraculously find one and take it then how will I hide it from Rich? I'm afraid of what he'll do.

"Then how do you know you're carrying his spawn?"

My eyes remain focused on his pursed lips. They're closed so tightly that they are to the point of restraint. It takes a minute to process what he's saying before I say,

"I can feel it, that's how."

His features soften once he sees me staring at my stomach. My hands blanket over the small bulge protectively.

Sighing heavily, he pulls me into a sudden hug. My shocked body stiffens before realizing that he isn't Rich, and he won't hurt me. I inhale a shaky breath, making sure to calm my racing heart. I haven't been hugged like this in a while.

He notices my reluctance but instead of pulling away he just holds me tighter, allowing me to latch onto the back his tee shirt.

"When we break out of here we're getting you to a doctor."

My sticky tears, along with my hands, cling to his shirt. I begin to sniffle once I realize I was crying. I can't cry because Rich says it's weak.

"I'm fine, okay?"

He sighs in agitation. If I could see his mesmerizing face I bet it would be contorted into a disapointed frown. He seems more bothered by this than I am. Is it bad that sometimes I don't feel anything at all for this baby?

He pulls away, making me wish he'd pull me in again. His arms are now secured on my hips while mine remain over his nape. I was hugging him back.

"Normally, I'd argue with you but I'll just let you keep thinking you're fine. I don't need a mentally weak Olive running with me when we break out of here. You're already a danger when you're in your right mind." He grins jokingly, making me want to pull him in for a kiss.

But, the longer I gaped at him, the more I was able to notice something else. Behind his teasing smirk was something deeper. The first thing I noticed was his tone.

He was trying to cover the burdening concern in his voice with small playfulness. The second thing I noticed was the frown that soon took up residence on his face.

My smile fades when I notice his solemnity. We both remain silent; glanicing at the floor in distilled contemplation. And then, I notice the reverence in his eyes when we finally decides to meet each other's gazes.

Without another word, he takes my hand- making my heart stammer- before walking down the rest of the hall.

He is mumbling something about finding a way out while I'm on the verge of another panic attack. My breaths are staggered with each cautious step I make. Closing my eyes, I imagine I'm at home, away from all of this. But by the time I open them, I'm hit with raw, unfiltered emotions.

Everytime I walk this hallway I feel an overwhelming sense of fear and anxiety as old flashbacks resurface. I try to block everything out before I can get upstairs but everytime I reach the last step, I falter.

"Hold...on." I pant heavily while trying to gain my balance.

Leaning against the wall, I close my eyes and ball my shaky hands into fists, willing myself to calm down.

"I said get up here. You're not getting out of this."

My arm is tugged so roughly that I struggle to keep standing. Without warning, my already sore body collapses on the hardwood floor. We're in the hallway and Rich is pissed.

It was only a few minutes ago he told me he loved me for the millionth time.

With it being our supposed "two month" anniversaery, he wanted to celebrate. And soon realized I didn't want anything to do with it. I was depressed, sore, tired, and bruised all over from his previous assaults.

So I stayed silent, choosing to keep my objective thoughts to myself. I wasn't prepared when he pulled me up and started dragging me upstairs.

"I meant what I said. If you love me so much then prove it." His eyes hold an unusual spark. It's as if he has some new, sick, twisted idea.

"Who knows, maybe I'll love you enough to let you go." He smirks sharply, making my stomach twist. Is what he just said true? Will he let me go if I prove how much I "love" him?

We're at the top of the stairs with him stealing my gaze seductively. My knees buckle while I fight the urge to cry. Can I really do this?

"Hey, no crying." With my throat in his hand, he holds me in a death grip while I stay completely still. I learned the hard way not to pull away.

My lips pucker when he moves his hand from my throat to my cheeks.

I notice the intrigued, mesmerized look in his eyes the longer he anatomizes me. It's like a vaccum sucking the life out of me.

My thoughts, my emotions, my soul, my everything is being sucked out of me the longer we stare. I'm staring out of fear while he is staring out of lust. My heart drops when I feel the sudden tingle from his hand as he traces the outline of my carving.

"So...beautiful." He breathes into my neck, making me shiver.

"I can't...I can't do this!" I shout whilst using my hands to push him off.

He stays silent while I shake and panic relentlessly. I don't know why he hasn't tried to shut me up yet. Maybe he finally sees the probl-

And just before my thoughts can leave, my head makes impact with the wall. I feel my vision blur before I'm pulled from the wall again and slammed repeatedly. I cough out, sputtering out blood along with saliva and tears.

"Crying is weak, Livie. Always remember that,"

This time, he pushes my back so hard that my bones shake. The vibrating throb in my head won't let up. I'm biting my quivering lip to stop myself from crying. The look in his dark brown eyes hold intolerance while I hold onto his shirt tighter.

I open my mouth to protest but all that comes out are small gagging noises.

The pain in the back of my head is crippling. It hurts to even blink.

"You finished?"

My eyes slowly close then re-open before nodding quickly. My head still hurts and I can feel blood but I don't say anything. Instead, I let him lay me on the floor.

The heaviness of his body overpowers me as I lay in shocked fear. I'll never get used to this. All I can do is make my mind go numb.

My body jerks suddenly, forcing a small groan to part my lips. It doesn't take a genius to know that he is disrobing me. I don't have the will to fight anymore. He could have killed me just to get a point across, and I don't want that to happen again.

Soon I feel my body being turned around only to face him. I feel a heavy lump in my throat when his umbrageous face comes into view.

"I'll make you love me."

I close my eyes and before I can brace myself I feel a jolt of fiery pain. The burning between my legs intensifies the harder he thrusts. I cry out, only to have my mouth covered. Only small, muffled squeals penetrate my lips.

My muscles contract, foricing me to arch my back to try to loosen the pain. It's natural for me to be rigid around him but now it isn't working in my favor.

He grunts before securing a tighter grip on my hip. This time I can feel him go deeper and deeper until I feel more blood pool. I feel like a floodgate has opened, but instead of water all I feel is blood and excruciating pain.

I can't prevent the blood curtling scream that forces its way past my lips. It's too much. I want it to end. Someone stop him.

"If you want it to... be painless... then prove to me... you love me." He collapses on top of me, panting heavily. The sweat from his body clings to my skin and seeps through, making me cringe.

I whimper when I feel his large hand grip my area, squeeezing to inflict more pain.

My mind tells me to do what I'm told but my body is too stiff to move. I'm afraid of being harmed again so I have to force myself to do the unthinkable. I have to force myself to do the most regrettable thing in my entire teenaged life. I place my lips to his. My body is filled with fear while my mind is pushing me to continue.

He receives it instantly, allowing his tongue to caress mine. The way he kisses isn't dominanting or filled with control. It's as if he wants me to lead him.

I feel myself being lifted before my back is pressed against the wall. His hands adhere to my bottom while my legs wrap arounf his waist. The more I give in to him, the more gentle he becomes. His lips suck on mine while I fight the urge to pull away. I don't want to feel anymore agony.

"That's better," He pulls away with a satisfied smirk before sucking on my neck. My body reacts with small pleasurable shudders. It's so intense and chilling that it's hard to fend off the goosebumps. What am I doing?

He pulls away, managing to strike a cunning smile. His eyes hold alluring naughtiness the longer he steals my gaze. Realizing that I've stopped smiling, I plaster a seductive smile on my face before wrapping his hair in my hands. This time, we kiss with more fervor. Good, he's buying it.

I'm pushed further up the wall suddenly, forcing my eyes to open.

His chocolate irises turn dark and with a look of dominating possessiveness, he grips my rump tighter.

The way I'm held makes it impossible to break from his grasp now. A heightenend sense of fear sneaks up on me, making my heart skip a beat. His arms wrap tighter around my waist to hold me up. I'm pressed against the wall while his body pushes into mine, making my core pulsate.

"Now, scream for me."

My hands grip the back of his hair when I feel him inside of me. This time it isn't harmful. No, this time it's gratifying. And this time I'm screaming for him as he penetrates my soul with lustful desire.

"Hey, you okay?"

I hear Jake call out to me, forcing my eyes to open. I'm leaning against the same wall it happened. I'm in the same spot I felt pleasure from Rich.

Regret attacks me to the point where negative feelings start to sink in again. How could I enjoy that? What is wrong with me? This baby is proof that I've shown my kidnapper affection. Why did I do that? How could I have been so stupid? What will my friends think when they see me?

My head collapses into my hands while I sob quietly. I can't do this. I can't live with this reminder of Rich growing inside of me. It's too much.

Don't get me wrong, I want my child to live but I don't want it to be subjected it to this life. And once Rich finds out he'll either kill it or make my life worse for having it.

My hands shake profusely at this thought. He's dangerous on a good day so what will I do when he finds out I'm pregnant. Worry overtakes my sore, tired body the more I think. Tears brim in my eyes and before I know it I'm crying.

I cry until my tears run out. I cry until my throat burns and my lungs scream out; pleading to be rescued. Pleading for freedom. My screams echo through the dark, shadowy hall as I continue releasing my turmoil.

By the time I stop screaming I notice that my teardrops have dried. I'm not feeling better, I just can't form anymore tears. I'm a pathetic excuse for a human being.

Sniffling and wiping my tears away, I'm greeted with the sound of his reassuring voice.

"I'll help you up." I see his hand extending so I take it. The look in his dark green, beguiling eyes tells me that he's worried about me.

I should be upset at the fact that he didn't console me but the truth is he didn't need to because I would have pushed him away. He did right by letting me cry it out.

As I stand, I fight the urge to vomit again. And this time it isn't from the baby.

We continue down the hallway. I tell him that there are five doors meaning five rooms up here. A bathroom, a hall closet, Rich's room, another locked room, and a door with a note on it.

Walking over to the door, we read what's on the note.

'This is your new room, Jakey boy. You'll be sleeping in here at night while Livie will be with me. Seems fair right? Well, If not then back to the basement you go.'

He leaves a smiley face at the end of the note, making it appear creepier than it already is.

"No way in hell I'm sleeping in this box." He grumbles angrily. We're outside of the door, standing side by side as we look in the room. The room is smaller than a toybox.

"You can't complain. Remember what you said? He wants to separate us so he'll jump at any chance to push your buttons. He wants to see if you've really changed." I try to explain.

I'm finally starting to understand. If Jake shows any signs of rebellion then our chance to escape is like leaves in a windstorm. I need to keep him from losing his temper for as long as possible. Because as soon as he does then we'll never get out of here.

"Come on Livie, look at this. Do you see this prison cell?"

"It's still better than the basement." Jake's room is basically a closet. It consists of one cot, and one chest. Talk about the bare necessities, right? He doesn't have a blanket, just a sheet and pillows. It's a step up from the dirty, dusty mattress in the basement though. At least he has a window. It's boarded up but it's a window, nonethelss.

"We gotta get out of here soon." He mumbles with foreboding.

I start searching the room while Jake starts patting the walls. I don't know what he's doing. All I know is that whatever he is trying to find, he is determined to find it.

"I noticed everything is locked and boarded. Does he have a key or something?"

"There's no key. I've already looked." Rich has secured this entire house to keep us here. The doors are locked and the windows are boarded to keep us in. No one is supposed to find us. Ever.

"What about weapons? Does he have any?" He asks while still patting the walls.

"I don't know." I gave up looking a long time ago.

He paces back and forth before stopping abruptly. His shoulders square while he rubs his chin in thought. I notice that he's gotten an inch or two taller.

"Since there aren't any weapons or keys for us to use then there must be a secret passageway somewhere in this house." He runs over to the wall to start tracing it again. This time it's more quickened and frantic.

"There has to be something. I mean how else does he leave this shithole?"

I stare at him in disbelief before going back to my task.

I can't focus on what he's doing because or some reason I feel compelled to find my baby some clothes. So now I'm currently looking through the chest drawers.

If I'm going to keep this baby then he or she will need clothes. My eyebrows pull into a frown the longer I search. There's a few shirts and pants but there doesn't seem to be any for babies.

"Hey, what are you doing? Nothing that can help us is in there."

He walks over to me to see what I'm doing so with a quick reaction I shut the drawer. I don't want him to know what I'm looking for. If he knows I'm focused on baby clothes instead of finding a way out then he'll think I'm even crazier than before.

"I'm just looking for a key." I lie quickly.

"But you just said you already...nevermind." He sighs dismissively.

"He went somewhere this morning. Where'd he go?"

His words are as quick as his frantic state. His eyes linger on mine, trying to get some information. I already what this is about. I'm the one with the info because I've been up here with him for six months. But what Jake doesn't realize is that I don't know where Rich goes when he leaves everyday. The only time he has told me anything would be this morning before he bolted out of the room.

"He said something about a job interview." I rub my tummy while I watch him.

With an alarmed look, his face suddenly pales, making me raise my eyebrows.

"What's wrong?"

"Oh shit." He starts backing out of the room with panicked eyes.

"What, what is it!?" I raise my voice to gain his attention.

"He's going to take my dad's job."

He runs out, leaving me standing in his sandbox sized room; anxious and scared. I'm left with no idea of what he is going to do. And no idea of what Rich will do.

26

· ◆ ·

CHAPTER 26

As I stand in the small room, waiting for Jake to come back I start to realize how dumb I must look. Can I think for myself? Why am I waiting for him to come back? He's been out of the basement for less than a day and he's already about to flip his lid.

Shit.

"Jake!" I call out while bolting down the mahogany stairs. He doesn't seem to realize that how he acts can make or break us. I can't do this without him and I need him to understand that. He is my ticket to freedom. Even if he is a selfish jerk sometimes.

If I can find him and try to convince him to hold his anger in then he'll be able to keep staying up here. And if he stays up here then we can get out of here sooner. I continue pacing down them until I get to the first landing. My breathing is rugged and my heart pounds fervently. I need to slow down, especailly since I've been so weak lately.

Once I make it to the empty foyer I call out to him. I've only been in the living room, bathroom and kitchen. I haven't been in the dining room or his office before. It's locked.

"Jake!" I shout.

"Come out, come out wherever you are." I whisper jokingly.

I don't know why I'm joking with him. Hell, I should still be pissed at him. I mean he didn't try to stop Rich from raping me. He just allowed it to happen. But then again, he did tell Rich not to hurt me. At least he sounded honest when he told me that. Hmm, maybe Jake isn't that bad afterall. I mean there isn't much he could do being chained to the wall so he used his words to try and protect me. Yeah, that helped.

I roll my eyes in annoyance. I don't know what to think anymore so I draw my attention back to finding him.

I make my way to the nearest room. It's the living room which looks better than how it did when I first got here. The walls are painted a silve gray with white borders. The old sofa and recliners have been replaced with new furniture. A deep blue sofa with deep blue chairs decorate the room. I notice the picture above the broken television. It's a picture of my mom and I. I don't know how he got it but it pisses me off.

Storming out of the room, I remember why I never go into the living room anymore. The entire six months I've been upstairs have been spent with me staying in Rich's room. I was too depressed to even get out of bed. But now that I'm pregnant I feel like my life is worth living again. I have someone to live for; someone to fight for.

Wiping my teary eyes, I walk to the kitchen. I spent the next several minutes searching the half bathroom and small closet. I was about to give up and head back upstairs untill heard it. A loud crash awakens my senses and forces my legs into motion.

"Jake!" My worried voice screeches while I run over to the office with the double glass doors.

This is my first time in here and it's surprisingly neat. Except for the overturned chairs and papers everywhere, everything else seems to be in place. There are a few Victorian paintings on the walls. They compliment the old, southeren theme of the room. Dark mahogany wood floors and desk, bookshelf with a thousand books and even a globe in the corner of the room. It's beside the window. Wait, there is a window in here and it's not boarded.

"We're leaving before he gets here. But I need to find something first." He continues rummaging through the drawers of the oakwood desk. All of his attention is focused on finding what he is looking for.

"How did you get in here? This door has always been locked." I look around the now cluttered room. This is unbelievable.

"Look behind you."

I frown before turning my head to see shards of broken glass on the floor. He broke the glass to unlock the door.

My first reaction is fury but then I stop myself. I stop to think about what he first said when I came in here. If we're leaving now then Rich won't punish us. I'll be safe because I'll be away from him.

"Oh my God! Look at your hand." I point to his bleeding hand. A few small cuts line his knuckles. It looks awfully painful. I hate the sight of blood and the feeling of pain so I'm cringing just staring at it.

"I guess I can't do everything in the movies." He shrugs with a modest grin, forcing me to suddenly smile.

"You need to sit, Olive? I could hear you snoring from all the way down here." He chuckles lightly, managing to change the topic and my mood. I love this side of him. This funny, sweet, caring side. The side that makes me smile.

"No, I'm okay." I was breathing hard because I haven't had proper excersie in over a year.

Walking over to him I decide to help him search. For what? I have no idea but I want to help.

We search for a few minutes before he stops suddenly. I notice him breathe laboriously with his hands gripping the edge of the desk. He looks frazzled which worries me. His eyes roam wildly while his dark hair is disshelved. He looks crazed.

"Think man, think." He murmurs to himself.

I'm still gawking at him when he runs his fingers through his tangled hair in distress. Even when he's stressed he looks cute.

Biting his lip, he runs his hands over his exhausted face before stretching. My eyes linger on his toned torso as his fitted shirt lifts slightly. When did he get those abs?

"I remember now." With focused eyes, he starts pacing suddenly.

This worries me but I can't stop him so I opt to just watch him in awe. I sill don't know what we're looking for or what he's doing. All I know is that he is acting crazy, and this room is a mess. Papers decorate the floor and the bookshelf that was once standing is now tilted. If not for the chair holding it up, it would have fallen to the floor by now. It's clear he tore this room apart before I got here.

"I remember this house. This room. It's starting to make perfect sense." He walks over to me in quick strides, making sure to grab my shoulders.

"Once I find it we're out of here, okay?" His tousled hair reaches his persistent green eyes. They hold a burning determination. A determination so strong it scares me.

"What are you looking for?" I ask, still awestruck by him.

He turns to me with a tempting smirk. "Our ticket to freedom."

The urge to kiss him is too strong, especially with the way he is holding my head in his hands. A small blush creeps up on my cheeks and heats my entire body when I realize how close our foreheads are.He makes me nervous in a good way. I want to kiss him but I know what he'll say, so with a defeated sigh I remove his hands from my cheek.

I notice a small frown grace his features but I quickly look away before I get sucked in. If I kiss him he'll tell me how much he loves Gia and that will upset me. I don't need us arguing right now.

"Livie, did you hear me?"

"Um no, what did you say?" I ask dumbly. I should be focused on what he's saying but all I see is his gorgeous lips moving.

He stands next to me, making a point to have our arms touch. I think he does it on purpose but I can't really call him out on it. He'll play dumb. He nudges me playfully, making another smile creep up so I keep my head down. My heart skips when I remember how good he felt when we hugged. His skin feels like cotton.

"It has to be in here..." I feel him start to rummage through the old desk again. His hands move as quickly as his mumbling mouth. He places a bunch of crumpled papers in front of us like a display before clasping both hands together.

"What is that?"

He releases a low laugh before pushing his hands in his pockets.

"It's a copy of the will to my grandfather's estate. It was first given to my dad because he's the oldest. But now that's he's been dead for five years it goes to his younger brother."

"Rich?" I finish in just as much shock as him. If Rich gains more power he'll be even more dangerous.

"He must have the real copy with him." His euphoric voice changes to a low, saddened tone. This makes me sad too.

"So what's going to happen now?"

He exhales slowly then says,

"Remember when I mentioned a secret passageway?"

Yeah I remember but I didn't think he was serious. He nudges me again, cuing my head to nod automatically.

"Well, there is one...it's just somewhere I can't really remember. We have to find it so I can stop him from taking everything my mom, brother and I own." His shoulders slouch while he frowns.

Whoa wait a gosh darn minute. He knows another way out?

"So you know how to get out of here? You knew this entire time and accused me of being the one who knew?" I narrow my eyes at him with a strong feeling of choler.

"I said I just remembered, okay?" He speaks with slight irritation. Is he seriously getting mad at me?

"Fine, where is it?" Out of all of the times to remember, he remembers now? A year after being trapped here.

With crossed arms, I see him roll his eyes before tilting his head downward. Why won't he look at me?

"I just said I don't remember where it is, exactly."

"This is just great." I mumble sarcastically.

"Why are you getting so upset? I said there's a way out." He shrugs. The tautness in the room is overwhelming.

"Yeah and you knew about it. You knew this whole time." I argue back.

"How many times do I have to tell you I didn't remember until now!" He heaves angrily. The way his jaw clenches reminds me of Rich. I see a flash of dark glint in his gray- green irises, making me slightly afraid. Normally, I'd back away but a slight feeling of courage bubbles inside of me. So with my arms crossed, I narrow my eyes menacingly.

"That's not something you fucking forget!" I spit just as acidically.

"Do you trust me, Livie? Because it sure as hell doesn't seem like it." His eyes plead with mine to trust him. He needs me to trust him but-

"I don't know who to trust anymore!" I admit before stopping myself.

We both pause, taking a minute to let everything settle. I see the hurt in his eyes before he flashes a quick recovery smile.

"Well you can trust me, okay. I'm not him." He reassures cooly.

My eyes shift to him before I look at the ground. I didn't mean to hurt his feelings. And judging by the way his voice lingers; small and solemn, I can tell he is still bothered by what I said. He isn't fine.

"Now what?" I change the topic quickly. I hate to admit that I don't really trust him. I want to but for some reason I can't.

"Good way to change the subject." A forced laugh escapes his lips while he stares at the floor. He's still offended that I don't trust him. Anyone could dismiss it as him being his usual self, but because I've been so observant, I caught it. He's trying to make himself feel better from that previous blow.

"Uh," He clears his throat nervously.

"This... this house is where my dad and his brother grew up. They lived here until he met my mom. They got married and then had Jackson and I." He glances at me before quickly turning away. A small feeling of anger overshadows me while I think about that. Why can't he look at me? I'm not mad at him. Am I?

Shaking my head, I raise an eyebrow then ask,

"So you mean to tell me that you know this house because you grew up here?"

That is probably how he knows about the secret passageway.

Nodding with a timid smile he continues, "We moved to Texas when I was ten but yeah, I grew up here." He states calmly. His eyebrows scrunch together while he recollects.

So that means he spent ten years in this house with his uncle until they moved away. But why did they leave? Were the two brothers feuding?

"My dad left the house to him because of ther constant fighting. With my dad being older he thought he could make Rich change. You know, lead him in the right direction but he was wrong. Rich got worse and my dad refused to live with him any longer so he called my grandfather to move back and take care of Uncle Rich." He explains, making me realize that I'm wearing my emotions my face again. He too can read me just like Rich.

"How old were they? Your dad and uncle?"

"Four years apart just like Jackson and I." He stares off, his voice hinting of sadness at the mention of his brother.

He once told me that he and Jackson were close. Well I hope they don't end up fighting like Rich and their dad. Siblings are supposed to always be there for you no matter what problems they face. Even when they fight they aren't supposed to stay mad at each other. Waylan and I never stayed mad at each other.

"Oh, and look what else I found."

He holds up another paper. But the harder I squint the more I begin to realize that it's not just a paper. It's a document with a signature. My mom's signature.

'On this day, October 28th, 2013, we give custody of Olivia Kelly Walters to the named person above, Richard Thompson Rhodes.'

My face drops when I see the date.

"It's dated on my sixteenth birthday." My mouth releases a panicked gasp when I realize that my mom really did give him custody of me. Why would she do that? How could she do that? This whole entire time I thought he was lying.

My knees buckle whule my chest heaves the longer I stare at my mom's signature. It's signed in black ink, staining the paper and my heart as well. My narrowed eyes linger on the document; trying to figure out how to feel. Should I yell, cry, or punch something?

I should punch something. My hands ball into fists the longer I allow my horrible reality to sink in. With tears falling down my cheeks, I grab the paper and crumple it up. It's just a piece of paper. It doesn't mean anything and they can't make me stay with him.

"Mia Katherine Walters? Is that your mom?" He asks curiously.

M.W. in the note stands for Mia Walters, my mother. The word 'soon' was written in that note. Could this be what it was referring to? Did Rich want custody of me just so he could have me since he couldn't have my mom?

My knees become weak and my body collapses suddenly. I can't even stand, and my throat burns.

"Livie!" I hear Jake call out before his body presses into my back. His arms wrap around me as I cry.

"No, no, no!" I start to shake, feeling rage and sadness consume me. Jake holds me tighter while we rock. His chin rests on my head while he tries to calm me down.

"We have to leave now." He repeats calmly. I hear him but I can't move. I can't think. I can't speak.

Soon, I feel cold air and then shuffling around me. I'm in a daze while he's running around the room. Why is this happening to me?

Shaking my head, I grab the roots of my hair before screaming loudly. My own mother gave me away to some sick sadist and she didn't even care. The more angered I become the faster I begin to rock. This isn't real. No, this is a dream.

"Let's go." He pulls my arm to get me to stand but I don't move. Instead, I stare idly ahead.

I hear more shuffling before I feel myself being lifted. One arm slinks around my waist while the other cradles my legs.

"How could... she do... this to me?" I hiccup. My tears continue to stream down my cheeks while I panic. This time I'm gripping his nape tighter as we ascend the stairs. He winces but doesn't say anything. He just allows me to continue breaking down.

A plethora of feelings overwhelm me all at once. Feelings of shame, anger, and sadness come crashing down on me. I feel heavy; as if I'm just deadweight. I'm sinking deeper and deeper into a pit of darkness. A depression overtakes me so unrelentlessly that I find it harder to breathe. I'm hyperventilating.

"Just breathe, " Jake commands in a soothing tone.

My shaky breaths subside to a steadier pace as I try to calm myself. I need to calm myself, but the more I think the more frightened I become because I'll never leave. The paper says he has custody until I'm eighteen. But I know he won't let me go. I'll never escape him. With no control whatsoever, I pour my tainted soul out, allowing all of my tears to cleanse me.

"I ca-an't spend th-the rest of my li-life wi-ith him." I stammer while being placed on a soft cushion.

I watch him close the door before moving to the chest. He pushes it over the wooden door effortlessly.

"W-what are you doing?"

He wipes the sweat from his brow before locking his gaze on me. His heart is beating frantically while beads of sweat pour down his dark blue shirt. He is panicking like I am, but the difference is he can't let me see him breakdown. Because once he does, I'll be even more upset.

"I'm," He swallows dryly. "I'm getting us out of here."

And before I can argue he runs over the wall the chest was once against. With cautious movement, he starts tracing the outline of the wall. I wait patiently until I hear a small 'yes' from him.

"Is this why he didn't want you upstairs?"

I'm still hugging myself but I'm able to see a small opening in the wall; a small door. It appears to blend with the charcoal colored wall. From the chest blocking it and the door sharing the same color, it's easy to miss at first glance.

"He was hoping I didn't remember."

He lifts me up again, making a point to grab my bottom. I don't complain. Instead I snuggle into his firm chest.

"You know how to hotwire a car?" He asks suddenly.

I'm now standing on gravel, looking confused and out of touch with myself. Why am I so weak? Why am I so hopeless? I'm not helping the situation if all I feel is emptiness. I feel displaced. Like I've left my own body and mind. I feel my body being placed in the seat of a car and then I hear a car door slam. I'm not in control.

Looking around with frantic eyes, I notice the atrocious smell of stale liquor. I see the ancient air freshner hanging from the mirror. The van is a cluttered, stinking mess. Wait, the. van? My mind panics when I realize I'm in Rich's van. How did I get here?

"Help! Someone help!" I start pulling on the door handle, trying to get out. My body is pulled back and then I hear him whisper.

"Can you save your 'crazy' for another time? We have to get out of here, Olive." He smirks teasingly at me. His dazzling smile lights up my darkness and makes me smile too.

Shaking his head with a happy grin, he starts the car and we're off in a flash. I don't ask him where he learned to hotwire a car, or if he knows where we're going. I only sit quietly; idly staring out the window. The sunlight feels invigorating against my skin. It warms me and for a moment I imagine that I'm home. I imagine I'm free from Rich and safe from danger. For a small second, I'm taken out of my dark pit of depression and placed intoa new world where I can spread my wings and fly free.

Staring out the window, I stare at the blurred trees. I get so lost in the trance of the greenery outside that I allow my heavy eyes to close. The small hum of the engine allows me to lull myself to sleep. This is the first time I've been able to sleep somewhat peacefully in a long time.

We keep driving until the engine starts to cut off. I open my eyes in an alarmed state. My mind automatically assumes the worst. Please don't tell me we're out of gas.

"Where are we? And why is it cutting off?" I sit up with wide eyes. We've come too far for Rich to catch us. I'm sill surprised we've managed to escape so soon.

"I don't know." He shrugs while putting the car in park. His yawning means he is just as exhausted as I am. I make a note to remind him to let me drive once he gets the car running.

"Well, can you start it back up?" I say with annoyance. It doesn't take a genius to figure this out. If the van has shut off then put the key in the ignition to start it.

He glances at me with a wrinkled nose and sorrow filled eyes.

"I don't have keys to start it back up because I hotwired it, remember?"

"So what now, Mr. genius?" I raise my eyebrows with a small grin.

"I'll figure something out, Olive." He opens the door and walks out.

I watch him open the hood before cursing. An entire cloud of smoke blankets over the hood and windshield, making it impossible to see. It's bad enough that it's already getting dark. We must have been driving for hours.

"Okay, yeah...we're out of gas!" He shouts to me. An exasperated look etches itself on his flawless face.

My first thought is to ask him why it took him so long to figure that out but I hold my tongue. That would only lead to us arguing. So, I decide to see if I can walk to a gas station. I'm not staying in this van alone.

"Okay, let's find a gas station!" I'm about to get out of the vehicle when he rushes back in. With heavy panting, he grips the steering wheel before placing his forehead on it.

"What are you doing? We have to find a gas station so we can get help."

He shakes his head before peering at me.

"We don't have any cash for gas. And help won't help us." He pauses while my brows crease in confusion.

"He has legal custody of you, Livie. No one is going to believe you when you tell them he's not your dad."

Wait, is that why he kept driving? Because he can't find anyone who will believe us? He can't find one person who won't send us back to Rich?

"How do you know? Did you stop and ask for help?" I question earnestly.

"I've been to two gas stations miles apart, and a Wal-mart." He sighs frustratedly.

I don't even ask how it went because us being stuck in the middle of nowhere answers that. He was ashamed to tell me we that we can't afford gas. That's why Rich didn't take the van.

Sadness swells in me when I realize that this could be it for us. Rich is probably home already which means we don't have much time to get to safety.

Fighting back tears, I gather the courage to say,

"But what about you? Can't you get help for me?"

He can be my witness. He can help me fight this.

"We can get you to a hospital. At least there, they can treat you and that baby."

My eyebrows pull into a discontented frown the longer I analyze his defeated frame. His forehead is still on the wheel while his arms rest on the beat up dashboard. The way his voice resonates, low and unsure makes me uneasy. I've never seen him this down before.

"Jake, please don't tell me you're giving up." My voice wavers while I choke back oncoming sobs.

"I'll always be here for you, okay. I won't let him hurt you anymore." He looks at me, this time with assurance.

"Repeat what I just said, Livie." His hands now cup my face, forcing me to look into his sea of deep green eyes.

Sighing loudly, I repeat after him.

"You...you'll always be here for me and you...won't let him hurt me."

"I should have thought this out better. But I just couldn't deal with him taking my dad's company. I just wanted to stop him." He chews his bottom lip while pulling me into hug.

He's right. This plan sucks. We have no idea where Rich's interview is and we have no way of finding help. I don't know what we're going to do.

"I'm sorry, Livie."

He pulls me tighter when I start to sob. What good am I if I can't help us break free? Now this plan has backfired and there is nothing we can do.

Clutching his shirt, I start to notice the way his arms wrap around my waist. It brings back memories of us in the basement. He's holding me the same way he did that night in the basement. It was the same night he said we needed each other.

Silence casts over us, filling our entire beings with dread. My watering eyes remain closed while I listen to his uneven heartbeat.

"A great director once said, we're born alone, we live alone, we die alone. Only through our love and friendship can we create the illusion for the moment that we're not alone."

He pauses then says,

"I don't know about you but I don't feel alone now." He rests his chin on the top of my head while his hands continue holding me in a firm grip.

I love this. He is trying to make me feel better by giving me the feeling of security and accompaniment. He is trying to help comfort me and it's working because I'm starting to feel protected in his arms; like he can protect me from anything or anyone.

"I should have done more to protect you." He breathes sadly. I can hear the heavy vexation in his voice. It's painful to hear.

"We still have a chance." I have no idea what we're going to do but I do believe we still have a chance. Even if we have to hide from Rich, we have a chance of not going back there.

"Livie, did you hear-"

Smiling timidly, I place my finger to his lips to silence him. I just need this. I need to feel loved. I'm not alone when I'm with him.

His eyes linger on mine, trying to figure me out. With a small smile, he places his forehead on mine.

My fingertips trace his jawline. I observe every inch of his perfect face. From his newly developed strong jaw to the stubble growing there. He looks older and sexier. Like he is maturing. I make a note of the way his eyes captivate mine, wrapping me in his alluring stare.

My heart beats faster when I feel his hand wrap in my hair. With a cute smirk, he gently rubs my full lips with his thumb. His touch is more than comforting, it's electrifying too. I feel a spark with him and it's more than just when we touch or kiss. I feel connected to him on a deeper level too.

"I never said happy birthday to you, Olive." He smiles apologetically at me. Is it strange that he makes me like him more and more. Or is it strange that he mentioned that at a time like this?

I frown before grinning excitedly.

"Thank-" I attempt to thank him but I'm stopped when I feel his lips abruptly brush against mine.

Closing my eyes, I bring my lips closer to his. They feel soft against mine and I love it. With his hands now gripping my hips, he pulls me closer to him.

We continue kissing, letting ourselves be set free. The deeper we kiss the more heated things become. He starts undressing me while I place my hand in his jeans. I give a playful squeeze, forcing a shocked grunt to part his lips.

I giggle when his lips go to my neck while mine starts trailing kisses along his shoulder.

I release a small moan when he sucks on my spot, making a point to make my body stir. The urge to fuck him right now is so strong that I can't hold back. My hands rub him all over while my body presses further into his. Whoa, what are we doing?

"Knew you couldn't resist me." I hear him laugh before tugging the rest of my jeans off. The sound of his laugh is just as sexy as him. Yes, there is no question as to what we're doing. A new questions linger; when are we going to do it?

Once we've undressed each other, I take a moment to memorize everything. Every gentle touch, every savory kiss, and every small moan he makes. His pulsing manhood pushes up on my thigh, making me even hotter for him.

He lays me down gently and I'm surprised we made it to the back so quickly. With our bodies still pressed together, I feel him trace my arm downward. A small electric shiver runs down my spine, leaving me wanting more.

"Don't stare too hard, Olive. I know looks can kill ." He winks at me, making my heart stop.

My hands cling to his cheesk while I bring him down to my lips. He sucks on my bottom lip while I allow my tongue to linger in his mouth.

A small satisfied hum rings in my ears. From him or from me, I don't know but I do know that he's just as aroused as I am.

He rubs my glistening chest while I trace my fingers over his sweaty spine. A shiver passes through him before he enters me. It's slow at first, making sure I'm okay. My body moves with his as I moan out. He gets the message so he takes the lead. He pushes further and I swear my breathing has just stopped.

He sees me grimace so he pulls out. With worried features, he removes my hair from my face then kisses me gently. He's telling me he isn't going to hurt me.

My arms wrap around him while goes in again. This time it doesn't hurt. This time I allow myself to feel ecstasy. This time I feel his skin on my skin. I feel every part of his soul sinking into mine.

The more synchronized we move, the further I escape into a world of sexual pleasure. I've never managed to feel this good with Rich. It felt so wrong and I had to convince myself it felt right. But not with Jake. No, with Jake it's different. And the more he penetrates my core, the more I begin to think; if this is so wrong then I sure as hell don't want it to be right.

"Hey, you okay?" I'm shaken awake by a hand on my shoulder.

I feel warm wetness on my cheek meaning I must have drooled. Crap. I was dreaming.

He laughs at me before saying,

"That must have been some dream, Livie. You kept moaning."

Oh my God, oh my God, oh my God.

My hand goes to cover my embarrassed face while he chuckles again. Can he stop doing that? He's only turning me on more.

"There's a hospital near here. We'll start walking tomorrow." He leaves the front seat to go to the back. Are we sleeping in here?

Looking around, I notice how dark it has gotten. The once orange sky is now shrouded in blackness. There aren't any street lights on this highway nor are there many cars. And judging from the way the van is parked, I'm guessing we've run out of gas. Shit, don't tell me it's my dream happening all over again.

27

— ❧ —

CHAPTER 27

Birds chirp loudly, creating a beautiful symphony of melonious sounds. Filling my ears with peace and making me smile. Restoring hope to me and making me content. I could lie here forever listening to the melodic sound of the birds.

I haven't heard the sound of birds singing in so long. The only birds that I've heard were crows, and they don't sing. It's ironic how those ugly birds portrayed my mood at that house; depressed, ill tempered, and fearful.

"Morning." A small squeeze on my tummy makes my eyes open.

But that lasts a second because the rays of sunlight beam through the windows, hurting my eyes yet warming my skin. I know it's morning but I'm not ready for today. I'm not ready for what we have to face.

He sits up so I turn to see him. His shirt is no where on him while his hair is a ruffled mess. Looking down, I notice that my shirt is off too. Where did our clothes go?

"Don't look at me like that. You had more fun than me." He smirks devilishly.

"So we...we um..."

Why does the previous virgin in me have to come out now?

"I dared you to strip so you did. And then you dared me so I did." He bites his lip, trying to hold in laughter.

"You're joking. Oh my...oh no." I sit up with wide eyes.

"Seriously Livie, you have to learn to calm your tits." He smirks smugly while eyeing my bosom.

My arms go to cover them which forces him to laugh harder. He isn't helping. I feel like I've been drugged or out of mind for the past eight hours. I feel like we did something and I don't know how I feel about it.

"I can't take it anymore." He wipes the fake tears of laughter from his eyes before saying,

"We fucked."

My cheeks turn crimson while my heart continues pounding. This is a dream come true and yet it's so wrong. I want him and yet I can't have him.

"So, we actually did...that?" I ask skeptically.

"You're surprisingly not that bad. You did way more than me." With his hands behind his head he leans back. Making a point to flex his muscles.

Is he saying I'm better than Gia? I stare at him, lost for words until I see his eyes drift to my naked form.

My eyes linger on him before looking for clothes.

"Over there." He points to a white spaghetti strapped dress with brown sandals.

"I did bring clothes for you, even though I prefer you wearing what you're wearing now." He smirks at me.

I laugh before running over to hug him. With his arms around me he leans in for a kiss.

After our savory make out session ends we decide to get dressed.

"I dare you to put your clothes on." I joke when I see he has yet to make an effort to get dressed.

"I dare you to take yours off." His sexy lips curve while his mesmerizing eyes hold amusement.

Shaking my head, I throw his khaki shorts at him.

He sighs while putting them on. We exchange a few more jokes while getting dressed. All I can do is giggle when he hits his head while trying to put his shirt on.

"So what's our plan?" I need a plan. We need a plan. Rich is probably hunting us down right now.

"I think we should walk..." He trails off.

Walk? The only time I've walked was to my elementary school when I was nine. We lived across the street so it was easy to get their on time. But now we're not even close to a Mickey Ds. No where near people or saftey. We're stuck on the side of a highway with no sense of where we are. Or, where to go. The only sign of civilization are the zooming cars around us.

"Walk where, Jake? We can't just walk around like zombies. We need to know where we're going." I turn serious, shocked at my tone and sudden mood change.

"Where do you want to go?" He speaks calmly, making me feel as if I'm important.

Home. I want to go home. But I highly doubt I'll get there so I opt for,

"The police station."

"Are you sure about this? Remember what he did to those other cops?" He whispers as we enter the prestigious building. There is an air about it. I feel safe here. Well, that's what I hope.

We enter through the front doors, greeted by fast feet and heavy chatter. The lobby is huge but the further we walk the more packed it becomes. The building is full of officers. Some heavy set, some small. Others dorky while some are straight up Greek Gods.

A few of them brush past us, not even giving us a second glance. Rows of desks and cubicles outline the room. Looking to my left I see a huge portrait of Officers Tommy and Lori. It's a portrait in remembrance of them. It's beautiful.

My sad eyes lock to the floor while I fight off tears. I feel Jake gently grab my hand before moving us along.

"You tracked them down using a tracker in your van?"

We hear the unbelief in the man's tone, making us stop in our tracks. The words 'van' and 'tracker ' echo in my head.

"It clunked out on me but it led me to the interstate. I figured this would be the first place they'd go."

I hear Rich's husky, frantic voice. And then I see him. I see him slouched in a chair across from a buff looking officer. A detective.

"Are you sure? We do have a report of your daughter running away last June. She was found at a neighbor's house." He places his file in front of Rich.

With an exasperated look, Rich sighs.

"I checked there already. Look, I really need to find my kids. I haven't slept since I found them missing. My baby girl is only sixteen years old." His voice cracks, on the verge of crying. My stomach lurches from the pain in his half teary eyes. He misses me.

"Okay, here's what we can do. We can patrol the area. I'll send some of my guys out to look for them, okay?"

I don't even get a chance to see them shake hands because Jake pulls me out of there.

"We were in there for way too long. Someone probably saw us by now."

I remain quiet, contemplating our next move. Wherever we go next has to guarantee our safety. We had spent about forty five minutes walking to the nearest police precinct so we're tired. But we can't stop.

"He said he tracked us." I say in a low, timid voice. I can only assume that Rich must have reached the van while we were walking. He didn't find us inside so he came to a place he'd think we'd go. The police station.

"We're going to the hospital," He starts tugging me when I don't move.

We're a few blocks away from the police precinct. It's close but where we're standing- in an alleyway- keeps us well hidden.

I smile when I hear children laughing. My eyes wander around, observing the very thing I've missed for a year. I've missed my parents, friends, and even life itself.

I've missed the beauty of being free. Speaking of beauty, this town is very beautiful. The children play in the park across the street while the locals run errands. There's even a fountain in front of the courthouse and an array of colorful flowers decorate the outside. June is so lovely.

"Come on Livie. We have to go," He pulls my arm but I don't falter.

"No, they'll know we went there. Didn't you hear them? They're looking for us."

"Livie where else are we going to go?" His eyes plead with me. The way his lips frown downwards indicates dread. He knows what will happen when Rich finds us.

"Let's go."

"We can't go to a hos-"

I'm knocked off my feet by something hard. My head hits the ground so suddenly that I'm shocked my eyes are still even open. I should have been knocked out cold.

Sitting up without thought, I realize how much pain I'm in. Groaning loudly, I clutch my bleeding head while trying to calm my racing heart. Blinking a few times, I'm able to shake my blurry vision before I'm surrounded by people.

"Oh dear, are you alright?" An older woman with caramel skin and platinum gray hair asks.

"Who-wh-" I sigh frustratedly, unable to get my words out. Where am I?

"That guy came out of no where." One man says in awe.

"Yeah, that asshole didn't even stop to see if you were okay." Another woman with high cheekbones and hazel eyes shakes her head.

I'm about to stand up when I hear heavy panting in front of me.

"Are you...okay?" His arms wrap around me, making me frown in confusion. Why is he so concerned about me?

We spent the next thirty minutes waiting for the paramedics to finish examining me. Apparently, I got run over by a cyclist. Jake chased him down and he ending up apologizing. I bet a hundred bucks it was by force. The only "talking" Jake does is with his fist.

"We have to take her to the hospital." A medic starts strapping me to the gurney.

No. I can't go to a hospital. I won't because once I get there Rich will know where we are. And the sooner he knows where we are, the sooner he'll discover I'm pregnant.

I'm silent the entire time. Choosing not to speak because what I'm thinking will offend so many people right now. Including Jake. He can kiss my ass.

"It's not my fault you're here so stop glaring at me." He quips cooly. He is sitting in a chair beside my bed with his feet kicked up.

My eyes remain focused on his while I glare harder. He starts making kissy faces to stop my staring, and fortunately for him it works. My middle raises instead, making him laugh.

"Alright Olivia, we have your results."

I was told that I suffered a mild concussion from the impact of falling on the concrete. They took blood and examined my vitals. I flinched from the pain of the sharp, cold needle digging into my skin when the nurse drew my blood. I hate the sight of blood.

"Hmm," She lifts the paper from her clipboard. "I'd say you're in the last stage of your first trimester." Her full lips curve into a warm smile.

So I was right. I am pregnant. Shit, shit. shit. I want the baby but I don't want to suffer from Rich's cruel wrath.

"Can you say that again? In clearer terms?" Jake raises his brows.

"She is three months pregnant. Congratulations you two."

I roll my eyes when she smiles again. It's a creepy smile. The kind of smile that belongs in a horror film.

"We'll call your parents and get everything sorted out." The lean doctor with jet black hair, and light green eyes turns to leave but is stopped by someone entering.

"I came as soon I heard." He heaves urgently.

I have to blink a few times to bring myself out of my shock.

There he is standing in front of the door, looking worried. Looking like a concerned parent who just found their children.

He's still dressed in his interview attire. Except this time, everything is flustered. From his dress slacks with small rips in them to his once tucked in shirt, now scrunched out. His black tie hangs loosely around his neck, giving the impression of how stressed he is.

From there, I see his face. The face of evil. The same face that haunts my dreams as much as my reality.

"And who are you?" The finicky doctor questions.

"I'm their dad." He answers with eyes focused on me. My heart drops to my stomach while my fists grip the white sheets. I know that look. The look that says,

"You're in deep shit. You know it as much as I do."

The same look that grasps my soul and gives me chills at the same time.

28

CHAPTER 28

There is nothing to say because I'm literally speechless. This has to be a bad dream.

"Wait, you're their dad?"

His eyes never leave mine as he nods. And once again, I too, find it hard to look away.

"Are you sure? Because the boy said-"

"Yeah he's sure." I hear Jake speak up, causing suspicion to raise. I never noticed how close he is until now. Or how his hand latches onto my trembling one while we both anticipate our ill-fated future.

"Well, I'll need you to sign some forms then Mr. Rhodes." She swiftly moves her glasses from her heart shaped face to eye him sternly.

"Why?" Rich's coffee colored eyes divert from Jake to me. His hands are now in his pockets while his eyes remain narrowed at me.

"I'm not sure if you know it, but your daughter is pregnant. Three months to be exact so I think as parent you should look into alternatives." She makes a clear point to change her happy tone to solemnity. Just a minute ago she was beaming as if she were the one expecting. And now she is talking about alternatives? I'm not giving my baby up.

"Can we have a minute to um, talk?"

There is a bitter taste in my mouth. It rises and makes my mouth water. My frozen body relaxes just enough to force it back down.

"Sure," She turns to me with a half smile before pattering out of the room.

Collected, lax, at ease? Those are just a few words that would describe Rich's reaction right now. His eyebrows scrunch like Jake's when he ponders in thought.

"Why are you here, huh?" He addresses us both.

I can't form words...or proper thoughts. I'm terrified of him.

"I leave for an interview. Something that will make our lives better and you just run...again." He grits his teeth, trying to ease the tension.

"She got hurt so I brought her here." Jake speaks cautiously. Is he taking the blame for this?

Unforgiving dread fills my insides at the thought of what he could do to Jake.

"So you make the fucking decsisions now!" He growls while knocking the vase from my nightstand.

I jump from the sudden sound while my heart speeds up sevenfold. A firm grip on my hand assures me that he is still here. Still standing beside me.

"Uh, no sir but I-"

"If you want to leave then go. But just know that I'll find you then kill you to keep you quiet. Now Livie- Livie stays with me. She isn't leaving no matter what."

My trembling hand goes to wipe my eyes. I'm crying without realizing.

"I can't...leave?" This is insane. I've tried and still managed to fail. Why is life playing with me?

"I have custody of you so no, you aren't leaving," He goes into his pocket to retrieve the copy. The final copy.

"I already showed the documents to the authorities. They know you're my underage daughter." He confirms with a heavy sigh in satisfaction. A smirk plays at the corners of his thin lips.

No. He doesn't have custody of me because my mom and dad do. Or, they were supposed to.

The more my thoughts reel the more it all starts to sink in again. My parents were still separated when I was sixteen, so in retrospect my mom was the one with full custody of me. She and dad must have agreed to give her full custody since he and I were basically estranged.

It's still quiet until he speaks again,

"Speaking of underage...why the fuck are you pregnant?"

My chest heaves when he paces over to me. Anxiety overtakes me when I feel Jake move in front of me.

"We can talk-"

Rich grabs his collar so suddenly that I have to blink a few times to confirm what I'm seeing. With one quick movement, he punches him in his gut.

My hands cover my mouth in shock when Jake topples over in an agonizing amount of pain.

"I'm... not... talking... to ...you!" For every word he says, there is a bone shattering kick to go along with it.

I'm off the bed and heading towards the door at a high velocity. If I can try to get help then maybe we won't be taken away again.

My hand reaches for the knob but instead of grasping the knob, my palms hit the floor.

I scream and thrash, only to have my mouth concealed by his rough hand. No, no, no. Please no. My eyes water when I'm placed on my back and greeted by his sharp, sepia eyes. The way they capture my soul, the way they make me forget every previous thought imaginable is something that will forever astonish me.

Lifting me up, I latch onto his hands. The same hands that are wrapped around my neck in a vice grip.

As we walk toward the hospital bed, I'm able to see an unconsious Jake. His entire mouth is filled with blood while his body is crumpled like paper. Is he still breathing? Please be okay.

"Pregnant...this is un-fucking-believable." I squirm when he snakes one hand under my hospital gown. His nails dig into my tummy, making an invincible scream penetrate my quaking lips.

"Scream one more time and I'll snap your neck." He threatens plainly. His forearm is around my neck, squeezing to the point of suffocation.

I whimper when he presses into my trachea, forcing me to cough and wheeze.

With malicious eyes filled with monstrous intent he then says,

"Now, here's what's going to happen. One: you will abort it, two: I'll make you abort it, Three: if you don't choose an option I'll choose for you."

His voice is ominous. His stare is even more unfavorable. The way the air from his nostrils kisses my neck makes me cringe.

"What will it be, Livie?" He spins me to face him, daring me to answer.

I can't kill my baby. I can't murder another human being. This is cruel, unfair, illogical even. I don't understand his reasoning for this.

"Why do you want me to kill...him or her?" I swallow the lump in my throbbing throat. There is surely a bruise there.

"I already told you I want you, not a kid!" He shakes my shoulders so hard that I end up losing my balance. It's more of a shove, forcing my body to fall backward.

The cool tile floor feels amazing against my clammy skin, and for a moment I picture myself falling into a refreshing pool. Swimming freely without limits.

Coughing loudly, I clutch my stomach in a reflexive way. I wasn't prepared for the powerful blow that I feel now.

It's like someone just grabbed the inside of my stomach and twisted it around. I groan and cough loudly when I feel a second kick.

"What's going on in here?" I hear the voice of an angel speak.

Looking up with weary eyes, I confirm my hopes when I see the doctor running over to me. I've never been so happy to see a doctor in my life.

"I do everything I can to protect her and she goes off and gets pregnant!" He shouts like a concerned parent.

Everyone is quietly dissecting the situation. The way the few nurses and policeofficers stare at him leads me to believe they're buying his lie.

"Don't...believe him." My raspy voice fills the silence.

Everyone draws their attention to me, making anxiety rise again. Ever since my virginity was stolen I've felt more exposed than ever. Like I'm covered by a shear cloth. I feel my clothes on me but I whenever I- or someone else- looks at me I feel like they can see all of me. My entire body.

"He's trying to kill it! He's trying to kill his baby!" I sob dishearteningly while wrapping my arms around her. I need a hug. I need a hug from my mother. The doctor stiffens but quickly recovers to hug me back.

I hear a few more shouts and cursing before officers cuff him. They question him about Jake, who is now awake. Dazed but awake. They question him about my pregnancy and if it's true that he's the father. Jake and I sit patiently, waiting for him to be arrested until-

"These are the custodial papers. I have custody of Olivia because her mom gave her to me before she died." He lies.

An officer assesses the papers laid out on the bed.

"Then why is she telling us how you abuse and torture them. And how you fathered her child?" A tall man questions while analyzing the document.

"I don't know why they choose to lie. "He simply shrugs then turns to me.

"As her dad, I love her too much." A warm, sinister smirk decorates his face.

"A little too much," Jake rolls his eyes.

"And what about you, kid? Is he your dad too?"

Jake eyes them with caution. He wrinkles his nose in thought before sighing.

"Actually," The look in his green eyes hint of uncertainty before he smirks at me.

"Yeah, Olivia is my little sister. And I promised to protect her from that prick at all costs." He wraps his arm around my shoulder. Nervousness floods my insides when I see Rich glare at us.

"Officers, I apologize for this. My kids never seem to stay out of trouble. They seem more concerned with having me arrested." He sighs pitifully.

What? What the hell is happening? And why isn't Jake speaking up?

"Well Rich, that's how most teens feel about their parents. I'm sure things will turn around." The same officer who questioned him sides with him.

"Wait, aren't you going to arrest him?" I question. I'm angry now and I'm going to be heard.

"We're not going to arrest your father for being a father." He walks over to us and places his hands on our shoulders.

"Listen guys, it's obvious he is trying. And as a single dad myself I understand how he feels."

My heart beat pounds in my ears, drowning out everything else that man says. I don't know what I did wrong to deserve this.

"You're an adult?" One cop points to him. Her eyebrows raise in questionable doubt. Most adults find it hard to believe he and I are the ages we claim to be because of our size. We have both lost weight from not being fed.

They continue to converse while I remain numb. I'm depressed, discouraged and hopeless. I can't go back there.

"Uh, yes sir. I'm eighteen." I come back into the conversation when Jake squeezes my arm.

"Then you don't have to stay in the house with your father. He's not holding you against your will." He chuckles at his joke. Yeah it's funny to him but it's real life for me. I am being held against my will.

"Are you sure there is no possible way Livie can live with me?" He all but begs. The edge in his sexy voice is so strong and willful. He is trying to help me.

"Unfortunately, Mr. Rhodes has custody of her because she is still a minor. Now with you it's different. You're a legal adult. So are you going back home or do you want to stay with your dad and sister?"

Why aren't they helping us? Can't they see Rich is a wolf in sheeps clothing. His warm, fatherly smile is a fraud. Everything about him is deceitful.

"I'm not lying when I say he kidnapped us." I sad eyes linger on his piercing blue ones.

They spend the next hour asking us more questions. Rich is outside of the room being questioned while Jake and I stay seated on the hospital bed. They told us a few minutes ago that our story sounds very convincing and that they'd send someone to investigate.

"Investigate? We don't have time for that!" Jake clenches his fists, anger bubbling inside of him.

"Well, if your time is so valuable then you don't need us wasting it." The officer with balding hair- the same one we've been talking to- folds his arm intimidatingly.

"No! He didn't mean it like that." I have to convince them to do something. To help us.

"Then how did he mean it? Because our time is just as valuable as yours. We don't want to find out you kids are lying." The blue eyed man points at both with stern solemnity.

"We aren't lying. Just go to his house to see for-"

"That will take weeks, possibly months so you have to be willing to wait. Is this a high priority case?" He rubs his fat chin while in thought.

"It's top priority. Any idiot can see that." Jake insults, forcing a smile to creep up on my lips.

The chubby officer places his hands in his pockets then says,

"Look kids, in all honesty I don't see anything wrong here. I don't see any bruises or any other indication of abuse."

"How would you fucking know if you haven't checked us out yet?"Jake spits venomously. This is one time I'm happy that he speaks with no filter.

"I handle these cases all the time. I would know at first glance if you were being mistreated."

I'm not sure if this doofus is just blind or incredibly stupid. Either way, he is making his entire police force look like idiots.

"Are you serious?" I ask in disbelief.

"Don't get me wrong, you two seem like nice kids." He exhales. "But acting out because you can't get your way is not the way to go."

"Can't get our way?" Jake and I both utter in unison.

My leg shakes while I think. Do they think we're some spoiled rich kids who can't get our way?

The sound of his static filled radio resonates through the room. My head drops when I hear them say Rich is in the clear. Meaning he is off the hook.

"We'll be by next week for a house visit." They all leave us alone with the man they assume is our dad.

My head is still down and Jake is mumbling cuss words. He's probably more angry than I am. I mean I'm numb right now.

I jump when I hear the door close. I feel Rich's evil, austere presence. I hear his slow, creepy steps approach us. Should I just run? Crap, Rich is standing in front of us. I couldn't get out of here to save my life.

Glancing at Jake, I see his head down with slumped shoulders. I'm surprised he hasn't walked out by now. But then I realize why he is staying. To protect me. He is keeping his promise.

"Welp kiddos, looks like it's moving day." Rich clasps his hands together with a triumphant smile. His brown eyes flicker like a flame. He is deranged and I hate him.

Richard Rhodes took us out of the hospital that day and made sure we would never see daylight again. We moved to a secluded cabin in the woods. At first, I didn't really know where we were going because we were both blind folded and hog tied. All I could feel was the bumpy road underneath us, and all I could smell was burnt rubber and stale liquor- the smell of his van.

We drove for about fourteen hours. I know it seems a bit odd that I counted that but one thing I've learned from being with Rich was that time was a very valuable thing. So valuable that I developed a way to count and keep track of the seconds, minutes, and hours that passed.

Once we came to a stop I knew it was final because he opened the van doors to let us out. Normally if we stopped he'd always leave, not allowing us to come out or anyone to come in. Now this was a huge problem considering the fact that I'm pregnant. And pregnant girls pee a lot.

Anyway, I held my water for hours until Rich dragged us out of the van. That was my first time peeing on myself since I was three. It was so sudden that it even scared Rich. His crazy ass thought my water broke.

Of course I got a slap when he realized I was still pregnant. Ruthless bastard.

He continued dragging us up the steps and into the cabin. It only lasted five seconds but I reveled in those five seconds. The air was crisp and smelled of maple trees. I could tell we were somewhere up north because the air was cooler. It was June when we escaped the second time but now it felt like late September. Humid yet milder temperatures. And even in September, it wasn't this chilly in Florida. Nope, we had to be in a northern state.

He put us in the attic for a few months as a form of punishment. Jake was on one side of the room while I was on the other. We were so far apart that we couldn't even hold hands at night. Rich did it on purpose to make us more distant. He separated us so we couldn't rely on each other anymore, and sadly it worked. We started to argue constantly.

At first, it was about small things like my snoring. And then I couldn't take his nitpicking anymore so I said,

"Would you rather be here with a girl who snores or a slut who can't keep her legs closed?"

He retorted with a scoff and then,

"Takes one to know one. Right Olive?"

I remember seeing red. And if my body was a grenade I would have surely exploded. From that moment on, our arguing would turn into huge shouting matches We would wake up angry and go to bed angry.

He'd say things to piss me off like how he really doesn't like me. Or how he felt sorry for me. I knew he was talking out of frustration.

I knew he didn't mean it. I knew because I felt the same way. I didn't mean what I said when I told him he was just like Rich. Or when I called him a spoiled dick.

We had been starved for days and hunger makes you turn into a monster.

Anyway, the hopeless weeks turned into desolate months. Rich would come to feed us. But often times, he'd come upstairs to rape me in front of Jake. He knew there was nothing Jake could do because we were so far apart. He was in one corner of the room while I was in the farthest. I pitied Jake just as much as myself because he'd always feel bad after. He'd always blame himself. That alone made me realize he didn't hate me. He hated Rich and was taking his anger out on me. That did make me feel somewhat better. Somewhat.

Every time he'd come upstairs, I would stay silent, choosing not to speak. I wasn't going to be heard anyway. After the first time I realized that screaming would cause more pain. So I pretended to like it. I pretended to want him. But in reality, I was dying. My soul was deteriorating. And afterward, I would be so sick that I couldn't stop vomitting for three days.

Every night I would hope, pray, plead for someone to rescue us. But everyday provided the same results. No one was coming because no one knew where we were. The police couldn't perform the abuse investigation because of our move. Life as I knew it was over for me. And I longed to be free from it. I longed to be free from Rich.

"It's your lucky day, Livie." He smirks while grabbing my ankle.

Oh no. Is it that time? No, it can't be. I'm not due until December thirty first. Or, so I thought.

"Up ya go."

My entire body stiffens while I shake my head. Tears flow down my red cheeks when he lifts me up. I clutch my bulging tummy while begging him.

"No, no, no." I know what he is planning to do and I know it won't end well for my baby.

He continues dragging me out of the room and down the stairs. My wobbly legs struggle to move because I haven't walked in so long. I'm stiff, sore, and tired from my pregnancy and I need relief. I need relief from this monster.

"Aw, don't tell me you aren't ready." He chuckles.

"Just...just take me to a hospital." I plead with sincerity. I need a hospital. I can't just give birth without a doctor.

"But it's snowing outside babe. And besides, isn't this what you wanted?" He lays me on the bed before closing the door.

Christmas is in a few days and his idea of a Christmas gift is cruel. If I give birth without proper care I could die, and so could my baby. I'm really nervous and afraid. I'm only eighteen and I've never given birth before. Where do I even start? Do I push when I feel a contraction? And when does my water break?

Oh shit. Why did I just think that? I Feel liquid underneath me, making my panic heighten. What do I do? I haven't even been to a doctor in seven months. I have no idea how I'm going to deliver this baby.

"I didn't want..." I swallow dryly when he puts his finger to his lips.

With eyes that have stolen my soul time and time again, he narrows them at me. The dark glint frightens me to my core. He is corrupted so therefore he has corrupted me.

"You wanted to have a baby so that's what you're going to fucking do." His lips curve sadistically while my body trembles unrelentlessly.

29

CHAPTER 29

One year later.

Sweat pours from my body the faster he rams himself into me. I feel like I'm in a sauna. A hot, stifling, merciless bath of flames. My body is on fire and the worst part is that it won't be extinguished anytime soon.

Pain.

That word was the realest word I've come to know. Pain is something natural. Something that is inevitable. Just like death. Everyone experiences pain; everyone has scars, things that taint them. And everyone has to die. It's a part of our messed up lives.

Pain is the one emotion that familiarizes itself with everyone. It doesn't discriminate. It just latches onto you, like a leech sucking the blood out of you. Sucking the life out of you. Too much pain leads to death and death frees you. That's all I wanted. All I needed, because death was my freedom. My only escape. That was until he-

An insuperable sensation overcomes me, making my body move purposefully and my thoughts sweep away like dust in a breeze. I feel myself slowly succumbing to the sensual movements he is performing on my bruised bottom. His aggressive hands claim me lustfully while I bite my lip to restrain myself.

He smirks daringly at me, knowing exactly what he is doing.

"Love..."

"You..."

"Feel..."

"Amazing..."

He whispers things in my ear, things as foul as he is. But I ignore him.

Instead of listening to his pointless lies, I focus my attention on the ceiling fan. It spins as briskly as my mind. My body is out of sync but my mind is still here. I'm able to feel every foul touch, and hear every animalistic sound he makes. From the creaky bed rocking against the wall to the pleasured grunts attacking my ears. Every bit of this is always leaves a horrible remnant. My tears are the only things that can escape.

My toes curl while my arms tighten around his neck. He's pushing to the limit now and I'm beginning to think it's done on purpose. My walls have already expanded and the more he pushes the harder it is for me to breathe. I find myself slowly slipping away. Slowly losing consciousness. Waiting to die.

That is until my throat betrays me. My eyes widen while I release a strained cry. Tears visible on my cheeks when he pulls my hair harder.

"Wake the fuck up and stop crying."

Swallowing my anxiety and fear as best I can, I nod quickly. Last time I passed out, he waited until I woke up to tell me that every hour I was out would be the number of days without going outside. I was out for two hours.

My body jerks while I blink rapidly, afraid that I might have passed out. I actually look forward to my thirty minutes outside each day. Even if Rich is there with me.

With my bare back pressed against the headboard in an upright position, I realize he moved us. His large hands coast my bottom all the way to my exposed chest. I've grown now and I embrace my curves. Let's just say that I'm not a scrawny sixteen year old anymore.

He kisses my neck ever so gently, allowing me to tilt my head back. I have to act like I enjoy this.

He continues rubbing and sucking my skin until stopping abruptly. It's as if he just had an epiphany.

With a cunning smirk and glistening, lucid chestnut eyes he orders me to spread further. I stay stock-still, not wanting to. I can't because I've gone as far as I can go. My sore legs are around his waist while he continues holding them genitively.

"Livie, if I have to say it again I'll make sure you won't be walking for a few days."

My throat burns and my body quakes fervently from his chilling threat. I'm sore all over and too tired to do this. Why does he want to hurt me?

Twenty nine minutes.

The bed continues to squeak with each powerful thrust. He moans in pleasure the deeper his erection slides into me. Closing my eyes, I grit my teeth while my nails dig into his perspired skin; sparkling like stars in the night sky.

It could be worse. I tell myself. Just go numb. Don't feel anything.

But instead of feeling nothing, I go from feeling like I'm sinking in quick sand to a drill digging into the sidewalk. The headboard is rocking with powerful force, banging against the wall speedily.

He loves this. He loves the feeling of me. Not me. But I don't love any of it. Not even myself at this point.

"You...can do...better...than that." He whispers huskily. My tense body jumps when I feel him slap my bruised side.

It's my right side, the same side that was pushed into the tip of the counter a week ago. That was the day I mentioned her birthday. The same day he came home drunker than a skunk and decided to take his anger out on me...again.

Rich pinches my side, making me moan. But my supposed "moan" turns into an instant a high yelp. I feel my chest heave unrelentlessly when he slows to a stop. He removes his face from the crook of my neck while his hand slowly trails upward. I wince when his hand clasps around my throat.

He doesn't have to say anything because the evil, vile look in his essonite eyes speaks for themselves. It's so powerful and dominating that I struggle to speak.

"I'm...I'm so- sorry but you were hurting me!"

My trembling hands grip his tightly while he squeezes my neck.

"Stop acting, Livie. I know you love this just as much as I do so stop groaning like this is the worse thing in the world." He commands, killing my already dead mood.

It would be perfect if I loved this or him. It would be easy to allow myself to utter moans of desire if I loved him. But I don't. I can't and I won't.

I've tried to trick Rich. I've tried to pretend like I was moaning. But the more violent he became, the more difficult it became to continue the lie. My body was yearning to flee from the aches and throbs that he inflicted upon me. I needed to release it but whenever I did it always sounded like a dreadful groan instead of a satisfied moan. I groan from the unbearable ail and Rich hates that.

So, instead of making a sound I choose to stay quiet. The quieter I am the sooner he'll finish. And once he is done I'll finally be able to sleep. I'll sleep until a nightmare startles me awake.

His eyes never leave mine as he grip on my neck loosens.

"You're all I have, Livie. I can't lose you."

Closing my dull, frightened cerulean eyes, I lift my hands to claim my previously restricted throat.

Inhaling shakily, I try to calm down until I feel my arms being lifted above my head.

Thirty eight minutes.

Our eyes linger on each others while his fingertips trail down my sides. Once he's done, I try to bring my arms down but he stops me.

"Keep them up."

We're still in the position he placed us in. His knees dig into the mattress while my back remains pressed against the wood headboard. He's still holding me,

"If you can keep your arms above your head without flinching, screaming, or shaking then I'll be kind enough to let you finish." He smirks at me, making my heart flutter. His eyes shine while he runs his fingers through his ruffled hair.

Rich has the potential to look really good if he'd just ditch the crazy act.

"But..I always flinch." I mumble in defeat. I know this game. The same game he's been playing this past year. He knows he'll win and he knows I'll always be left with unfinished business.

"Is it because I use a knife?"

He doesn't need to wait for a reply because he already knows the answer. I've been terrified of knives ever since the first time he slit my throat.

"Well, don't worry. This time I want to swim just as bad as you do."

I hate how he knows my deepest thoughts. My secret desires.

Despite the pain, there was a point when he did make me feel good. He knows I haven't reached my climax yet- in fact, I can still feel my area throb with want while the overflowing juices drip from me. As fucked up as it sounds, I need this release. Just in a less excruciating way.

He goes over to a secluded part of the dimly lit room. The room we're in isn't large. It's average. There aren't any decorations nor are there any currtains. Only blinds. A full size bed sits in the middle of the room while a small night stand sits on my side. The right side. The wallpaper is old enough for a fifties decor magazine, and provide nothing to this room except depression.

"This should both give us what we want." He sighs before inhaling whatever is in his hand.

Steady is my breathing while my eyes narrow in curiousity.

And then he turns around.

Looking down, I see a tiny baby wrapped in my arms. Her blue eyes with small specks of brown slowly close. I smile at how beautiful she looks. Like an angel. My little angel. From there, I notice a small button nose. My dad's nose. Smiling to myself, my eyes land on her attractive rosy cheeks and tiny yet full pink lips like me.

Her small strands of brown hair sit neatly atop her head, complimenting her already radiant beauty.

I, Olivia Kelly Walters has a baby now. Wow. I wonder what Margaret, Kelly, and Nathan will think. I wonder how I'm going to get all three of us out of here now.

I hear Rich walk over to us. He takes her from me to give her a small light pink blanket. The gesture is nice but it still doesn't dismiss the fact that I could've died twelve hours ago.

"Just keep her warm." He hands her back to me then stands in front of us with his hands in his pockets.

I cradle her while watching him.

His eyes are closed while he deliberates. Not moving, not troubled. Showing absolutely no emotions whatsoever, and making me more anxious.

"Look at it!" He shouts with such ferocity that my own thoughts scatter. My hands grip the sheets while I forbid my mind to think about it.

Grabbing my chin, he forces my head up. His fingers press into my skin but I still keep my eyes shut. I don't want to see it. Once was enough.

"We're addressing this now without you attacking me." He breathes out while pulling me closer to him. Our bare bodies touch, filling my cheeks with heat. Too much heat. Too much warmth. I need to feel cold. I need to be cold.

He is now seizing my body in a tight grip while my soul pours out. His arms wrap around my waist, rocking us gently.

"Police! Get your hands off of her!"

Rich freezes for a second. And in that small amount of time I'm able to feel his fingers curl into my flesh. This means something but I don't know what.

"Don't turn this into something worse Richard. Let go of her."

His hands never leave my waist when he pulls away from me. I notice the self- indulgent look in his eyes. The look that is holding me captive. Pain. Pain is clear as day in his eyes. Just like in mine. He rubs his thumb on my cheek then sighs heavily, fanning my face with a mixture of my vanilla scent and his light aftershave.

"Off the bed. Now!" The person commands.

I feel his once relaxed muscles tense and then he kisses me on my lips. It's light yet still impactual. How do I feel? Fear, relief, stoic? I don't know.

"Love between two people can have limits, Livie. Even if that limit is death,"

I don't have time to process what he just said because the bone chilling sound of a gun being fired fills my ears.

Screaming loudly, I feel a heavy body fall on me. His body falls on me, causing me to fall back on the bed. Crimson liquid pours from his chest onto me, staining the bed and everything else inside of me.

"Stay still, Olivia." One agent commands. They are all dressed in black uniforms with guns aimed to shoot.

The cool air from the open door forces me to involuntary shiver. Rich is covering my sporadically beating chest. My terrified eyes linger on the grim scene before me.

A nest of guards surround the entire room, probably the outside too, while Rich lies motionless on top of me. I'm not sure if he's even breathing. Wait, am I even breathing?

The slow, thick liquid alarms me to where it all sinks in. They shot him. His blood is all over me, covering me like a blanket.

"Get him... off! Get...get him off...of me!"

A few run over to me while another is ordered to check his pulse.

I'm still hyperventilating when they turn him over. I watch in astonishment, not noticing that someone has covered me. I'm now protected by a wool blanket.

Is this real? Am I really being saved? My mind goes to something else. It embraces the feeling of cool air sinking into my hot, clammy skin. It embraces the glorious sounds of police entering.

And then I hear shouting.

"Get her to an ambulance!"

The shouts get louder, forcing me to try to sit up to see the source of the commotion. I cry out in agony when I struggle to move my legs. I didn't realize I was in such an irrefutable amount of pain. I can't even move.

"Can you walk, sweetheart?" One agent moves my head to face her. I don't how they got in or where they came from but I'm so thrilled they're here.

My arms extend to hug her. I hold her in a death grip while thanking her repeatedly.

"Come on. We'll take you to a hospital."

I scream when I try to close my blood infested legs. They're still spread, only this time they're covered by the blanket.

"How long have you been..." She trails off, unsure of how I'll react. She helps me slide into some black sweats.

"I don't...know. I lost count... after forty... two minutes." I pant loudly, trying to fight through the aching pain in my vagina. My throat feels drier than a desert and my body is excreating enough water to create a new ocean.

"You counted?" She asks quizzically while helping me into a pink tank top.

This time I'm up, barely able to stand. My knees tremble, threatening to give out. The blood on my legs stain the sweats and I'm instantly grateful she gave me black instead of gray.

"It's...the only...way...to take...my mind...off of it."

I've always had to make it seem like I enjoyed this. Like all of my pain didn't exist because I felt pleasure. Every moan, sensual movement, and pleasure filled scream was a front.

Underneath it all was a scared girl in an undeniable amount of pain. And if Rich found out I was hurting, he'd hurt me more. He'd cause more pain thinking he was only relieving me.

"Is there anyone else in here?" One officer addresses me with a concerned expression.

"Check...check the basement."

Another stream of blood flows down my legs, making me feel as if I peed on myself. It's similar to how I felt when I gave birth to- No Livie. Forget it. Forget everything that prick has done to you. You're safe now. You're free and you don't have to live with it anymore. Nodding to myself, I close my eyes to keep myself from remembering. I have to forget.

Looking up, I catch a few officers stare in utter disbelief. It's hard to believe that a nineteen year old girl has been trapped here for three years; being raped by a man who has kidnapped her only because she reminds him of her mother.

"Go look in the basement!" I shout, on the verge of panicking. A few move while others remain focused on getting me downstairs. I always forbode this activity because it hurts so much.

"Who is down there?" The same woman asks in sympathetic concern. She has given me a jacket to wear because it's cold outside.

"My friend..."

Jake's been down there for three days now. He tried to protect me again and failed. Rich beat him unconscious.

Ever since that day in the hospital he has been trying to fight for me. He promised he wouldn't let Rich hurt me and most times he has fullfilled that promise. Instead of leaving me in the hospital he stayed. He stayed here with me because he knew I couldn't leave. He knew Rich had custody of me. But now that I'm nineteen I can finally leave. I'm finally free.

Stepping out into the cool, January air I notice a huge group of people perched outside of the house. A line of reporters. There's yellow tape that separates them from me.

Shouts and camera flashes attack my face, forcing me to blink a few times.

"Olivia, are you okay? Can you tell how you're feeling right now?"

"Are you and Mr. Rhodes in love?"

"Olivia Walters. Is that even your real name?" Another asks.

"Are you the girl who went missing three years ago?" They feed off each other's questions.

They escort me to a police cruiser until the ambulance can arrive. My feet are frozen from the snow but I don't care. I need to cool off. A small breeze uproots tiny strands of my wavy blond hair, making small shivers run down my spine. Something isn't right. Pulling my blanket tighter, I allow my eyes to search for Jake.

"Where's Jake?" My raspy voice fills the cloudy air.

"We took him to the hospital." Is all she says before I hear another familiar voice.

"Olivia!" A tall, lean woman with short brunette hair runs over to me.

"Aunt Casey?" I strain to see her. I haven't seen her since Waylan's funeral.

Most people say that my aunt and I are the complete opposite. And not just in looks. But I wouldn't really know because I haven't seen her in so long. She went to New York after my brothers' funeral.

"I'm sorry Olivia, I'm so sorry this took so long. I was overseas with my agency but I came as soon as I heard." She grabs me and starts bawling her eyes out. Her slender arms wrap around me tightly. I hug her back, happy to be with my family again. She is the closest thing to family for me.

A loud, chaotic voice erupts, making my heartrate spike again. I pull away, not caring about the hurt look on her face.

I see Rich on a gurney, tied down like a prisoner of war. I see his chest heave in and out while his once closed eyes open. His haunting brown eyes lock on mine for a second before he whispers,

"I'm not losing you like Mia."

Everything is frozen- and not from the snow. My rigid body remains trapped in panic and fear. I'm freaking out and not many people are noticing.

"What? What is it?" Her large, hazel eyes latch onto my scared form. This is the first time I've seen my playful aunt turn serious.

Should I tell her? Did I even hear what I think I heard? He said he isn't losing me like my mom. I heard him mumble that.

"Is it him? Because he's unconscious Olivia. He isn't going to hurt you anymore." She assures in a motherly tone.

By this time, I'm too enamored with what he said to notice that I'm being lifted onto a gurney. The loud sirens mix with my troubled thoughts, drowning out my peace of mind. He's alive while I'm still dead on the inside.

30

CHAPTER 30

I can't sleep. Three words that annoy the hell out of me. Actually, I don't really think it's the words. It's the fact that I can't close my eyes. I can't drift off into a safe, peaceful dreamland because I have way too much on my mind. And it's difficult to sleep over the sound of your own thoughts.

"Olivia,"

Oh, and the hospital too. It's really hard to sleep here. They come in like thieves in the wee hours of the night to poke and prod me. You'd think I was some government experiment with the way I'm kept here.

"This is Doctor Wilkes. He'll be assessing you today."

Here we go again.

Groaning loudly, I shift onto my side to face the window. I'd rather face away from them because they'll get my messsage quicker. Leave me alone.

"It's just a discussion about your surgery and how well it went." The bubbly nurse with the shrill voice says excitedly.

Oh yeah. I had to go into surgery as soon as I arrived because I suffered from heavy internal and external bleeding. My vaginal ligaments were torn so badly that they had to perform a procedure to fix it.

Thankfully, the bleeding has stopped and it's less painful to walk. The doctors and nurses explained how miraculous it was for me to have survived all of that. He went on to tell me that most girls who experience severe tearing can't have anymore kids. I still can though. But do I want to?

"Actually, it's not so much about your surgery, Olivia. It's about what I examined during it."

I sit up quickly, only to realize that my sudden movement has caused a steady ache in my head. I rub my forehead gingerly while giving him my undivided attention. This sounds serious.

Sensing my acceptance to hear him out, he says,

"The wounds on your wrists concern me." His gray eyebrows raise while he anaylzes my face.

"Wounds on my wrists?" I frown in confusion, not thinking to check the very place he is talking about.

"You know I meant scars." He shakes his head with a small chuckle.

"Oh those. They're nothing serious. That was a long time ago." I admit sheepishly.

It was a darker time in my already shitty life. I was depressed everyday, and couldn't keep anything down. Now they're healed, only scars remain. I shudder while trying to supppress the awful memory. But once again, my mind wanders away.

My legs swing over the bed and with a tired sigh, I grab some advil off the nightstand. Last night he was violently rough. Nothing like how he was before. He was so much more worse because he walked in on me cutting. He was angry because I tried to off myself.

I've never been one to contemplate suicide or even go through with it.

But last night was different. Something in me snapped and I couldn't bear it anymore. I couldn't even bear to think about it so my mind focused on my other problems. They'll all be resolved.

At first I thought I could keep this up. This pretending to be in love with him but I can't. I can't keep making him think I love him when I don't, because that just makes him lust after me more.

So an hour before he was supposed to come home I decided to take myself out of here. I decided to rid the world of terrible me. I couldn't take it anymore. The pain, the hurt, the anger. I just couldn't carry it all so I went to the bathroom and-

"How are your wrists?"

His fingertips trail my spine, making me clench my fists. My throbbing wrists scream at me but I push the pain away. I mentally stop myself from feeling it. Now, I just want to punch someone. I've gone from fearful to vengeful. There is so much hate in me now that I'm surprised I'm able to be in the same room with him. I don't think I've ever hated someone as much as I hate Rich.

"You promised not to hurt yourself." The bed creaks from him sitting up. Over the raspy, tired voice he sounds genuinely concerned. But I don't fall that easily. Last night he was a completely different person. He was livid, and now he is calm? No, he's crazy.

"Leave me alone. I just want to be alone." I whisper with sorrow filled eyes. My eyes won't even shed tears anymore. That's how much I've cried.

"I'm trying Livie. Trying to make our lives better. What happened to Reyna was for the best. Please try to understand, babe." His poisonous words slide off his tongue so easily that I can't hide the shudder that swims through my veins.

It disturbs me how he can be okay with this. A week old infant doesn't just die in her sleep. Does she?

"How can you say her death was for 'the best'? How can you just pretend like you didn't do anything wrong?" I turn to him with ill intent in my tear brimmed eyes. It's been a few days since her supposed death, and a part of me still feels like she's here. I feel like my baby is here with me; her momma.

"You're stressed and tired all the time. I did you a favor." His false concern makes me want to play darts. Only this time, knives are my darts while his eery face is the target.

"What did you just say?" I narrow my eyes while clenching my already bruised jaw.

"I said it's not good being stressed about her death." He tries to reach for my hands but I jump off the bed, giving us space apart.

"No. You said you did me a favor." I call him out on his lie. I've had enough of this. The lying, the scheming, and the way he tries to justify his hellacious actions.

Before this, I was prepared to try to raise my baby until I could escape. But now escape and freedom are gnawing at me. Waiting for me to jump at the chance to leave. A chance that never comes.

"Yeah, I knew you couldn't handle seeing her like-" He stops mid sentence then closes his eyes. I've learned what that means. He is trying to calm himself.

My heart pounds when he paces toward me, sending my scared frame to the wall. With his palms pressed against the gray colored wall, I watch him lean his forehead on mine.

"She's buried out back, if you want to see her." He sighs sadly, not meeting my gaze.

I try to fight it. I try so hard to keep my emotions under control, but everytime I think about her lifeless body I falter. I carried her for almost ten months. This life was growing inside of me. A life that Rich and I created.

When I first conceived I was terrified. I was afraid of having a kid and mostly afraid of him finding out.

But then, when I felt her kick for the first time I knew I would love her forever. My baby was the only family I had and now she is gone. Just like my parents, she is dead too.

My eyes close as I feel myself overheating. This is so wrong. This is so messed up. My body trembles with violent outrage the more my infectious thoughts spread. I want to see her alive, not buried in the backyard like some lost pet.

"Oh, and I left this for us to remember her by."

My eyes remain closed as I'm met with a shower of nostalgia. I need my daughter here with me. I need to hold her and protect her. I need to keep her from being afraid like me.

"Livie, just look at it."

Rich told me she died in her sleep a few days ago but I refused to believe it. I couldn't believe that a week old infant could just pass away without any explanation.

I spent that entire day searching the house for her. But once day turned to night, I began to realize that she was gone. Dead. So, in that moment I decided I wanted to die too. Her death was my real breaking point.

My chest heaves when I see the light pink blanket in his hands. It still has her and my dried blood all over it. The light carmine color tortures my soul and taunts my thoughts. The stains leaving unwanted memories in its' wake.

I remember. It was the same blanket he covered her with after I gave birth to her.

"Wh-why?" I begin to sob while sliding the down the wall. Burying my head in my hands, I cry louder. Why would he show me this?

"Look at your fucking wrists, Livie!" I jump from his sudden crescendo but my head stays buried.

"I said look at your wrists!" He shouts again, making me look up. It alarms me to the point where I automatically hug myself. I'll never see her again. I'll never get to hold her or rock her to sleep. Her death came too soon and I feel like I failed her. I failed my daughter because I couldn't protect her. It's not her fault though,-

"It's your fault my wrists are like this not hers!" I know what he is trying to do. He thinks accusing my Reyna will solve this. Well he's wrong. Everything bad that has happened to me is and will always be his fault.

"I'm not losing you! Not to her, not to that bastard of a nephew, and not to anyone else!"His hands grip my shoulders, locking me in place. My wide eyes continue to spill tears the more I think. He killed her. He killed her because he didn't want her taking his place.

"You're a sick bastard and I hope you rot in hell!" I push him away from me to run to the bathroom.

If I can make it there then I can lock myself in and finish what I started. The razor blade is hidden under a rotted floorboard. Something he knows nothing about.

"Don't turn your back to me when I'm talking to you." He growls before yanking my arm. I'm brought back to him and then spun around to face his muderous face.

It happens so quickly that I don't even get a minute to gather myself.

Before I can cower, a large fist connects to my jaw. My body falls to the ground and before I can get up, my back is being stepped on.

I'm being crushed by his boot. My head is pressed between him and the floor.

"We're going to address this now!" His thunderous voice sends my quaking body squirming.

"I didn't kill her and I'm not letting you kill yourself!" He roars venomously.

A small pinch attacks my tingling scalp when he lifts me up. I'm now pressed to him while he inhales my hair. From there, he lets his tainted lips plant a firm kiss on mine.

All I can do is remain deathly still because I've grown accustomed to it. This is what he does. He hits me then expects me to forgive him because of a false apology and a few foul kisses.

"I'm sorry, Livie. I shouldn't have snapped at you like that." I feel claustrophobic when he engulfs me in a tight embrace. His arms are entrapping me while my head remains pressed to his chest.

"I've just been on edge lately. It's been stressful trying to keep you happy and keep my job."

I stay quiet, sobbing into his shirt.

"I've already lost Mia and I can't lose you. I won't fail you." He exhales, fanning my nape with warmth.

He may claim to love me but deep down inside we both know how untrue that is. And even though he claims he is innocent, I still get the feeling that we both know how untrue that is.

I'm brought back to reality when a hand is placed on my shoulder.

"Olivia, if you keep this up then I'm afraid your ass is going to die." He states blatantly, getting straight to the point.

Doctor Wilkes is one of those doctors who tries to have a filter but fails drastically. I don't mind it though beause I'm just as messed up as him.

"Shit, you're on to me." I grin at his frown of diaspproval.

"This is serious, Olivia. I'm concerned and I just want to know that you'll be safe when we release you." His frownlines are as clear as imprints in the sand.

I've been here for a few days now and I just want to leave. Aunt Casey wants me to move in with her but I don't know if that's a good ideas. I've heard stories about her outrageous parties. Not to mention her gig as a model. She's been modeling in France for five years.

I still have no idea why she wants to take in a depressed nineteen year old. That still baffles me.

"If I feel that you're still not ready then we'll keep you here longer. I know you love low sodium pizza and low sugar vanilla cake." He smiles timidly, knowing I hate this place just as bad as adults in crocs.

"I'll be okay once you release me." I've promised myself I wouldn't go back to that. I cringe, remembering the pain after. Sore, blotched and bloody. Ugly incisions decorating my already fragile skin. I don't want that again. I already have to worry about covering these.

Dr. Wilkes spent the rest of his time checking my vitals. You know, heartrate, blood pressure, weight, height, etc.

I was even allowed a shower instead of a sink bath. And once I was out I was given a clean gown, some more tasteless food, and the nurse re-dressed my wounds.

"He must have been one fucked up man to make you resort to that." He mumbles before sliding out of the door. Another thing I've learned about Dr. Wilkes. His opinions are as brash as his exits.

After my assessment, the local police department came to visit. They bought me flowers and a large pink teddy bear with the word 'Survivor' on it.

Once I took pictures and thanked them, I took the opportunity to speak to the lady who helped me walk out of that awful prison.

I remembered her curly, dark brown hair and light mocha skin. I didn't realize how pretty she is until now. Her hair is pulled back into a ponytail, revealing a feminine, oval shaped face with low cheekbones.

Her bright, golden eyes pop while her bright smile illuminates the room, and the few male officers around her. It's a pity she doesn't even realize it. Just like my friend Margaret. Most guys at our school had a secret crush on her because of her personality alone. Kelly had the looks but Margaret oozed perfection with her loveable aura.

"How ya feeling?" She stands with her hands in her pockets, eyeing me cautiously. Her stance is just as broad as her shoulders.

"Better." I smile when she pats my shoulder.

It's loud for a few seconds until she kicks them out. They all look terrified of her and I suspect that she's more than a pretty face. She's a team leader.

"Now it's better." She sits down beside me before continuing.

"Now, I know this might be the last thing you want to here but trust me you need to hear it." She stares at me with concern.

I know what this is about. And she's right, I don't want to here it but I need to.

"Rich has been in jail for three days now. It's only because we're waiting for the judge to give us his arraignment date."

I know what that means. They're waiting to see when he goes to court so they can end their case sooner. The sooner he goes to court the sooner he'll be sentenced.

"But don't worry. He's not getting out of this. He'll be arrested and charged with you and Jake's kidnapping. Then, he'll be set to stay in jail for a long time without parole." She explains viably. Her happiness seems to linger more than mine at the moment.

"What about my parents and Jake's dad?" And my baby.

"What about them?" She asks with raised brows.

"They're dead because he killed them." I admit solemnly. He'll get more time on murder charges, that's why they have to charge him with murder.

She sighs then says,

"We've already looked into those cases from the Glennville area. The coroner deemed them as suicides."

Suicides? No, that isn't right. My parents were screwed up but they were never suicidal. I know that for a fact.

"But he told me he killed my dad."

This makes her lean back in her chair while rubbing her chin. I'm hoping my statement makes her think. I hope this makes her rethink their case.

"Olivia, I'm sorry but there is nothing we can do about it. That was over three years ago and handled by Florida authorities. The case is closed. Now what we can do is arrest him on kidnapping, sexual assualt, and fraud charges. "

My shoulders slouch in defeat while I wipe my teary eyes. There has to be some way.

"Where am I now?" I ask in a low voice.

"Just a few miles outside of Harrisburg, Pennsylvania."

I need to get back to Glennville to prove he murdered them. If I can prove he's a murderer too then he'll definitely receive the death penalty. Yes, I want Rich to die. I want him to die over and over again because he has killed me over and over again.

Her phone rings. It's a catchy tune but I don't know the exact name of the song. It's been three years since I've had my IPod or even listened to the radio. I miss music so much.

"Olivia,"

Looking up, I have to blink a few times to realize she is standing at the door.

"I'm sorry but I have to cut this visit short. Got a call from my daughter's school. I left my number on your table so just phone me when you need me." She smiles politely then leaves.

Once she is gone I'm forced back to my thoughts. And I'm forced to weigh my options: move to New York with my Aunt Casey and move on with my life. Or atleast try to.

Or, move back to Florida to show them how much of a liar Rich is.

Once the sun started to set, I decided that now would be the best time to sneak out to find Jake. If I'm going back to Florida I'll need his help.

Walking through the sterile halls is surpsisinlgy smooth sailing for me. The nurses on my floor were too busy flirting with the male doctors. I couldn't help but laugh when one told him she'd look better on him than his white coat would.

They didn't hear me which made it so much easier to get to my location quicker; the nurses station so I could search the files.

Luckily, his room is a few down from mine. 335A.

I'm a little nervous because this is the first time I'll be seeing him since we were separated. I wonder if he's even awake now. Hypothermia is serious stuff.

The door is already cracked so all I have to do is just push it open. With my hand on the knob, I take a deep breath, trying to fight off the nagging nerves overtaking me. I'm anxious, scared, and hesitant to see him again, but I need to do this. I need his help. Plus, I think he's the reason why the police were able to find us. And for that, I want to thank him.

But before I can enter, I hear voices. Whispering voices. Jake must still be asleep.

"So what do we do?"

"Just tell him. It's not some big secret anymore." The guy sounds like he doesn't care much about anything.

"No, I'll tell him when he's ready." She decides.

The sudden motion of the door swinging open sends me stumbling back. I feel a small hand clutch my wrist, preventing me from falling on my ass, and making me wince slightly.

"Hey, aren't you the girl who was in that freak's house with my Jay bae?" She frowns in a somewhat sympathetic manner. I should be bothered by her curtness but I'm not. I'm more agitated with the stupid nickmane she gave him; Jae bae. I cringe even thinking about it. At least mine- Jakey cakes sounds better.

"What are you doing at his door?" She raises her perfectly waxed brows while crossing her fit arms. I notice how toned they are and come to the conclusion that she is the typical, cliche cheerleader. But she's no longer in high school. She's in college.

"Hello, do you speak?" Her eyes, the color of sapphire glare into mine with annoyance.

"Don't be so rude, Gia. She's probably here to see if he's okay. Right, Olivia?" His naive, blueish green eyes dart from Gia to me. This must be Jackson, his older brother. They have similar looks. Dark hair, green eyes, narrow bridged noses, and full lips. Jackson is just an inch or too taller, and less active from the looks of it. His dark rimmed glasses sit perched on the bridge of his nose while he smiles warmly at me, revealing his dimples. I conclude that he must be the studying all day and night type.

Gia sighs, knocking me out of my thoughts.

"Do you want to see him or not?" I notice her eyes roll while she removes her jet black bang from her model like face. She's prettier than I am, and she knows it. She reminds me of someone I used to know. Someone I was best friends with. Kelly Adams.

"Uh, yeah." I swallow my nerves quickly. Hoping she doesn't notice. People like her feed off of my fear so I need to do my damndest to hide it.

It's been quiet. Too quiet. I think I may have interrupted something because Jackson won't even look in his brother's direction while Gia keeps glaring at me.

I swear I'm about to slap her. She shouldn't be glaring at me. I never did anything to her- Oh wait.

My eyes shift from Jake, who is sleeping peacefully, to Gia, who is now holding his hand. I'm forced to watch her caress and coddle all over him. A small form of envy tries to creep up but I suppress it. I can't be jealous. She had him first. She may not deserve him but she did have him first.

Dammit, have I turned into one of those girls? The same girls I despise? The ones who fight over a boy. Oh no, oh no, oh no.

But wait, is he even a boy? No, he's a man. He's a very sexy man who can take me all over again.

Shit, did I just think that? He's in a relationship with the female devil.

Without a second thought, I quickly turn on my heel and speed walk out the door.

I shouldn't have visited him. What was I thinking? Even if he did wake up he wouldn't glance twice in my direction. He loves Gia. That much is clear. And I doubt he'll want to help me now that she's here.

I slip into my room and back into bed. Snuggling in the blankets I sigh heavily because I don't know what to do anymore besides try to sleep.

31

CHAPTER 31

My heart thuds in my chest the longer I stare into his grave eyes. With the way my heart is beating, I wouldn't be too surprised if joggers were jogging on my chest.

It heaves sporadically while streams of sweat continue to flow down my entire body. I'm beyond nervous and anxious. I'm petrified. He can't do this. He can't expect me to give birth like this.

"Please..." I sniffle, trying to control my sobs. I need to convince him to take me to a doctor.

"Just take me to a hospital." I breathe out tiredly. I've been trying to breathe like how they do in movies but it's not working.

My terrified frame jerks when he grips my arms violently, making a point to cause pain.

"What. Did. I. Just. Fucking. Say? You wanted a baby so you're going to have one." He speaks through gritted teeth. The anger seething out of him is unreal and makes me very uneasy.

I open my mouth to plead again but before words can form, my airways release a small moan. My hands instantly clutch my pulsing tummy while I grimace. Contractions.

"How far apart are they?" He asks suddenly.

My mind is spinning. My thoughts are jumbled and so are my breaths. I can't think or speak. I'm a panicked mess.

"Stress isn't good for the kid, Livie. Now tell me how far apart they are."

This time I feel my legs spread. Oh no. Why is he parting my legs? What is he trying to do?

"N-no!" I try to push him away but his grip on my knees warn me. He is serious.

"If you took the time to realize that I'm helping you then things would go a lot smoother. Now, calm your ass down and count how far apart your contractions are." He commands, making me swallow dryly.

Nodding quickly, I begin to count out loud while he inserts his finger in my cervix.

"What...what are you doing?" My eyes flicker to him nervously.

"I'm measuring. Are you finished counting?" He peers at me with curious eyes. I notice him frown while he continues "measuring" me.

"Uh, I'm six... six minutes apart." By this time, I've started rocking while rubbing my baby bump.

"Shit, longer contractions means longer time in labor." He mumbles to himself.

My eyebrows frown while I observe his placid demeanor. He is way too calm and it bothers me. No one should be this calm, especially since there isn't a doctor around.

"How do you know this?" This isn't making sense. He has no idea how to deliver a baby. That's why I need proper medical attention.

"Keep your legs apart and focus on breathing." He covers my shivering body with a blanket then walks to the bathroom.

I'm left in the bed, looking more confused than a boy ladybug.

Another shiver passes through me so I pull it closer to me.

I hear shuffling in the bathroom and then he walks out. My eyes linger on the items in his arms. Two blankets. One light pink and the other blue. A small tube that drains mucus, a blood pressure monitor, a pair of scissors, some gloves, gauze, and shiny metal that looks to be stitching utensils.

I groan loudly when another intense contraction strains my body. I need to stop this pain so I try to lay on my side.

"Shit, shit, shit." He walks over to the bedside table and begins organizing the items. I get a sense that he knows what he is doing. Like he has prepared for this.

"Are they closer?"

I'm about to ask 'who?' when I feel another sharp pain constrict my abdominal muscles. The pressure below is immense and I need to release it. I have an urge to push so I do.

"No! Don't push yet." He paces over to reclaim his spot. The entrance of my area.

"Why...why not?" I retort in irritation. I can't help it. The urge to push this baby out is too strong.

"If you push too soon you'll tear, and tearing is bad because you'll swell." He explains bluntly.

He doesn't need to say anymore because I get it. Pushing too soon could cause more pain. I don't have any proper medical care and if I make a mistake then things will go downhill quicker than how they are now.

Another painful contraction attacks my stomach, forcing my teary eyes to water while I bite my lip. They're getting closer.

"You're doing great, Livie. Just wait a few more minutes and then you can push." He looks up from me with a different, more frightening expression. Worry.

In and out. In and out. I focus my attention on breathing while pushing. Rich ordered me to push several minutes ago so that's all I've been doing. Pushing and breathing instead of freaking out. I can't panic because if I do then I put the baby in harm's way. And I don't ever want to do that.

There's an immense amount of pressure in my lower parts but that doesn't hinder me. It just makes me push harder. Soon I'm told to stop and then I hear loud crying. I'm a little dazed but that doesn't stop my ears from perking up. I shake the nausea off before using my elbows to prop myself up. I want to see it.

A small head comes out first. Blood and film cover the tiny baby while I watch in shocked awe. He removes the placenta from her neck then cuts her umbilical cord. I watch him use the tube to drain the mucus from her nose and mouth. I watch him do this with precision and care, all while she lays on my tummy, crying loudly. I sing to her while rubbing her tiny stomach, hoping to get her quiet.

Without words, he lifts her up and places her in my arms. Looking down, I see a tiny baby wrapped in my arms. The slimy blood and mucus cover her like a second skin. She is dirty but despite her grimy appearance, she is still gorgeous. Her blue eyes with small specks of brown slowly close. I smile at how beautiful she looks. Like an angel.My little angel.

From there, I notice a small button nose. My dad's nose. Smiling to myself, my eyes land on her attractive rosy cheeks and tiny yet full pink lips like me.

Her small strands of brown hair sit neatly atop her head, complimenting her already radiant beauty.

I, Olivia Kelly Walters has a baby now. Wow. I wonder what Margaret, Kelly, and Nathan will think. And then, I wonder how I'm going to get all three of us out of here now. Jake, myself, and my little angel.

I hear Rich walk over to us. He takes her from me to give her a small light pink blanket. So that's what the blankets were for. The gesture is nice but it still doesn't dismiss the fact that I could've died twelve hours ago. Even if he thought he knew what he was doing he should have taken me to a hospital.

"Just keep her warm." He hands her back to me then stands in front of us with his hands in his pockets.

His eyes are closed while he deliberates. Not moving, not troubled. Showing absolutely no emotions whatsoever, and making me more anxious.

I hear a faint sigh and then, "So, what are we naming her?"

I hold her closer to me while rocking her gently. Did he just ask what we're naming her? Does this mean I get to keep her? Happiness shows in my lips before my eyes slowly travel to Rich. He runs his hand down his face before meeting my gaze. With a half smile, he nods, expecting an answer.

"Reyna." I respond timidly. "Because her eyes remind me of rain in a forest. Clear blue with specks of brown. Refreshing and beautiful."

I'm sleeping peacefully. Dreaming about my baby and how perfect she is. In my dreams I see her, I hold her, I play with her. In my dreams she is with me and I'm with her. In my dreams, my daughter is never dead but always alive.

A loud crash awakens me from my quiet slumber. My eyes are the first to open before I'm sitting up quickly.

Panting loudly, I scan the dark room cautiously. My eyes search every angle until a lamp flickers on. My nightstand lamp.

"Livie," The voice whispers.

I feel intrusive hands latch onto my arm so I go into automatic defense mode. My legs kick while my hands punch his chest.

"Ouch!" I hear him grunt out. Good, I got him. My legs spring into action but before I'm off the bed, I feel my body fall backward.

"Get off!" I shout when he sits on my abdomen. I'm now pinned down, defenseless. His hands wrap around my arms while he continues straddling me.

"Not until you aplologize first." The familiar voice replies playfully.

There is only one explanation for that voice.

"Jake?"

"You wanted to talk to me, right?" He eases off of me, now he's just straddling me.

My whole body warms at the sound of his seraphic voice and how close we are. Our intense heat reminds me of the night in the van. It was perfect like him. And not to mention his voice. It makes the corners of my mouth curve whenever I hear it.

"How did you know that?" I ask, bewildered by him. He was asleep when I went to visit him.

"I could smell you in my room." He pinches his nose while fanning the air to make fun of me.

My knee goes up to kick him but he shouts,

"I'm kidding, Olive!" A small chuckle is heard from him while I glare.

"Jack told me. He and Gia left earlier but he told me you came by to see me." He turns solemn staring off in thought.

"Yeah, I just wanted to make sure you were okay." I mumble while trying to remove the sleep from my eyes. I'm sitting up now while he's still at the foot of the bed.

"Move over." He commands smoothly.

Without question, I eagerly scoot over to give him room. The bed isn't that small so we can both fit comfortably. Our bodies touch, his hand wraps around mine while we lay in darkness and silence.

"I'm leaving for New York tomorrow."

Tomorrow my Aunt Casey is moving me further up north. We're moving to Manhattan. Tomorrow I'll never see Jake again. And I'll never be able to prove Rich murdered my parents.

"Why so far?" The dissapointment in his tone is clear. But he quickly covers it with a small cough.

"My aunt thinks distance will help me heal faster." I sigh in disappointment. She may be right but I don't want to move away from Jake. Deep down inside, he's the main reason I want to go back to my home town. I want to be with him.

"Well, what do you think?"

"I think proving Rich is a murderer will help me heal faster." I blurt out too quickly. Maybe I should tell him the main reason; I think being with you will help me heal faster.

There's a thick silence in the air. Like we're both thinking. And then, I turn to see him staring back at me. With a wry smile he says,

"That's the shit I've been waiting to hear."

We spent the rest of the night plannig and talking about everything under the sun.

First, we talked about how he was able to get the police to find us. I needed to know so I asked him. He told me he spent a year expanding a tunnel in the basement. When I frowned he clarified.

He said he was planning on traveling through it to get help. It was already there, covered by a thick layer of wood.

He found it when he had one of his anger spells. He explained how he was throwing rocks, sticks, whatever he could get his hands on. He picked them up and chucked them at the wall.

He said he heard something break through the wall. Well, it wasn't a wall. He later discovered it was a large board of wood. Rotted and ancient. It was blocking a small passageway. A tunnel.

My reaction was a wide grin because he is a genius. Rich rarely allowed Jake upstairs. And when he did it was just to torment him by using me. So I guess that gave him time to dig or expand, as he calls it.

"So that's what you were doing down there?"

"You'd be surprised what kind of tools you find when you're bored." He shrugs.

"So, what'd you do after he beat you that day?" He was knocked unconscious. I remember because I was there. They had been arguing because Rich found hidden food in the basement. I would sneak food to Jake because the crumbs Rich gave him weren't enough. So Jake took the blame for me that day.

"I pretended to be unconscious, basically. I needed those three days to finish."

My eyes close while I snuggle closer to him. From there, he tells me he spent nearly a day walking in the snow and cold. That's how he developed hypothermia. He didn't have a coat nor shoes. Just a long sleeve tee and some jeans. He experienced intervals of cold; frozen limbs, dry throat, and fervent shakes until he went completely numb.

Once he made it to town, a few people stopped to help him. He managed to tell them how far he walked and the direction he came from before he passed out. He said his vision started to blur and then soon he was falling down. The next thing he knew, he was waking up in the hospital.

"They told me they found you. I remember feeling accomplished. Like I was finally able to keep my promise for once." He smiles triumphantly.

My eyes begin to water because he is right. He kept his promise. He promised to protect me and he did. It may have taken him a year but he followed through with it.

After he finishes I sit up to gawk at him. His green, intriguing eyes remain focused on mine, reading me too.

I take in his scruffy appearance. I stare at his strong jaw upward. He hasn't shaved in months, meaning his five o clock shadow is full. His lips are the same full pink and his nose is slightly crooked, but still looks cute. He has one scar above his right eye and underneath his dark, scrunched eyebrows. I notice his hair is longer too. With all that has happened I can see that he is flawed like me. His scars tell a story. Our scars tell a story.

I'm not prepared for what happens next because my body freezes, not knowing what to do. I feel his lips on mine, kissing me gently. Soon, I'm falling backward onto the bed. My body presses into his while I return the kiss.

My heart skips a beat when I feel his hands trace over me, making me more turned on than I already am. I feel invigorated when I kiss him. Like he's the breath of fresh air I need. He is everything I need to feel. I need love, friendship, passion, to feel beautiful. And he makes me feel all of those things.

"I think I love you," I breathe out when he starts undressing me.

In a matter of seconds I feel coolness on my perspiring skin but I don't get chills. Instead, I smirk while disrobing him. I feel his erection press into my thigh, making my core pulsate.

I trace my fingertips down him, making him shiver with desire.

His sculpted and toned body clings to me while our kiss deepens. I trail my hands along his strong biceps. When did he get those?

Maybe from all of that work he did in the basement, I don't know. All I know is that he makes my eyes shine with lust and my mouth water.

He positions himself, his hand grip my rear while my legs wrap around him. With a glint in his sharp, attractive eyes he says,

"I think you do too."

My body is the first to respond because my back arches when I feel him enter.

Gripping the sheets, I allow myself to feel him. I feel his soul enter into me, giving me what I want and making me feel needed. My chest elevates the faster we move. He feels amazing. Like a bubble of energized pleasure has exploded inside of me.

The longer he goes, the more I let go of my worries. I don't care if we get caught or if he didn't say the three words I was expecting. No, I don't give anymore thought to what we're doing. I just move with him, making sure he feels just as much enjoyment as I do. We continue moving and moaning in sensual pleasure.

With my arms draped around his neck, I sit up. We need a new position. He figures out what I'm doing so he lets me lead. I have no idea what I'm doing but I do know one thing, I'm going to dominate.

"Whoa Livie, finally being a leader?" He raises his brows while I shake my head playfully.

With the way he is sitting, I can understand why he made that joke.

He's pressed against the headboard while I straddle him. My hands trail down his chest to his abdomen, stopping above his V. I could do one of two things here. I could tease him or just devour him.

He grips my thighs, squeezing to let me know he's waiting. And in that instant, I know what I'm going to do. I press my lips to his neck, sucking until I get a rise out of him.

His body jerks up, startling me and even startling himself.

He chuckles then surprises me with his own move. He penetrates me again. But this time, it's without warning. I squeak from the sudden feel of his hard member sliding into my core. He pushes until I'm soaking wet down below.

By this time our hearts are beating as quickly as our movements. Up, down. Back and forth. The closer we come to climax the more intensified the heat feels. I tilt my head back while he massages my chest. Low moans of pleasure part from my lips.

My body quakes when he finishes, spilling his fluid inside of me. It feels indescribably good. So good that I can't prevent the moan that escapes. It's loud enough to wake the entire floor.

"Oh shit," I cover my mouth while he laughs.

"No one... heard us." Panting loudly, he pulls me into a hug. Our sweaty bodies glisten in the moonlight from the window, shining like stars. I fall into him, hugging him tighter.

"What the hell is going on in here?"

My head shoots up to the door. A nurse with burgundy scrubs and eyes sharper than a knife glares at us.

"Is this supposed to help you two heal?" The uptight nurse with eyebrows thinner than a string walks over to us.

The blood in my body rushes to my ears and then back down to my cheeks. Embarrassment takes up residence on my face.

"It's sexual therapy." Jake shrugs, making me burst into laughter. I try to hold it into but I can't. I laugh harder.

"Sexual therapy my ass, pretty boy." She grabs his arm, yanking him off the bed.

"No thanks ma'am. I've had my go." With a sly grin, he wraps himself in the towel she handed him.

I continue laughing as she drags him out by his ear. I hear a loud crash and then her yelling. My door opens again. With his back pressed to the door, he locks it.

I watch him run over to me so fast paced that I can't keep up with my own thoughts. He pulls me in for a long kiss. This time it's filled with passion, fervor, and desire. This time it tells me that he needed this just as much as I do.

"Jacob Oliver Rhodes." The door swings open, forcing our eyes open.

I'm met with a sea of emerald, captivating me with just one stare. Our foreheads touch while his thumb traces my thin lips. Her approaching footsteps get louder until she stops.

He smiles at me with sincerity then says,

"I'll be back,"

Nodding my head, I watch the shrewd nurse drag him out of my room. She slams my door, leaving me with happy, hopeful thoughts instead of depressing, foreboding ones.

These are good thoughts. The kind that make me bubbly inside.

Jake loves me too? That's my first thought, and then my second one comes. Of course he does. He wouldn't follow your plan to take Rich down if he didn't.

32

CHAPTER 32

Jake asked no questions when I told him my plan. He was just as eager as I was to get Rich the death penalty for murdering his dad. Except, my dad wasn't the only victim. I lost my mom and my daughter. My daughter. It feels weird to say that. Maybe because it's been a year since I've lost her. It's been three hundred and sixty five days since our bond has diminished. Sometimes I think about Reyna and how well off she'd be. Would I have really kept her? Or would I have given her up after six months? I don't really know. I mean I had her for one week and I couldn't keep my hands off of her. I carried her everywhere with me. She was my only family, and now she is gone. Tears swell in my eyes, and my throat burns as old memories re-emerge. I need to forget. I have to forget everything.

"So we're really going through with this?" He asks once we make it to the parking lot. It's currently six a.m. and we've just crept out of the hospital. I know it seems impossible to do but you'd be surprised how many nurses fall asleep during graveyard shift.

"They can't really stop us. We're adults now." I pull my jacket tighter. We've been away from Rich for a week, and yet it feels like an eternity. A small ache settles in my chest at that thought.

"Do you miss him?" His concern is strong. So strong that it stops me in my path. This moment reminds me of the first time he told me Rich liked me.It caught me off guard. I wasn't expecting him to ask me that.

"What's your real reason for wanting to go back there? And don't say it's 'cause of me?" He chuckles at the last part.

I'm forced to smile at the melodic sound of his sexy laugh. I love everything about him.

"Jake, not everything is about you." I giggle when he pouts play-fully.

Sighing heavily, I admit the rest of the truth.

"I... I just need some evidence first. And some of it is in that house."

We're still in Pennsylvania, meaning the house he kept us in has plenty of evidence. Evidence we need to have for the police.

"Evidence or closure, Livie?"

He turns me to face him. I can feel his stare on me. His unadulter-ated, raw stare dissecting me piece by piece. But instead of meeting his gaze, I aim mine to the ground.

Tears form in my eyes at the thought of closure. All of Reyna's belongings are in that house. Every memory of her being is there. A mother's worse nightmare is losing her child, and I faced that head on. This is why I need to forget. But no matter how many times I try to, I just can't.

"Her blanket is there...it's-" I start to cry softly. My eyes sting while my body locks onto Jake's as he holds me tighter. I need her with me. I need something that reminds me of my daughter because I feel lost without her.

He consoles me while I sob hysterically. His arms wrap around my back while mine grip his jacket. I know he feels my salty droplets and mucus but he doesn't say anything. He just let's me cry it out.

After two buses, a taxi, and walking three miles we finally make it to the cabin. I fell asleep in the taxi and was surprised when I didn't wake from a nightmare. My cheeks heated when I realized Jake's arm was wrapped around my shoulder while I leaned into him. His intoxicating smell of sweet lemon made my insides twist. Not only does he look good, but he smells good too.

We walk through the forest in silence, stepping on rugged ground full of snow covered sticks and rocks. My arm is draped around his waist while his rests on my shoulder. I close my eyes, allowing myself to be enamored in him. Just the thought of him makes my heart beat faster, and the way he smiles at me; confident yet playful makes my knees weak. I sigh in content, thinking about us. Wondering if he feels the same. Or, if I'm just some easy thing to him. I mean I said I loved him and he didn't really reply the way I thought he would.

Maybe I'm over-reacting, I don't know. But I am sure of one thing. I want him to break up with Gia the ugly, bitchy dragon.

"Good thing my brother gave me that cash." He pants out when we arrive at the cabin. We're currently standing on the wrap around porch, shivering. The cabin gives me chills with the eerie appearance leering off of it. The dark shadows looming over us reminds me of our old prison in the basement. The two story cabin appears larger than the last time I've seen it. Large, dark, depressing. There is even police tape on the front door. This place exudes creepiness.

"Yeah, we wouldn't have been able to walk the whole way." Between the cold, February air and winter elements, and the long distance from the hospital, we would not have made it.

He nods before using his body weight to open the door. His hand grips the knob while his tilted body slams into the door.

I wait patiently, allowing my eyes to glance around. I notice the frost exit from our noses as we inhale and exhale the brittle air. My eyes scan the perimeter, observing every foot of snow on the ground. A blanket of pure white ice enshrouds the entire yard. I notice small footprints in the snow. A baby's footprints.

Without any questions, my legs set into motion. I'm trekking through the deep snow before I can stop myself.

"Livie," Jake calls after me.

A heavy chill passes through me, making me pull my coat tighter. I have to follow these steps. My eyebrows furrow when I hear crying. It's so familiar that I can't help the attraction to it. I feel the need to comfort the upset child. The hollering gets louder, making my veins run cold. Is that my baby? Oh no. I start a brisk run, trying to find her so I can keep her warm.

"I'm coming! Coming to sav-" I'm cut off by the frigid precipitation in the ground. With a small 'oomph,' my entire body lands in the snow face first.

"Livie!" I hear Jake's deep voice call out but I don't reply.

Instead, I stay frozen in shock. This can't be real. Blinking a few times I reach out, gliding my fingertips across her porcelain face. A small smile plays at the corners of my lips when I see her smile back at me. She appears older now. Twelve months old to be exact. Tears continue to spill over while I take in my baby. Her brown hair clings to her rosy cheeks and makes her bright blue eyes pop.

She's shaking so I scoop her up. I hold onto her for dear life. Afraid of letting go. Afraid of losing her again.

"Momma's here, angel." I whisper to her. My body goes into a steady rock while she whimpers softly.

I'm here and I'm never leaving her again. Her tiny finger clutches my heart shaped necklace. The same necklace aunt Casey gave me the first day I woke up in the hospital.

"You like it?"

She peers at me with scared, blue Bambi eyes. Her small mouth forms a smile at the sound of my voice. I close my eyes, fighting off more tears. Although it's been a year, I've missed so much of her life. It's like everything about her has fast forwarded. She can say momma- not too clearly but clear enough for me to understand- and her body has grown too.

Opening my eyes, I'm greeted by the sound of her excitement. Her gums present and her eyes shine as she pats my chest to let me know she wants it.

"It's yours then. This is for you, Reyn." My hands go up to unclasp my necklace to give to her. We're both sitting in the snow, completely captivated by one another's presence. The sun is now up, blessing us with rays of light and heat. It makes her face appear brighter; lovelier. And the snow sparkles like glitter.

"I love you Reyna. Mommy loves you." I whisper while rocking her to sleep. This action brings back so many memories. The best memories of my life. Every night she'd cry without taking a breath, and every night I was there to comfort her. Those seven days and six nights were the best days of my life. And now, now I'll have more of them to look forward to. Smiling to myself, I hug her tighter.

"Livie, what are you doing?"

Looking up, I see Jake standing with his hands in his low rise jeans pockets. I notice his eyes on me; pity and worry occupying his handsome features.

"And where'd you get that?"

I'm about to ask him what on earth is he talking about but I'm stopped when I see a small pink shoe box in my hands. My heart sinks to my stomach when I remember where I am. In the backyard. The same place Rich claimed he buried her. I know this because for thirty minutes each day, I'd stand out here, looking at the ground. Staring at the grave that is haunting my conscious because I was too afraid to dig it up myself.

"It's nothing." I stand up to dust the snow off my jeans. My hand holds the box in a strong grip, not wanting him to grab it.

"Okay," Is all he says while straightening his black North Face jacket.

With one last glance behind me, I see the hole in the snow. The hole I managed to dig up.

Swallowing the bile in my throat, I follow Jake. My boots sink into the snow while we walk to the side of the house. My mouth remains silent and my eyes stay focused on the winter wonderland beneath my feet. I'm contemplating, still shocked by what just happened.

The winter breeze sweeps past us, sending my loose strands astray. My dirty blond hair is pulled into a high ponytail so it doesn't get out of hand like the rest of my hair.

The trek to the house seems long but it probably isn't. Maybe less than a minute.

Anyway, we enter through the door and I'm hit by a flood emotions. Emotions so strong that I can't control how I'm starting to feel. Anger, hurt, despair, depression, joy, anxiety, fear. The louder my breathing gets the more my fingers pull on the hem of my light pink sweater. From there, they go to my neck. I feel my skin and collarbone but I don't feel my necklace. Where's my necklace?

You gave it to your daughter.

A small voice confirms. Inviolable anxiety shakes my core as I ponder. She was really here. My daughter came to meet me here. Chewing on my bottom lip, I try to keep myself intact. I try to prevent myself from breaking down. So instead of crying, I smile.

I smile because she came. I gave her my necklace and she gave me her box. Now she has a part of me and I have a part of her.

My eyes close while uncontrolled tears spill out.

This is too much. Why did I come here?

And why is this wool sweater so itchy? An abrupt warmth attacks my body, making me extremely hot. Quickly removing my jacket, I feel the box fall from my hands. I hear a thud as it lands on the floor. My first thought is to pick it up, but I'm stopped when I feel my throat tighten and my knees buckle.

"Whoa," Jake catches me before I pass out. His arms push me further into his chest, making me warm and tingly inside.

"Are you sure you're okay with this?" He peers at me, crease lines forming in his soft features.

I wiped my tears soon after that. I need to stay strong for me, for Reyna. Because crying is weak and the weak don't make it.

"Did you find anything?" He asks, clearly exasperated.

I'm not too certain how long it's been but my limbs are tingly and my mouth opens to yawn.

"Nothing..." I sigh, sorrow filling my insides. It's been nothing but pointless searching in an empty house. There are only two rooms up here. An empty one and Rich's room. The attic is at the end of the hallway and downstairs is the living room, kitchen and basement.

Jake was just downstairs while I searched the upstairs. We chose places we were most familiar with. And since he spent the majority of his time downstairs I figured he knew it better than I did.

"Once we're finished here we're going to his house in Florida, right?" He is now leaning against the door frame. We're in Rich's room and the stench is overwhelming. It's a solid mix of blood, sweat, and tears. Literally.

"You remember those locked rooms?" I pull my sleeves down when I notice him eyeing my wrists.

"Well do you?" I ask, more sternly this time.

With narrowed eyes and a slightly tilted head, he nods cautiously. From the way his arms fold and his lax posture I conclude that he is trying to understand what I'm thinking.

"Well those rooms could hold the key to Rich's future. Death." Those rooms could reveal so much about him. All of the things he's stolen, including the weapons used to commit his crimes could be the evidence we need to get him charged with murder.

And even though he says he is honest and works for a living I know that isn't true. I knew him before he became a business man. Nothing has changed except his cunning words and stunning attire.

"And what if they don't? What do we do then?" He frowns at me, obviously doubting my plan.

"What do you mean?" Those rooms are locked for a reason and I'm going to uncover it.

"Livie," He runs his fingers through his hair. "I think your plan is cool and all, but can we wait until he gets sentenced first? Who knows, they could give him life in prison."

No. That isn't good enough for Rich. He needs to die.

"If we don't think it's fair then we'll go after him." He tries to reason with me.

"Are you serious? You're just giving up?" I cut my eyes at him, making a point to show him how serious I am.

"What the fuck, Livie! How is that giving up? I went along with this plan to make you happy. To make you think you aren't crazy. But what if-" He stops abruptly.

Clearing his throat, he avoids my eyes then says,

"All I'm saying is let's be nineteen and twenty. Let's get our lives back first." His eyes linger on mine, begging for me to agree. But I can't.

"What life do I have, Jake? Can you tell me that?" I don't have a mom dad, brother, or boyfriend to go back to. I have nothing. Only remnants of a broken spirit and damaged body.

"You can make a life for yourself. A great one." He assures calmly.

Heavy doubt settles in me at his words. He wasn't supposed to say that.

"We can make a life for ourselves, Jake. What about us?" I emphasize the word 'us'.

Silence engulfs us for a few moments, leaving us with our own sound breathing, and rapid thoughts. I'm thinking of him agreeing with me. I'm hoping he does want to be with me. But then he says it. He says the few words that make my ears burn.

"What about us?" He stares at me with a dumbfounded expression. It's as if he wasn't expecting me to be so upset.

With a frustrated groan, I cross my arms. This is why I didn't want to bring it up. My stomach gets butterflies at the thought of a relationship, but despite how nervous I am I want one. I'm starting to want one. And it's with him.

"You want to marry me?" He smirks with a look of apprehension.

It takes every bone in my body to stop myself from shaking him. Why is he playing dumb?

"Because it's a little too soon for that, Olive." He jokes, making my cheeks flame.

"No, I don't want to fucking marry you! But I'd appreciate it if you'd stop leading me on, making me think you did." There is some distance between us, and for that I'm grateful. We need to stay as far away from each other as possible.

"Oh, I get it, Olive. I understand what you're so pissed about." He shakes his head at me like I'm some pathetic thirsty bitch.

"You're mad because I'm still with Gia." He finishes with narrowed emerald eyes and crossed arms. His demeanor exudes rudeness as we stand face to face.

"No, I'm mad because your dick is bigger than your head." I insult snidely. It's not right for me to keep giving him what he wants sexually if he's only going back to that evil vermin. I'm tired of the mixed signals.

"You're the one who kissed me back." He admits plainly. The look in his placid green eyes; confident, assured, reigning makes me want to choke the shit out of him. He knows I have deeper feelings for him and yet he wants play with me like I'm a toy. And what's worse is that I allowed him to do it.

"Oh, and if I recall, you wanted it just as bad as I did." His tone is softer now, as if he is endorsing his own thoughts. He believes what he is saying is true, and he's right. It is.

The deeper I search into his jeweled irises the more my hard glare softens. He's right, I did kiss him back and now, I want to kiss him again. What the hell is wrong with me? I turn away from him while gripping my hair in frustration. Is this sexual tension? Because it sure as hell feels like it.

"Wanted what?" A sudden small voice breaks through the silence. It sounds like a voice more broken than mine. The sadness in her tone isn't masked by innocence. It's depth is so strong and pure that it forces me to stop in my tracks. It's the sound of heartbreak.

My head whips up, only to be met with a crowd of spectators. Only this time, they aren't just police or my aunt standing in the doorway. No, this time Gia and Jackson are in the center of the group.

She is looking like the perfect, exotic princess while I look like a desperate, broken victim, ready to implode with all of these emotions. I won't explode, no. Everything that I'm feeling needs to stay hidden deep inside, because when my emotions are out in the open I get hurt.

"What did she want? What did you want?" She points at us both, looking a bit distraught. Her eyelids flutter while she mock sniffles. Meaning she is trying to ward off tears that aren't even forming.

"Hey babe, calm do-"

"Shut the hell up, Jake!" She shouts, making me jump slightly. Looks like I'm still startled by sudden noises. Or maybe, it's the sound of her shrill voice. Her vocals resemble nails on a chalkboard.

"Livie," The feeling of a hand on my shoulder forces me to stiffen. I hear the person whisper to me; telling me that everything will be okay. I wish I could believe my aunt but I can't. Everyone has lied to me so why is she any different?

"Gia, I'm telling you right now I want you." He asserts with his hands on her arms. I can't see his face but I'm able to hear the pleading in his voice. A small part of me feels sorry for him.

Her dark eyebrows pull into a frown while her red lips curve evilly. I notice this look; a look of taunting but Jake doesn't.

"Go fuck yourself...OR better yet, that skeleton looking whore." She shakes her head at me before storming out of the room. And of course, like the obedient whipped boy he is, he follows after her. I hate that bitch.

Jackson stares at me with pity in his dark green eyes. From the way his jaw clenches to the sullen look in his irises I can see that the horrible expression on his face matches the horrible feeling inside. He mouths the words 'I'm sorry' to me before walking out the room.

"Look Olivia, running away won't solve your problems. You're moving to the big apple with me and I promise you'll love it." She smiles warmly, her natural glow revealing more attractive features. I can see why she is a model. My aunt is gorgeous.

By this time I've ignored everything everyone has said to me. I grab my baby's box without anyone noticing. I'll keep her with me forever.

My aunt wraps me in a sideways hug and begins a steady walk. I'm claustrophobic. My tumultuous thoughts overcrowd my mind while my horrid scars haunt my body. A permanent reminder of the man of my nightmares. Richard Rhodes.

"It's time for change. Time for a fresh, new start." She sighs happily. The bitter wind slaps my face and turns my cheeks crimson.

On my way to the car I hear Jake and Gia. I hear him pleading with her and I hear her scoffing at him. It makes me sick to see this. To see him be so willing to change for her but not for me. I know she had him first but I want to be his last. I want to be his everything. I can see the hurt in his eyes. The same hurt in mine. And the more I watch her play her role of heartbroken girlfriend, the more I get a intuitive feeling. A feeling that is so obvious even a blind man could see. I can't help but feel like she is acting and is stringing Jakey cakes along. Yeah, I can't help but think that her and Jackson are the real couple.

33

CHAPTER 33

F our months later.

Time. It is said that time heals all wounds. That those wounds turn to scars, and those scars fade away eventually. Well, it's been four months and these marks are still here. The carving on my right thigh is plain as day, and so are the cuts on my wrists. They have a light pink hue now; slowly changing to brown.

Absence. It is said that absence makes the heart grow fonder. That the longer your special someone is gone, the more you grow to love and appreciate them. Well, that is true. It's true because I miss Jake. I honestly miss him and hate him, and I don't know what to do about it.

As I sit on my twin sized bed, staring at my wrists I can't help but close my eyes. A range of images flash through my head like a movie. Each vivid detail being depicted word for word, play by play. I can see everything unfold before my eyes. I can see my parents; my mom's loving, vibrant smile, and my dad's stern eyes; cautious yet friendly. The days before our family grew distant. Those were the days my brother was alive.

Then, in an instant I see eyes. Smoldering green eyes, submerging me in a canopy of ebullience. Staring into Jake's eyes made me feel vitality, hope, and courage even. He's the reason I'm out of Rich's grasp. But with the way I'm feeling now I'd rather be back there with Jake. At least I wouldn't be out of his life completely.

Thinking back on Rich, it's been a while since I've heard anything about him. The detective, Miss Lovelace told me that he will be going away for a very long time. That was back in February though, and I still feel like they aren't telling me everything.

So when she visited me in April I demanded she tell me the truth. I did manage to get some information out of her which made me feel more at ease. He is in a state prison in Florida, serving a fifteen year sentence for kidnapping and assault. After she told me that I flipped. I just lost it because he is alive while my baby and parents are dead. It's not fair. She reassured me that he had a heavier burden to carry because he had to live with himself.

I guess she was right, but I still feel like he deserves worse though. He deserves to suffer how he made me suffer. Every time I think about Rich I get angry. And my therapist says anger isn't good.

Opening my dull, teary eyes, I release a tense breath while un-clenching my fists. I've been stressed and distant because of all this aggression I'm holding in. I'm just so fucking angry and there isn't a damn thing anyone can do about it. Not even my therapist can help me. I'm cold, distant, and disturbed now. I feel like I'm drowning in my own insanity. I'm slowly drifting away to emptiness. It's like I'm not myself anymore. Happy, caring, fun loving Olivia is gone, only to be replaced with angry, vengeful, depressed Olivia.

I've lost my true self and I don't know how to bring it back. All I know is that I'm so tired of feeling pain. I'm sick of feeling afraid, ashamed, unloved, and depressed. Without a second thought, I fall back on the full sized bed with cotton blankets. Inhaling deeply, I take in my surroundings. The same surroundings I've had to adjust to these past few months.

My room is nice. Spacious and refreshing. I'm not closed in; I can breathe here.

Sitting up, I notice the pastel hues add more color to this once drab room. My walls are a darker shade of pearl while the wood floors are light. My bed, nightstand, and dresser are an off white with a mauve stripe on each.

When we first moved in the room was bare and boring; just a bed, nightstand and dresser. I didn't have a problem with it because I was just happy for a bed. A bed I could sleep in alone. I spent my days and nights in my room laying on the floor, staring at the ceiling. I cherished that time because I could think.

All of my thoughts, good or bad, would occupy my mind, and there wasn't anyone telling me how or what to think. I was okay with reminiscing about my baby, about Jake, and even my parents.

One day, after my G.E.D class had ended I went straight to the bathroom and locked myself inside. I didn't realize I was having a panic attack until the police had to break down the door. Turns out that I was upset because I saw a little girl who looked like my Reyna. The more they explained the more I started to remember. She had the prettiest blue eyes and rosest of cheeks. I remember one of my classmates holding her and telling me how much she loved her daughter. And in that moment, tears started to pour and my legs started to sprint.

Aunt Casey made a promise to help me take my mind off of everything so we started decorating my room. Things have gotten better and I'm progressing, but I'm still left with a broken heart. I still feel pain but now I conceal it. I can't heal it so I just conceal it.

"Olivia," Casey's friendly, welcoming voice fills my ears.

Ever since I've been discharged from the hospital she has been by my side. Everything I need and want is right here for me. I know my aunt loves me but sometimes I need space. A lot more space.

"Want to go to the photoshoot with me today? It can be a reward for completing your classes." She clasps her delicate hands together while focusing on me.

I'm proud to say that I have my diploma. I may not have graduated but I'm able to say that I completed the twelfth grade. And now I can start looking at professional chef schools. I plan on going to a school here in New York. Los Angeles is too far of a place for me to be alone.

"How about some pizza? Wanna get a bite to eat?" She all but pleads. The begging in her tone is beyond pathetic. Why can't she just go without me?

"Shopping? Shopping is always good," She plops down beside me, making little impact to the bed.

Ever since I arrived she's been talking to me non-stop about how much I'm going to love New York and how great the food is here. She says she is going to show me how to look and feel like a girl again. That made me happy because ever since I've been locked away with Rich, I've been forced to wear baggy tees, faded jeans, or old dresses.

But now that I'm really in the Big Apple I don't want to go any-where or do anything. The only places I went were to school and therapy. I'm not afraid of people. I'm just too depressed to do any-thing. It's funny how quickly my mood changed once I got here. I used to be excited but now, I'm just over everything.

"If you won't go anywhere or do anything then maybe we should move to a place where you can." She places a gentle hand on my shoulder, trying to comfort me.

"Move? What do you mean?" I just want to stay in one place. I was a hermit before and I'll keep being one now.

"Remember that phone call I received the other day?" She stares at me with large hazel eyes. I notice the light makeup on her square, model like face. Her long lashes makes her eyes stand out while her medium sized pink lips, and flawless skin make her appear more youthful. I can honestly say that I'm glad she is letting her hair thick brown grow out.

"Olivia, do you even know what I'm talking about?"

Staring with curious eyes, I nod slowly. It was only a few days ago she received a phone call from her manager. I just remember her squealing like a sixteen year old girl who just got asked out by her crush. She stayed on the phone calling every friend in town to invite them out on the town. She invited me but I was too tired. Well, that's what I told her. Truthfully, I didn't feel like partying with a bunch of twenty something year olds.

"Continue," I smile shyly, making her chuckle.

"I have a few opportunites in Florida that I need to take advantage of. We'll be in Daytona for a few months until I can finish this project." She kisses my cheek then skips to the door.

"Oh, and we leave in two weeks!" She shouts on her way out.

Welcome to Daytona Beach, the sign reads.

I feel the jeep stop after she pulls into a park. I'm still strapped in with my head leaning against the window.

"Why are we here?" My hands go to remove my shades so I can take in the scenery. The ocean is enormous; a large body of water stretching across the horrizon and beyond. I stare in awe at the beauty of the waves rolling into the shore. The bright sun illuminates the sand, making it glisten.

"I figured you haven't been in a while." She gets out and starts to stretch.

My lips spread into a warm smile while I open my door. Stepping out, my sandals are the first to touch the ground. I make my way to where my aunt Casey is standing. In front of the entrance. Just a few feet away from the jeep.

"But, I don't have my swimsuit." I walk over to her. She's still standing in the same spot, staring at the crystal blue water. Anxious excitement in her hazel eyes.

"Don't tell me someone wants to swim." She eyes me with a teasing smile.

I've told her several times that I didn't care if I ever went to the beach. I didn't care if I ever made friends or even got married. I told her that I didn't want to live because I was dead on the inside.

"I'm glad you're back, Liv." She grabs my hand to pull me into a hug.

I hug back, allowing her happiness to invade my insides. I went from hating her happy, infectious spirit to loving it. She helps me feel better.

She pulls away before making her way to the boardwalk. I watch her make it all the way to the trash cans before she turns around,

"Are you going to be okay by yourself?" Her concerned voice resonates across the crowded atmosphere.

Nodding my head, I wave her off. I'll be fine as long as I stay by the car. And if anything goes wrong I'll just lock myself inside and call the police.

Leaning against the trunk, I look around at all the people having fun. Families with small kids, couples walking their pets, and even teenagers in groups, all laughing and dancing to the reggae music blaring through the speakers. There's a cafe a few ways down. The Caribbean food smells amazing. Maybe I'll ask Casey if we can eat soon.

Anyway, I coninue people watching. Giving a few snickers and giggles at unsuspecting people. Some dig in their noses while others trip over their own two feet. It's quite funny, especially when they see me laughing at them. Yeah dude, I just saw the small embarassment on your face.

I'm having fun, not so subtly laughing at people until something catches my eye. There's a figure in a hood with his hands in his pockets. I can't make out a face, all I know is whoever it is gives me chills. I watch him inhale one last puff before throwing the bud to the ground. My heart skips a beat when his eyes meet mine. They're chocolate brown just like-

"I hope you like this."

I'm interrupted by a tiny hand holding a bag up to my face. Blinking a few times, I'm pulled out of my trance by Casey. She hands me the bag with a huge smirk on her glossed lips.

Shaking my head I make my way to the bathroom to change. It ended up being a bikini and a pair of white shorts. My aunt knows how self conscious I am now that I have so many scars. She knows how much I hate showing skin now, and yet she comtinues to try to make me.

"Come on out Olivia! Embrace your beauty," She encourages from outside the stall.

With my hand tightly gripping my towel to my chest I slowly walk out.

Glancing at the tiled floor nervously, I wait for the shocked gasps and the looks of disapproval, but no one makes a sound.

"It's just us in here. So, do you like it?" She speaks with hesitance.

Looking up, I make eye contact with the mirror. My mascara filled eyes widen when I remove my towel. The bikini is a halter top with teal stripes while the bottoms are a solid teal. I love how the colors compliment my cream skin.

I continue staring at myself. I have grown some since I was found. My legs have gotten a bit longer, I have curves in the right places and my chest is sizable. I'm not a size four anymore. I'm an eight and I'm satisfied. Smiling to myself, I even notice how lengthy my dirty blonde hair has gotten, it's now past my shoulders, half way down my back. Before I was taken I rocked short hair but now it's longer. Rich made me grow it out and now I'm so used to length that I'd feel bald if it were any shorter.

Anyway, we claim a spot near the water. Close to the waves but not close enough to get wet.

I lay my towel on the sand before placing my bag on it. Aunt Casey sets up the large umbrella and cooler while I start preparing my skin. You know, the usual moisturizer and suncreen.

We spent the next forty five minutes chatting and enjoying the beach; making sand castles and taking funny pictures.Everything about this place gave me life. From the vibrant atmosphere to the laughing people, to the sound of the waves crashing into the rocks. This place was a breath of fresh air. It took my mind off my current problems.

"Hey." A male voice calls, making me jump slightly.

With my aviators still on, I squint at the intruder. He's tall with caramel skin and looks to kill.

"We need another girl for our match. You wanna play?" His brown eyebrows raise while I stare at him, baffled by the fact that someone wants me to join their game. I'm not in the least bit athletic.

"Please, we need four people but we only have three." He pleads then sighs,

"One of our players decided to be a little bitch." He shouts at him, making me grin.

Looking behind him, I notice three more people. A guy with short hair, and glasses and a girl with long, black hair. It's obvious they're a couple. There's a guy sitting off to the side who has his finger raised in our direction.

"Um ok." I stand up, managing to dust the sand off my legs.

"This is my first time playing though." I admit sheepishly as we approach the others. There's a volleyball net and a ball on the ground. It's obvious what game this is.

"It's fine, Gia can't play either." He replies teasingly.

I'm about to ask him to repeat that name but the sound of a whiney, bitchy voice confirms it.

"What's taking so damn long?" She huffs in aggravation.

It's really Gia. The female devil in the flesh. Her dark hair shines in the sunlight while her lips spread into a evil smirk. She knows who I am.

"Guys, this is...wait, I didn't catch your name." He turns to me, expecting an answer.

They all stare at me, as if I'm some foreign alien who just invaded their little world. Gia is giving me a look of disgust while her boyfriend, Jackson gives me a half smile. The guy sitting in the sand continues drawing stick figures, completely ignoring the scene before his eyes.

The tension is so heavy a knife couldn't cut it. Swallowing dryly, I feel a bit intimidated. It's clear I don't fit in with this group.

"Um, actually I don't think I-"

"Come on, Livie. Don't be a mood killer." The guy who was sitting to the side waltzes over to me.

My eyes grow wider when I realize who he is. Remember when I said I had grown? Well, Jake has too. His medium dark brown hair is rugged and still sexy. It's taken care of because he now has products for that. His body is toned too. It's as if he's grown three sizes since I last saw him. He had a body before but it wasn't as fullfilled as now. It's like his previous years in athletics has done him a huge favor.

"Are you going to stand there the whole time?" He asks with an amusing smirk.

I want to smile but the inner protective me is screaming, " Run, Livie! Run! Don't let this guy break your heart again." I want to punch him, hug him, kiss him, and love him all at the same time. But I can't do that. So I settle for this,

"Are you going to keep asking me dumbass questions?" I move my hair to my shoulder while analyzing him. He seems happier now too. His bright green eyes shine while he wipes the sweat from his brow.

With a small chuckle he asks,

"You want to swim?" The look he gives makes me more nervous than I already am. This look startles me because he actually looks happy to see me while I look confused.

Gia scoffs, making me glare at her. If she is with Jackson now then it's none of her business what Jake and I do.

"But what about the game?" The other guy asks dissapointedly.

I later found out that the guy who invited me to play is Dylan, Jake's best friend. I don't know why I have a feeling Jake sent him over to me.

"You and Jack can play. It'll be even because the hairy beast doesn't want to play." He points at Gia with a bored expression and folded arms. I want to laugh at the astounded look in her azure eyes but I hold back.

"Whatever Tiny Tim." She makes a joke about his manhood, making everyone burst into laughter while he steams with annoyance. Okay, these two definitely aren't together anymore.

"So, how about that swim?" He asks once everyone leaves. He's staring down at me with the cutest emerald eyes.

My eyes lock onto him instantly, seizing his entire being. The longer I gawk at him the more all negative thoughts about him diminish. I don't know what to do or say anymore. I mean this moment is here. The moment when I finally get to see him, talk to him and now I'm afraid too. Because I'm terrifed of losing him all over again.

"Suit yourself," He shrugs passively. I watch him turn to the water and before I can blink an eye he's diving in head first.

I want to swim too. And not because of Jake- actually, it is because of him. I want to be near him so with slight anxiety, I make my way to the water. The sun kisses my skin, making my insides warm. Warmth. I haven't felt that in a while. It's something I've missed.

The sunlight is blinding but I don't care because it's beautiful. With my hands up to the sky and a delighted grin, I embrace this freedom. This freedom that so many people take for granted, including myself.

I decide to keep my shorts on- no need in revealing my carving- before running in the water. It's warm and feels invigorating against my skin. I swim purposefully, feeling free in the water around me. There are no limits to what I can do in the water and I love it. I'm exalted in the sea.

We continue swimming. He splashes me first and before I can stop myself I'm using my body weight to hold him under water. I scream when he lifts me up and throws me under. We play like there is nothing wrong between us.

As if we've been friends since the beginning of time. Every playful splash, shove, and friendly small talk is natural between us. I love this feeling. The feeling of being with him. He makes me laugh, and I'm able to be myself around him. Even if he makes crappy jokes about me. I've missed him so much, and judging from the way he keeps staring at me while we converse he has missed me too.

We keep joking and laughing for hours. Just enjoying each other's company. That is, until our stomach's start growling.

The bass booms out the speakers and invades my eardrums. It's loud and crowded in here but the food is really good. I ordered the Caribbean chicken salad while Jake and Casey ordered burgers.

The first few minutes were kind of awkward, considering the fact that Casey interrogated Jake. She was there when everything un- folded between Jake, Gia and I so that made it easier for her to talk to us.

She told him to never treat me that way again, and that a woman's heart is a very open yet complicated thing. She explained to us both that love never comes easy. It takes effort for a relationship to work. But first we need to establish some sort of commitment.

She lectured us both about our involvement in infidelity. Explaining how completely unacceptable it was.

I never realized how much my aunt knew about me until now. I never really thought about all of the things she explained until now. Truth is, I'm afraid of commitment. Because once I commit I'll be even more vulnerable than I am now. And vulnerability leaves room for heartbreak.

Once she finished we sat in silence, listening to the caribbean music and watching the sunset on the waterfront.

"I'll leave you two to talk," She eyes Jake with warning eyes before giving me a quick peck on the cheek.

"Text me when you're ready."

Nodding my head, I turn to Jake. He's fiddling with his fingers while the inside of his cheek is being chewed.

"So..." I trail off, unsure of what issue to address first. There are way too many problems between us, and the fact that we just had a good time makes me extremely hesitant to speak my mind.

"So, you still hate me?" He lifts his head to peer at me. His nose wrinkles, making me blush. He's too cute. Shit Livie, don't fall for it.

"I hate what you did," I sigh sadly.

He rubs his face tiredly. I watch him take a swig of his sprite before staring at the ocean. The sun is starting to set, giving way to night. The sun setting on the horizon is absolutely beautiful. I get so lost in watching the waves and sun that I'm startled when I feel a body sit next to me.

"Is it okay to say that I do too?" His low tone is enveloped in melancholy. He seems sincere but I still can't fully trust him. I still love him but I can't trust him. He could apologize today and betray me tomorrow.

Tears spring in my eyes, forcing me to look away from him.

"Livie, I'm sorry okay. I know I've said that a thousand times but even still, I haven't said it enough. I'm sorry for hurting you." His arm cocoons my frame then pulls me closer.

"Are you just saying that because you realize I'm the only option you have?" My voice cracks, unable to permeate control. I'm still facing away from him. I can't even look at him because if I do I'll forget every wrong he has done to me.

"I'm saying that because you're the only girl I want." He pauses for a brief second then says, "You're the only girl I want but don't deserve."

The pain in his voice causes my heart to sink. It makes more tears spill out. And in that moment, I allow my eyes to travel to his glassy ones. They aren't lively and vibrant.No, they're dull and sullen. He is truly suffering too. But from what? Heartache or guilt? I may not know. But one thing is certain, I'm not suffering alone and neither is he.

"Say something," His eyes search mine and the longer I stare at him the more my mind starts to wander. I can't forgive him; not yet at least. But we can still do one thing.

"We can start over." I don't have to force a smile and neither does he. I let him bring me closer before planting a soft kiss on my forehead. He makes me feel so many emotions at one time, and I can't tell if that's a good thing or a bad one. All I know is that I love him. And all I want is for him to love me too.

34

— ❦ —

CHAPTER 34

If I could use one word to describe this moment; one word to describe this feeling, there wouldn't be one. There are absolutely no words to form right now.

And as I stand face to face with Jacob Rhodes, completely absorbed in his alluring jade eyes, I can't help but hold more than a smile on my face. I'm finally reunited with my Jakey cakes. That alone holds a spark in my heart. A spark so strong that I know he feels it too.

"Did you hear me?" He brings me out of my bubble of happiness when he gently grabs my hand.

"Hell no," Batting my lashes, I form an innocent smile.

He laughs too, making a point to pull me closer. The way he uses his large hands to consume my waist fills my insides with warmth. Just being in his presence makes me forget every bad thing he has done.

"I'll call you tomorrow. Maybe I can give you a tour of the town and then hit up a movie after. " He smiles sweetly.

With my lips spread into a modest grin, I give him a playful nudge.

"Are you asking me on a date, Mr. Jakey Cakes?" I stop myself from pulling him in for a kiss.

"Depends. Are you saying yes, Olive?" He quips while conquering my hips.

The feeling of his warm hands on my body makes my heart race. And even though I feel a huge attraction to him, I can't make him think that all is well. I have to make him prove his love for me.

"Actually," My hands clutch his to subtly push them off.

With his head down, I notice a small frown. It's obvious he took the hint because his hands are now in his shorts pockets.

"I'm saying another time," It takes everything in me not to scream at myself. That sounded a bit harsher than expected.

"Okay then...I guess good things are worth waiting for,"

My eyes go up to his to read him. But instead of seeing what I expect to see- teasing, I see modest honesty. His jeweled eyes stun me to the point of silence. I'm speechless. I seriously was not expecting him to say that.

The small creak of the door opening keeps me silent. We're too captivated by each other.

"What the hell, Olivia? I'm your aunt not your big sister. It's two a.m and I told you to be home before twelve." She rubs the sleep from her eyes before crossing her lean arms. The daunting look in her caring eyes tells me she is serious. I guess aunt Casey don't play.

After hugging him goodbye, I went straight to my new room. All of my furniture is here, I just need to unpack. With an exasperated sigh, I make a decision to organize the cluttered boxes and disarrayed furniture. I know it's two in the morning and I should probably be preparing myself for slumber, but I just can't sleep. This needs to get done so I might as well get it over with now.

Pulling out my iPhone, I turn on Pandora. Hopefully blasting Ed Sheeran will keep me on task.

Oh, but how wrong I am. While I start unpacking I start singing until my lungs bleed. Like I've said before, I don't care if it's two in the morning. I'm happy, dammit.

While I'm setting up, I can't stop myself from thinking about Jake. I think about our conversation at the restaurant. He really apologized to me and meant it. And he said I was worth waiting for. Wow, this is a huge breakthrough for him, and I'm more than pleased.

After I told him about starting over he re-introduced himself, making me giggle. Once I smiled, he told me how pretty I looked, which made me blush even more.

His compliments always make me happy but some part of me feels like he is just being nice. In my opinion I'm not pretty. I'm as average as can be. And let's not mention my lack of confidence. That is in a league all its own.

And if he didn't realize then I wasn't going to tell him that.

Anyway, I later discovered that my aunt Casey along with his brother Jackson, played a huge role in bringing us back together in the first place. It was no coincidence that he happened to be at the beach the same time as me.

Apparently, Casey wanted to see me happier so she did some online stalking. She found Jackson's number and called him.

At first, he was hesitant because he and Jake had stopped talking for a while. In fact, the first conversation they had was on the beach today and that was only because Dylan forced them to talk. Jake didn't elaborate on their conversation; all I know is that Jackson refused to dump Gia- the center of their feud in the first place.

Once I finish organizing my room, I toss my iPhone on my bed before heading to the bathroom to shower. Once I've pushed all memories of Rich aside, I step into the warmth of the shower. I lather up and begin a brisk scrub all over. Every time I shower I have to keep my mind off of Rich. I have to remind myself that it's just a shower and he isn't here anymore.

Turning off the shower, I wrap my towel around my shivering body before stepping out onto the cold tile. The previous condensation has diminished now and the door is now open, making my eyebrows furrow in high suspicion. That wasn't open before.

"Aunt Casey?" I call out worriedly. She and I are the only ones here in this two bedroom house so the only way to explain my bathroom door being open is because of her.

I focus my breathing while drying myself off. It has to be her. She must have opened it to check on me. Nodding to myself, I make a mental note to check on her after I get dressed.

Pulling my oversized Mickey Mouse tee shirt over my head, I notice how damp my hair is. It clings to my overly moist neck and back. Why am I sweating?

"Calm down, Livie," I release a tense breath before grabbing my black shorts. My hands tremble while I slide them up. The intense heat overpowering me makes my throat dry and my stomach twist. For some reason my body is anxious and my breaths are short and rugged. Why am I so afraid?

"Livie," The voice. The voice of evil resonates off the walls and sinks into my ears.

My world beigins to spin, making me nauseous. There's a loud ringing in my eardrums and I find it hard to focus my vision. It's him. It's really him. He is here, in my room. My eyes remain glued to his intrusive stature as I find it hard to speak.

He is wearing all black; black hoodie, black shirt, dark jeans. Even his aura is dark; like a thief in the night. The only thing I can see are his defying garnet eyes, holding me captive again. The little light shining from the bathroom shines on us as we stand a few feet apart. He's in the doorway while I'm backing away.

"Tell me something," With his hands in his jeans pockets, he starts to stroll towards me.

My mind is telling me to scream but once again, fear consumes me.

"Did you miss me as much as I've missed you? Did you think about me as much as I've thought about you?" He smiles tauntingly at me. The devilish look he holds sends chills down my spine.

I watch him take slow and cautious steps toward me. And as he nears my frightened frame, I can't help but force my body further into the wall.

"Because if you didn't then that means I didn't do my job." His eyes narrow, mirroring anger as he knots his fists in my hair.

"I told you not to leave." He sighs sadly while pushing my trembling body to his chest.

My mind is blank; void of thinking. I don't know where Casey is or how Rich even got in here. All I know is that my tears won't cease and my heart won't stop racing.

"Remember when I said love has limits, Livie? Remember when I said that limit was death?" He pulls my head back, allowing me to see and feel the black glock now pressed to my cheek.

"Well, guess who is going to die?"

That one word attacks my muscles, making me freeze in an instant. That one word forces my knees to buckle and makes my bones grow cold. I'm still afraid to die.

"Don't ki-kill... me, don't! Ple-please... don't kill...me!" I hiccup violently. That's all I can do right now. All I have left is to plead for my life.

"Shhh," He covers my whimpering mouth with one hand while we back away. I never realized how strong his hold is until now. One arm is pressed into my neck while his hand- the hand with the gun- is still locked in place, on my cheek.

"Give me one reason why I shouldn't?"

With regret lingering on my tongue, I say,

"Because...because I'll go with you." My head is down in defeat while I cling onto his arm for dear life. He could pull the trigger any second, and that could end my life. I need to say what he wants to hear if I want to live.

But instead of him releasing me, I feel the rumble of his chest as he laughs cynically.

"Just like your mother."

My mouth becomes unbearably dry as my knees grow weaker. This is what fear feels like. This is what I've grown accustomed to all because of one man. Because of Rich.

"Your mother said the exact same thing. Except, she didn't mean it." He exhales slowly, willing himself to calm down.

"I'm not like her! I mean it. I'll go with you." I've started to beg while tears stream down my puffy cheeks.

Without another word from either of us, he sets the gun on the sink before turning me to face him. His stubble is rough on his prominent jawline. Glancing up further, I see the tightness in his lips, and the pain lingering in his dark eyes.

"This...this is why I love you," He breathes out, fanning my face in the process.

I'm stiff as a board when he brings me closer to him, wrapping me in a posessive embrace.

Should I fight? Do I have time to knock him down? If I can run to my phone then I have a better chance at surviving this.

But before I can make my move- or any moves at all- I feel myself being lifted onto the counter.

"Stay still," He demands while sliding his hands inside my shirt. My quaking lips remain pressed while I fight the urge to push him away.

His fingertips trail upward until they seize my chest. I feel a gentle squeeze, causing my throat to hum.

Biting my lip, I close my eyes. What do I do now?

I gasp when I feel his lips on my neck and collarbone, staining my flesh with poisonous kisses. His large hands slip into my shorts, tugging on my panties.

Small droplets leak from my eyes while my mind is spinning. I'm trying to gather my thoughts so I can get away from him. But the longer I ponder, the colder my body gets. A shiver passes through me when his fingertips graze my perspired flesh.

Realizing that my shirt is being lifted, I latch onto his hands to stop him.

"Don't... hurt me again." I whisper fearfully.

"Hey, remember what I said about crying." He wipes my tears with his thumb before lifting the gun.

"No," I flinch away but he grips my chin to pull me closer. I'm literally staring into the face of death because the black gun is inches from my mouth.

"You do everything I say when I say it. Got it?"

My eyes close while I listen to my pounding heart. Is he trying to take me again? And how did he get out of prison? There hasn't been any reports of a criminal on the run.

An abrupt pulsing ache forces me to moan while my eyes roll in the back of my head. Gripping his shirt tighter, I blink rapidly while a stream of crimson glides down my face.

"You got that!" His booming voice vibrates the entire bathroom, making my body jerk. Nodding my head, I let him lead me out of the bathroom. I'm a bit dazed but I don't let that interfere with my ability to walk.

We're hand in hand until I feel my body falling. I don't have time to scramble up or even see what is happening. All I can hear is shouting and cursing. And then, in an instant a shot is fired.

Screaming, I curl myself into a ball. Make it go away. Make it stop. With my eyes shut tight, I start rocking while thinking of my Reyna.

"I said get up!" The voice dictates loudly. It's filled with callousness and evil intent. The sound is familiar and I know it isn't directed at me.

Sitting up, I'm met with a fuming man with a gun in his hand. Rich's gun. The man I'm staring at has a face made from the angels above. His lips curve into a sinister smirk while his green eyes hold undeniable focus. I notice the way he holds the gun; firm and strong. Unlike how he held the butcher knife years ago. That was a standoff against Rich and he lost. But judging by his serious tone, and wrathful eyes, he isn't going to lose this time.

Rich stands with his hands up defensively. His cold, essonite eyes never leave mine the entire time.

"Betraying me again, Livie?" He grins while I continue backing away.

It's clear Jake has had enough because fires. The loud pop of the gun forces me to claim my ears. It's a horrible sound. A frightening sound.

"They're blanks, Jakey boy." Rich smirks devilishly.

I watch in horrified awe as they fight. For a few seconds Rich has the upper hand. Punching, tacking, and kicking Jake. All I can do is scream for him because I'm too stoic to move. Jake has to make it, he has to live. I remain huddled against the wall, watching the brawl until Jake finally makes a move. He kicks Rich in his groin before tackling him to ground. Slug after slug is being inflicted on Rich and the more Jake punches, the more Rich loses consciousness. I now realize why Jake was on the floor so long; he was tiring Rich out.

A relieved smile raises on my lips when I see Jake stand weakly. Running over to him, I try to support his weight.

"You were supposed to come another time." I joke while snuggling my head into his side. My arms are wrapped around him while he continues breathing heavily.

"Oh, you...were...serious?" He pants out tiredly.

Without a second thought, I laugh while shifting my body to give him a tight, suffocating hug. Thank God he came when he did. Regardless if he was sneaking in to see me or not. I'm glad he came when he did.

"What do... we do now?" He questions, still out of breath. His arm squeezes my waist while I continue clinging onto him.

With a small exhale, I pull away from him before turning my head to the unconsious man behind us. Rich's proportional body is sprawled out on the floor. Blood stained and bruised. His eyes are closed but his chest is moving. He's alive so he'll be able to feel pain. He needs to feel what I feel.

A bright idea pops into my head, and in that moment, I know exactly what we're going to do.

"We take him, and we hold him until we're finished with him."

But first, I need to see if my aunt is alive. I need to make sure she is okay first.

35

CHAPTER 35

"What the hell did you just say?" He frowns at me. His nose is wrinkled while his brows furrow.

Now normally this would bother me because I hate when he thinks I'm being irrational or crazy; but right now, I could care less about his opinion. I've been waiting for this opportunity for a long time.

"Tie him up. I'll be back."

My mind is focused on finding Casey. I need her to be alright. With that thought, I leave a puzzled Jake standing in my room. I know he is skeptical about this plan, but I don't really care. All I care about is making Rich suffer, even if it's just for five minutes.

He calls after me but I don't reply. Instead, I focus on finding my aunt. Pacing down the hallway, I stop at her door. This is it. She may be in there alive, or...I don't even want to think about it. Losing my aunt will destroy me even more. It will feel like someone pouring salt into my already opened wounds. I don't need anymore pain in my life. I've been through enough.

With steady breathing, I try to calm myself before getting worked up. I mean with all that just happened, I probably need a heart monitor right now.

Opening her door, I peek my head in. The room is quiet; almost too quiet. And the darkness overtakes my eyesight, forcing my eyes to squint. I can't see anything. Stepping in further, I leave the door cracked to allow light into the room. I'm afraid to turn the lights on because I'm afraid of what I'll see.

"Aunt Casey," I run over to her. She's lying in her bed, completely still.

At first my heart stops briefly because I don't see her chest rising and falling. But then I see her turn over. With a sigh of relief I quietly leave her room. I won't wake her.

"How is she? Is she alive?" Jake's concerned voice fills my ears as soon as I enter my room.

Putting my hair in a ponytail, I ponder some more. He doesn't need to know I left her a note. It's vague but at least she won't worry too much about me. I really do need to clear my head, and I know the right way to do it.

"Yeah," Nodding my head, I make my way over my closet to change. I'm feeling a bit daring but instead of going for my black XO cropped tee with high waisted shorts, I choose something more reserved. A light blue chambray top with faded skinny's and canvas shoes.

"Whoa," he eyes my body hungrily, making me blush slightly. I didn't expect to look this hot either but with Aunt Casey anything is possible. She chose every one of my outfits for me and she didn't dissapoint. I'm tired of old tee shirts and jeans anyway.

Looking at him too I can see he looks just as good. His shoes are navy blue addidas while his khaki pants are cuffed. I smile at the dark purple tee and sleeveless gray hoodie that reveals his toned arms. His eyes smolder while he evinces his approval of my outfit.

He keeps staring at me with soft eyes until I say,

"We're taking your car." With my hands on my hips, I stare down at Rich. There's mischief to my tone, and unrelenting wrath in my heart. I'm so enamored with getting even that it's not even funny anymore.

"Where to?" He asks dumbly, completely baffled by the turn of events. He is now staring grimly at Rich's constrained body just like I am. I notice the duct tape over his mouth, hands, and feet. That makes me even more excited.

"We're going somewhere he'll be very familar with." I smirk devilishly.

Once we get him into Jake's 1967 Camaro, we drive off into the darkness. With my eyes now closed, I lean my sweaty head against the cool glass window. My entire body feels overheated, and not because of anxiety. Nope, I'm sweaty because of Rich's heavy ass. We had to lift him to put him in the trunk of the car.

Before doubts can flood my tumultous mind, I turn on the radio. It's some country station that I'm unfamiliar with. I love all kinds of music so I don't change it, I just hum to the catchy tune while gripping Reyna's box tightly. I'm bringing it with me because she is just as apart of this as Jake and I are.

Anyway, we drive in silence. Just me thinking about my life while Jake drives to our destination.

I don't know exactly what I'm going to do to Rich but I do know that I'm willing to wing it. I'm willing to do everything in my power to make his life hell. Whether it's for thirty minutes or thirty days. I am determined to make him feel how I felt. I am bent on making him experience what I've experienced. Fear, pain, heartache. I want his already dark soul to crumble right in front of my vindictive eyes. Yes, I want to break him.

Before, I wanted him to die. I wanted him dead because death was the quickest way to remove him from my life. But I now realize that death isn't an option for him anymore. No, that is too easy. A man like Rich needs to linger in suffering.

The sudden jerk of the antique vehicle makes my head rise to see what's going on. All sinful thoughts diminish while I eye Jake apprehensive.

"What's wrong?" I question while sitting up in my seat.

His knuckles grip the steering wheel tightly while he stares at the road ahead. Beads of sweat glide down his forehead while he swallows nervously.

"Thought I saw cops." He admits, completely mortified.

Without stopping myself, I let the sweet sound of laughter rip from my throat. I laugh until tears brim in my eyes.

"This shit isn't funny, Livie. Do you know what will happen when we get caught?" He huffs in aggravation. I notice his knuckles have turned juts as pale as his face.

"Jake grow some balls. We're not committing a murder." I force a laugh to lighten the mood.

"Yeah, tell that to the cops when they arrest our asses." He shakes his head while pulling into the gravel driveway.

"Are you in or not?" I ask once he puts the car in park. Enough is enough, and right now I don't have time for his bullshit.

He sighs before opening his door and stepping out. Believe it or not, I think he wants to do this just as bad as I do. But the only difference between he and I is the fact that I have the courage to do it.

Once I step out, I notice how beautiful the dreary sky is for three a.m. Instead of the usual benighted sky with few clouds and few stars; there are countless numbers of stars and a moon so full it could swallow me whole. The large moon illuminates the early morning sky, giving light to our path. We're parked a few feet away from the same house we were previously captive in. The same house Rich and Jake grew up in.

Before I can even check to see if the front doors are locked, Jake grabs my hand. The way he squeezes forces my irises to linger on his. The worry, concern, and fear showing in his eyes is so strong that even I can feel it too.

"Remember what I told you?" He is now rubbing circles in my hands. His eyes remain locked on the ground while his warm hands continue seizing mine. The action melts my insides while I nod.

"Do you remember my answer when you asked me what I was afraid of?" He exhales before peering at me. His green, powerful eyes capture mine while we remain entranced in each other's magnetic presence.

"Not caring was your answer." I shrug, not really understanding where he is going with this.

"I'm afraid of not caring about anyone or anything, Livie." He acknowledges his flaw while I chew on my bottom lip. I'm feeling a bit uneasy because I know where this is headed, and I don't want him to dissect me. I don't need anyone gazing into my soul with microscopic eyes. So I steer the conversation back to him.

"What kind of fear is that?" I frown in curiosity. He never elaborated before now.

"It's my kind." He replies just as quickly. "Because when you don't care about anything then you give up. And giving up is quitting."

Thinking back on the previous times I've spent with Rich one vivid memory stands out more than the others. It's not being taken or having my throat cut, or him carving my thigh; no, it's something more gruesome, and twisted than I ever thought possible. The sickest thing I remember while being captive with him was the time I slit my wrists. I tried to bleed out because I thought that would be the best solution to my problems. I gave up on my self.

For a minute, I felt the pulsing pain fade away, only to be replaced with alleviation. I remember my eyes rolling in the back of my head as I allowed my head to lean against the cool wall. My crimson stained wrists remained in an upright position while I felt every soul aching defilement flow out of my veins. Like droplets of rain gliding down a window, my cherry red poison escaped. All of my negative emotions went with it. And while I laid on the floor bleeding out, I yearned to be free too. I longed to escaped as quickly as my blood did.

The feeling was euphoric and then, I closed my eyes. I wasn't prepared for what I saw. I was not prepared to see my deceased brother holding Reyna in his arms. I wasn't prepared to hear him chime the very words that chilled my soul.

"Reyna wants you to live; even when you think there's nothing to live for."

Opening my salty eyes, I cover my mouth while nodding my head. I remember too much. I need to forget. But what if trying to forget is the essence of my problems? Trying to forget won't make them go away. It only buries them deep within me, resulting in a future regurgitation of sullied memories. That explains my horrendous nightmares and flagitious flashbacks.

"Remember when you told me you weren't quitting. That you were just accepting your fate?"

Silence is the best response so that's what I give him. This reminds me of the many arguments we had in the basement those few years ago. I used to think they were petty and that he was being a bully, but in retropsect he was right. He saw potential in me. Potential to be the courageous woman I was destined to be. He didn't want me to just give up. He wanted me to keep fighting even after I thought Rich had knocked the fight out of me.

We may have only been two sixteen and seventeen year olds but we were smart enough to rely on each other to survive.

With his hand under my chin, I feel him lift it up. My excreating eyes blink while trying to erase the blurry tears. This is why I love him. No, this is why I am in love with him.

"Livie, I want you to have the courage to accept the things you cannott change. Even if that means walking away from this." His eyes hold deep, soul clenching meaning. And even in the darkness of early morning, I can see his sincerity.

And even though he is trying to stop me from torturing Rich, I get a sense that even he knows his efforts are in vain.

The basement is still moldy and depressing. It's filled with an unrelenting stench and a malevolent presence. To say it still creeps the hell out of me would be an understatement.

We place a semi conscious Rich in the chair then start using rope to tie him to it. His arms are tied behind the chair while his feet are tied to the legs of the chair. He is right where he needs to be. Only this time, he isn't the one barking orders.

Before we dragged him down here I told Jake I would do this with or without him. His only response was a small head shake.

I don't like seeing him like this but there is nothing he can do to stop me because my mind is made up.

After we came to an agreement- an agreement to disagree- we took the time to scope out the place. Turns out he already had it set up for us.

Once we got down the stairs there was a chair in the center with a flickering fluorescent light that shined down on the center like a spotlight. Walking in further we saw a wall with shelves straight ahead. On the bottom shelf were tools like a saw, drill and hammer. The sight made my stomach churn while Jake rubbed his face in distress. Maybe we were in over our heads but that still didn't stop me from wanting to go through with this plan.

Anyway, we stared in horror at the brutal tools that were meant for me. But the few instruments on the bottom shelf weren't it. There were more. The large red toolbox sat on the second shelf while a huge axe hung on the wall next to it. My eyes began to water and in that exact moment, I realized that he really was planning on torturing me.

My hands tremble so I place them in my pockets to conceal it. I can't let him see me weak. No, I can't let him win. The entire room seemes to be emmersed in darkness. Like a cloud of sin covering us in it's harsh blanket. I keep my eyes focused ahead while Jake is facing Rich. I keep eyeing the utensils cautiously, trying to figure out which to use.

I walk over to the shelf with a tense breath. Ever since I've stepped down here it's like all of my emotions have hit me harder than a ton of bricks. Every raw, pure, unadulterated emotion I've ever felt has attacked my insides, making me more anxious than I already am.

One.

Two.

Three.

I start counting, trying to steady my breathing. I really need to calm down and execute this without flaking out. I can't back out now.

My delicate hand hovers over the array of shiny metal. knives.

With a small sigh, I lift the tiny blade. It's small but deadly. Meaning it's tiny but sharp enough to cut someone's finger off. I think I'll get my point across with this.

I'm about to walk over to him so I can wake him up, but the sound of a Skrillex ringtone fills my ears.

It's so alrming and unexpected that it even wakes up Rich. He is now bobbing his head while groaning loudly.

"Why didn't you silence it?" I ask a caught off guard Jake. His phone is now to his ear while he continues to ignore me.

Really? Is he really doing this right now. I stand in front of Rich, fuming from ear to ear. That better not be Gia on the other end of that phone. Because if it is he'll be eating it.

"I know what you're thinking so stop thinking it." He says before jetting upstairs.

In automactic habit, I dart upstairs after him. The blade is no longer in my hands. I must have dropped it. Giving no more attention to that, I keep running until I reach his car.

"Where... are you going?" I breathe out tiredly. By this time a small breeze has picked up around us. It cools my scorched skin for a few seconds.

"To get Jackson." He starts the old engine, making it rumble.

"His car is down so he needs a ride. Get in, I'm not leaving you here with him." He reaches over to open my door but I shake my head. Is that who called him?

"Just go without me." I know what I need to say, and I also know that Jake doesn't need to be around to hear it.

His pained expression makes my heart sink but I never allow my emotions to show. Instead I kept reassuring him I'd be okay. I know deep inside I'd break down but like I've said before, I have a pressing issue that only Rich and I can discuss. No one else.

After Jake's persistent begging for me to get in his car and my persistent refusal, we finally agreed on keeping our phones on so we could call each other in case of an emergency.

Once I get back down to the basement I'm greeted with a simmering Rich. His burdening silence is unsettling as his inexorable aura resonates throughout the entire basement. It's clear he isn't the happiest camper right now.

With a quick glance in his direction, I'm met with his intense gaze. It burns through to my soul, destroying my inner being yet again. But I'm not phased anymore. He has successfully tainted me.

A small chuckle parts from his sinister lips, making my head snap toward him.

"Come on, Livie. We can talk about this, baby." He flashes a cunning smile. His dark eyes and taunting smirk make him appear more daunting than he already is. I wish I could tell you that he doesn't make me nervous. I wish I could say he never gets to me. But if I said that then I'd be lying.

"Why did you do it?" My small voice fills the silence while I stroll to the shelf of weapontry.

His silence is heavy and makes my blood boil. I need him to answer me. I need to know why he murdered my daughter.

"Answer me!" I shout whilst clutching a piece of metal. It's a scapel.

"I...I didn't kill her! I loved her too!" He shouts with just as much intenstiy as me. His chest rises and falls while his pleading eyes focus on me. My heightened tone must have startled him.

"Yeah right," With a simple head shake and a scoff, I graze my fingers over the other tools.

"Aha," I rejoice when I find the perfect piece of revenge. The perfect way to get the truth out of him is to pull every single fucking tooth until there's nothing but gums left.

Closing my eyes, I give myself a few moments to compose myself. I wipe my tears before staring at the rusty old pliers. Holding these things makes me feel powerful. It gives me more control than what I know what to do with. I have all of the power right now, and in some sick twisted way I relish in it. Not sure if that's sick or exhilarating.

Turning to face him, my mouth gapes open at what I see. And before I can even process what he is doing I'm falling backward. My head hits the concrete with so much force that it causes an ache to erupt in my head.

The next thing I hear is the sound of the pliers sliding across the floor along with any hopes I had. In one quick motion, I'm pinned down by my wrists with Rich hovering over me. I don't have time to beg or plead because my mouth is suddenly covered by his palm.

"I didn't... kill her, I've... told you this before," He pants softly.

His entire body weight is holding me hostage while I try to reach for my phone. It's in my pocket. The suffocating feel of his fingertips gripping my hand makes me freeze. Damn it, my hand was half way in my pocket.

"Did you hear me?" His rough voice infects my ears. I haven't heard his frightening voice, or felt his bone chilling presence in a while.

"If you didn't kill her then how'd she die?" I question, on the brink of tears.

All I remember is him being extremely angry the first week after her birth. All I know is that he was constantly on edge and distant to Reyna. That alone, gave me reason to believe he killed her.

The earsplitting screams coming from the small infant fills my ears, forcing me out of bed. I rub my exhausted eyes before sitting up. Glancing at the clock I supress a growl.

5:33 a.m.

It's been two hours since I put her to bed and now she's awake again. I've fed, changed, and rocked her but still no results. I don't know what to do anymore.

"If you don't shut her up I will." Rich sneers venomously. There is fire when he speaks but now warmth in his vocals.

My jaw clenches while I try to hold in boiling anger. This is only day two and he's already irritated. But what he fails to realize is that I am too.

"What the hell do you think I'm trying to do? I don't know what's wrong with her!" I hold her close to me, rocking her again, hoping to lull her back to sleep. I walk around the room while humming to her. Her small voice is raspy from crying so much while tears overlap in her blue eyes.

The sudden sound of the floorboards creaking makes me freeze. My eyes close when I feel a strong presence behind me. Rich. He snakes his arms around me, holding my waist in a vice grip.

We walk to the corner of the room, where her bassinet is. My hands clench onto her tightly, not wanting to let her go.

"Maybe if you put her in her bassinet she'll fall asleep." He suggests calmly. A little too calmly.

My worried eyes close, and then with a reluctant sigh, I nod. She is still crying uncontrollably when I place her in her warm crib. I notice her small face is contorted as if she is in pain. My heart literally aches because there is nothing I can do. Rich refuses to take her to a hospital.

The crying continues and seems to be getting worse. I know newborns cry but this is unusual. She has been crying all day. With my hand on her tummy, I kiss her forehead while she squirms.

I really hope she can fall asleep. She needs to rest.

Lifting my head from her crib, I turn around. A pained cry escapes my lips when I feel a powerful blow to my cheek. Stumbling back, I grab my bruised cheek while tears start to stream. An intense ringing fills my ears while my body quakes in fear.

"I told you to put her in her crib, that's it. Don't get too attached." He says coldly before storming out of the room. The heavy slam of the door shakes the room and my bones too. He leaves me standing beside her crib, completely shocked and confused.

He was the one who asked me what we were naming her. He was the one who gave me the pink blanket to wrap her in. In fact, it still has her dried blood on it. And it's the only thing used to keep her warm because Rich didn't buy her anymore blankets. Just diapers.

Rubbing my tummy, I reminisce about Reyna and her box. That box keeps her with me. That's why I'll never get rid of it. Because every part of her is with me. Including the blood stained blanket.

"Livie, she was sick..." he admits with shame. "I knew she was sick,"

"I didn't tell you because I knew you'd be even more upset." He continues while my sobs force me to make choking sounds.

This time I feel my body being lifted and then in an instant large arms wrap around me. My average sized frame is pressed into his chest while his arms wrap around me, trying to comfort me.

"You could have taken her to a hospital." My low, weak voice erupts through the small silence.

"I know, but I was afraid I'd get caught. They would have questioned me about her birth and why she didn't have a birth certificate. " His arms wrap around me tighter while I cry louder and harder.

"I'm sorry, Livie. I never meant for her to die. This is what I mean when I said don't get attached. It's easier to cope when you don't get attached." He repeats while rocking us.

Shaking my head, I refuse to live with that. I refuse to agree with what this twisted asshole has to say. With a spark of ignited courage, I stand abruptly.

"You accepted it just like that? Without trying to save her, you just let her die!" I can't look at him and the more he speaks, the more vomit rises in my already sore throat.

He stands to face me then shouts,

"I accepted it to make it easier for me! It was either take her to a hospital, risk getting caught and losing you. Or, lose an already ill baby. I was willing to live with her death if that meant living with you forever." He whispers the last part hauntingly. It's haunting because the realization of him allowing her to die chills me to my core. He may not have killed her but he still let her die. And that to me, is just as bad. He is still a cold blooded murdering rapist in my eyes.

"I love you, Livie. I really do despite how you feel about me. And I'm going to show you how much I do."

His soothing tone is used to mask an underlying manipulative one. I know what he is trying to do. And I'll avoid going back to that at all costs.

"N-no, just...just stay away fro-from me" I start backing away with fearful eyes and a tense body. I'm still stunned by his previous words. Still distressed with no way out of this.

And that's when it happens. Before I have time to run he lunges forward with such ferocity and strength that I'm on the ground before I can blink an eye.

His malicious, ill saturated glare penetrates my soul while I suddenly lose my ability to speak. With stealth and caution, he brings his nose to my neck before inhaling a giant gulp of my scent. Panic stricken and teary eyed, I start hyperventilating when I feel cold metal slide up my abdomen until stopping at my chest.

My small whimpers increase when I hear my shirt rip open. Squriming I try to fight him but the blade on my neck forces me to cease.

"I told you that love has limits, Livie. Even if that limit is death." The sound of his monstrous, painful voice echoes through the basement before understanding sinks in.

I finally understand what he meant when he told me that. There comes a time in everyone's life when you lose the one person you love the most. But I know Rich isn't referring to losing the love of your life in that sense. He means that the only way for me to escape him is for me to die.

I feel my limp body jerk as he pulls apart my bra. I allow him to violate me. I think it's funny how I used to run from death. It's ironic how the very thing that I feared is the very thing I embrace now.

"Do you want to die?" He plants small, soft kisses on my collar bone before lifting me up.

His hand grips the back of my hair while I close my eyes. I can feel the sharp tip of the blade resting on my stomach, yearning to plunge into me.

From his steady heartbeat and silent lips, I confirm my suspicions. He is waiting for my reply.

"If not then say it back. Say you love me too,"

My mouth is drier than the Sahara but my eyes are spewing gallons of water down my cheeks. I can't say it back.

And I'm not going to. Ever.

I'll never convince myself that I love him because I'll always be imprisoned. I'll always be confined to his cold heart. And when you force yourself to love a monster it tears you apart from the inside out. I know firsthand because my scars on my wrists tell that story.

When love holds limits it slowly dies. It fades away because it was never limitless to begin with. And to me, a limitless love is the most sacred love of all. Because loving without limits means that nothing holds you back. It's like a first class flight to freedom. You're freefalling out of an infinite sky of possiblilites. The freedom to discover who you are as well as the person you're in love with is right at your fingertops. I never felt free with Rich. In fact, I felt the complete opposite. I was as mentally captive as I was physically. Held. Restricted. Chained. I hated myself and I hated him.

Going back to what he said I conclude that he is right; our love had limits. It had limits because I refused to love him back. There was even a point when I had decided that I'd rather be dead than love him. But this time, I'm not forced to kill myself.

"Do you love me, Livie?" his intrusive tongue lingers on my lips, pleading for entrance.

Shaking my head I close my eyes, preparing myself for what is to come. A flood of emotions attacks me but this time I embrace them too. I look forward to seeing my Reyna again. I look forward to my parents wrapping me in stifling hug.

An alarmed gasp escapes me while my body jolts upward. And as I feel the blade enter further into my flesh I can't help but feel complete and utter satisfaction. He can take my purity, innocence, body, and loved ones away from me. But he can't steal my spirit. No, he'll never have my soul because Jake has that.

36

EPILOGUE

The leaves fall from the trees in scattered intervals as the wind blows around me. A few even fall on my lap, making me flinch slightly. I've been sensitive to light touches.

Once my heart rate steadies, I use my right hand to pick one up. It's the shape of a star and has crumpled brown edges. I observe it with a small smile because this is so familiar. A very familiar memory because the hues of yellow, orange and red remind of the time my brother and I piled leaves outside. That was the last time I played with him.

With my head bowed, I close my eyes. I can cry but I won't. Instead, I think of my mom, dad, and brother. I think of my friends, and I think of how much I've changed. I'm more courageous now.

While I'm quietly reminiscing I hear the crunch of leaves behind me. Someone is walking toward me but who? With my hand now free, I spin the wheelchair around. When I first arrived three months ago I couldn't walk, so now I go to physical therapy to help me recover.

"Ready to go back?" The boy in front of me raises his brows. His ruffled dark hair makes his green eyes appear more intriguing. More inviting, even.

Not really.

"Um, what time is it?" I ask while rubbing my casted arm. Believe it or not, my arm suffered more tearing than my neck and abdomen. It really is a miracle I survived. If not for the help of Jake and Jack, I'd be dead. They brought the police to me.

"It's three." He places his hands in his pockets while I frown.

That number carries so much weight. Three is a significant number. Three is the number of times the knife punctured my flesh; after stabbing me in my abdomen, he pushed me down. I held my bleeding stomach with my right hand while trying to fend him off with my left arm. I remember him ranting about how much he loved me and because of that he was going to make sure I died in his arms.

I shiver from the vivid memory of my throat rattling scream when the blade slashed into my left arm. Once he did that, it fell to my side and I was in so much pain that I could barely lift it up. He saw the frightened look on my face which made him close his eyes before violently slicing my throat. At the time, I was ready to die but I wasn't expecting him to be so vicious. I was not expecting him to make me suffer. And the more tears rolled down my cheeks the more he felt compelled to wipe them away with his blood stained fingers. I wasn't expecting him to lift me up and hold me closer to him. I was not expecting to hear the muffled cries that escaped him while I literally choked on my own blood.

Three. Three is significant because it is the number of words he said to me while rocking me in his arms.

"I love you." His domineering voice was cold as ice. No warmth lingered on his tongue.

And as I stayed pressed to him, shaking and gurgling, I couldn't help but be forced to listen to his lies. I couldn't pull away or even talk back. I couldn't escape him because he wanted me to bleed to death in his arms.

"I did it because I love you, Olivia."

I couldn't focus on the pain, or the fact that Jake hadn't arrived yet. No, I couldn't focus on anything else because I just wanted out. I just wanted to die.

There are three things in life we all experience; love, loss, and pain. And as I bled out, I allowed my heavy eyes to slowly close, willing myself to die. But then it happened.It happened so fast that I was barely alive when I heard the three gunshots that brought Rich to the ground. Yes, he was shot three times before I blacked out. That was the day I was engulfed in darkness and later realized that I didn't have to be the one to die anymore. I finally realized that Rich's death was the only way I'd truly escape him; the only way he'd escape himself.

We arrive in the spacious, well lit lobby with just a few nurses speed walking by. No other patients are here, just me. I've been going to physical therapy to help me recover.

And because I live on the third floor, I never miss an appointment. After the attack I was hospitalized because I went into a coma. My life was hanging by a thread and I remember every vivid detail of my unconsciousness. I remember who I saw, what I saw, and what I heard during those two months asleep. My memories are staying with me because I'm not telling anyone. I'm not telling anyone about how I reunited with my brother, and how I taught Reyna how to speak. Those memories are what keep me moving. Every time I feel sad; like I need to die all over again, I think of what Reyn told me.

"Wake up mommy. You have to live for me so I can live in you."

I remember her patting my cheek while tears streamed down my cheeks. I didn't want to wake up. I didn't want to go back to my reality. I just wanted to be with her. I wanted to stay with my daughter.

But the more I cried, the louder everything else around me seemed. The more my heart poured out the more my peaceful surroundings faded. I wasn't in the field of dandelions or the tree house Waylan and Reyna built anymore. No, I was in the hospital. My hearing was the first to develop, then my sight, then my feeling.

I awoke to the blurry sight of Jake. His head down and eyes closed while standing over me. I was lost for words until he opened his eyes. His sea of emerald staring down at me, making my entire body freeze. He gave me chills in a good way.

No one moved or spoke. He just kept staring at me with wide green eyes until suddenly bolting out the door. He didn't give me time to'open my mouth, or even sit up. He just ran out the room.

Only when he re-entered with my Aunt and a few doctors was I able to see his red, swollen eyes. He was crying too.

That was a few weeks ago though. Right after that I started going to physical therapy. And now that I have my voice back I can start going to counseling. I can start mending my mental scars.

"Chipotle when you're done?" He flashes a knowing smile. His hair is still dark but shorter now. It's swept upward. I notice his masculine jaw of facial hair makes him appear older than twenty one. His birthday was in August and I missed it. I was told he spent the entire day waiting for me to wake up.

His lips instantly press to mine, making me warm and bubbly inside. He still makes me feel like a schoolgirl who's crush just glanced at her. He makes me so happy and I don't know what I'd do without him.

Pulling out of our kiss, he stares into my eyes. "I had to get your attention somehow,"

Smirking flirtatiously, I pat his cheek before saying,

"Don't get my order wrong, Jakey Cakes" I laugh when he frowns. Last time he ordered guacamole and chips instead of my burrito.

"I make no promises, Olive." He pecks my cheek then stands.

"Seriously," I groan at his playful aura. If he is planning on getting it wrong on purpose then I'm going to throw his food on the floor. Childish I know, but I don't care. Alll care about is the savory taste of beef, salsa, and rice igniting my tastebuds.

"Fine, I'll get two combos." He grumbles before walking out.

This has always been our routine since I woke up. He stays with me, talks to me even when I couldn't talk back, and even buys me Chipotle for lunch. It's kind of funny how you truly get to know someone after thinking you've known them for so long.

3:15 p.m.

The four walls are decorated with one theme on each. The wall adjacent to me, on my right, has a huge rainbow with white clouds at the top. It would make anyone smile but not me. I hate rainbows so I choose to look at the one to my left. That one is even worse because large clowns with red hair and noses dance around like there's no tomorrow. Which doesn't help my fear of clowns.

The wall behind me holds the most windows so it's only fitting to make it appear to resemble an ocean with boat sailing on it. Looking at it, I feel like I'm on my way to a deserted island. Far away from harm. Far away from the one man who caused such turmoil. Far away from Rich. Is it weird that I still feel his presence even though he's dead?

The sudden sound of the door opening sends my eyes to the wall across from me. It's simple princess theme is set to make any little girl feel special. I was that way too. Sweet, guiltless, and naive. But once innocence faded away, my life quickly changed. And now, it will never, ever be the same.

I watch the group of about four walk in and take their seats. One boy with spiked blond hair walks over to me. With a high look of irritation, he crosses his arms while staring down on me.

I stare back because I know what this is about.

"That's my seat, " He points a beefy finger at me.

"So what, go find another." I shrug with emotionless eyes. The Olivia three years ago would have gotten up but not this new Olivia. No, she's staying seated.

"Bitch." He huffs then goes to take a seat next to another girl with short, black hair and tan skin. Her attire is black everything. Black shirt, black jeans, black shoes, and black eyes. I don't think she even owns another color. I would truly hate that because no matter how depressed I get, I still need color.

"Sorry about this room guys. The young adult room is being renovated." A familiar voice fills my ears.

A shocked gasp nearly escapes me when I see my old friend, Margaret standing in the front of the room. Her fiery red hair is straight and evenly cut now, no longer knotted and tangled. I realize her porcelain face is brighter, happier. The broad smile outlining her strong features makes me smile too.

I've always known her to volunteer but I never suspected she'd be counseling abuse victims. In high school, she'd always renovate, plant flowers outside, and donate furniture to help restore deteriorated buildings. Margaret, or Grit as I called her was the angel. The "good good, good girl." She was the one considered a saint at our school not a bible freak. I think it was because she never condemned anyone to hell like some people do. She never judged either so it made it easier for our classmates to talk to her about anything.

"So, who'd like to go first for the introduction?" She clasps her hands together while eyeing us eargerly. Her attire is more feminine now. She's wearing a light gray off the shoulder sweater with denim jeans and brown boots. It's funny how we look now. I used to dress cute and girly. Now all I wear are jeans and long sleeve tee shirts.

After her moment of silence she decides to go first. She introduces herself as Mrs. Greene. Noticing the small diamond rock on her finger, I instantly make the connection. Her and Nathan must have gotten married. I knew she liked him.

Anyway, she has two dogs, Darth and Vader. Probably Nathan's idea but a funny one nonetheless. She went on to tell us that she had two sisters but one was kidnapped three years ago. My heart dropped to my stomach when I realized that I was the one she was referring to.

The next introductions went by so quickly that some of them sounded more like greetings. The goth girl went after . She's twenty one and had been with her violent boyfriend for seven years. That's all the information she gave.

The next person, the dirty blonde douche bag told us how he isn't angry, depressed, or abused. He just hates life. Which is a lie. You have to have a reason. Turns out he is nineteen and suicidal but he refused to explain why.

The other two, a Latino boy about eighteen, and an Asian girl about twenty two told us how they grew up as siblings because they went through the same thing. Their families were murdered by drug lords. From there, they were put into foster care and spent their childhood trying to protect each other. Now, Lilly is trying to prevent Brian from going down that same path.

I was last of course. I didn't want to lie, and besides, how could I with my status? Everyone in town knew my story, so I opted to tell them a few things. I explained how my parents where murdered when I was sixteen. I told the group that I spent three years with the psycho who kidnapped, abused, and tortured me. I told them about how I first thought he took me because he didn't want to go back to prison but I later realized it was deeper than that. I didn't go into anymore detail but I think they caught the gist of it.

"Hey, you need a ride?" A cheerful voice makes me turn my head.

She strolls up to me with her hands in her jacket pocket. It's cold here in Glennville for late October and we're not used to it.

"Actually, I'm waiting on someone." I smile sheepishly. Besides the fact that I'm starving, I'm also nervous to hear what she has to say to me. I mean it has been over three years since we've spoken and our last conversation was left on bad terms.

"Oh," She continues standing next to me until I hear,

"Liv, it's been a while...and I want you to know that I forgive you." She turns to me with a small grin. Her freckles on her cheeks lift, making me smile too. I've missed my best friend.

"You knew it was me the whole time?" I raise my eyebrows in genuine curiosity.

"Your first clue should have been when I said I had two sisters." She giggles.

That's true. I knew she considered me as her second sister because we were closer in age than her older sister. Grit has four older brothers and one sister.

"How's your family?"

"They're great. Toby and Micah room together at Florida State while Alec, Riley and Hannah attend University of Miami." She explains happily.

"That's nice." I always knew Toby and Micah would attend the same school. They're teammates and brothers.

"What about you?" I'd love to know where she ended up. She always joked about being a nun.

"Married, remember?" She smiles a wholehearted smile then says,

"I hate school so I decided to follow my true passion. I mentor young people because some need guidance. And besides, I've been told I'm re-latable so that helps too." She shrugs.

We keep talking. I'm sitting in my chair while she chats about her life and how much everyone has missed me. I know that's a lie but I smile and nod anyway.

She tells me that she and Nathan decided to marry once they graduated. Even though he was a grade ahead of us he told her he wanted her to graduate first. I had no choice but to smile at that because that's just like him. Always a sweetheart.

"Girl, you should totally come over to my house. I'm having a small get together tonight. Maybe Kelly can drop by too."

"How about you guys come to my house?" A voice breaks the silence, making me grin. I know who that is and I also know he has food. I can smell it and my stomach can too.

"Livie met my friends but I don't think I've met hers." He places the bag- the same bag I'm reaching for- under his arm then extends his hand.

"I'm Jake,"

They shake hands before Margaret's eyes shift to me. By this time Jake has handed me my burrito.

"Livie? She lets you call her that?" She points a skeptical finger at him while scoffing.

He nods before taking a bite of my burrito. She watches us for a few moments in awe.

"And I didn't know she liked dick," She continues, making me stop chewing to glare at her.

Did I mention how honest she can be? Sometimes more brutal than me.

"Just because I never dated anyone in high school doesn't make me a lesbian." I roll my eyes at her while she smiles apologetically.

Soon after lunch in the lobby ended Jake, Grit, and I decided to ask my nurse if I could leave for a few hours.I waited anxiously while they pleaded with her. They used the whole, 'she's been good, let her free' speech. And when that didn't work they tried the, "it's her twentieth birthday and you only turn twenty once."

All I could do was shake my head at that. I don't want to remember my birthday ever again.

The plump nurse stares at me with folded arms then says,

"Fine, she can go out. But first, I need to see if she passes this test." The brown haired nurse with purple highlights walks over to me.

With an encouraging smile on her nude lips, she says,

"Remember what you did in therapy last week?"

Nodding eagerly, I position my arms and legs. Once they're in the right position, I use my upper body strength to lift my lower body up. My weak knees bend while I continue to slowly lift myself. Biting my lower lip, I close my teary eyes to help fight off the pain. It hurts to stand but I'm willing to endure it.

"Open your eyes," A soft, masculine voice commands.

My eyes open to the sight of a gorgeous sunset. From there, I notice a large pile of branches in the center of the yard. I notice a group of people huddled around it; talking, laughing, singing, dancing, making out, being young. My eyes travel to the football field sized yard then back to the pile of wood in the center. This is a-

"Bonfire!" I hear two obnoxious voices shout in unison.

I already know who it is. Kelly and Gia. Margaret must have introduced them.

Anyway, Jake and I chat while snacking on Doritos, honey buns and sprite. He knows my favorites because some are also his favorites. We continue talking about everything under the sun. Games, sports, and even his school. He is attending University of North Florida and he seems to be doing very well in his classes.

The vibe is more than chill at this point and I'm slowly starting to enjoy myself. Jake and I even dance together.

"Remember when you told me how you always wanted to go to prom?" He pulls me closer to him. His arms wrap around my waist while I squeeze his nape.

"Yeah, what about it?"

"This isn't it but it's pretty damn close."

Nodding happily, I place my hands on his cheeks to bring him in for a kiss. The first time I woke up in the hospital he stayed by my side day and night. And even when I couldn't talk he would do enough for the both of us. I never got tired of him talking to me though. Even at night, when he would confess how much he loved me. My eyes would be closed to make him sleep, but he never did. He couldn't sleep and neither could I.

"Okay everyone, before we start I have a surprise for Livie," Jake announces proudly.

My cheeks heat when I hear singing from behind me. My entire face lights up when I see Nathan, Kelly, Margaret, Aunt Casey, and Jake's mom Christy standing in front of me with smiling faces. Margaret is holding a cake with cream frosting that reads,

'Liv and Not Die

Happy Birthday Livie!'

--in pink frosting.

After blowing out my twenty candles, we cut the cake. Jake shoves cake in my face while I grimace. He bursts out laughing when I try to throw some in face but fail.

This feeling; this happiness I'm experiencing makes me forget about all of my other problems. It helps me go back to a time when I knew what happiness even felt like. Happiness is loving yourself. Happiness is loving those around you as much as you love yourself. I love myself. And I finally know what it feels like to be myself. It's smiling through your in pain, dancing in the rain, loving against hate, and finding someone just as insane as you are. Happiness is amazing and europhic, and so is love.

Jake pulls my hand, knocking me out of my thoughts. We take our seats on a bench and so does everyone else. Nathan and Grit are sitting on the one next to us while Dylan, Kelly, Gia and Jackson sit on the other two.

"Hurry up, we're cold!" The evil twins shout while shivering. Kelly is wearing a pink sweater with a knee length mini skirt and ankle boots. While Gia is covered in a cropped tee, black leggings and a pair of UGG boots.

They continue shivering while Jackson and Dylan scramble to gather blankets.

"Dress warmer next time." Margaret tells them.

"I'm sorry Margaret but we don't need to hide our bodies like you and Libby do." Gia scoffs, making a point to pronounce my name wrong.

Jake pulls me closer while I groan loudly. Forget her insult about my scarred body. I'm more bothered by what they're wearing. Who wears summer skirts and thin leggings to a bonfire in late October?

The two continue cracking jokes while I stay silent. Margaret surprises me when she tells them to quote: "shut the fuck up before I make you."

The tense air turned into hysteric laughter from the guys and I was glad someone shut them up.

Looking at my phone, I see it's eight thirty which means it's dark enough to light the fire. So with more cake in hand, and my body snuggled into Jake, I watch Dylan and Jackson light the pile of sticks and branches. The scene is amazing and spine chilling all at once. The flames disperse upward; spewing heat and small embers. It gives light and warmth to our small group.

Staring into the flames, I lean my head on his shoulder. He sighs before placing his chin atop my head. I love him. I know I've said it more than a million times but that's because it's true. He brings out the best in me. Like he said before, he sees potential in me that I don't even see in myself. He is the glue to my macaroni, the sunshine in my sky, and the love of my life.

"Livie, I might not be perfect but I think this is the perfect time for me to tell you."

What? What is he talking about? Lifting my head I see his lips curve to form a modest smile. He closes his eyes then exhales. Whatever is on his mind has been nagging at him for a while now.

"What's wrong?" My heart starts to sink because I think he is going to break my heart all over again. Am I ready for that? Is anyone ever ready for heartbreak?

"Out of the many times you told me you loved me," His words are slow and steady. "I never told you that I loved you too."